THE CURSE OF ILL-GOTTEN GAINS

GAINS

THE CASEBOOK OF BARNABY ADAIR
BOOK TWELVE

STEPHANIE LAURENS

ABOUT THE CURSE OF ILL-GOTTEN GAINS

THE TWELFTH VOLUME IN THE CASEBOOK OF BARNABY ADAIR NOVELS

#1 NYT-bestselling author Stephanie Laurens is back with a complex case in which her favorite sleuths must wade through the attendees of a ton house party to discover which one was moved to murder their host.

When the genial and highly regarded Sir Montague Underhill is found murdered in his own orchard, Inspector Stokes is dispatched, together with Barnaby and Penelope Adair, to Patchcote Grange to uncover the culprit. But a fashionable house party provides a large cast of potential suspects, and when the investigators learn what business Sir Montague had been dabbling in, the challenge before them grows even larger.

Richard Percival has bowed to familial pressure and agreed to attend a tonnish house party at Patchcote Grange, where the gathering's unabashed aim is to introduce eligible gentlemen to suitable young ladies. Two of Richard's elderly aunts have assured him that Miss Rosalind Hemmings will make him the perfect wife, and after meeting Miss Hemmings over dinner on the first evening of the party, Richard is sufficiently intrigued to be willing to learn—indeed, he's even looking forward to learning—more of the unusually direct young lady.

But on coming downstairs the following morning, he hears an anguished scream for help. On racing outside to the orchard from whence the scream came, he finds his possibly-intended standing over the very dead body of their universally well-regarded host, Sir Montague Underhill. This is clearly a matter for Scotland Yard, and Richard wastes no time in summoning Barnaby and Penelope Adair and Inspector Stokes to the company's aid. For, indeed, very soon, it becomes blatantly clear that the murderer is one of those presently residing in the house.

On arriving at the Grange, Penelope, Barnaby, and Stokes are confronted with a dauntingly large cast of potential suspects. Wedding through the throng takes time, but on uncovering Sir Montague's private means of earning a little extra cash, it becomes ever more likely that his murderer is, indeed, one of the guests at the house. All too soon, the questions facing the investigators become whether Sir Montague learned a secret someone was desperate to conceal, and if so, what secret was powerful enough to compel an otherwise reasonable man to murder?

A historical novel of 85,000 words interweaving mystery, crime, and a touch of romance.

PRAISE FOR THE WORKS OF
STEPHANIE LAURENS

"Stephanie Laurens' heroines are marvelous tributes to Georgette Heyer: feisty and strong." *Cathy Kelly*

"Stephanie Laurens never fails to entertain and charm her readers with vibrant plots, snappy dialogue, and unforgettable characters." *Historical Romance Reviews*

"Stephanie Laurens plays into readers' fantasies like a master and claims their hearts time and again." *Romantic Times Magazine*

Praise for The Curse of the Ill-Gotten Gains

"Fans of Penelope and Barnaby Adair will be pleased to see them once again step forward to unravel a mystery involving members of nineteenth-century England's high society. When the host of a country-house party is murdered, the Adairs and Inspector Stokes are called in to discover who among the dozens of guests could have committed the crime. Their investigation uncovers secrets, betrayals, blackmail, and even romance. Sedately paced but precisely plotted, this story will keep readers engaged from start to finish." *Kim H., Proofreader, Red Adept Editing*

"A house party in the English countryside goes dreadfully awry when the host is bludgeoned to death in the orchard, but it turns out that quite a few of the guests had a reason to want him gone. Enter Inspector Stokes of Scotland Yard and his sidekicks, the aristocrats Barnaby and Penelope Adair, and this becomes one house party that intriguingly combines the exploits of the haut ton with some good old shoe-leather investigating." *Angela M., Copy Editor, Red Adept Editing*

"Fans of Regency-set fiction with a taste for murder mysteries will enjoy The Curse of Ill-Gotten Gains." *Virge B., Proofreader, Red Adept Editing*

OTHER TITLES BY STEPHANIE LAURENS

Marriage and Murder

The Murder of Thomas Cardwell

The Curse of Ill-gotten Gains

Who Killed the Earl of Moran? (March, 2026)

Bastion Club Novels

Captain Jack's Woman (Prequel)

The Lady Chosen

A Gentleman's Honor

A Lady of His Own

A Fine Passion

To Distraction

Beyond Seduction

The Edge of Desire

Mastered by Love

Black Cobra Quartet

The Untamed Bride

The Elusive Bride

The Brazen Bride

The Reckless Bride

The Adventurers Quartet

The Lady's Command

A Buccaneer at Heart

The Daredevil Snared

Lord of the Privateers

The Cavanaughs

The Designs of Lord Randolph Cavanaugh

The Pursuits of Lord Kit Cavanaugh

The Beguilement of Lady Eustacia Cavanaugh

The Obsessions of Lord Godfrey Cavanaugh

Other Novels

The Lady Risks All

The Legend of Nimway Hall – 1750: Jacqueline

Medieval (As M.S.Laurens)

Desire's Prize

Novellas

Melting Ice – from the anthologies *Rough Around the Edges* and *Scandalous Brides*

Rose in Bloom – from the anthology *Scottish Brides*

Scandalous Lord Dere – from the anthology *Secrets of a Perfect Night*

Lost and Found – from the anthology *Hero, Come Back*

The Fall of Rogue Gerrard – from the anthology *It Happened One Night*

The Seduction of Sebastian Trantor – from the anthology *It Happened One Season*

Short Stories

The Wedding Planner – from the anthology *Royal Weddings*

A Return Engagement – from the anthology *Royal Bridesmaids*

UK-Style Regency Romances

Tangled Reins

Four in Hand

Impetuous Innocent

Fair Juno

The Reasons for Marriage

A Lady of Expectations An Unwilling Conquest

A Comfortable Wife

THE CURSE OF ILL-GOTTEN GAINS

THE CURSE OF ILL-GOTTEN GAINS

Copyright © 2025 by Savdek Management Proprietary Limited

ISBN: 978-1-925559-78-1

Cover design by Savdek Management Pty. Ltd.

First print publication: October, 2025

Savdek Management Proprietary Limited, Melbourne, Australia.

www.stephanielaurens.com

Email: admin@stephanielaurens.com

The names Stephanie Laurens and the Cynsters and the SL Logo are registered trademarks of Savdek Management Proprietary Ltd.

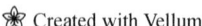 Created with Vellum

CHAPTER 1

JULY 19, 1841. PATCHCOTE GRANGE, SURREY, ENGLAND.

*N*o one had seen.

No one was around that side of the house.

Breathe—no need to panic.

The red haze of fury was slowly ebbing, leaving in its wake a strange lassitude.

Rational thought rose through the miasma, urging caution.

Still…it had felt so *good*. That moment when the stake had connected with Monty's skull had brought such a surge of satisfaction.

As if that outcome was exactly, precisely how things had to be.

Now…

Breathe deeply and think about what lies ahead.

The next step was to find that wretched document. In fact, that was the only thing left to do.

The only thing that stood in the way of a comfortable and carefree life.

The Honorable Richard Percival closed the door of his room on the first floor of Patchcote Grange and, carrying his three recently completed letters, walked toward the main stairs. Idly, he wondered what the day would bring and inwardly admitted he was not as unexcited by the prospect as he'd expected to be.

Attending house parties had never been a favored occupation, but having requested his aunts' assistance in identifying a suitable bride, he'd felt obliged to come to Patchcote Grange and cast his eye over their prime prospect. That said, he'd fully expected to spend his time in Surrey discovering and subsequently demonstrating why his aunts' selected candidate would not do.

Indeed, he'd had little faith that a lady both suitable and compatible even existed.

After meeting Miss Rosalind Hemmings at dinner the previous evening, he was no longer so certain that was the case.

She was in her mid-twenties, and far from tripping over her toes to capture his attention and impress him, she'd regarded him assessingly—almost suspiciously. Certainly measuringly and with reserve, as if she was expecting to be disappointed and to summarily dismiss him. That reaction alone had made him look twice. He wasn't a coxcomb, but he knew how highly he rated in the eligible-bachelor stakes.

Then again, the Hemmingses were wealthy and well-connected, which was at least in part why his aunts had chosen Rosalind to bring to his attention. Presumably, she could and would make her own choice in the matter of selecting a husband.

Rather unexpectedly, he was willing to explore the possibility that he might want to be that man.

He reached the head of the stairs and started down the first long flight.

In his earlier years, he'd never thought of himself as the marrying kind. But then, his brother, Robert, the late Viscount Seddington, had died in mysterious circumstances along with his wife, and Richard's nephew and niece had disappeared, and he'd discovered just how important family was to him. Through his own endeavors—but even more through those of Robert's stepdaughter, Rose, and her husband, Thomas—Richard's nephew, William, and his niece, Alice, had been kept safe from the cousin who had sought to murder them and have Richard accused and convicted of the crime, thus clearing the way for that cousin to inherit the Seddington title and the exceedingly large entailed estate.

In the wake of that drama, Richard had reunited with William, Alice, and Rose and had formed a close friendship with Thomas Glendower, Rose's husband. Given Richard was a bachelor and Rose and Thomas were very willing to keep William and Alice with them, over recent years, the pair had spent most of their days in the Glendower household. But it was Richard who currently managed Seddington, the significant estate that would ultimately fall to William, as Viscount Seddington, to run, and given Rose and Thomas lived outside tonnish society, it would be Richard's responsibility to steer William into that world and, equally pertinently, to oversee Alice's emergence into the ton.

It had been Richard's evolving understanding of the role he would need to play in securing his nephew's and niece's futures that had prompted him to rethink his attitude to marriage.

To do the best for William and Alice, to best repay and keep his silent vows to Robert, Richard had accepted that he needed a wife.

The right wife. One who would stand by his side, perform as required, and not irritate him beyond all measure in the process.

Despite his aunts' knowledge of the ton and of him, he hadn't expected to find that elusive lady at Patchcote Grange, yet it seemed Fate might have taken a benevolent interest in his plans.

As he crossed the landing and started down the last flight, he was conscious of rising expectation. The muted sounds of female voices reached him, with the *clack* of billiard balls a staccato counterpoint.

Looking ahead down the length of the front hall and through the open front doors, Richard saw the sunlit lawn stretching beyond the forecourt. Should he indulge in the quiet of the library or head outside?

The company assembled for the weeklong party was large, with a good selection of eligible, older, and younger gentlemen to complement the gaggle of young ladies and their mothers. No doubt, he would find other gentlemen of his ilk in the library, perusing the news sheets.

He was on the second-last stair when a scream ripped through the sleepy somnolence of the summer morning. A scream for help.

Richard halted.

The scream had come from outside. A second scream followed, its tone even more urgent.

Swallowing a curse, Richard leapt to the hall tiles and sprinted for the open doorway. Passing the hall table, he tossed his letters toward the silver salver resting on the polished surface and continued headlong for the front porch.

He raced past the open library door and heard the men in the library rousing.

He cleared the doorway and leapt down the porch steps, then skidded to a halt on the gravel forecourt and looked around.

Lawns, trees…where?

The next call was fainter. "Help! The orchard!"

While strolling the previous evening, he'd noticed the stone-walled orchard in one corner of the grounds. He ran toward the entrance archway, which stood at the nearest corner.

As he closed the distance, through the archway, he saw Rosalind Hemmings standing halfway along the first row of trees, her hands to her white face as she stared at something in the grass at her feet.

Unexpected emotion clutched at his chest.

He cleared the archway and slowed. His gaze tracked to what Rosalind was staring at, then, as horror-struck as she, he couldn't look away.

He halted beside her and stared at their host stretched out, face down, in the grass, with the back of his skull cracked open.

No more able than Rosalind to draw his gaze from the grisly sight, Richard reached out one arm and gently drew her to him, exerting just enough pressure to turn her into his shoulder so she was no longer looking at the murdered man.

She didn't sag against him, yet neither did she resist his direction. The scent of her glossy brown hair reached him and, together with the warmth of her slender form, at some deep level, reassured him.

"Dear God." The horrified whisper fell from his lips, and he took a step back, drawing Rosalind with him.

Montague—Monty—Underhill lay sprawled a few feet from the trunk of an old apple tree. He lay with his face in the longish grass, his head closer to the trunk, his skull caved in to the extent there was no need to check for signs of life. A pool of blood had gathered beneath and to one side of the body.

Richard felt Rosalind draw in a huge breath, then she raised her head from his shoulder. Her voice choked, she managed, "I was out walking… and there he was."

Richard squeezed her arm, then carefully released her. He could hear others rushing their way. He stepped to the side of the body, crouched, and for form's sake, set two fingers to Monty's throat, but as anyone could have predicted, there was no pulse to find.

Watching him through wide lavender-blue eyes, Rosalind gulped. "I already checked. He's dead."

Richard glanced at her, then rose. He looked over his shoulder at the approaching men, then moved back to Rosalind. Her gaze had returned to the body. Focusing on her face, he asked, "Are you all right?"

"Hardly." She swallowed, then raised her head and met his eyes. "But I'm definitely better than he is."

The crisp reply assured him that she wasn't about to dissolve into hysterics.

He nodded, then turned to the others striding, rather uncertainly, into the orchard.

He waved to halt them. "Better you keep your distance."

"Oh, I say!"

"Good Lord!"

A chorus of shocked exclamations filled the air as more of those arriving—most of the gentlemen, as far as Richard could see—caught sight of the body.

Richard raised his head and looked over the orchard wall and saw that the ladies were gathering in an agitated cluster on the lawn, but none, thank heaven, was showing any signs of venturing closer. Among the group, he saw Mrs. Hemmings, Rosalind's mother, both his aunts, and Lady Pamela Underhill, Monty's wife.

"Great heavens!" Lord Wincombe, one of the older gentlemen, spluttered. "We have to do something, but what? What should we do?"

Richard thought the answer obvious. "We need to send for the local magistrate and the police." He delivered the pronouncement in a tone that brooked no argument. He was aware that several there, having no wish to become embroiled in any official investigation, let alone one for murder, might think to somehow sweep the business under the proverbial rug.

He was relieved when all the younger men and those his age agreed without question.

Several of the older gentlemen frowned.

Elliot, a sensible man, said, "I'll get the butler to send for the magistrate."

Grateful, Richard added, "Ask Gearing to send a footman with a sheet. The footman will need to remain on guard until the authorities get here."

Elliot nodded and retreated, trailed by several of the younger gentlemen who looked rather wan.

"I say, Percival." Lord Morland, another of the older men, shifted his bulk uncomfortably. "Shouldn't we at least have Monty carried to the house?"

"That will risk the ire of whoever is sent to investigate." Richard had already decided to dispatch his groom hotfoot to Scotland Yard. "Underhill's been murdered. There's no getting around that. No denying it. The police will be summoned."

A strangled cry drew everyone's gazes to the gathered ladies. One of the men returning to the house had told them what had been found. Indeed, Lady Pamela would have insisted on being told, and now she'd heard the news, she'd fainted into her sister's arms, and the other ladies were closing supportively around their hostess.

The men with wives in the group promptly returned to their ladies' sides.

A footman came flying from the house with a folded sheet in his arms.

Carrington, one of the eligible bachelors, helped the footman unfold the sheet and decently cover the body.

With that done, solemn and concerned, the remaining gentlemen turned and slowly filed out of the orchard and walked heavily back to the house, following the ladies, who were already retreating.

Richard checked with the footman that he knew he was to remain on guard.

Standing ramrod straight, the lanky man declared, "Until the police or the magistrate say I can go."

With an approving nod, Richard turned to Rosalind. His gaze following the men crossing the lawn toward the house, he murmured, "Did you see Vincent Underhill?" Aged about twenty-five, Vincent was Monty and Pamela's only son.

"No." Rosalind softly snorted. "He's probably still abed."

"That is a possibility." Richard had noted that others—Vincent's friends—had also not appeared.

Rosalind glanced at the sheet-draped form resting in the grass. "That might be just as well."

The retreating gentlemen had reached the forecourt. Richard saw a rider appear from the rear of the house and gallop hard down the main drive.

Richard looked at Rosalind. "Are you up to facing the inevitable inquisition?"

He'd dallied to give her time to regroup.

She looked at the house and sighed. "If they get too bad, I'll pretend to feel faint."

He almost laughed, but, instead, offered his arm. "Come, then. I'll escort you back."

She regarded his raised sleeve, and her brows arched. "Into the lions' den?"

"Worse. Into a gathering of ton gossips who know you know what they want to find out."

That surprised a faint laugh from her, and she took his arm and raised her head. "Onward, then."

With her on his arm, he strolled as slowly as was reasonable out of the orchard and over the lawn.

As they neared the house, Rosalind cynically observed, "What would you wager that all too soon, many of the ladies, both young and old, come to view this house party as one they were especially lucky to have attended?"

"Because once they return to town, they'll be in high demand to divulge every scandal-laden detail?"

"Exactly."

Supporting her up the low steps to the front porch, equally cynically, Richard replied, "Betting against the ton's rampant curiosity is a wager I would never take."

Penelope Adair sat behind the desk in her garden parlor and doggedly slogged her way through the remarkably boring yet difficult translation she'd agreed to complete for the British Museum's history department.

"For my money," she muttered to herself, "this is one scroll that could have vanished beneath the sands with no one the poorer."

But she'd agreed to do it, so she would.

The knowledge that this would be her last project before August and the family's regular summer excursions to visit her sisters at their homes and then Barnaby's family at Cothelstone Castle helped to keep her focused on the arduous, not to say mind-numbing, task.

Finally—*finally!*—she reached the last page, the last line, the last character.

"There!" Triumphantly, she blotted her last line, read it over to make sure she hadn't made any mistake, then sat straight in her chair and set aside her pen. "Wonderful!"

"And you haven't even heard the news yet." Barnaby walked in, a letter in his hand, a smile on his face, and an intrigued expression in his blue eyes.

Penelope opened her eyes wide. "What's happened?"

Advancing, Barnaby waved the missive. "Monty Underhill's been killed, and Percival is there, at Patchcote Grange, attending a house party, and he's written to beg us to come down and help Scotland Yard investigate."

"Have they been notified?" Penelope held out her hand for the letter, and Barnaby handed it over.

"Richard says he sent for Stokes directly." Barnaby paused while she read, then asked, "How's the scroll going? Can you manage a few days away?"

Having perused Richard's scant and uninformative few lines, Penelope looked up and beamed. "I've finished! That's what I was celebrating when you walked in."

"Excellent." Barnaby grinned back.

Penelope glanced again at the letter. "A house party at Patchcote Grange. That's Pamela's regular event, which is always devoted, first to last, to matchmaking. Especially now that her daughter has made her come-out and her nieces, Susan's two, have as well. And Richard's there?" Dark eyes gleaming, she looked at Barnaby. "Well, well…"

Trying to hide his smile, Barnaby shook his head at her. "I expect it's his host's murder that Percival wants our help with, not his love life."

Penelope pushed back from the desk. "I can't see why he shouldn't have the benefit of our expertise on both fronts."

As she rose from her chair, the doorbell pealed. She met Barnaby's eyes and arched her brows. "I wonder…"

Barnaby waved her on, and letter still in hand, she led the way along the corridor to the front hall.

Sure enough, Stokes had arrived.

He looked up as she and Barnaby neared. "Have you heard?"

Penelope waved Richard's letter. "That Monty Underhill's been murdered? Just now. And yes, we're free."

Stokes blew out a breath. "Good. Because I've been instructed that in light of the personages involved, your assistance is highly recommended. Indeed, the Commissioner's tone suggested that he considered your inclusion in the investigative team all but mandatory."

"In this case," Barnaby said, "the Commissioner's instincts are sound. I can guarantee that some there will be only too keen to quash any investigation."

"And that's regardless of whether they have anything at all to hide,"

Penelope added. "For some, keeping the police at bay is still second nature—an ingrained habit."

Stokes huffed. "So we'll have our work cut out for us."

"At least," Barnaby said, indicating the letter with a tip of his head, "Percival is there."

"True," Stokes said. "That means we've at least one pair of reliable eyes and ears among the company."

"I suspect his aunts will be there, too," Penelope said. "Lady Campbell-Carstairs and Lady Kelly. Both are old, but they're observant and will know more than I about many of the guests. The ladies, at least."

"So what do you know about this gathering?" Stokes asked.

"It's a regular event—a summer house party hosted by the Underhills at Patchcote Grange, with the primary focus being on introducing marriageable young ladies to suitable, eligible gentlemen." Her gaze distant, Penelope paused, then refocused on Stokes. "And you might need to be aware that Patchcote Grange—the house and attached estate, which is considerable—is owned by Lady Pamela."

Stokes frowned. "Not Mr. Underhill?"

Penelope shook her head. "Lady Pamela is one of two daughters of the previous Marquess of Skeldon. Patchcote Grange was the property her father settled on her for her lifetime, and on her death, it will pass from her to her eldest son, Vincent Underhill."

"Is that a common arrangement?" Stokes asked.

Again, Penelope shook her head. "However, when it comes to daughters of the nobility, it's not without precedent. It ensures that the property, which was originally a part of the marquessate, ultimately passes to the marquess's grandchildren and cannot be diverted via a spouse gaining control."

"I see." Stokes continued to frown, clearly working his way through the implications.

Helpfully, Barnaby confirmed, "Because of that, there's no inheritance involved in Underhill's murder. Whoever killed him, it wasn't in order to inherit Patchcote Grange."

Stokes grunted. "Well, that's one motive less." He eyed Barnaby and Penelope. "Regardless, the sooner we get down there the better, so when can you leave?"

Penelope volunteered, "Patchcote Grange is in Surrey, a stone's throw south of Beddington Corner, so only about an hour away."

"That close?" Stokes looked hopeful. "With any luck, we'll be there by the afternoon."

Barnaby had been exchanging a look with Penelope. He raised his brows. "Can we set off from here in half an hour?"

She beamed. "I can't see why not." She turned to Stokes. "So half an hour from now, and don't be late."

Stokes huffed and turned for the door.

After returning to the house and escorting Rosalind to the morning room, where her mother and all the other ladies had taken refuge to talk in hushed tones of the horror of the discovery, Richard had diverted to his room and dashed off two notes that he'd dispatched with his groom to be delivered poste-haste to London. Subsequently, he'd remained in his room, staring into space while trying to fix in his mind all he'd noticed in the orchard, before finally stirring and making for the library, where, predictably, the gentlemen had gathered. Most had helped themselves to tots of brandy from the tantalus. All appeared shaken, some more than others.

Sinking into a spare armchair close by the door, Richard noted that most of the men of the company were there. The sole exception was Vincent Underhill, whom Richard had glimpsed supporting his distraught sister upstairs. Vincent's friends—Patterson and Fentiman—had joined the company at some point. Richard wondered if they'd been abed or somewhere else on the estate.

"Dreadful business," the Earl of Leith quietly stated.

Lord Morland, standing with Leith a few feet away from the chair Richard occupied, took a healthy swig of brandy. "I gather there's nothing much we can do until the magistrate gets here."

Lord Wincombe walked up to the group. "Gearing said the local magistrate, Sir Henry Coutts, lives quite close, so hopefully, he'll be able to get here soon."

Richard noted that while it was plain every man there heartily wished Underhill had not had his head bashed in, as yet, none had voiced any opinion as to who had done the deed, much less why.

That, he had to admit, was hardly surprising. While without much thought, Richard could name any number of ton gentlemen that no one would be all that surprised to learn had been violently murdered by persons unknown, Monty Underhill definitely didn't belong in that category.

Apparently, Morland was thinking along the same lines. His brow deeply furrowed, he ventured, "Can't for the life of me imagine who would want to do that to Monty. Gentle soul, always helpful. Never a malicious bone in his body."

Frowning, Wincombe nodded. "It's certainly perplexing."

"And potentially worrying," Leith put in.

When the others, Richard included, looked questioningly at Leith, he shrugged. "It would be worrying indeed if the killing was some random act and Monty being the victim was simply a case of being in the wrong place at the wrong time."

Morland tipped his head in acknowledgment. "Possible, I suppose."

Richard bit back the observation that murder victims were rarely so conveniently unconnected to their killers. Leith and Morland were merely putting words to the thoughts of most in the room. Indeed, possibly most in the house.

Gradually, the quiet conversations drifted to more normal subjects, such as the outcomes of recent race meets and sales at Tattersalls and the latest prize fight.

Time seemed to crawl as all there tried to distract themselves from the image of their host bludgeoned to death in his own orchard on a bright summer day.

Eventually, to everyone's unvoiced relief, Gearing, the butler, appeared. Glancing around, Gearing spotted Leith and Richard and headed their way. He stopped beside Richard's chair and bowed. "My lords. Mr. Percival. Lady Pamela has retired to her rooms, but she suggests the company should carry on with normal activities, at least until the authorities arrive. To that end, I am here to inquire whether the gentlemen wish to partake of luncheon. The ladies have announced they will do so and have gathered in the drawing room. Lady Campbell-Carstairs dispatched me to alert you and invite you to join them."

Richard and Leith exchanged glances, then looked at Morland and Wincombe. It was an awkward situation, but starving themselves wouldn't help, and perhaps acting normally for the time being might help people find their mental feet.

Correctly divining the general consensus, Leith said, "Thank you, Gearing. We'll join the ladies."

The rest of the gentlemen had drawn nearer. Richard and those seated rose, and as a group, they followed Gearing out of the library and across the hall to the drawing room.

Richard was among the first of the gentlemen to enter the long room. Spotting Rosalind standing by a window halfway down the room, he made his way to her, noting, as he did, the hushed voices and wide eyes of the female contingent. As husbands joined their spouses and the younger gentlemen approached the younger ladies, in the quick, quiet questions and the murmured answers, Richard sensed welling curiosity over what, exactly, had happened. Over who had killed Monty Underhill and why.

Given Monty's character and personality, the general feeling of complete bewilderment, of being unable to reconcile that such a thing had happened, wasn't surprising. Quite literally, no one could conceive of what might have moved anyone to such an act.

Rosalind was standing a little apart from the other guests. She registered Richard's approach and acknowledged his presence with a vague nod, but her attention remained fixed across the room.

Richard halted beside her and tracked her gaze to the group of younger ladies and, now, younger gentlemen. Rosalind's expression carried a frowning quality as she stared at her younger sister, Regina.

Richard looked back and forth. He sensed Regina was aware of Rosalind's regard but was pretending to be oblivious. Returning his gaze to Rosalind, he quietly asked, "Are you all right?"

She glanced his way, considered him for an instant, then replied, "Well enough." Then she grimaced faintly and added, "I'm not the swooning sort."

Richard nodded. "Duly noted." *With a certain relief, what's more.*

From the doorway, Gearing announced, "My lords, ladies, and gentlemen. Luncheon is served."

With Pamela and her family absent—including her sister, Susan—Richard's aunt Agatha, Lady Campbell-Carstairs, was the senior lady present. She rose from an armchair by the hearth and waved her cane at Leith—the senior nobleman—and he obediently crossed to offer his arm.

Together, Agatha and Leith led the company forth. While some of the elders present made an effort to observe precedence, most simply fell into line with whomever they'd been standing beside.

Meeting Rosalind's soft blue gaze, Richard offered his arm. "Shall we make our relatives happy?"

Her lips lifted a fraction, then she laid her hand on his sleeve and raised her head. "Why not?"

Rosalind walked with Percival out of the drawing room and fought not to let her awareness slide sideways, yet her senses seemed irresistibly drawn to the gentleman pacing with easy grace beside her.

Percival was proving to be something of a conundrum. While on the one hand, fully half her mind was focused on her sister and what was going on in Regina's head, Percival was proving to be an effective distraction.

And if she wished to be seen as behaving normally, then it was unquestionably he to whom she should be paying attention.

Over six feet tall, broad shouldered, lean, and powerful, he exuded an air of effortless control somewhat at odds with his undeniably rakish handsomeness. Sable-brown hair, slightly wavy locks in fashionably rumpled disarray, combined with unusually dark-blue eyes set beneath black eyebrows, well-defined cheekbones, and the spare angular planes of a face that veritably screamed his aristocratic antecedents to create an image of male beauty that any female with eyes would notice.

She'd noticed, but she'd told herself that beauty was as beauty did, and Percival's reputation as a hedonistic rakehell was of far more weight in the matrimonial scales.

And yet…

She'd expected to instantly take against him—on meeting him, to immediately have any number of sound arguments with which to quash the suggestion that he and she might suit. Instead…

The gentleman she'd met the previous evening had been…something other than what she'd imagined he would be.

He'd been—and still was—attentive without being pushy, supportive and willing to step in and assist her as she wished, not as he deemed he should. Certainly, he was far more intelligent and capable than she and, she suspected, wider society had assumed. He was incisive, decisive, and rational in a way that appealed to her. She preferred stability, and with his innate understanding of their world and his straightforward way of dealing with it and, it seemed, her, he was—entirely unexpectedly—shaping up as an excellent prospect, possibly her best prospect, for achieving all she wished for in life.

As they passed into the dining room, she slanted a faintly puzzled, distinctly curious glance his way.

He seemed to feel her gaze. Briefly, he met her eyes, then they reached the table, and he drew out a chair for her almost midway down the board.

She owned to feeling pleased when he claimed the chair beside her and sat. For some incalculable reason, she felt safer with him near. She told herself it was because, with him beside her, she didn't need to make conversation with anyone else, and he seemed amenable to eating and observing the company without needing to chat all the time.

She used the moment when everyone was shuffling about and sorting themselves into a semblance of appropriate seating to locate her sister. To Rosalind's eyes, Regina appeared unusually pale, and as she sat between two of the younger gentlemen—Patterson and Fentiman—farther down the table on the opposite side of the board with the other younger ladies and gentlemen, Regina seemed notably subdued.

With typical youthful resilience, the rest of the younger crew had largely rebounded from the shock and uncertainty their host's murder had evoked. Judging by their expressions and the comments traded back and forth, a sense of curiosity and readiness to be intrigued and, indeed, entertained had taken hold.

Percival offered a platter, and Rosalind was forced to pull her mind and her gaze from her sister. But once the wider company settled to consume the cold collation the staff had put out, as, understandably, most felt weighed down by the unexpected and inexplicable murder, conversation grew sporadic, allowing Rosalind to continue to ponder Regina's strange behavior.

She and Regina were sharing a room, and from the moment they'd risen from their beds, the tension gripping Regina had been obvious. At least to Rosalind. She'd asked if anything was wrong. Far from easing her mind, Regina's brittle assurance that all was perfect had only increased Rosalind's concern.

She'd kept a watchful eye on Regina through breakfast, but after they'd left the table and Regina had stated her intention of joining the bevy of younger ladies making for the conservatory, Rosalind had elected to go upstairs and quietly read in their room.

It had been pure chance that she'd glanced through a window and seen Regina hurrying across the rear lawn, apparently set on being somewhere.

Concern flaring, Rosalind had rushed downstairs and started out in pursuit. Of course, not wanting to attract attention, she'd had to pretend to be merely strolling the grounds. Then, she'd realized Regina was making for the orchard. With thoughts of her impressionable and inexperienced younger sister rushing to keep some clandestine meeting circling insistently in her head, Rosalind had *strolled* as fast as she'd dared toward the orchard.

On reaching the archway, she'd looked in but hadn't seen anyone. Puzzled, she walked down the row of trees…

The shock of finding Monty Underhill's body had thrust all thoughts of Regina from Rosalind's mind.

However, half an hour ago, when Rosalind had gone upstairs to wash before luncheon, she'd found her maid, Cilly, in the room she and Regina shared. Cilly had been grumbling under her breath as she'd scrubbed at the hem of the gown Regina had worn to breakfast—and to rush around the gardens and, possibly, into the orchard. When Rosalind asked Cilly what was amiss, Cilly had shown her the thin line of blood staining a short section of the hem.

Cilly had groused, "Why she had to get so close to a dead body as to get blood on her hem, I have no notion!"

Rosalind hadn't corrected the maid's assumption.

But Rosalind knew beyond question that Regina hadn't approached Monty Underhill's body at any time after Rosalind had come upon it.

She'd thought Regina had gone into the orchard. Now, she knew she had. So where had Regina gone? Had she found the body, panicked, and fled through the orchard into the wood beyond?

Why hadn't Regina raised the alarm?

Consumed by that question, with her gaze fixed on Regina, Rosalind realized that Percival was watching her. She glanced his way and met his eyes. The shrewd, assessing look she found there had her drawing in a breath. He was far too observant for her peace of mind.

Casting about for distraction, she looked toward Regina again. While the rest of the younger crew were growing more animated, Regina remained subdued.

Of course, Percival had followed her gaze. In a faintly questioning tone, he said, "At their age, a dead body is more cause for excitement than concern."

"Hmm. Apparently." *But not so for Regina.* Determinedly, Rosalind asked about Percival's estate, which she'd heard was in Lincolnshire.

He held her gaze for an instant more, then smoothly, obligingly, followed her lead and replied.

CHAPTER 2

A s the Adair carriage wended its way up the long Patchcote
Grange drive, Penelope peered out of the window at the large,
sprawling Jacobean mansion with its many chimney pots rising to the sky.
The building appeared in excellent order, and the extensive grounds were
in similar condition with thick plantings of established trees and mani-
cured lawns enclosing the mansion in a green embrace.

The carriage drew to a smooth halt on the graveled forecourt. As she
waited for Stokes and Barnaby to descend, Penelope checked her small
watch. They'd made excellent time from Mayfair; it was only just two
o'clock.

Having heard the clop of hooves, Richard walked out of the house
with the local magistrate, Sir Henry Coutts. They paused on the porch,
and recognizing Phelps, the Adairs' coachman, on the box of the carriage,
Richard owned to some relief.

He and Sir Henry, a sensible sort, had just come down from speaking
with Lady Pamela. Despite the shock and, somewhat unexpectedly, very
real grief Pamela transparently felt, she was bearing up well and had
insisted that the investigators Richard had taken it upon himself to
summon were given free rein to find and apprehend her husband's
murderer.

Stokes descended from the carriage first. At a trifle over six feet tall
and of solid build, the experienced inspector exuded an aura of command.
His harsh-featured face and dark hair and eyebrows added to the image,

and his steely gray gaze, already scanning the house assessingly, suggested that little escaped him. Richard had encountered Stokes in a professional capacity before, and in the present circumstances, there was no other police officer Richard would rather see. Stokes was gentry born, well-educated, and able to move within the ton, navigating society's shoals as few others in the force could.

Early in his inspector days, Stokes had crossed paths with the Honorable Barnaby Adair, and immediately, the pair had struck up a friendship. Shared values and a mutual thirst for justice had seen friendship deepen into a lasting bond.

Now, Barnaby followed Stokes from the carriage and, like Stokes, paused to look around. An inch or so taller than Stokes but with golden curls and striking blue eyes, Barnaby was the epitome of a tonnish gentleman—the sort many young gentlemen aspired to become. No one seeing his aristocratic features and the understated elegance and quiet assurance that clung to his broad shoulders like a cloak could doubt that he was an earl's son. His knowledge of the ton and government institutions and his connections within those spheres were extensive, and his influence opened doors that would otherwise remain closed to Stokes and most others. His unwavering focus on seeing justice done regardless of the victim's status had, in more recent years, broadened into social projects aimed at improving the lot of those less fortunate.

After glancing around, Barnaby turned back to the carriage and offered his hand. The third member of their investigating team, Barnaby's wife, Penelope, grasped his fingers and climbed down the carriage steps.

In marked contrast to Barnaby and Stokes, Penelope was petite, a pocket Venus with dark hair and beautiful dark eyes perennially screened behind the spectacles she'd worn since girlhood. On other women, spectacles might detract from their appearance, but with Penelope, they were simply a part of her mystique, and she remained strikingly pretty and, it had to be said, precocious. If Barnaby represented the apogee of the conventional gentleman, Penelope was deliberately and determinedly unconventional in many ways. Although now the mother of two young boys and the undisputed general who ran their household, she was also an expert in ancient languages, much in demand as a translator and widely respected in academic circles. With her unrelentingly curious, inquisitive, and inventive mind combined with her intuitive grasp of people's feelings, she brought to the group an intellectual and emotional depth, the importance of which was impossible to overstate.

As she was even more auspiciously connected with the major ton families than Barnaby and was also an accredited darling of the ton's grandes dames, she was a force to be reckoned with on many levels, and her knowledge of ton mores was beyond compare.

Richard couldn't think of a trio of investigators he would rather have dealing with this case. He glanced at Sir Henry. "Come. I'll introduce you."

On firm ground, Penelope shook out her skirts in preparation for greeting Richard and the older man with him. But before the pair could descend from the porch, the sound of heavy carriage wheels rolling up the drive had them all pausing to watch as the ponderous police wagon drew up behind the carriage.

The wagon was still rocking on its springs when the door burst open, and Findlay, Scotland Yard's medical examiner, leapt to the ground. His black bag in hand, he strode forward.

Stopping beside Penelope, Barnaby, and Stokes, Findlay scanned what he could see of the grounds. "The orchard, you said. Where is it?"

Footsteps crunched, and they turned as Richard and the older gentleman joined them.

The unknown man was in his late fifties, perhaps even sixty. He appeared a solid country-squire sort and carried himself well. His curling gray hair matched his wiry eyebrows, and his features, surely initially craggy, had softened with the years, although at present, those features were set in serious and sober lines.

Despite the circumstances, Penelope smiled delightedly at Richard.

Returning her smile in more muted fashion, Richard gestured to the older gentleman. "This is Sir Henry Coutts, the local magistrate." To Sir Henry, he continued, "Allow me to present Inspector Stokes of Scotland Yard, the Honorable Mr. Barnaby Adair, and Mrs. Adair."

"Inspector." Sir Henry offered his hand to Stokes, then turned to Barnaby and Penelope.

Before Sir Henry could ask, Stokes supplied, "Mr. and Mrs. Adair act as official consultants to the Yard, and they are here at the Commissioner's behest."

Still puzzled but now curious, Sir Henry shook Barnaby's hand and nodded politely to Penelope.

She smiled understandingly and explained, "We assist Stokes in dealing with cases involving members of the ton."

"Ah. I see." Sir Henry glanced back at the house. "I can imagine that in cases such as this, your presence would be beneficial."

"Exactly so." Penelope fixed her gaze on Sir Henry. "Now, what can you tell us of this murder?"

Sir Henry grunted, and his features clouded. "Bad business. I've known Monty Underhill these past decades. Utterly harmless fellow. Good man. But a young lady out walking this morning found his body in the orchard. Bludgeoned to death, it seems."

Findlay appeared around Stokes's shoulder. "The body?"

Stokes introduced Findlay as the Yard's and London's premier medical examiner—which was, in fact, Findlay's growing reputation—and Sir Henry looked duly impressed. He pointed across the lawn to the far corner away from the drive. "Still in the orchard. Percival here was the first man on the scene and knew not to move him, so he's as he was found."

Richard added, "I confirmed Monty was dead but otherwise didn't disturb the body, and we've had a footman on guard since then."

"Excellent." Plainly pleased, Findlay half bowed to the company. "If you'll excuse me, the sooner I get to it, the sooner I can return to town and the morgue and the other bodies awaiting my attention."

Penelope hid an appreciative grin as Findlay strode off across the lawn, his black bag swinging.

"Now," Sir Henry continued, "I've had all the guests gather in the drawing room and asked them to remain there for the nonce. I've spoken with Lady Pamela, and she's given the authorities—specifically Scotland Yard—free rein to uncover the dastard who murdered Monty. She's understandably overset, but bearing up." Sir Henry paused, then somewhat uncomfortably added, "I did gather that she expects the culprit to be taken up in short order."

Stokes eyed the color in Sir Henry's cheeks and wryly asked, "Did she suggest that said culprit will likely be a passing vagabond?"

Sir Henry's eyes widened. "She did."

Barnaby smiled faintly. "It's always easier to believe a murder happened through some unpredictable, unforeseeable outside agency rather than being the action or reaction of one of the victim's peers."

Sir Henry nodded. "Human nature, I suppose."

Stokes had glanced toward the open front door but turned to Sir Henry. "Findlay will want to remove the body to London as soon as he can, so we'd better take a look at the scene first."

Richard waved them on, and he and Sir Henry fell into step beside Penelope, Barnaby, and Stokes. Stokes beckoned his men—O'Donnell, Morgan, and Walsh, who had come in the wagon with Findlay—to follow.

As they left the forecourt and started across the lawn, Richard dipped his head and murmured to Penelope and Barnaby, "Thank you for coming."

Penelope shot him a wry grin. "You knew very well that we'd answer your call." She looked ahead. "It's not every morning one is invited to investigate a murder."

"Especially," Barnaby added, "a murder of one of our own."

Richard raised his head. "It does strike closer to home." As Sir Henry and Stokes drew ahead, Richard glanced at Penelope and Barnaby. "You were acquainted with Underhill, weren't you?"

"Indeed," Penelope replied. "Although I'm more familiar with Pamela, of course."

Richard arched a brow at Penelope. "A connection?"

"Very distant on Mama's side," she replied, "but a connection never-theless."

"I knew Underhill," Barnaby said, "but only socially, in passing, as it were."

"That's much the same as me," Richard said. "One couldn't have said we moved in the same circles." He glanced shrewdly at Penelope and Barnaby. "But what you know of the family will be helpful. You'll have some understanding of the familial and social dynamics at play."

From his tone, Penelope deduced he was referring to the issue of Pamela being the actual owner of all they were presently surveying. The orchard was quite some way across the lawn; Penelope could only just make out an entrance archway. "The orchard's walled?"

"Yes. All the way around," Richard replied, "but there are at least three archways—the one we're approaching, another giving onto the shrubbery, and one at the rear corner, which leads into the wood."

Barnaby asked, "How many guests are presently here?"

"The rest of the immediate family—so Pamela, the son, Vincent, and the daughter, Cecilia. Also here are Pamela's sister, Lady Susan Goodrich, along with her daughters, Enid and Samantha." Richard went on, "None of that group were at luncheon, and there were twenty-three around the table, including myself."

Penelope slanted him a glance. "Also including your aunts?"

Richard met her gaze and warily admitted, "Including my aunts."

"And the Hemmingses?"

Richard sighed. "I suppose it was too much to imagine you wouldn't know about that. But yes, Mrs. Hemmings and her daughters, Rosalind and Regina, are here. It was Rosalind who discovered the body and raised the alarm."

With the orchard nearing, Penelope slowed her steps to ask, "What's your family's connection with the Underhills? I can't place it."

"My aunts are close to the family via an old and longstanding friendship with the late marquess."

"Pamela and Susan's father?" Penelope clarified.

"Yes. And courtesy of that, Pamela has always had a soft spot for my aunts, so when they asked, she was happy to oblige them by inviting not just them but me and the Hemmings ladies."

Penelope nodded. "And the rest of the company? Why are they here?"

"As I'm sure you're aware, the principal purpose of Pamela's house party is to promote suitable matches. To that end, I gather Pamela hopes to entice Leith into offering for Cecilia. I imagine that would be hailed as an acceptable match on all sides, and it seems that Leith is interested enough to look. As for the others, Mrs. Waterhouse has hopes of snaring Elliot for her daughter, Alison. The Waterhouses and, indeed, most of those here are close acquaintances of one or another of the Underhills, and I understand most of the middle-aged set are reasonably frequent visitors, either here or at Wyndham Castle."

Stokes had reached the orchard archway and paused, waiting for them to catch up. He'd heard the last comment and arched his brows. "Wyndham Castle?"

"The seat of the Marquess of Skeldon," Barnaby supplied. "It's in the Midlands."

"The castle was Lady Pamela and Lady Susan's childhood home," Penelope added. "On their father's death, the title, castle, and estate passed to their cousin, Bradley Hurstbridge."

She looked past Stokes into the orchard. Some way inside, she could just make out a white sheet tossed aside and a still form stretched on the ground beneath a tree. Findlay was already crouched beside the body.

Penelope, Barnaby, and Richard hung back, allowing Stokes and Sir Henry to approach the body first, then the three followed the pair deeper into the orchard, with the uniformed officers at their backs.

As they neared the scene, Barnaby noticed a footman standing back against the stone wall a few yards from the body. On seeing the man, Stokes asked his name, then sent him to wait at the archway. Patently grateful, the footman decamped, leaving the rest of them to take in the scene.

Quietly, they drifted wide around the body, observing and cataloguing what they could see while Findlay continued with his necessarily cursory examination, yet not that much study was required to establish the cause of death.

Finishing his circuit, Stokes halted beside the crouching Findlay and glanced at Richard. "Do you know Underhill's movements prior to him coming to the orchard? When was he last seen alive?"

Standing nearer the tree trunk, Richard replied, "He came down to breakfast later than I. He arrived a few minutes before I left the dining room, which must have been about seven-thirty. I've heard others say he was at the table with them, and by all accounts, he was one of the last to leave. At a guess, that would have been closer to nine o'clock, when the staff would have wanted to start clearing the board. Several gentlemen had settled in the library with the day's news sheets, and they say he looked in and chatted for a few minutes before wandering off, apparently outside."

Stokes had fished out his trusty notebook and was busily scribbling. "When was the body found and by whom?"

"One of the guests—Miss Rosalind Hemmings—was taking the air and came this way. She saw the body, realized who it was and that he was dead, and screamed for help. I was on the stairs at the time—I'd been writing letters in my room and was on my way down to leave them for posting when I heard the scream. That must have been about ten o'clock. I came racing out, and others followed."

Stokes nodded, paused in his writing, and looked down at Findlay. "What can you tell us?"

"He's dead. Definitely. And judging by the depth of that"—Findlay nodded at the indentation in the back of the corpse's skull—"he was dead within seconds of being struck." Findlay paused, head tilting as he studied the wound. "He was hit with something entirely unforgiving. Something heavy. You might want to look around."

Stokes turned and looked at his men.

O'Donnell saluted, and the other two nodded, and the three fanned out, searching through the thick summer grass.

Stokes returned to Findlay. "Anything else?"

Findlay rocked back on his heels, then blew out a breath. "This is more an educated guess, but I'd say he didn't hear his assailant approach. He was distracted." Findlay raised his gaze to the tree trunk and, with his head, indicated a large hollow about six feet from the ground. "He might have been poking around in there."

Penelope bustled over to look, and Barnaby followed.

Penelope was too short to see inside the hollow, but Barnaby peered in easily enough. "There's nothing in here but leaves and twigs."

From beside them, Richard said, "Monty was shorter. I doubt he would have been easily able to see inside, not unless he went up on his toes."

"Or he felt inside." Penelope demonstrated, then retrieved her hand, frowned, and brushed debris off her fingertips.

"Guv!" O'Donnell called.

They turned to see the experienced sergeant deeper in the orchard.

He pointed at something in the grass. "Looks like this might be the weapon."

The rest of them waited by the body as Stokes strode across, ducking beneath branches heavy with fruit to where his sergeant stood. Morgan and Walsh, deeper in the orchard, ceased their searching and started back, eager to see what O'Donnell had found.

On joining O'Donnell, Stokes halted and stared downward, then he bent and carefully picked up what appeared to be an iron stake. After examining the stake's end, Stokes nodded to his men and carried the stake back to Findlay.

As Stokes approached, those about the body saw tufts of light-brown hair and other matter crusted along a section of the stake.

Findlay grunted, got to his feet, and reached to take the stake from Stokes. Findlay squinted at the encrustation, then hefted the stake. "This'll be it." Stepping across the body's legs, Findlay lowered the stake and held it just above the corpse's caved-in skull. It wasn't hard to see that the hair color and fineness matched that of the body and that the indentation in the skull held a similar shape to the edge of the stake. Findlay raised the stake. "I'll take measurements back at the morgue, but I don't think you need to search further. This is the murder weapon."

Barnaby eyed the stake. "Could a woman have wielded that?"

Findlay's brows rose. He weighed the stake, then looked at Penelope.

She sighed and rounded the body and took the stake. She raised it easily enough.

"Wait!" Findlay ducked around to stand behind her. "Now, slowly lower it."

She complied.

Once she was holding the stake horizontally, Findlay grunted. Reaching around to retrieve the stake, he looked at Stokes and Barnaby. "Clearly, any woman could have lifted the stake. But given his height"—Findlay nodded at the corpse—"only a woman of at least average height could have struck that blow." He turned to smile at Penelope. "For instance, Mrs. Adair could not have been the murderer. The angle of the blow would have been more vertical."

Penelope sighed. "Sadly, saying someone must be taller than me won't narrow our suspects list much at all."

The men smiled.

Barnaby caught Findlay's gaze and arched his brows. "Would our murderer have had blood on their hands or clothes?"

Findlay lightly shrugged. "It's possible." He looked at the corpse, then at the length of the stake. "That said, I think it's unlikely. I think the victim collapsed under the blow. It was quite ferocious, so I tend to think you're looking for a man. However, the victim fell forward, and most of the bleeding you see occurred after he hit the ground, so any splatter at the moment the blow connected would, I judge, have been minimal, and the length of this stake means the murderer was standing a good yard away from his victim."

"All right." Stokes looked up from his notebook. "Time of death?"

Findlay glanced at Richard. "With the body being outside, exposed to warmer temperatures, it's difficult to be accurate, but if he was last seen in the house at just after nine o'clock and he was found dead at around ten, then that window—say between nine and ten o'clock this morning—is consistent with what I see."

Stokes grunted. "Good enough." He looked at the others. "So we have our murder weapon, the scene of the crime, and the hour during which the murder occurred."

Barnaby observed, "I can't remember when we've had so much to work with, straight off the bat."

Penelope narrowed her eyes at him. "Don't jinx us."

Stokes looked at Findlay. "Anything more you can tell us?"

"Well." Findlay held up the stake. "I can't see any more of these lying around, and if you look closely, there's a number painted on this end"—

he offered the end he'd been holding, not the end used to crack a skull—
"a good long while ago. Reddish paint, number thirty-five."

Barnaby moved with Penelope and Stokes to peer at the number on
the stake.

"What could that mean?" Penelope asked.

"I suggest you ask the gardeners," Findlay said. "They might be able
to tell you where this came from."

"And that," Stokes said, "might tell us where the murderer was before
he set off to follow Underhill with murderous intent."

Findlay nodded. "Exactly."

Sir Henry, who had been a silent observer throughout, shifted
nervously. When the others looked his way, he grimaced faintly. "I fear
the natives will be growing restless."

Penelope inclined her head. "Indeed. You're right." She looked at
Stokes. "We need to return to the house and do what we can to reassure
the company."

Stokes nodded and turned to Findlay. A discussion ensued over who
got to keep the stake, but in the end, Stokes prevailed, and Findlay grudg-
ingly cleaned off the gory end and kept the rag as evidence.

Satisfied, Stokes handed the stake to O'Donnell and ordered Walsh
and the footman to help Findlay move the body to the police wagon.

"Once I get the body to the morgue, I'll send the wagon back."
Findlay nodded to Sir Henry, Richard, Barnaby, and Penelope. "I'll send
word if my detailed examination turns up anything new that might prove
useful."

Stokes thanked him, then waved Sir Henry, Barnaby, Penelope, and
Richard toward the house. Stokes joined the group, and O'Donnell and
Morgan followed.

As they crossed the wide sweep of lawn, Stokes said to Sir Henry, "It
would help, Sir Henry, if you could share with us what you know of the
Underhills."

Sir Henry obliged, painting a picture of a family well established in
the county, but not as connected with local society as might be supposed.
"Her ladyship is a bit high in the instep, if you know what I mean. She
doesn't spend much time playing gracious lady of the local manor.
Against that, Monty was always a genial chap. He and his son ride with
the local hunt—they have quite decent kennels and stables here—and you
were likely to bump into Monty at the local markets and occasionally at

the local inn. He kept in touch with the farmers—well, he had to, given the number of tenant farms and the acres and fields within the estate."

"It's quite large, I gather," Barnaby said.

Sir Henry confirmed, "It's a significant holding in these parts."

"And Underhill managed those farms and acres?" Stokes asked.

"Indeed, he did. Well," Sir Henry explained, "it's not something a lady can do, is it?"

"Speaking of that," Penelope said, "it's widely known among the ton that Lady Pamela and Monty's marriage was arranged as one of simple convenience." She looked at Sir Henry. "From what you saw of them, did they get along well?"

Sir Henry frowned, then said, "They were contrasts in character and personality, certainly, but strange to tell, they actually seemed to rub along well. Very…undramatically. No fuss, just got on with it." He shrugged. "It seemed to work."

They reached the forecourt and stepped onto the gravel.

When they arrived at the porch steps, Sir Henry halted. He looked at the maw beyond the house's open door, then faced Richard, Barnaby, Penelope, and Stokes. "Inspector, I see no reason to intervene in your investigation. I'm happy to leave this case in your hands."

His expression impassive, Stokes inclined his head. "Thank you, Sir Henry."

As if released from some burden, Sir Henry smiled and rapidly made his farewells. With a last cheery wave, he strode off, making for the stable around the corner of the house.

Stokes, Barnaby, Penelope, and Richard watched him go.

Stokes ventured, "I take it he didn't want to tangle with Lady Pamela and her guests."

Richard snorted. "And who can blame him?"

Penelope threw him a disapproving glance and led the way inside.

With Penelope, Stokes, and Richard, Barnaby walked into the cool shadows of the front hall of Patchcote Grange. The drawing room lay to their left; the double doors were cracked but not open, and a low murmur of conversation emanated from within.

A butler came hurrying from the depths of the house. "Good afternoon, gentlemen." His demeanor distinctly solemn, he bowed. "Ma'am."

Richard gestured to Stokes. "Gearing, this is Inspector Stokes of Scotland Yard. He's in charge of the investigation, and Sir Henry has consigned the matter of finding your master's murderer into the inspector's capable hands."

"Indeed, sir." Gearing looked at Richard hopefully.

Richard obliged. "And these are Mr. and Mrs. Adair, who at the request of the Commissioner will be assisting the inspector in making his inquiries."

"I see." Judging by his expression, Gearing didn't see at all but was too well-trained to say so.

"My men"—Stokes directed Gearing's gaze to O'Donnell and Morgan, who had halted just inside the door and been joined by Walsh—"will be moving about the house and estate. It would help if you would notify the staff that it's possible they might be questioned about the movement of people they might have noticed and that you and your mistress, who I understand has already given the investigation a free hand, have no reservations over the staff sharing whatever they might know."

Gearing didn't look delighted but inclined his head. "I'll make that clear to the staff, sir."

A rise in the babel coming from the drawing room had everyone glancing at the doors.

"Before we address the guests," Stokes said, and Gearing's relief was instantly visible, "could you confirm when this house party commenced?"

"Well," Gearing said, "the family have been here for nearly two weeks, and the guests arrived yesterday—Sunday—from after lunch until just before dinner. Everyone was here before six o'clock."

"And the party was to last until when?" Penelope asked.

"Until next Sunday, ma'am. The guests were due to leave after Sunday luncheon."

"Thank you." Stokes shut his notebook. "It will save time if we speak with everyone presently residing under this roof simultaneously. If you would gather the staff and have them join us in the drawing room, we'll endeavor to keep the disruption as brief as we can."

The last phrase was plainly music to Gearing's ears. He bowed. "I'll assemble the staff immediately."

"Meanwhile"—Stokes turned to the drawing room—"we'll introduce ourselves."

With Richard, Penelope, and Stokes, Barnaby walked toward the drawing room.

As they reached the almost-shut doors, Richard held up a hand and whispered, "Give me a minute to slip inside." He met Stokes's eyes. "No reason to make a point of my connection to those investigating."

Stokes nodded. "Good point."

He, Barnaby, and Penelope stepped to the side of the doorway. While Richard slipped into the room, pushing the doors almost closed again, Stokes beckoned to his men. When they joined the group, in a low-voice, Stokes said, "I'm not yet sure what we need you to search for, but as we're liable to be in the house for the next hour, you may as well scout out the surroundings. Look for anyone out and about—gardeners, field workers, and the like."

"You might take that stake to the gardeners," Barnaby suggested. "See if they can at least confirm it belongs on the estate."

Morgan, who now held the stake, nodded.

With a tip of his head, Stokes sent the three on their way.

Then, Stokes met Barnaby's and Penelope's gazes. "Ready?"

Penelope arched her brows at Stokes. "Who gets to lead?"

Stokes grinned. "You do. This is more your arena than mine." He tipped his head at Barnaby. "Or even his."

Penelope tilted her head in regal acknowledgment and advanced on the double doors. She set them wide and swept inside, putting an abrupt end to every last conversation.

Clothes rustled as guests turned to look expectantly at the newcomers.

At the entirely unexpected newcomers. Surprise rippled through the crowd as several there recognized Penelope and Barnaby. Judging by the sudden hiatus that followed, recognition was swiftly superseded by recollection of their frequent successes in assisting Scotland Yard.

From the corner of his eye, Barnaby saw Richard standing by the windows with a group of male guests. Barnaby recognized the majority of the gentlemen present, although, unsurprisingly, he hadn't previously encountered the younger men.

Penelope halted and swept her gaze over the assembled company. Her expression solemn, she inclined her head, including the entire group with the gesture. "Good afternoon. Many of you will know or recognize my husband and me. For those yet to meet us, I am Mrs. Penelope Adair, and"—with a wave, she indicated Barnaby, who had halted to her left— "this is my husband, Barnaby Adair. The Commissioner of the Metropolitan Police has requested that we assist Inspector Stokes"—she gestured to Stokes, standing behind and to her right—"in apprehending the murderer of Mr. Montague Underhill."

A murmur rose from the company, carrying hints of approval and, especially from the younger members, burgeoning curiosity.

The doors opened, and Gearing ushered in the staff, who hurried self-consciously to take up positions along the inner wall.

When the sound of shuffling shoes subsided, Stokes caught Penelope's eye, and as she stepped back, he stepped forward. To the company at large, he stated, "For those not yet aware, I am Inspector Stokes of Scotland Yard, and I've been sent to lead this investigation. In that endeavor, I will be assisted by Mr. and Mrs. Adair. I can formally confirm that this morning, Mr. Montague Underhill was found murdered in the orchard of Patchcote Grange. His body has been examined by Scotland Yard's medical examiner, and the body has been removed to the morgue in London. With our arrival, the investigation into Mr. Underhill's murder has officially commenced. I must advise you that, until such time as the investigation at the Grange is deemed complete, you will need to remain on the estate." He turned to address the staff. "The prohibition on leaving the estate also extends to all staff normally resident in the house or in other buildings on the estate."

Rather stiffly, Gearing nodded.

Turning back to the guests, Stokes continued, "Lady Pamela has granted Scotland Yard a free hand in conducting our investigation. We will seek to identify the culprit with all speed, but until we do, no one may leave. Any attempt to do so will be interpreted as an indication of, at the very least, having something to hide and, at the worst, as a confession to the crime."

Barnaby struggled to keep his features impassive as he watched the guests' incipient protests die upon their lips.

To make matters even clearer, Penelope added, "We understand all here were planning to remain at the Grange until next Sunday, and we hope to conclude the investigation well before then."

Stokes turned to Gearing and the staff. "Thank you for attending. You may go."

As the staff filed out, Stokes exchanged glances with Barnaby and Penelope. When the door shut behind Gearing, Stokes informed the guests, "Given the hour, we, too, will take our leave, but we'll return tomorrow to commence interviews with each of you separately. At this time, you're free to move about the estate as you wish."

"But…" One of the older matrons looked confused. "Why do you need to speak with us? What can we possibly tell you?"

"As to that," Penelope replied, "we won't know until we ask our questions. We will want to learn what each of you saw or noticed around the time of the murder, and the sooner we learn that, the sooner we'll be able to clarify who killed Mr. Underhill."

"Rest assured," Barnaby said, "our sole purpose here is to identify Underhill's killer."

Stokes waited, but when no one responded, he inclined his head. "Until tomorrow." With Barnaby and Penelope following, he turned and led the way to the door. Stokes opened the door and held it for Penelope to sail through. After Barnaby followed her into the hall, Stokes walked out and quietly shut the door behind him.

As he joined Barnaby and Penelope by the foot of the stairs, he arched his brows. "That went better than I'd anticipated."

Penelope murmured, "It helped that Pamela had already declared her support."

"Indeed." Barnaby swung to face Gearing as the butler walked quickly toward them. "I believe we need to speak with her ladyship, Gearing. Will you show us up?"

As Penelope followed Gearing up the stairs and along a corridor, she rapidly reviewed all she knew of Lady Pamela Underhill. She and Barnaby and Pamela—and by extension, the late Monty, too—moved in similar, sometimes intersecting circles. Pamela had been born a Hurstbridge, and that family was as old as Barnaby's and Penelope's.

Given that, Penelope knew she would need to be on her mettle during the coming interview. She would need to guard against Pamela taking charge.

Gearing led them to a door toward the end of the central wing. He tapped on the panel, then, hearing a command to enter, opened the door and announced Barnaby, Penelope, and Stokes.

Penelope swept past, into a chamber wreathed in shadows. The curtains had been drawn against the westering sun, and the three occupants—Pamela, her daughter, Cecilia, and son, Vincent—were seated in the gloom on a sofa and in an armchair with their backs to what little light there was.

As Penelope approached, she saw that Pamela, who was sitting ramrod straight with her fingers tightly clenched in her lap in one corner of the sofa, flanked by Cecilia on the sofa and Vincent in the armchair, was already garbed in deepest mourning. Cecilia and Vincent, too, were in somber attire. However, the clothes were not in the latest fashion, suggesting the outfits had originally been acquired to honor an earlier death in the family.

Possibly the late marquess.

Pamela had never been even passably pretty. Of above-average height and gaunt, spare figure, she was hatchet-faced, with a mannishly square jaw and large, staring eyes. She wore her dark hair drawn back into a severe bun, an unflattering style that only rendered her unfortunate features even more starkly obvious.

Cecilia appeared to be a slightly softer version of Pamela, while Vincent, dark-haired and with features similar to his mother's—although on him, those features weren't such a negative—slouched in the armchair, exuding the studied ennui of an idle young gentleman about town.

Understandably, all three Underhills were staring in surprise at Penelope and Barnaby. Stokes, they'd expected, but not his assistants.

"Mrs. Adair?" Pamela blinked, then her slightly protuberant eyes shifted to Barnaby. "Mr. Adair."

Recalling the need to remain in control, Penelope stated, "Barnaby and I are here at the request, indeed, the insistence of the Commissioner of Police. You will, no doubt, have heard that we occasionally assist Scotland Yard with cases involving members of the ton. As I'm sure you will appreciate, our backgrounds give us insights that, in general, policemen lack." She softened her tone. "In the case of Mr. Underhill's murder, the Commissioner wished to ensure the investigative team included the very best minds possible."

As Penelope had expected, Pamela saw that as her and her family's due and also drew some degree of reassurance from Penelope and Barnaby's involvement. "I see." Unbending from her rather rigid stance, Pamela gestured to the second sofa facing the one she occupied. As Barnaby and Penelope moved to sink onto the cushions, Pamela fixed her challenging gaze on Stokes.

Before she could haughtily inquire, Stokes half bowed and stated, "I'm Inspector Stokes, my lady. Mr. and Mrs. Adair and I have successfully worked on many cases involving the deaths of members of the ton."

Stokes's grammar-school diction and his ease in this rather formal setting further reassured her ladyship. She inclined her head graciously and waved Stokes to an armchair.

"Firstly," Penelope said, keen not to let the reins of the interview slip, "allow us to offer our condolences on your recent loss." While uttering that and several similar anodyne phrases, she noted that, although all three Underhills showed signs of being blindsided by the murder, still appearing shocked and stunned, there was not a tear to be seen between them, and as yet, none of the three were pretending to be overcome with grief.

Grief might yet come, but this, Penelope felt, was their current true emotional state. They hadn't started to shape their reactions to what they thought they should show. Safe in Pamela's private parlor, presumably, they saw no need.

Quietly, Stokes added his condolences and those of the Commissioner as well. "Allow me to assure you that we have every intention of identifying and taking up the perpetrator as soon as may be."

Judging by her demeanor, Pamela—well known for being extremely starchy—was softening somewhat, clearly mollified by the apparent attention being paid to her family.

Penelope seized the moment to say, "Purely by way of confirmation, you are the elder daughter of the late Marquess of Skeldon, and your husband was one of the Hertfordshire Underhills."

Pamela nodded. "That's correct."

"And your son, Vincent"—Penelope indicated the young man in the armchair—"and your daughter, Cecilia, are your and Mr. Underhill's only children."

Pamela glanced at Vincent, then looked at Cecilia, seated beside her. She squeezed Cecilia's hand and attempted a faint, encouraging smile. "Indeed." Pamela paused, then faintly frowning, added, "It's really so… *inconsiderate* of Monty to get himself killed, and on the very first morning of my house party." Pamela looked at Penelope. "As I'm sure you will understand, Mrs. Adair, we had such hopes…"

Cecilia shifted and patted her mother's hand. "It's all right, Mama. I've plenty of time."

Cecilia's soft words did not noticeably impinge on Pamela, who continued to look rather peeved.

"Perhaps," Penelope said, "you could tell us whether the family has a house in London and how much of the year you spend there." When Pamela turned her gathering frown on Penelope, she explained, "We need to get some sense of what Monty's life was like in order to understand what might have led to his murder."

Pamela's frown only deepened. "Well, we hire a house, one in Mayfair, every Season, but other than that, we live here."

Vincent stirred. "We also spend weeks at a time at Wyndham Castle."

Pamela nodded. "Yes. Of course. We visit there regularly. My cousin, the marquess, is a widower and likes to gather the family around him."

"And," Penelope pressed, "there were no particular tensions or arguments with others that you know of?"

"For instance," Barnaby put in, "any imagined social slight or any difficulties with tenant farmers. Any disagreement with anyone at all."

"No. None." Pamela's declaration was absolute. Penelope noted that neither Cecilia nor Vincent showed any hint of disagreeing or of having a different view.

Barnaby stated, "I know Monty was a member of White's." He looked at Vincent. "Did he belong to any other club?"

Vincent shook his head. "Not that I'm aware of."

"Was he fond of any particular pursuit?" Barnaby asked. "Horses, carriages, racing, guns?"

"He and I ride—rode—to hounds, with the local hunt." Vincent drew in a tight breath, as if the verb change had suddenly brought home to him that his father was dead.

"So," Stokes murmured, "would it be correct to say that each year, Mr. Underhill spent about four to five months in London, engaging in the usual gentlemanly social pursuits, then perhaps a month or more at Wyndham Castle and the rest of his time here? I assume he was involved with running the estate."

"Well, yes. That is what he did with his time." Pamela looked at Stokes, then, plainly puzzled, shifted her gaze to Penelope and Barnaby. "But I don't understand why how and where Monty spent his time is at all relevant. He was out in the orchard. Goodness knows why, but surely, in the circumstances, it must have been some passing itinerant—a gypsy or some such person—who saw him there and killed him."

Declining to point out the illogicality of that statement, Penelope inclined her head. "Even so, surely, you and your family will expect us to investigate every possible cause. The Commissioner will certainly expect us to do so."

Pamela looked as if she couldn't quite understand what Penelope meant.

Seizing the moment to change tacks, she ventured, "It's widely known that your marriage was one of convenience. How did that come about?"

Pamela blinked. Penelope was counting on Pamela's reputation of having little reservation about anything she said, on any subject, to carry the moment.

"Well." Pamela shrugged. "The simple truth is I lacked for suitors, and Monty, like all the Underhills, lacked funds, so when he offered for my hand, my parents suggested I accept, and as Monty wasn't a difficult sort to rub along with, it suited me to do so." She met Penelope's gaze and candidly declared, "I never had reason to regret that decision. Monty and I...worked well together. I suppose you could say our goals, while not exactly the same, aligned well. There was never any drama, which we both appreciated."

All of that fitted with Penelope's understanding of the Underhills' marriage. All practicality and no passion.

Penelope shifted her attention to Cecilia. "Do you know of any reason anyone might have wished your father ill?"

Cecilia's frown held a sullen quality. "No. I can't think why anyone would have killed Papa." The impression she gave was that she felt it was a personal affront that anyone had dared. She added, "He was just Papa. He never gave anyone cause to dislike him."

Penelope glanced at Barnaby.

Correctly interpreting her look, he turned his gaze to Vincent. "Did your father ever confide any difficulties he had to you? Any arguments with other gentlemen in the ton?"

Vincent looked less certain than his sister, but even he said, "Papa wasn't really one to have arguments." He paused, then said, "I often wondered if, beyond what he did day to day, much mattered to him at all." Vincent met Barnaby's gaze. "And if nothing matters, there's little reason to bestir oneself over anything, is there?"

That, Penelope thought, was an interesting observation.

She listened as Barnaby drew Vincent out regarding his own aspirations. It quickly became clear that Vincent saw himself as entitled to whatever he wanted of life, and he was obviously spoilt by his mother, but throughout, Penelope caught no hint that Vincent had any issue with nor harbored any animosity toward his father.

Indeed, all three had painted Monty Underhill as an uncomplicated and accepted constant in their lives.

When Barnaby smoothly yielded the investigative stage to her, Penelope refocused on Pamela and, once again hoping that lady's renowned frankness would come to her aid, said, "I believe you're the actual owner of Patchcote Grange, the house and estate, and also of the funds with which the property was endowed."

Pamela curtly nodded. "Indeed. I keep a very tight rein on the total expenses, but Monty—as Vincent alluded to—handled all the day-to-day disbursements."

"So he acted essentially as your agent?" Penelope asked.

"Yes." Pamela's lips tightened. "I suppose one might say that."

Penelope glanced at Stokes, who had done his best to fade into the background. He met her gaze and fractionally shook his head.

Pamela had followed the interaction and now pounced. "What I would like to know is how long you imagine this investigation will take and what, if any, disruption it will cause for our guests." She fixed her large eyes on Penelope. "I do not want our guests subjected to any distressing experience. I appeal to your insights, Mrs. Adair, Mr. Adair, to ensure that is the case."

Barnaby inclined his head. "We will do our utmost to ensure that no guests, or indeed, anyone else, is inconvenienced more than is absolutely necessary. That said, our primary task here is to identify and take up your husband's murderer."

Pamela dipped her head. "Of course. Nevertheless, I cannot imagine that Monty would wish any search for his murderer to cause additional harm to our family." She focused on Penelope. "Mrs. Adair, with your experience of such cases, what is the ton's reaction to Monty's death and the manner of it likely to be?"

Will it harm my standing and that of my children and family more broadly?

Penelope heard the unvoiced query clearly. Suppressing her reaction to the implications of the question, she answered factually. "At this point, most of the ton will have yet to hear of the murder. By the time they do, depending on how cooperative people are, we would hope to have already closed the case, and then the matter will largely feature as old news. A happening to be noted, but of little ongoing interest. The ton, as you know, will always move on to the latest titillating news."

Digesting that, Pamela nodded. "I see."

Stokes stirred and offered, "Your guests will only be asked to account for their movements and what they know of your late husband's movements over the hours before he was killed. It's unlikely we'll need to know more than that."

Barnaby added, "Finding the murderer as quickly as possible will be in everyone's interest, and collating the guests' recollections of Monty's movements will be key to that."

"For instance," Stokes said, "regarding why he was in the orchard this morning, was Mr. Underhill a birdwatcher? Was he interested in birds?"

All three Underhills looked mystified.

"No," Vincent said. "He had no interest in birds."

"He might just have wandered out to the orchard," Cecilia offered. "No real reason, just to take the air."

Stokes inclined his head. "Maybe so."

"On the question of guests," Penelope said, "do you have a list we might borrow? It will save us from having to ask everyone's names."

"Yes, of course." Pamela sent Cecilia to a writing desk across the room. "In the top right-hand pigeonhole."

Cecilia returned with a sheet of paper and, at her mother's nod, handed it to Penelope before returning to the sofa.

Penelope scanned the list. "I see." There were twenty-three names plus the family, which included Susan and her two daughters. "If I may…" Quickly, she asked, guessed, and ultimately received confirmation of why each guest had been invited. As they'd already learned, the primary purpose of the house party was to facilitate suitable matches by introducing eligible gentlemen to the selected young ladies—all daughters of the family or of close connections or friends.

Pamela's unrestrained candor was a blessing, her fabled lack of tact distinctly helpful in this case. Her comments proved that, despite any other shortcomings, her knowledge and understanding of her guests was sound.

Once Penelope was sure she had all the details she would need, she glanced at Stokes and faintly arched her brows.

He caught Pamela's eye. "We'll need to glance over your husband's papers to ensure, for instance, that he's received no threats. Where does he keep his correspondence?"

Pamela looked blankly at her children. "His study? Or in the library?"

"The study," Cecilia stated, quite categorically.

Penelope noticed that Vincent frowned at his sister, but he said nothing.

"Thank you." Stokes rose, and Penelope and Barnaby got to their feet. Stokes bowed to Pamela. "We appreciate your assistance and your support. We will do our level best to complete this investigation in as short a time as possible."

Regally, Pamela inclined her head. "Thank you, Inspector. I have instructed the staff to assist your endeavors in whatever way you require."

Penelope and Barnaby made their farewells, then trailed Stokes to the door.

Vincent rose, followed them, and slipped through the door behind them.

With Barnaby and Stokes, Penelope turned toward the stairs, aware that, after closing the parlor door, Vincent had gone the other way.

They walked into the gallery, and Stokes halted at the head of the stairs. He turned to Barnaby and Penelope. "Should we start interviewing the guests or the staff, or should we check the study first?"

After noting the time—past four o'clock—and briefly debating their options, they accepted that it was too late to commence any interviews, especially as they'd yet to decide on their questions, and opted to examine the study instead.

"Who knows what we might find?" Penelope said as she started down the stairs.

Gearing was waiting in the front hall. As they stepped onto the tiles, he asked, "If I may inquire, Inspector, sir, ma'am, will you be staying at the Grange?"

Barnaby smiled understandingly. "No. We prefer to put up at a nearby inn."

Penelope asked, "Is there one you can recommend?"

Greatly relieved, Gearing was happy to point them toward the Red Lion in the village of Hackbridge. "It's not far at all from the entrance to the main drive. Just head a short distance north on the London Road, and you'll see the sign."

"Thank you." Penelope smiled at Gearing. "That sounds perfect."

"We plan to start interviewing the guests tomorrow morning," Stokes told Gearing. "And at some point in the next few hours, the police coach will return from London. Please redirect them to the Red Lion."

"Of course, Inspector."

"Now," Barnaby said, "we need to examine Mr. Underhill's study." He looked at Gearing. "Which way?"

Relieved of his earlier apprehension over having to accommodate them all, Gearing readily led them down a corridor and into another wing of the house.

CHAPTER 3

*T*hey followed Gearing to a door at the end of the wing.

"Here we are." Gearing opened the door and stood back.

Penelope walked in and immediately halted.

Following at her heels, Barnaby came to a screeching stop. Over Penelope's head, he stared at Vincent Underhill, who was standing in the middle of the room and looking faintly chagrined. And guilty, too.

Having left his mother's parlor behind them, Vincent had to have come directly there, presumably for some purpose.

Barnaby stepped aside as Stokes came in and, on seeing Vincent, firmly shut the door.

"Vincent," Penelope said. "What are you doing here?"

Her tone suggested she was merely curious, but Vincent colored, then glanced around in the same vague fashion he seemed to have been doing when they entered.

When he looked at them again, he'd managed to summon a bored expression.

When the three of them simply waited, plainly expecting him to answer, he shrugged. "Now Papa's gone, I suppose this room will be mine. I came down to take a look."

Knowing we're interested in the contents of the study.

Barnaby glanced around. The three internal walls were lined with shelves, all packed with ledgers and account books with rolled maps tucked between. A heavy mahogany estate desk sat before one side wall, while on the opposite side of the room, facing the desk, a fireplace was inset between the bookshelves. The external wall featured a pair of glassed doors that gave onto a small, paved area beyond which the lawn rolled away to a distant line of trees. Long curtains framed the glass panels, which were flanked by two pedestals supporting ivory busts of Greek philosophers.

Penelope made for the desk. Walking past Vincent, she rounded one end and pushed aside the large admiral's chair to stand directly behind the expanse. Studying the piles of documents stacked on the desktop, she frowned. "These have been searched."

Vincent had swung to track her. "What?" He, too, frowned. After a second, he suggested, "Perhaps it's just as Papa left it...although he was usually neat and tidy with his papers." Frowning more definitely, Vincent nodded at the desk. "As you can see."

"Indeed, I can." Penelope started opening drawers, pausing to stare at the contents of each before closing it and opening the next. Going from one drawer to another, she shook her head. "People know where they keep things in their own desk. They rarely forget and so don't need to rummage through everything to find whatever they're after. They don't need to disturb every pile, every drawer. So, I repeat. This desk has been searched. Recently. Since Monty was last here."

She shut the last drawer and looked at Vincent.

Stokes and Barnaby also fixed their gazes on him.

His eyes now wide, Vincent shook his head. "It wasn't me." He paused, then added, "You saw me leave Mama's parlor behind you. I came straight here, but I hadn't even had time to decide what to look for before you arrived." Somewhat sulkily—shades of his sister—he admitted, "I thought you were going to start talking to guests or something. If you must know, I came down to see if there was anything valuable lying about that I should take before you lot came and searched."

Stokes tipped his head. "And did you find anything worth taking?"

"No!" Petulantly, Vincent insisted, "I just told you. You arrived before I had a chance to even look."

For a second, they allowed silence to reign, then Barnaby mildly asked, "Given you are here, is there a safe?"

Vincent glanced at him from beneath his brows—as if wondering if there was some trap in the question—then he pointed at the painting of some ancestor that hung above the fireplace. "Behind that."

As Barnaby crossed to the painting, Vincent added, "I don't know where Papa kept the key, but I think he hid it somewhere in here."

"Ah." Penelope opened the top drawer of the desk and extracted a heavy key. She held it up. "I suspect this will be it."

Stokes reached across the desk and took the key. "Let's see." To Vincent, he added, "As you're here, you can bear witness to what we find inside."

Vincent had lost his sulky look and, with every appearance of being perfectly amenable, followed Stokes to the fireplace.

Barnaby had swung back the painting, revealing a standard wall safe. He stepped aside to allow Stokes to fit the key into the lock and glanced at Penelope. "I take it our searcher would have found the key?"

"Most definitely," she assured him. "It was tossed on top of everything else in the drawer, with no attempt at all to hide it."

With Vincent holding aside the heavy painting, Stokes swung open the safe's door.

Barnaby joined Stokes and Vincent in peering inside.

For Penelope's benefit, Barnaby reported, "Jewelry cases, as one might expect. And cash—quite a stack of notes." He reached inside and picked up a red pouch. It clinked. He hefted it, then replaced it. "Guineas —the pouch is full of them. Nothing else."

"No ledgers or anything like that?" Penelope asked.

Barnaby shook his head. "Just the cash and jewelry."

Stokes looked at Vincent. "Is this what you expected to find in here?"

Vincent grimaced. "I really don't know." His gaze returned to the pile of cash. "But such an amount doesn't seem…well, unusual."

Stokes looked at Barnaby. "What do you think?"

"I think," he replied, "that this is a working estate of some size, with a large household and associated staff. There'll be wages to pay and supplies to be bought and so on." He glanced at Vincent. "This doesn't seem excessive. More like the usual amount one might expect Underhill to have on hand."

Stokes turned his gaze on Vincent. "Your father dealt with the estate, didn't he?"

Vincent nodded. "Well, him and the estate manager, Simms. But Simms lives in Wallington and only comes in once a week to meet with Papa and go over the books and what's happening in the fields. Papa was always the one who held the money to pay for things." Studying the contents of the safe, Vincent tipped his head. "From what I recall seeing before, at this time of the month, that's about what I would have expected him to have in there."

"Right." Stokes swung the door shut and locked the safe.

Vincent asked, "Can I have the key?"

Stokes pulled the key from the lock and slid it into his pocket. "The key will be handed to the executor of your father's will." At Vincent's faint frown, Stokes added, "You might speak with your mother, and if she hasn't already done so, send word to the family solicitor. They will need to attend the funeral, whenever that's held, and bring and read your father's will. The police will hold the key until we can hand it to either the solicitor or the will's executor."

Vincent digested that, then glanced at the clock on the mantel. "I'll go and speak with Mama now, before she starts dressing for dinner."

Penelope had wondered whether Pamela would rejoin the company and decided Vincent was probably correct. Pamela would want to know how her guests were reacting to the situation.

Vincent nodded to Penelope, Barnaby, and Stokes and left the study, closing the door behind him.

Stokes regarded the door, then shook his head. He looked at Penelope. "Was he the one who did the searching?"

"I seriously doubt it, and only if he'd searched before, and I don't think he did." She gestured to the desk. "Whoever went through here was thorough and reasonably careful. *I* can see they've pushed things around, and they'd just dropped the key back in the drawer on top of everything else, but in general, if one didn't know what signs to look for, the searching wouldn't be obvious."

"So whoever it was," Barnaby said, "they weren't in a tearing rush."

"No. They were thorough and deliberate, and if Vincent had done this earlier, I can't see why he would have been standing in the middle of the room for us to walk in on."

"More telling," Barnaby said, "is that it seems the searcher found the key to the safe and, presumably, opened it."

"Yet all that money," Stokes said, "is still there."

Barnaby nodded. "Exactly. So whatever our searcher was after, it wasn't money. Or jewelry."

Stokes grunted. He looked at the shelves of ledgers. "So, what now? If this place has already been searched—and I suppose we can assume the searcher was also the killer—what are the chances that there's anything incriminating still lying around for us to find?"

Barnaby had also been glancing around. "There's no sign our searcher grew frustrated, but can we therefore assume he found what he came for?"

Penelope hummed, then replied, "I'm not sure we can. He was careful and methodical, presumably intent on leaving few clues that he'd searched at all. So even if he was unsuccessful, he might be clever enough not to have let his temper get the better of him. He might well think to come back and continue his search later." She surveyed the myriad ledgers. "He can't have searched all those. He can't even have pulled each of them out and looked behind them. That alone would take hours."

"True," Stokes said. "So we know the desk, at least, was thoroughly searched and the safe as well, but we can't tell whether our searcher found what he was after."

Penelope nodded. "That's the situation in a nutshell."

Barnaby glanced at the clock. "Time's caught up with us. I vote we call it a day and head for the Red Lion. We can eat and think through what we know to this point and clarify what our next steps should be."

"That," Penelope said, "is likely our wisest course."

"Even wiser," Stokes stated, "given that our murderer is very possibly in the house, and just in case there's something in here he hasn't yet found, I'll leave a constable on guard overnight."

Barnaby nodded. "An excellent idea."

He waited while Stokes organized for Walsh to remain in the study with the doors and windows locked, with Morgan to relieve him in the early hours via the external doors. Meanwhile, Penelope idly sifted through the papers piled on the desk, but as with the safe, there were no clues to be found as to why Monty Underhill was murdered.

Barnaby sat beside Penelope on the settle in the comfortable private parlor they'd hired at the Red Lion and stretched his booted feet toward the fire. The serving girls had just gone out, ferrying away the plates and platters that had previously held a succulent dinner of roast beef and vegetables and a scrumptious apple pie.

Replete and content, the three investigators relaxed and turned their minds, individually and collectively, to their latest case.

Her gaze on the flames leaping in the hearth, Penelope opened the discussion. "Could Vincent be our searcher? Theoretically, he could have searched the study while we were examining the body or even earlier and simply gone back to make sure he'd left nothing incriminating behind, and then we walked in on him."

Barnaby shook his head. "I can't see it. Why would he wait until his father was dead to go searching? Even if there was something he wanted to remove from the study—regardless of whether he murdered his father, something he thought would implicate him or that he simply didn't want us to see—why risk searching during the day? When he knew we were around? He's in the house overnight, every night, and he couldn't have known we would leave someone on guard."

Seated in the armchair to Barnaby's left, Stokes grunted. "I think when he followed us from his mother's parlor, he overheard us discussing interviewing the guests. Regardless, he assumed that's what we would do next, so he thought the way was clear to look in the study and see if—as he said—there was anything valuable he should remove. I don't think his actions were more deeply thought out than that."

Penelope grimaced. "He's inexperienced and naive enough to think we might 'take' or 'confiscate' money or valuables."

Barnaby nodded. "If we hadn't gone straight to the study, the odds are good that he would have remembered the safe, opened it, and cleared it out."

"And that would have thrown us for a loop." Stokes sank deeper into the chair. "Lucky we found him before he had the chance."

"And," Penelope pointed out, "his surprise on learning the desk had been searched was, I think, utterly genuine. He wasn't the searcher."

"I agree," Stokes said. "He's not the searcher, but does that mean he's not the murderer?"

"No," Barnaby said. "But I suspect we'll discover he isn't the murderer, either. He showed no sign of harboring the sort of intense feelings toward his father that could have prompted a murder of this sort." He looked at Penelope. "In fact, I would say that's one of the more peculiar and puzzling aspects of this case. Apparently without exception, Monty Underhill was viewed as a pleasant, genial sort. Why anyone would feel strongly enough to bash in his skull is difficult to see."

"Equally," Penelope said, "the notion that Monty did something that incited such a murderous reaction from someone…well, that seems entirely out of character." She looked at Barnaby and Stokes. "We'll have to hope that our interviews tomorrow shed some fresh and unexpected light on our victim."

"Because"—Barnaby inclined his head—"if this isn't a case of the archetypal demented passing vagrant striking out of the blue, then presumably, Monty had a falling-out with someone, and that someone murdered him because of it."

"Before we start speculating about motive," Stokes said, "returning to already known fact, namely the search, presumably clandestine, of Underhill's study, when do we think that occurred?"

"I doubt it would have been before the murder," Barnaby said. "The study was Monty's private domain. Not only might he have walked in at any moment, but he would have spent time there each day. He would have noticed the place had been searched."

"He would have taken away the safe's key, if nothing else," Penelope stated. "That said, the house party guests were under the Grange's roof over Sunday night. The searcher could have searched during the night, and Monty might not have gone there before heading out to the orchard."

"That will need to be one line of inquiry during the interviews," Stokes said, "to establish Underhill's movements this morning prior to the murder. But your theory suggests that the searcher—who, at this point, we're inclined to believe is also the murderer—came to the house party intent on removing something Underhill had in his possession."

Penelope tipped her head. "Or on learning something—perhaps some information—Monty had written down."

Silence fell as they considered and weighed what they knew.

Eventually, Stokes stirred and looked at his coinvestigators. "So regarding our interviews, where do we start? What are we looking for or trying to learn?"

"Clearly," Penelope said, "we need to learn more about Monty Under-hill, and given the circumstances, with him just being murdered and in such grisly fashion, I suspect we'll find people will be only too willing to fill us in on all his foibles, real, imagined, and suspected."

Barnaby lightly grimaced. "What we, personally, know of him isn't all that helpful." He glanced at Penelope. "Monty was one of those who passed through ton life with a gentle smile and an amiable nature, leaving barely a ripple in his wake."

Penelope inclined her head. "That's an accurate description. I've never heard anyone disparage him in any way at all. As far as I know, he is—was—universally well-regarded."

"Where does he hail from?" Stokes asked.

"Hertfordshire," Barnaby replied. "The Underhills have been an established family in that county for centuries."

"Deep connections, some land, but little cash?" Stokes ventured.

"Exactly." Barnaby continued, "Monty was a member of White's and moved in all the best circles of the ton's upper echelon. He was received everywhere. Of note, however, is that his status derived entirely from his birth, his name, and his personality, not from Pamela's wealth."

"So that's society's view of him based on contact in social settings," Penelope stated. "That isn't to say that he wasn't quite different in private."

Barnaby inclined his head. "Or within the family, but with Pamela as his wife, I find the concept of Monty lording it over his roost difficult to believe."

"Indeed." Penelope added, "I think we can discount infidelity or even jealousy as a motive. This might have been a crime of passion but not of that sort." She looked at Stokes. "As you saw, there was no passion in the Underhills' marriage, and I really can't see Pamela or Vincent, much less Cecilia, finding a wandering eye sufficient reason to upset their social applecart." She paused, then added, "It bears stressing that, despite Pamela being a marquess's daughter, her social standing and that of Vincent and Cecilia are significantly underpinned by Monty's."

Barnaby elaborated, "With his background and his genial, hail-fellow-well-met personality, his acceptance was always absolute and unquestioned, and in large measure, that bolstered his wife's and his children's acceptability."

"Many assume," Penelope said, "that acceptance by the ton is guaranteed by birth. That birth alone will open all doors. But certainly, within the upper echelon—the haut ton—that's not actually the case. Regardless of birth, if someone has an abrasive personality or significant character flaws—and Pamela has both—they are likely to find themselves ostracized. Not overtly so but through simply being ignored." She looked at Stokes. "Cast your mind back to Prinny. He was a prime example. The haut ton deserted him, eventually despised him, and wanted nothing to do with him even though he was regent and, later, king."

Stokes frowned. "I see."

"With Pamela being a marquess's daughter," Barnaby said, "by birth, she and her children are unquestionably acceptable, but by character—

hers, especially... That's where Monty's reputation and wide-ranging social acceptance came into play."

"From the first," Penelope stated, "that's what he brought to the marriage. An excellent pedigree and a universally liked and respected character and a steady, appealing personality."

"All right." Stokes nodded. "I think I understand. So unless we find firm evidence to the contrary, we're not imagining this to be a murder committed by one of the immediate family."

"At this point," Barnaby said, "we know how Monty was killed, where he was killed, and we have a defined window of time for when. What we have no clue about is why."

Looking at Stokes, Barnaby added, "Monty truly was the most jovial, gregarious, and utterly innocuous sort. There was nothing at all that made him stand out, let alone that might incite the degree of animosity that would goad someone into bashing in his skull with an iron stake."

"Hmm." Penelope frowned. "We haven't yet learned why he was in the orchard and, possibly, looking into that hollow in the tree."

"True." Stokes pulled out his notebook. "We also need to follow up with Morgan about the stake. Hopefully, the gardeners can help us with that. If we can learn where it came from, that might give us a clue as to who the murderer might be. Or at least, where the murderer was prior to committing the murder."

"I can't see any of the guests walking around carrying an iron stake," Barnaby said. "Presumably, the murderer picked it up from somewhere nearby."

"That," Penelope said, "suggests the murder was not premeditated. That the murderer saw Monty out walking and, for some reason, decided to seize the opportunity and kill him. The killer didn't plan to use the stake—I doubt anyone planning a murder would. The stake was simply the weapon the killer found to hand."

Both Barnaby and Stokes frowned as they considered that insight.

Still frowning, Barnaby said, "Seeing an opportunity and grasping it suggests that the underlying reason the murderer killed Monty existed prior to that moment. And as, presumably, everyone was together throughout the previous evening, and as yet, no one has mentioned any altercation or falling out over that time... If, in our interviews, we don't hear of any recent disagreement that occurred on Sunday or this morning, that will imply that the motive behind the murder existed before the murderer came to Patchcote Grange."

Also frowning as they followed that logic, neither Penelope nor Stokes disagreed.

After a long moment, Penelope ventured, "That's confusing. I agree that, barring any evidence of some recent altercation, it seems the motive must have already existed, yet whatever triggered the killer to act in what appears to be an impulsive, opportunistic way, that trigger had to be something unexpected. Something that happened this morning." She looked at Barnaby and Stokes and firmly stated, "This murder wasn't— couldn't have been—premeditated. Ergo, the murderer didn't expect to kill Monty this morning."

Neither man argued.

Eventually, Stokes glanced at his notes, then shut the book and tucked it away. "Given we're keeping the guests at the house, we'll need to do as they expect and work our way through interviewing them all." He looked at Penelope. "How many are on that list?"

"There were thirty attendees, all told," Barnaby said, "including Monty and the three other Underhills."

"And Pamela's sister, Susan Goodrich, and her two daughters— Monty's nieces—are also in that number," Penelope said.

Stokes sighed. "So twenty-six guests to interview, including the Goodriches and Percival."

"I think we need to interview Vincent and Cecilia Underhill separately as well," Penelope put in. "Who knows what insights into their father's character or activities they might have?"

Barnaby met Stokes's long-suffering gaze and faintly smiled. "That's twenty-nine interviews if we include Pamela as well, and for completeness's sake, that might be wise."

"No help for it," Penelope stated bracingly. "We'll need to interview each and every one, because, for my money, no matter how unlikely it seems at first glance, someone in that group is almost certainly the killer."

Stokes huffed. "Unless, of course, we find some sighting of a demented vagrant."

Lips twitching, Penelope shook her head. "In all our cases, we've yet to come across one of those."

"And so, for us," Barnaby wryly said, "that means tomorrow will be one long day of interviews."

"And, I warn you," Penelope added, "some if not several will try our patience."

~

The following morning at nine o'clock, Barnaby trailed Penelope and Stokes as the pair strode into Patchcote Grange.

As was customary at country houses hosting summer house parties, the front doors had been propped wide, and Penelope marched through and down the long hall, inclining her head graciously to the footman who, alerted by their footsteps, came hurrying to see if anything was required.

"We'll be in the study," Stokes informed the footman and followed Penelope down the corridor leading to that room.

Barnaby brought up the rear, quietly amused at his wife's determination. She'd won an argument to get them there at that hour, which was too early to commence their interviews.

A hum of muted conversation drifted from where he imagined the dining room would be. Luckily, the study lay in the opposite wing.

Speaking over her shoulder, Penelope reiterated, "I know we think the murderer already searched and, presumably, removed anything incriminating, but that's an assumption. What if they didn't find what they were after? He or she must have had limited time, even if they'd searched by lamplight during Sunday night. And regardless, you must admit there's a decent chance that, even if they did find something and take it away, there might be something else still there. Something that will shed light on why Monty—of all men—was murdered."

Stokes sighed. "The only reason I'm going along with this is because —as you've been at such pains to point out—none of the guests, much less the family, are likely to consider themselves available for interviewing until at least ten o'clock."

"Exactly!" Penelope nodded decisively. "So we have time to indulge my whim." On reaching the study door, she paused and arched a brow at Barnaby.

Letting his amusement show, he halted beside Stokes and said, "I'm going along with your notion because, given our singular lack of insight into why anyone would want Monty dead, casting an eye over his private papers might yield some clue."

Stokes grunted, opened the study door, waved Penelope through, and followed.

Barnaby stepped inside and closed the door as Morgan rose from the chair behind the desk.

The now-experienced constable nodded respectfully. "Morning, all."

To Stokes, he reported, "No attempt to gain entry overnight. Not while Walsh was here, either."

Penelope halted by the desk. "That means that either the searcher found what they were looking for..." She wrinkled her nose. "Or that they didn't and are now searching elsewhere."

"Or have given up," Stokes said. "At least while we're here."

"If," Barnaby said, "as we're assuming, the killer is the searcher and, presumably, killed for what he's searching for, then he's unlikely to simply give up and walk away."

Penelope tipped her head in his direction. "True. So either way, it behooves us to search."

Stokes asked Morgan, "Did you get anywhere with that stake?"

"Not really," Morgan replied. "The gardeners were all out and about, and O'Donnell thought it more useful for us to take stock of the lay of the land immediately around the house rather than go searching for men somewhere farther afield."

"Fair enough," Stokes said. "But fetch the stake now and hunt down the gardeners and see what they can tell us. That's our murder weapon, after all. O'Donnell and Walsh should already be speaking with the indoor staff."

"Aye, guv." Morgan snapped off a salute and made for the door.

Penelope rounded the desk and claimed the chair behind it. "Now, let's see what we have." She proceeded to retrieve an assortment of papers, documents, and letters from the desk's drawers and set them beside the smaller stacks already on the desktop.

Barnaby and Stokes drew up armchairs and sat facing the desk.

"Here." Penelope divided the piles roughly into thirds and pushed a pile each toward Barnaby and Stokes, then settled back in the chair to peruse her allocation.

After a moment of sorting and scanning, Stokes grunted and sat up. "Better you two read the letters. The people he mentions and any references made will mean more to you than me." He worked through his pile, separating the letters and pushing them randomly toward either Barnaby or Penelope, who added them to their piles.

Silence descended, broken only by the crackle of paper and the shuffle of documents being rearranged.

Stokes came upon several banking statements and sent them Penelope's way. Absentmindedly, she took them, then sat back and scanned them more carefully. On reaching the end of the last page, she sighed and dropped them onto the desk along with the other documents she'd studied. "Nothing. Absolutely nothing to suggest anything at all amiss."

Barnaby tossed the letters he'd scanned onto the desk. "Monty seems every bit as unthreatening and innocuous as I'd thought him."

Stokes reached the end of the last document in his pile and dropped it, too, onto the polished surface. "I've seen nothing the least bit remarkable."

"Well, it was worth a try." Disaffectedly, Penelope gathered the papers and returned them, more or less, to the drawers from which they'd come. After dropping the final set into the open bottom drawer on her right, she pushed the drawer shut, but it stuck.

She frowned, jiggled the drawer, and tried again. "This won't shut."

Frowning, she pulled the drawer all the way out, then slid from the chair to kneel on the floor. Ducking down, she peered into the opening. "Hello."

Both Barnaby and Stokes rose to look over the desk.

"What is it?" Stokes asked.

Reaching into the gap, Penelope stretched her fingers along the bottom of the drawer above. "I think…" Touching the cover of the small black book she'd spied, she gripped, wiggled it, and managed to dislodge it from where it was wedged. Rocking back on her heels, she examined her find, then rose and dropped back into the chair. "This was tucked in a notch made to hold it on the bottom of the drawer above. It had shifted, and that's why I couldn't shut the drawer."

The book was of the kind many gentlemen carried to keep track of names and addresses. She opened the cover and flicked through the pages.

After a moment, Barnaby and Stokes rounded the desk and stood on either side of her so that they, too, could see what was making her frown.

At first, she wasn't sure what she was looking at, but the deeper into the book she went, the more obvious it became. When she reached the end of the entries, she lowered the book and, her tone severe, said, "I believe we've found one possible motive for why Monty wound up dead."

Barnaby reached for the book, and she let him take it.

He, too, flicked through the pages. Incredulously, he said, "Blackmail?"

Grimly, she nodded. "That's what it looks like." She swiveled and studied Barnaby and Stokes, who'd moved to Barnaby's side. The pair were examining the entries as she had. "As far as I can make out, each page relates to one person."

"This is all in Underhill's hand," Stokes stated. "We've seen enough of his writing to be certain of that."

"Lady Carville." Barnaby glanced at Penelope. "She's one of the guests."

Penelope nodded. "I saw several others as well. But if you look at Lady Carville's page, you'll see a code at the top. *I*. Knowing Lady Carville, that likely means 'infidelity' or 'indiscretion.' I also saw the code *T*, which might mean 'thief.' Also *L*, which might mean 'liar.'"

Stokes pointed at a page. "Lord Morland. He's one of the guests, too. Another *I*."

Barnaby continued to turn the well-thumbed pages. "This has to be the motive. We've found nothing else, have heard of nothing else, that might have moved someone to murder Monty Underhill, but this"—he brandished the book—"surely would."

Stokes nodded. "Depending on how scandalous or threatening the subject of the blackmail was."

"These dates and figures beneath each name." Barnaby arched a brow at Penelope. "Payments?"

"I think so." She looked at Stokes. "Before we start our interviews, we need to determine which of the victims named in the book are here and whether any were scheduled to make payments yesterday morning."

Stokes looked struck. "You think that's why he was in the orchard, probably looking into that hollow in the tree?"

Penelope raised her hands. "We've found no other explanation, and if a payment was to be made yesterday morning, that would fit. Hollows in trees have a long history of being used to leave items for others to collect at some other time."

"Finally"—Barnaby handed the book back to Penelope—"Underhill being killed is starting to make some sense."

"He was clearly a wolf in sheep's clothing." Penelope settled to page through the book again.

Stokes drew out his notebook and returned to his chair. "We need to make a list of the victims who are here and whether he expected to receive payments from any of them yesterday."

Barnaby sank into the other chair. "He would have had to make contact and arrange the details of the payment—how much and where and when—before the victims left their homes, or they wouldn't necessarily have the cash."

"The book only gives date and amount," Penelope said, "or in some cases, especially from the ladies, jewelry, like a ring or a necklace." She hunted in her pocket and drew out the list she'd extracted from Pamela. She waved the list and held the black book out to Stokes. "Start at the beginning and read out the names, his code for whatever hold he had over them, and whether they were slated to make a payment yesterday, and I'll note that on this list."

She spread the list on the blotter and picked up a pencil, and Stokes dutifully worked his way through the book.

When he reached the end, Penelope had placed asterisks beside five names. "Five victims in the house," she reported. "Lord Morland, Lady Carville, Lady Wincombe, Mr. Nevin-Smythe, and Miss Regina Hemmings, but only two—Lady Wincombe and Miss Hemmings—were due to make payments while here, and both were expected to make those payments yesterday."

Stokes had flicked back through the book and was squinting at one page. "I'm not sure what this code is. It's for Lord Morland, who, as you noted earlier, has an *I* beside his name, but he has a second code letter that looks like an *E*. Nevin-Smythe has a *C* beside his name—presumably 'cheat.' What could *E* be?"

Penelope held out a hand. "Here. Let me see."

Stokes surrendered the book, and she held the page close to her glasses. "It's not an *E*. It's an *F*." She looked at Barnaby. "Fraud?"

He shrugged. "I'm not aware of any likely fraud involving Morland."

"Regardless"—she studied the page on which Lord Morland's payments were recorded—"Morland's been paying Monty for several years and quite tidy amounts, too."

"Enough to murder to get out of?" Stokes asked.

Eyes on the page, Penelope tipped her head. "Actually, I wouldn't have said so. These amounts should be well within Morland's capacity to pay without any real difficulty." She flicked to the next page and then to the next. "In fact, I would say that the amount Monty extracted from each of his victims was carefully calculated to be well within their ability to pay without causing any real hardship."

Barnaby observed, "None of the five who are here, or indeed, any of those named in the book, would wish to risk those sorts of accusations being made public if they didn't have to. It seems Monty gave them an option they preferred to take."

"It also means he must have had knowledge or even evidence of their transgressions that he could cite." Penelope closed the book and set it on the desktop, but the cover remained angled upward.

She stared at it for a moment. With one fingertip, she pressed the cover closed, but when she raised her hand, the cover sprang up again. "Hmm." She picked up the book and studied the page at which it seemed to want to open. "What's this?" Holding the book close to her glasses, she examined the inner spine. "A page has been torn out." She lowered the book and ran a fingertip gently along the groove between the pages. "And quite recently, too. The edge is still firm and crisp. If time had passed, it would have softened."

"Let me see." Stokes held out his hand, and she gave him the book. He studied it, then passed it to Barnaby. Stokes nodded at Penelope. "You're right."

"So…" She narrowed her eyes in thought. "We know the study was searched before we arrived, possibly in the hour or so after Monty was killed." She looked at Stokes and Barnaby. "Are we thinking it was the killer who did the searching?"

"Given the evidence of this book, that seems likely," Barnaby said, "regardless of whether the searching was done before or after the murder."

"So," Penelope went on, "the question, then, is, was it the killer who tore out the page? Presumably because that page referred to him or her."

Stokes looked stern. "That's very cold-blooded and calculated. To find the book but only remove their entry and, presumably knowing that others here, at the house party, are listed in the pages and therefore also victims, put the book back and leave it for us to find."

"That would be an effective way of sending us down the wrong track," Penelope observed.

Stokes looked at her, then shifted his gaze to Barnaby. "Is that what happened here?"

"I hesitate to leap to conclusions," Barnaby replied, "but based on what we've thus far uncovered, the murderer leaving the book in order to mislead us seems plausible."

"The alternative," Penelope said, "which, in fact, is equally likely, is that Monty himself tore out that page because whoever was listed on it has died or left the country or for some other reason is no longer a viable victim."

His frowning gaze fixed on the book, Stokes said, "As far as I can see, at present, there's no way we can be sure who tore out the page. And if it was Underhill, then whoever was named on the missing page is not involved in this case."

"Agreed," Barnaby said. "But if it was the murderer who tore out the page…"

"That," Penelope stated, "means that none of the victims still named in the book is the killer."

"And," Stokes grimly capped, "that one of the other guests is."

He met Penelope's then Barnaby's eyes. "If he tore out the page, he's definitely here, in the house, waiting and watching and expecting us to go after the other victims."

CHAPTER 4

*T*hey'd aimed to commence their interviews at the acceptable hour of ten o'clock. Now, however…

"Having unearthed a motive as well as several potential suspects among the guests, we need to rethink our approach." Barnaby met Penelope's eyes. "We have to move carefully so we don't impugn anyone's reputation unjustly."

"We also don't want to give this murderer any hint of what we're thinking," Stokes added.

Penelope nodded decisively. "We should make a plan tailored to elicit answers to the questions we have now. After finding Monty's little black book."

Stokes glanced around. "My first suggestion is that this room isn't best suited to our purpose. The lighting's dim, and it's too cramped to put people at ease. We want people relaxed enough to talk freely."

"Agreed." Barnaby met Penelope's eyes. "The library will be a better venue."

Penelope nodded. "It will also be seen as more in keeping with our guests' social standing."

Barnaby dispatched the footman, who had been waiting in the corridor, to fetch Constable Walsh and Gearing.

After leaving Walsh on guard in the study, they followed Gearing to the library, which lay on the opposite side of the hall from the drawing room at the front of the sprawling house.

They walked into the library, halted, and surveyed the space. The chamber was as large as the drawing room and offered several groupings of comfortable chairs. A cluster comprising a leather-covered Chesterfield sofa and four matching armchairs faced the fireplace, which was located in the center of the long inner wall, opposite the windows overlooking the forecourt. Nearer to hand sat another group of three armchairs, mirrored by a similar setting at the far end of the room. The long inner wall and both side walls hosted numerous glass-fronted or open-shelved bookcases, all well stocked with leather-bound tomes interspersed with porcelain vases and statuettes, while the wall broken by the windows sported occasional tables in the gaps between the windows. The tables displayed several busts, a sextant, and an armillary sphere.

Angled before the far inner corner of the room sat a handsome rosewood desk. Although the desk bore a crystal pen-and-ink set, its pristine leather-edged blotter suggested the placement was more for ornamentation than use. The beautiful inlays and rich patina of the desk's panels underscored that conclusion.

With a smile, Penelope turned to Gearing. "This will do admirably."

"Very good, ma'am. Please inform me if you have any further requirements." Gearing added, "Lady Pamela made it clear that the staff are to do everything we can to assist the investigation."

"That was helpful of her." With a nod, Penelope dismissed Gearing. He retreated, and as the door shut behind him, she turned to Barnaby and Stokes. "I suggest we appropriate some armchairs"—she waved to the grouping farther down the room—"and conduct our interviews in a more conversational setting."

Barnaby nodded and, with Stokes, went to shift the chairs. "That should help put our interviewees at ease."

They settled on having three armchairs arranged in an arc facing a fourth chair in which their subject would sit.

Penelope had just claimed the central chair of the three when a tap on the door heralded O'Donnell.

The experienced sergeant looked in and spotted them. He entered and closed the door, then crossed the room to halt before the chairs, politely bob his head, and report, "I've spoken with all the indoor staff—all those who were here yesterday morning—and by all accounts, they were too busy to have noticed anything."

Penelope nodded. "That's entirely believable. With twenty-six guests in the house plus the family, the staff will be at full stretch."

Stokes drew out his notebook. "What was their view of the master of the house?"

"One and all, they liked him," O'Donnell said. "Not often one hears that, but all used words like 'kind' and 'easygoing.' Apparently, he was never one to get riled or on his high horse, and everyone below stairs are rather shocked that someone up and killed him." O'Donnell paused, then added, "Like her ladyship, they tend to the notion of the villain being some passing madman."

Stokes grunted. "It seems their master, however kind-hearted and genial, led a much more complicated life than they imagine."

"One with a darker side," Penelope stated.

"We've discovered evidence," Stokes said, "that Underhill had a sideline in blackmail."

O'Donnell's eyes flew wide. "That'll cause a huge shock, I'd say."

"And not just among the staff," Barnaby added.

"Indeed," Penelope concurred.

"We're still feeling our way over how best to follow the leads Underhill's blackmail offers," Stokes said, "so keep that news to yourself."

"Yes, guv."

Stokes tapped his pencil on the cover of his notebook. "Meanwhile, I want you to go around the tenant farms and into the surrounding areas—the estates, houses, farms, and villages—and see if there's been any sightings of anyone lurking. The usual suspects—itinerants, vagabonds, gypsies, vagrants, and so on. It would help if we could strike that possibility entirely from our list."

"Aye, sir." O'Donnell saluted, nodded to Penelope and Barnaby, and departed.

As the door clicked shut, Penelope, who had been consulting her list of guests, observed, "We have two blackmail victims who were due to make payments yesterday. Miss Regina Hemmings—she's only twenty years old, which seems rather heartless of Monty, but the Hemmingses are rather well-off, so presumably, he thought his demands were reasonable. She was scheduled to hand over a string of pearls, but as was his habit, Monty hasn't noted exactly when or where."

Penelope ran her finger down her list and stopped at another name. "And then we have Lady Wincombe. She—or I suppose, officially, her husband, Lord Wincombe—is the guardian of her ladyship's orphaned niece, Harriet Cranton, who is also among the guests." Penelope tipped her head. "What indiscretion Monty was holding over her ladyship and what leverage it gave him—why it's important to her to keep said indiscretion concealed—is difficult to guess. However, while I can't immediately see what, exactly, Monty was threatening Lady Wincombe with, judging by her continued payments, his threat of exposure was effective."

"Who are the others on the victims list?" Stokes asked. "Presumably, they have the strongest motive to do away with Underhill."

"They and their nearest and dearest," Barnaby put in.

"In addition to Lady Wincombe and Miss Hemmings," Penelope said, "we have Lady Carville, Lord Morland, and Mr. Nevin-Smythe."

Stokes grimaced. "With a company of this size, I would normally favor concentrating on those five, but in this case…" He slanted a questioning look at Barnaby.

"Given that the murderer's name might no longer feature in Monty's book," Barnaby said, "we should avoid alerting the company to us having any reason to focus on anyone in particular."

"No need," Penelope said, "to start unnecessary speculation and rumors about people who are no more guilty than most but whom Monty nevertheless made into his victims. As matters stand, we have no reason to believe any of them is his killer."

Somewhat glumly, Stokes nodded. "Obviously, we'll tip our hand to the five victims when we speak with each of them, but I think we can be certain they won't spread the news they were being blackmailed by Underhill." He looked at Penelope. "So in light of recent findings, what do we need to know?"

Penelope arched her brows. "Let's think through that logically."

Stokes and Barnaby exchanged faintly amused glances, then each claimed one of the chairs flanking the one in which Penelope was sitting.

The ormolu clock on the mantelpiece ticked on while they debated and discussed not just what they needed to know and how best to ask those questions but also in what order those questions should be posed to elicit the most informative responses.

"We need to give them the opportunity to be as expansive as they wish." Penelope faintly grimaced. "In some cases, that might result in far more verbiage than we might like, but jewels are often found amidst dross."

"Sadly true." Stokes had written their proposed questions in his notebook. "Right. These are the questions we'll put to each interviewee." He held up the book and read, "One, when did they arrive at the house party and why are they here? Two, when did they come downstairs on Monday morning and where did they go? Three, where were they between nine and ten o'clock? Four, do they know if anyone else left the house during that period? Five, what was their view of Underhill? And sixth and last, do they know of any reason why anyone would want to kill him?"

Penelope observed, "That should give us enough to start with, and when we speak with those who were Monty's victims, we can probe further and see what they say."

Barnaby stated, "We should hold the information in Monty's black book close to our collective chest until and unless we feel we can learn more by revealing what we know."

"Indeed. The murderer is the one we want to leave guessing," Penelope said.

"So," Stokes asked, "in what order should we have people in?"

"Hmm." Penelope frowned. "I suspect the company—both the innocent and the guilty—will be agog to see how we proceed. If we don't want them trying to read anything into our order of interviews, let's use an order that's based on some obvious criteria." She looked at Stokes. "Like social rank."

"That makes sense," Stokes allowed. "It's also what some might expect."

"Right, then." Penelope waggled her fingers at him. "Give me your pencil and let's see what that translates to."

"Leith first?" Barnaby suggested.

Penelope frowned. "He's an earl, but as Susan is the daughter of a marquess, some would argue that she ranks higher." Penelope paused, then added, "And, of course, as the elder of the pair, Pamela ranks higher still." She looked at Stokes. "It might be useful to have Pamela in first. We can cast it as outlining for her what questions we intend to put to her guests—and that will, indeed, reassure her—while at the same time getting what insights we can from her."

His fingers steepled before his face, Stokes nodded. "Good idea."

"And then"—Penelope consulted her list—"we could alternate between male and female as we go down the ranks. Given the company is evenly split between the genders, that, too, might prove useful."

"Meaning the ladies will have more to offer from observing the gentlemen?" Barnaby suggested.

Penelope nodded. "Just so."

∼

With her sister in tow, Rosalind walked out onto the rear terrace. As she'd hoped, at that moment, there was no one else inhabiting the long expanse of flagstones. She led Regina, subdued and rather wilting, to the balustrade beyond the steps leading down to the lawn.

Rosalind folded her arms and leaned on the stone coping. She glanced at Regina as her sister came to stand, much less relaxed, beside her.

Regina's gaze was fixed on the trees at the far edge of the lawn. "Are you sure telling Percival is a good idea?"

"Perfectly sure." Rosalind infused the words with as much crisp certainty as she could muster. It had taken some time to get the full truth of what Regina had done the previous morning from her. Following Regina's gaze to the trees, Rosalind stated, "Percival said he was going for a ramble and would be back in good time for lunch." Straightening, she turned to the wrought-iron tables and chairs set out farther along the terrace. "If we wait here, we should be able to intercept him when he returns to the house."

Somewhat warily, Regina trailed Rosalind to the nearest table, drew out a chair, and sat on its edge. For a few moments, the sisters looked out over the lawns, then Regina asked, "Are you sure he'll help and not just be shocked?"

"He knows the investigators. I'm certain he'll agree to help." Rosalind was a trifle surprised by how firmly she believed that. She hadn't known Richard for long, but thirty-six hours of acquaintance had, apparently, been sufficient to convince her that his reputation as a hedonistic libertine—while possibly valid in earlier years—no longer applied. He was a man who was focused and deliberate, and she sensed that doing the right thing was important to him.

She couldn't explain why she was so sure of the last, yet she absolutely was.

That said, she hadn't answered the second part of Regina's question. She felt certain Richard would be as shocked as she had been on learning what had been going on. Given she and Regina were sharing a room, Regina hadn't been able to avoid Rosalind's nighttime inquisition. When confronted with the evidence of the blood on her gown's hem, Regina's brittle defenses had crumbled, and the entire story had tumbled out, after which Regina had begged Rosalind to help her.

Rosalind knew her sister. She unequivocally believed all that Regina had told her. Regina wasn't devious enough to have invented such a tale. Moreover, every action Regina had taken was precisely how Rosalind would have predicted her young and impressionable sister would behave when faced with such circumstances.

Yet Rosalind could see how the facts might appear to others, especially the investigators. Indeed, she couldn't fault Regina for attempting to hide her involvement nor for her reluctance to make that involvement known to the authorities.

Like Regina, Rosalind had been shocked to learn of what now appeared to be Monty Underhill's little sideline. She'd always viewed him as a genial, pleasant, and trustworthy gentleman. Of course, there could be some other, perfectly innocent explanation for why he'd been in the orchard, apparently looking into the hollow in the tree shortly after Regina had been due to leave her pearls there.

Having heard Regina's story first to last, Rosalind didn't think that likely.

She glanced at the door leading onto the terrace. Before they'd come outside, she'd checked that all the matrons and older ladies, their mother included, were safely ensconced in the morning room. They'd all been there, gathered around Lady Pamela, who had come downstairs after breakfast.

Most of the younger ladies and gentlemen were strolling in the rose garden or shrubbery or playing a round of croquet. Rosalind could hear the *clink* of balls from the distant green. No doubt, her mother thought she and Regina were with one of those groups, doing what they were at Patchcote Grange to do, namely make connections with suitable gentlemen.

Being a touch older than the other unmarried ladies and having a particular gentleman she was supposed to be getting to know had subtly set Rosalind apart from her less directed juniors.

I suppose asking Percival for help in this matter qualifies. How he reacts will be revealing and will say quite a bit about his character.

When it came to it, while she hoped she'd guessed correctly, she had no guarantee as to how he would behave.

She shifted on the hard wrought-iron seat, then settled again, doing her best to project an air of calm assurance.

She'd arrived at Patchcote Grange believing that, once she'd met Richard Percival, it was highly unlikely that she would want to encourage the connection. She'd imagined him as his reputation painted him—a hedonistic rake, albeit a discreet, handsome, elegant, and eligible one—and that was not at all what she wished for in a husband.

The events of the past two days had shown her a different man. One whom, possibly…

Rosalind glimpsed movement under the trees, then Richard strolled out of the shadows, and she felt a tiny yet undeniable thrill shiver through her.

As Richard approached the house, he looked ahead and saw Rosalind sitting on the terrace. Unexpectedly, his pulse skipped, then he realized her sister was sitting alongside her.

Keeping his stride slow and steady, he noted that both sisters were watching him with… Was it anticipation?

He focused on Rosalind, and as he neared the steps and she shifted forward, ready to stand, he realized she was waiting for him.

Specifically, him. For some purpose.

Instincts and intellect fully engaged, he went quickly up the steps and turned her way.

Both sisters rose, and he greeted them with a smile and an equable nod. "Ladies."

Rosalind waved to the vacant chair at their table. "We were hoping you would join us."

He didn't need to be asked twice. Calmly, he drew out the chair, waited until the sisters subsided into theirs, then sat.

He didn't miss Rosalind's quick scan of the terrace before she said, "We have a situation with which we hope you'll be willing to help us."

She hadn't said "able" but "willing." He met her eyes. "Consider me entirely at your disposal."

She searched his eyes, then exhaled. "Well, then. I've discovered a little more about what occurred yesterday morning. Before Monty was killed."

Wholly focused on her, he nodded curtly. "Go on."

She eyed him assessingly as she said, "It appears that our late host had a rather shocking secret life. As a blackmailer."

He blinked slowly, then refocused on her face, her eyes, and confirmed she was deadly serious. Again, he simply said, "Go on."

"We don't know who else was a victim, but Monty had been blackmailing Regina since last summer."

Richard shifted his gaze to the silent, younger sister. Her blush as she stared at her clasped hands was even more telling than her woebegone expression.

Despite the—entirely understandable—shock he felt at the news that

Monty, of all men, had been blackmailing anyone, he didn't for a second doubt Rosalind's word. Or indeed, Regina's. Slowly, he nodded, then returned his gaze to Rosalind's fine eyes. "All right. Tell me the whole."

Once he'd heard the full tale—and in truth, it all made terrible sense —he met Rosalind's watchful gaze. After a moment, he admitted, "I confess I'm…flabbergasted." He shook his head. "I don't doubt your word"—he glanced at Regina—"either of you, but what Monty was doing is…a lot to take in."

Rosalind leaned a trifle nearer. "We were hoping you might advise us as to what we should do."

Instantly, he replied, "Trust me, the answer to that is exceedingly straightforward. You need to tell the investigators all you've told me and as soon as possible." He met Rosalind's eyes, then Regina's, and the hesitation he saw prompted him to say, "I can vouch for their integrity and also their acuity." He found a wry and, he hoped, reassuring smile. "I'm speaking from experience in saying that of all those who might have been sent to investigate this case, the Adairs and Stokes are the team you should most welcome. I can promise you they won't leap to unwarranted conclusions, and they'll do their level best to protect all those who are innocent of this crime."

Rosalind looked reassured. "That's quite a recommendation."

He nodded. "And as I said, it's drawn from personal experience." He looked at Regina. "They are very good at what they do. Quite literally the best."

Regina was still reluctant, but Rosalind leaned across and closed one of her hands over her sister's tightly clasped ones. "You need to tell the investigators all you've told us." She squeezed Regina's hands encouragingly. "I'll come with you."

"I will, too." Richard caught Regina's startled gaze, pushed back his chair, and rose. "There's nothing to fear in doing the right thing. And ask yourself this—if Monty Underhill was blackmailing you, who else was he blackmailing?"

That brought a slight frown to Regina's face. Rosalind waited— hopeful but, Richard judged, too wise in the ways of her sister to prod.

Eventually, Regina raised her gaze to his face. "There will be others, won't there?"

"I think we can be certain of that," he replied.

Regina glanced at Rosalind, then looked back at him. Her delicate chin firmed, and she nodded. "All right. But"—she glanced at Rosalind and then him—"you will come with me, won't you?"

"We'll come with you now." Richard waited as Regina drew in a fortifying breath, and the sisters rose. Rosalind linked her arm with Regina's—a subtle show of solidarity—and hiding an appreciative smile, Richard escorted them into the house.

They found Gearing in the front hall. Luckily, no one else was around.

"Where are the investigators, Gearing?" Richard asked.

Gearing nodded toward the closed library doors and the footman standing outside them. "They're in the library and, I gather, preparing to commence their interviews with the guests."

"Excellent. Thank you, Gearing." Richard glanced at Rosalind and Regina. "That will suit our purpose well." He ushered the sisters toward the library. "We'll just go in and have a word."

Penelope sat behind the ornate library desk with Barnaby in a chair by her elbow. She'd just completed their list of interviewees when a sharp rap fell on the library door.

The investigators exchanged glances, then Barnaby called, "Come."

To Penelope's surprise, it was Richard who opened the door and ushered Rosalind and Regina Hemmings into the room.

Curious, Penelope rose, as did Barnaby and Stokes.

Richard closed the door, then, herding the ladies before him, stated, "Miss Hemmings has information you need to know."

Penelope looked at the sisters. Rosalind looked resolute, but solicitous of her younger sister, while Regina looked overwhelmed and increasingly nervous.

"Thank you for coming to see us." Stokes inclined his head to the pair. "We'll be grateful for any light you can shed on the situation."

Penelope bustled out from behind the desk and joined Barnaby and Stokes in being as encouraging as they could while they added two chairs to their conversational grouping and guided the sisters and Richard into the seats.

Once everyone settled, Rosalind looked at Regina and gently prompted, "It would be best if you start at the beginning. When the black-mailer first contacted you."

Instantly, Penelope fastened her gaze on Regina, as did Stokes and

Barnaby. Not by a flicker of an eyelash did they reveal they already knew that Regina had been blackmailed.

Under their scrutiny, Regina colored painfully.

Penelope caught the girl's eye and, with patent sympathy and sincerity, assured her, "I promise we won't bite."

The unexpected comment made Regina's lips fleetingly lift. Then, she drew in a breath, gripped her fingers tightly in her lap, and tipped up her chin. "It started early last summer, with a note delivered to the back door of our London house. A few weeks before, I'd visited with Mama and Rosalind at Wyndham Castle, and while there…" She drew in a shallow breath and blurted, "I let a footman kiss me. On the back stairs. Just once." She ducked her head, and her fingers twisted in her lap. "I know it was wrong—and silly! But I just…wanted to know. To see."

Rosalind reached across and bracingly gripped her sister's twisting fingers. "We all know what that's like. It truly wasn't any great thing."

Regina's head came up. "But that was just it. He—the blackmailer—said it would be." She focused on Penelope. "He knew what had happened—he made that clear in what he wrote—but he said he would make out it was so much worse. That if I didn't pay him, he would make the moment into something utterly tawdry. He said that if my sordid act became public knowledge, I would be banished from society. And he pointed out how that would affect the whole family's standing"—she glanced at Rosalind—"and dim Rosalind's prospects as well."

Reassuringly, Penelope said, "He was exploiting your innocence. For the record, Rosalind is correct—what you did was no terrible thing. A slap on the wrist from your mother and perhaps a few disapproving frowns from the starchiest matrons, but truly, as ton scandals go, that wouldn't even rate."

"Oh." Regina sat up. Clearly, she found Penelope's assessment far more bolstering than her sister's.

Barnaby gently asked, "What did the blackmailer want of you?"

"He first asked for money, but it was just ten pounds, and I had that put by." Regina was growing more comfortable and confident. "He told me to leave the money in a particular urn on Lady Selbridge's side terrace during her ball two nights later."

"So he—the blackmailer—knew you would be attending that ball." Stokes shot a glance at Penelope.

Regina frowned. "He must have, mustn't he?" After a moment, she went on, "I put the money in the urn early in the evening, just after we arrived. It was a fine night, and guests were out on the terrace more or less constantly. Obviously, I couldn't stand and watch to see who came to fetch the money. Before we left the ball, I peeked in the urn, and the money was still there. I had to leave it, but I didn't hear from the blackmailer the next day, so I assume he took it later."

"When did you get his next demand?" Stokes asked. "And how did you receive it?"

Regina's defensiveness had fallen away. "The same as the first time —a note delivered to the back door by a messenger boy. That was in"— she screwed up her face in thought—"late September, I think. We were back in London by then and going out to balls and parties." She sobered as she remembered. "This time, he wanted a pearl-and-amethyst brooch I'd been given by one of my great-aunts." She met Penelope's gaze. "I didn't want to give it up, but the note stated he didn't want anything else."

"Where were you told to leave it?" Barnaby asked.

Regina sighed. "In a particular Venetian-glass vase on the shelves in Lady Hamilton's music room. We were there two nights later for a musicale. I slipped the brooch into the vase and tried to keep watch on it through the performance, but up to the time everyone filed out of the room at the end—and I had to go, too—no one had gone near the vase."

"I see." Penelope resisted the urge to consult the black book. Instead, she asked, "How many more 'payments' have you made?"

"Two more between then and this week." Regina added, "It was always the same—a note sent to the back door, asking for money or a piece of jewelry that I was to leave in a more or less public place. One was a spot in the museum."

"Shifting to his latest demand," Stokes said, "was that communicated via a note as well?"

"Yes. A boy delivered it to the back door on Thursday morning. He— the blackmailer—always seemed to know when we were in town and what events I would be attending." Regina's expression grew troubled. "This time, he asked for the pearl necklace my grandmother had left me. I'd worn it to a ball the week before. It's all I have from her, and I didn't want to give it up." Her shoulders slumped, her lips turning down. "But, of course, I couldn't afford not to. Or so I thought."

Penelope nodded understandingly. "And you were told to leave the necklace…?"

Regina tipped her head in the direction of the orchard. "In the hollow in the apple tree in the first row of the orchard, five trees along from the entrance archway."

Penelope looked at Stokes and Barnaby, then returned her gaze to Regina. "I don't suppose you've kept this note?"

Regina's eyes widened. "I did. I have it here. He always ended with an instruction to burn the note, but I was worried I'd forget which tree it was, so I brought the note with me."

Penelope straightened. "Where is it?"

"Upstairs. In my reticule in our room," Regina answered.

Rosalind caught Penelope's eye. "Perhaps I could go and fetch it while Regina answers the rest of your questions."

Stokes inclined his head. "If you would, Miss Hemmings, that would help."

Richard also met Penelope's gaze. As Rosalind rose, he did, too. "I'll come with you."

Rosalind accepted his escort without demur, and the pair left and quietly closed the door behind them.

"Now." Penelope refocused on Regina, who had plainly recovered a great deal of what, Penelope judged, was her usual composure. "That brings us to yesterday morning. Start from when you woke. Did you come downstairs with your mother and Rosalind?"

Regina nodded. "I share a room with Rosalind, so I couldn't slip out early and put the necklace in the hollow. I had to behave as if nothing was wrong, that I wasn't on edge and rushing off somewhere. So after breakfast, when Rosalind left to go upstairs and read, I went with the other younger ladies, and we made for the conservatory, but before we got there, I pretended I needed something from my room and headed up the stairs. I stopped on the landing, and once the other girls had gone down the corridor, I slipped downstairs again and onto the terrace and from there onto the lawn." She pulled a face. "I hadn't expected Rosalind to see me, but she did, and of course, she followed me. She called, but I pretended not to hear and hurried on. I was sure I was very late by then—the note had said to put the necklace in the hollow before nine o'clock, and I was sure it had to be close to that time already. Then, I realized Rosalind was gaining on me! I went around into the woods, then circled back. I thought I'd lost her, so I rushed to the orchard."

The color ebbed from her cheeks. "I had the pearls in my pocket, and I was reaching for them as I ran along the first row of trees—and I tripped over him! I was so *shocked*, but I managed not to scream. I was petrified. Frozen. But after a few seconds, I made myself creep closer and see if he was still alive, but he wasn't. Then, I heard Rosalind calling and coming nearer. I didn't know if others were around. I panicked and rushed on through the orchard and into the shrubbery. Then, I heard Rosalind scream for help and knew she'd found him. I didn't know what to do! The shrubbery gives onto the woods, and I went out into the quiet and found a log and sat there." She paused, then more calmly added, "I don't know how long I sat on that log, but while I was there, I realized what finding Mr. Underhill in the orchard, stretched out like that, meant." She met Penelope's eyes. "*He* was the blackmailer. It was too coincidental for him to be going to look in that hollow when I was supposed to have put Grandmother's pearls into it by then."

Briskly, Penelope nodded. "We know Mr. Underhill was blackmailing you as well as quite a few others."

Regina brightened. "You do?"

"We have evidence of his crimes," Stokes said.

Regina's relief was palpable. "So you believe me?"

When Penelope, Barnaby, and Stokes nodded, Regina's tension wholly evaporated.

"Where did you go once you left the wood?" Stokes asked.

"I could hear all the ruckus in the orchard," Regina replied, "and I knew Rosalind would look for me, so I circled around to the terrace and went up to our room." She paused, then added, "That was when I realized I had blood on the hem of my gown—from crouching to see if Mr. Underhill was alive. I changed gowns and gave the dirtied one to our maid to wash, but she showed it to Rosalind later, so Rosalind knew I'd been in the orchard before her." Regina shared a smile with Penelope. "That's why she wouldn't let up until I'd told her the truth—all of it."

"We and you," Barnaby said, "should be very glad she did."

Regina's smile lit her face. "I am." Then, her smile faded into a faint frown. "I now understand how the blackmailer knew so much about me, about the family and our lives. But knowing it was Mr. Underhill—it's still a shock. I quite liked him." The betrayal she felt echoed in the words. Then, her features hardened, and she looked at Stokes. "But I do know that he was at the Selbridge ball and at Lady Hamilton's musicale. If that helps?"

Stokes nodded as he jotted. "Thank you. It does."

The door opened, and Rosalind and Richard came in. As Richard shut the door, Rosalind came forward and offered a folded note to Penelope. "I think this makes all clear."

Penelope took the note, unfolded it, scanned it, then stated, "The entire note is in Monty Underhill's hand. The instructions he gives are 'to place the pearl necklace you wore to Lady Hampton's ball in the hollow in the apple tree in the first row of the orchard, five trees from the entrance arch, before nine o'clock on Monday morning.'" She looked at Stokes. "I believe that's fairly conclusive."

Then she looked assessingly at Regina. "But to settle the matter beyond question." She handed the note to Stokes and, rising, waved Regina to her feet. "How tall are you compared to me?"

They stood back-to-back, and it was clear to all that Regina was the same height as Penelope.

"Certainly no taller." Stokes made a note.

Stepping away, Penelope smiled at Regina. "The significance of height is that the evidence shows that whoever bashed Monty Underhill over the head had to be taller than me. Or you. So you could not have killed Monty Underhill, and of that, there is no doubt."

Regina's face brightened. "Oh, thank you! That's *such* a relief—to know that I can't possibly be a suspect."

Stokes was flicking back and forth through his notes. "When you were in the orchard, did you notice an iron stake lying in the grass?"

Regina shook her head. "Was that what he was hit with?"

"We believe so." Stokes glanced at Rosalind. "If you could just clarify, Miss Hemmings, did you see anyone while you were following your sister to the orchard?"

Rosalind shook her head. "I hurried down the terrace steps, but Regina was a good way ahead of me." She flicked a smiling glance at Regina. "I was quite cross with her because I knew she was deliberately avoiding me. I followed her into the wood, and she circled around a bit before heading out again. I was farther back by then, but I reached the edge of the trees in time to see her whisk around the corner of the orchard wall, I assumed through the archway into the orchard." Somewhat ruefully, she glanced at Penelope. "I'm sure you can guess what I was thinking."

Her lips quirking, Penelope arched a brow. "That Regina was engaging in some clandestine meeting with some utterly unsuitable man?"

Rosalind lightly grimaced. "Something like that."

Regina faintly huffed, but she was smiling at her older sister as she reached out and squeezed Rosalind's hand. "I'm just so glad you did come after me, and I'm sorry I left you to deal with it all."

Rosalind squeezed Regina's hand and smiled back. "That's what older sisters are for."

Stokes had been studying his notes. He shut his notebook, looked at Regina, Rosalind, and Richard, and inclined his head. "You did the right thing in coming to us with your information. As matters transpired, we already knew Regina was one of Underhill's victims and that she is by no means the only one. He left a book with a list of those he preyed upon and the dates and descriptions of their payments. That evidence makes it clear he'd been practicing his extortions for years." Stokes paused, meeting their frankly surprised and not-a-little-shocked gazes. "We're trusting you with that information, but please, keep it to yourselves." He focused on Rosalind and Regina. "Don't tell your mother." He shifted his gaze to Richard. "And definitely do not tell your aunts."

Soberly, Richard nodded. "Consider my lips sealed."

Stokes glanced at Penelope.

She smiled at Regina, Rosalind, and Richard. "Although we'd already learned about the blackmail, your information has considerably improved our understanding of Mr. Underhill's activities."

Barnaby inclined his head to the three. "Because of your information, the investigation will proceed at a much faster pace." He briefly glanced at Stokes, then went on, "However, we should warn you that there is every possibility that Underhill's murderer is one of the guests residing under this roof. That being so, the less he or she knows about what we know, the better for all concerned."

"Because of that," Penelope said, "we would counsel you to make every effort to behave as if you know absolutely nothing about the murder. That won't necessarily be easy, but no matter what leading questions anyone poses, please act as if you have no idea whatsoever of any of the information we've just discussed."

Richard had grown increasingly serious. He nodded to Penelope, Barnaby, and Stokes. "We'll follow that advice."

After a final round of thanks all around, Richard solicitously ushered the sisters from the room.

The instant the door clicked shut, Penelope turned to Stokes and Barnaby. "Well! That truly has clarified matters considerably."

Stokes nodded. "We've a clearer idea of what was happening around the time Underhill was murdered, and our understanding of how he conducted his blackmailing scheme has improved significantly."

"True," Barnaby said, "but what are the odds that the other guests who are Monty's victims also have no idea who their blackmailer was?"

Stokes grimaced. "Sadly, I fear those odds are stacked against us. He was obviously very careful to conceal his identity from his victims."

Penelope nodded. "Even with a victim as relatively helpless as Regina Hemmings."

"Thinking further," Barnaby went on, "if none of his victims knew their blackmailer's identity, was Monty's blackmailing the cause of his death? Or was the motive something else entirely?"

They pondered the point, then Penelope suggested, "Let's start our interviews—finally!—and see whether we stumble on any hint of another motive."

Stokes agreed. "That's likely our best way forward."

Barnaby turned to the mantelpiece and tugged the bellpull that hung beside it. When Gearing responded, Barnaby instructed the butler to convey their respects to Lady Pamela and ask if she could spare them a few minutes of her time.

CHAPTER 5

$\mathcal{W}$hen the library door opened and Lady Pamela walked in, Penelope was standing before the chairs, waiting to guide their hostess into the comfortable armchair at the focus of the investigators' "conversational grouping."

Pamela looked wan and even a touch haggard. Her dark mourning gown rendered her gaunt and pale. After favoring the investigators with a severe nod, Pamela sat as directed, and Penelope sank into the chair directly facing her, with Barnaby on Penelope's right and Stokes to her left.

Penelope opened with "Thank you for your support in our efforts to apprehend your husband's murderer. We thought it appropriate we speak with you first and outline the questions we intend posing to your guests and to advise you that, in the circumstances, we believe it will be wise to speak with each and every guest so that none will be seen to be singled out in any way." She clarified, "While we are in need of information, which we believe the guests can provide, we do not wish to imply that we suspect anyone of the crime."

Pamela's frown had been deepening, but Penelope's last sentence gave her pause. After a moment, Pamela haughtily inclined her head. "I suppose that's sensible."

Smoothly, Penelope continued, "We felt that the best way to demonstrate how unthreatening our interviews will be is to put the same questions to you." Penelope opened her eyes at her ladyship. "If you're willing?"

Pamela clearly wasn't eager but felt compelled to agree. "If you think it best."

Penelope smiled understandingly. "Our first question is when did you arrive at the Grange?"

"I arrived with Monty, Vincent, and Cecilia on the Monday two weeks back. We'd been at Wyndham Castle, which, as I'm sure you're aware, is my family's principal seat. We often spend time there with my cousin, the marquess."

"I see." Penelope went on, "Shifting focus to Monday morning, when did you come downstairs?"

"I came down early, at a little before eight. I like to be there, in the dining room, on the morning of the first day of any house party to ensure the guests enjoyed a restful night and have everything they require for a pleasant stay." Pamela added, "Cecilia came down with me. Naturally, many of the gentlemen were ahead of us and already at the table."

"And after breakfast?" Penelope strove to keep her ladyship's gaze on her rather than Stokes, who was taking notes. "Where did you go, and who went with you?"

"My sister and I left the table together with several of the matrons and older ladies. We went to the morning room for our usual morning coze, and Cecilia and the other young ladies went to the conservatory so that their chatter didn't impinge on our conversations."

"The third item on our list," Penelope said, "is to ask where you were between nine and ten o'clock."

"I remained in the morning room."

"Are you aware of anyone who left the house during that time?"

Pamela frowned, then offered, "I didn't see anyone outside, but Susan left the morning room and went for a stroll, I imagine to the rose garden. It's a favorite haunt of hers when she's here."

"Excellent." Penelope skipped their next question. They didn't need to ask Pamela what she'd thought of her husband. "Our final query is whether you know of any reason why anyone would want to kill Monty."

Pamela's frown deepened. "No." She appeared truly perplexed. "I've thought and thought, yet I cannot imagine why anyone would want to kill him. He was amusing in his way and, otherwise, perfectly harmless. He had to have been killed by someone who didn't know him. A passing vagrant, an itinerant—someone of that sort."

Penelope shared a glance with Stokes, then rose. "Thank you for indulging us, Lady Pamela."

Pamela blinked, then hauled herself to her feet. Somewhat suspiciously, she demanded, "Is that the full sum of your questions?"

Barnaby and Stokes had risen, and Barnaby replied, "For now. Our purpose is to check if anyone saw someone we can't account for."

"Oh." The comment clearly fed into her ladyship's belief that someone unknown had ventured into the orchard and murdered her spouse. "I see." She glanced at Penelope, who met her gaze with a look of limpid innocence. Pamela huffed. "Yes, well. If that's all, I'll leave you to it. I've told Gearing to arrange anything you wish for."

"Thank you." Penelope ushered Pamela to the door. "We'll be sure to let you know if we learn anything definite from the guests."

After Penelope had seen Pamela out, Barnaby rang for Gearing and dispatched him to invite the Earl of Leith to join them.

When Barnaby returned to the armchairs, Stokes arched a brow at him. "That'll sound as if we're inviting him to give us his opinion."

Barnaby grinned and resumed his seat. "I think we can reasonably predict that curiosity over our investigation is running high, so a bland request for attendance is sufficient to bring anyone through the door."

"Hopefully, in the right frame of mind to answer our questions," Penelope put in. "Fully yet succinctly."

"So," Stokes said, "before he arrives, what do I need to know about Leith?"

"He's an interesting character," Penelope remarked. "His name is Frederick Armstrong. He somewhat unexpectedly inherited the title from his uncle a little over two years ago. His uncle's son should have inherited, but he—the son—vanished decades ago and hasn't been heard from since, so he was duly declared dead, and the title passed to Frederick."

"Nothing untoward known about him," Barnaby put in. "In general, he's a straightforward character, well-liked and well-regarded."

"I should probably mention," Penelope said, "that prior to inheriting the title, Leith was solid bachelor material—connected to the earldom, a gentleman, certainly, but not one to court attention. Now, of course, the title has transformed him into a rich matrimonial prize. He's much sought after, and I gather he's accepted the responsibility of keeping the line going and has started, rather warily and carefully, to look about him for a wife. I suspect that's why he's here."

A tap on the door heralded the Earl of Leith.

Barnaby rose and, with a smile, gestured for Leith to join them. As, urbane and composed, the earl traveled the long length of the room, Barnaby seized the chance to match his memory with the current fact.

Somewhere in his late thirties, Leith was of above-average height, a few inches shorter than Barnaby and Stokes. Leith possessed a solid build and an imposing presence and wore the mantle of earl well. He had brown hair, thick but neatly trimmed, and mid-brown eyes set in an angular, rather squarish face with a strong, patrician nose. His was not a handsome face but was sufficiently striking and pleasant to attract and hold attention. As he approached the investigators, Leith's expression remained relaxed and confident, and as Barnaby had predicted, a gleam of curiosity shone in his eyes.

With nods to Penelope and Barnaby and a curious glance and a dip of his head to Stokes, Leith complied with Barnaby's unspoken invitation to sit in their interviewee's chair.

Barnaby sat and opened the questioning with their agreed query as to when Leith had arrived and why he was there.

Leith readily replied, "I drove down from town in my curricle and arrived in the latter half of the afternoon." He glanced at Penelope and smiled. "As to why I'm here, you could put that down to wishing to stay in Lady Pamela's good graces. She was most insistent that I attend." He paused, then, head tilting, self-deprecatingly added, "As I have yet to marry, I suspect she hopes that I might find her daughter appealing."

Catching Penelope's eye, Leith lightly shrugged. "As I will need to marry at some point, I'm amenable to casting my eye over the field."

"You spent Sunday evening with the company, I assume?" Barnaby inquired.

"Indeed."

"Moving on to Monday," Barnaby said, "at what time did you come downstairs?"

"I breakfast early, usually just after seven o'clock—I reached the dining room about that time." Without further prompting, Leith continued, "After I rose from the table, I came in here to check the news sheets. That was a little before eight, I believe, and they'd just come in, but nothing caught my eye, and as I knew I had several letters I needed to write, I returned to my room to do so."

Barnaby inclined his head in acceptance. "Do you recall where you were between nine and ten o'clock?"

Leith's brows rose. "Over the time Monty was murdered? I was still in my room, writing. I heard the commotion—people rushing downstairs —and after a little time, I came down to see what the fuss was about."

"You didn't hear Miss Hemmings scream for help?" Penelope asked.

Leith shook his head. "The window was shut."

"Do you know if anyone else left the house during that period—nine to ten?" Barnaby asked.

"No. But I wasn't paying attention to anyone or anything beyond my writing."

Barnaby glanced at Penelope, then at Stokes, then proceeded with their next question. "What was your view of Underhill?"

Leith's face clouded, and his expression turned somber. His gaze grew distant as he said, "I knew Monty quite well—better than I know Pamela. Although he was older, the Underhills and my family, the Armstrongs, have a long history. Our lands lie in the same part of the country, and the families have been friendly for many generations. When I first came on the town, Monty went out of his way to ease my path into society." A faint smile flitted over Leith's face as if he was remembering happier times. "He was a bit like a favorite uncle crossed with an older cousin to me. I held him in high regard." After several seconds of being sunk in his memories, Leith stirred, raised his head, and stated, "I always found Monty to be a genial fellow, an excellent host, and an all-around pleasant man. We often crossed paths at White's, and he always had time for a few words." Cynically, Leith added, "Even before I came into the title."

"Do you know of any reason someone would want to kill him?" Barnaby asked.

Confidently, Leith stated, "No. None at all." He paused, then added, "In truth, I find it quite shocking that someone has." He met Barnaby's eyes. "Do you have any idea who did it?"

Smoothly, Stokes replied, "At present, we're collecting information regarding what everyone here saw and heard. Once we've assembled those facts, we'll have a clearer view of what happened."

"I see." Leith's gaze, which had shifted to Stokes, flashed to Penelope.

Barnaby rose. "Thank you for your assistance, Leith."

With a charming smile, Leith got to his feet. "In the circumstances, I can hardly say it was a pleasure, but weathering your inquisition really wasn't too difficult." He bowed to Penelope, nodded to Stokes, and joined Barnaby, who guided him from the room.

After Leith left, still at the door, Barnaby glanced inquiringly at Penelope.

She consulted her list. "Lady Susan's next."

Barnaby informed Gearing, and while the butler went to look for her ladyship, Barnaby returned to the armchairs.

Stokes looked at Penelope. "So what can you tell me about Lady Susan?"

"She's Pamela's sister, younger by several years. As I recall, the sisters have always got on, always been quite close. Neither made any splash within the ton, and by ton standards, neither were attractive partis, as both have...*difficult* personalities. In particular, Susan is known the length and breadth of the ton as unrelentingly blunt and lacking all tact. However, being a marquess's daughters, both sisters eventually married. Despite the shortcomings of her distinctly sharp and frequently unrestrained tongue, Susan is widely credited with making the better match in ultimately snaring Lord Goodrich." Penelope met Stokes's gaze. "If you found Pamela a trifle haughty, I should warn you that Susan is distinctly snootier and more inclined to keep her nose in the air. She often presents as quite rude."

Stokes grunted, but, as the door opened, said nothing more.

Penelope, Barnaby, and Stokes rose, and Penelope thanked Susan for her attendance and directed her to the chair facing Penelope's.

Susan nodded curtly and strode toward them. In general appearance, she was a younger version of her sister, perhaps an inch or so taller and a trifle more robust, more Junoesque. She, too, wore her dark hair drawn back from her face in an unflattering style that did nothing to soften the mannish line of her jaw.

Once Susan settled and the investigators resumed their seats, Penelope opened with their agreed first question.

Susan regarded her with a direct gaze. "My daughters and I arrived in our carriage on Saturday. We came early to spend an extra day with my sister and her family. As for why we are here, well, because we were invited, of course, and we—my sister and I—had hopes of fostering an attachment between my younger girl, Samantha, and Vincent." Susan glowered, and her lips crimped in transparent annoyance.

Sensing something more to be learned, Penelope lightly inquired, "And how are matters faring in that regard?"

"They aren't," Susan bluntly replied. "It turned out that Monty had other ideas and strongly opposed the match." That she deeply resented her brother-in-law's attitude was beyond question. "In light of his staunch opposition, I suppose you might say I'm here to cast the net more widely for both of my girls."

"Were you and your family at Wyndham Castle recently, with Pamela and her family?"

"Yes. We went home for ten days, then came here."

Mildly, Penelope asked, "On Monday morning, at what time did you come downstairs?"

"We—my daughters and I—came out of our rooms at about eight o'clock. We gathered in the corridor, and several other ladies and girls joined us—the Hemmingses among others—and we trooped downstairs together and went into the dining room."

"And once you rose from the table?"

"A group of ladies left the dining room all at once. With the other matrons and the older ladies, I settled in the morning room at first. The young ladies took themselves off to the conservatory, except for Rosalind. She went upstairs."

"And you remained in the morning room?"

Susan's gown rustled as she shifted in the chair. "No. I routinely walk of a morning after breakfast, and I found the chatter a bit much, so I left the others and went out via the terrace to the rose garden. It's a favorite place of mine here, at Patchcote. This estate used to be one of our family properties, so I've known the house since I was a child, and I've watched the roses develop over the years." She paused, then exhaled and said, "I was standing among the roses when I heard Rosalind scream."

"Do you know if anyone else left the house that morning?" Barnaby asked.

"I've no idea." Susan frowned. "I believe the younger crew had spoken of going for a walk around the grounds at some point, but I don't know if any of them had got that far before it happened." She glanced at Barnaby. "I didn't see anyone else while I was outside, if that's what you want to know."

Barnaby inclined his head.

Penelope leapt in to ask the question she hoped would elicit a possibly revealing answer. "If you would indulge us, what was your view of Monty?"

Susan's lips primmed in overt disapproval. After several seconds of glaring at nothing, she replied, "It's common knowledge that I always thought Pamela could have done much better for herself. Then again, she's known for being stubborn, and there's no accounting for taste. So for love of her, I had to accept him, didn't I?" She uttered a harsh bark of a laugh. "The irony of Monty then declaring that Samantha wasn't good enough for his son! That didn't escape me, I can assure you!" Smoldering resentment underlaid the words.

When it was plain she was not about to volunteer anything more, in an even tone, Barnaby asked, "Do you know of any reason why someone would want to kill Monty?"

Susan regarded him dismissively. "No. Of course not." She waved the point aside. "I might not have liked the man, but most found him a genial sort. A likeable fellow. I find the notion that he was murdered quite incomprehensible."

Penelope glanced at Stokes, who fractionally shook his head, then she rose, encouraging Susan to do the same. "Thank you for your time, Lady Susan. And your confidences."

Susan snorted. "Can't see that they'll get you much further. You should be out looking for some vagrant—it's the only thing that makes sense."

Penelope accompanied her ladyship to the door, then sent Gearing to summon Richard.

As she returned to the central armchair, Stokes humphed. "She was out of the house, supposedly in the rose garden, which, I believe, is on the same side of the house as the orchard. Given the obvious rancor she bore the victim and her general attitude and temper, until we have her whereabouts confirmed over the period between nine and ten o'clock, she will remain a definite suspect."

Penelope frowned, apparently unconvinced, but Barnaby agreed. "She's more than tall enough and strong enough to have delivered the killing blow."

The door opened, and Richard came in. As, with a quick smile, he came down the room to join them, Barnaby waved him to the interviewee's chair and explained, "We're speaking with all the guests, more or less in order of precedence so no one can be viewed suspiciously for being singled out."

Subsiding into the indicated chair, Richard nodded. "A very wise move, given the guests and the circumstances."

"Speaking of which," Penelope said, "how are the other guests reacting to the investigation?"

Richard sat back. "Truth to tell, now the initial shock is wearing off, most are increasingly consumed by curiosity. It's not every day one gets to observe a murder investigation at close range."

Somewhat airily, Penelope asked, "And how are the Hemmings sisters coping?"

Barnaby watched as Richard wisely answered rather guardedly.

Hiding a smile at his wife's abiding interest in matchmaking and intercepting a long-suffering look from Stokes, Barnaby seized the reins. "To get down to business, to get some idea of who was where and when, we're asking all the guests a standard set of questions, the first of which is, when did you arrive at the Grange?"

Very happy to switch tacks, Richard promptly replied, "I traveled down in my carriage with my aunts. We arrived on Sunday, midafternoon."

"And you're here because…?" Barnaby asked.

"I'm here because my aunts engineered an invitation, and to keep them quiet, it was easiest to fall in with their plans." Richard glanced at Penelope. "As I suspect you already know, my aunts have suggested that Rosalind Hemmings might make me a suitable bride, and this house party provides an opportunity to explore the possibility."

Before Penelope could pursue that topic, Stokes asked, "At what time did you come downstairs on Monday morning?"

"At affairs such as this, I come down early to breakfast to avoid the ladies and all the chatter. From the dining room, I went upstairs to my room again. I had several letters I needed to write."

"And between nine and ten o'clock?" Stokes inquired.

"I was writing in my room until just before ten. I finished the letters and brought them with me when I came downstairs. I was on the stairs when Rosalind screamed. I tossed the letters on the salver on the hall table and ran outside."

Stokes was jotting, so Barnaby asked, "Do you know if anyone else left the house during that time—nine to ten?"

Richard paused, clearly thinking back. "No. There were other gentlemen seated in here—I glimpsed them as I ran past the open doorway. They'd heard the scream, too, and followed me outside."

"You didn't see anyone outside while you were upstairs?" Stokes rumbled.

"No." Richard shrugged. "I wasn't looking."

Barnaby asked, "What was your view of Monty? Did you know him well?"

"Not well, no. Much like you, I was acquainted with him well enough to exchange nods and stop and chat at social events or in a club. As to how I found him..." He blew out a breath. "If I ignore what we've recently learned about his illicit activities, then up to now, I'd always found him to be a likeable chap, good-natured, usually full of bonhomie with rarely an unkind word to say of anyone and only when it was well-deserved. He was more convivial than most, a harmless gentleman of good family." Richard raised his brows. "Many in the ton will be deeply shocked to learn of his murder, primarily because it's hard to imagine why anyone would want to murder a man like him."

Barnaby's lips twisted. "You've largely answered our next question, namely, whether you know of any reason anyone would want to kill him."

Richard's features hardened. "Other than him blackmailing members of the ton?"

Penelope sighed. "Everything we're hearing suggests that has to be the motive."

"But for the record," Stokes said, "you're not aware of anything else that might constitute a motive for Underhill's murder?"

Richard shook his head. He glanced at Penelope and Barnaby. "Surely, Monty's blackmailing stands a very good chance of being the reason he was murdered."

Barnaby dipped his head in agreement.

Richard regarded the investigators, then added, "It's worth remembering that there are more secrets within the ton than most will ever know, and many of those secrets are powerful ones—the sort that, should they become widely known, will change powerful men's fortunes dramatically, literally from prince to pauper."

Stokes was nodding. "A powerful secret births a powerful motive."

"Exactly," Richard said.

Head tilted, Penelope murmured, "What are the chances that, during his lengthy career in the ton, Monty had stumbled upon such a secret?"

"If he was in the habit of seeking to learn others' secrets," Barnaby said, "as we now know he was, then given the circles in which he moved, I'd say the chances were high."

All pondered that insight for a moment, then Stokes shut his notebook and nodded to Richard. "That's it for you."

Richard rose, and Penelope rapidly consulted her list, then looked at Richard and smiled. "If you could send in your aunt Agatha, that would be a great help."

Richard's smile turned wryly cynical. "I'm sure she'll be delighted to oblige."

Penelope was unsurprised when, mere moments after Richard had left, Agatha, Lady Campbell-Carstairs, stumped into the room. She leaned on her cane as she surveyed the space, then she saw them, waved, and came slowly toward them.

Barnaby and Stokes rose, and smiling, Penelope went to help the old lady to the interviewee's armchair.

Agatha was of the older generation; she wouldn't see sixty again. She had a soft, round figure and a soft-featured face, but there was a shrewdness in her still-blue eyes that suggested a sharp mind resided behind them. With steel-gray hair drawn back in a loose bun and a paisley shawl draped about her shoulders, she accepted Penelope's assistance with a grateful nod and sank into the chair with a sigh.

As the others sat, Agatha declared, "I'm happy to tell you whatever I know about this incident, which is blessedly little, and I'm itchingly keen to learn what on earth Monty did to get himself killed."

She folded her hands over the top of her cane and looked at them expectantly.

Seated opposite and thus directly in the line of fire, Penelope explained, "We're asking everyone about their whereabouts on Monday morning, but first, could you tell us when you arrived at the Grange?"

Agatha waved. "Didn't Richard say? We came down with him in his carriage on Sunday. Arrived about three o'clock."

"And you're here in order to…?"

"Prod Richard into looking properly at Rosalind Hemmings with a view to offering for her hand. She'll make him an excellent wife, but steering a gentleman like my nephew is no mean feat."

"Indeed." Penelope caught a warning look from Stokes and reluctantly continued with their agreed questions. "On Monday morning, at what time did you come downstairs?"

"We—m'sister Miriam and I—had breakfast together in our room. We came downstairs at about nine and joined the other ladies in the morning room."

"And from then to ten o'clock?"

"You mean when Rosalind screamed?" When Penelope nodded, Agatha went on, "We were sitting and chatting, as you might expect."

"Did you notice if anyone left the house that morning, before the scream?"

"Monty—he was going out through the front door as Miriam and I came down the stairs. Oh, and that popinjay, Nevin-Smythe, came out of the dining room, crossed the hall before the stairs, nodded to us, then walked on down the other corridor. Probably to the billiards room. We could hear balls clacking." Agatha paused, then went on, "And after we'd joined the company in the morning room, Susan went out to take a walk in the garden."

Penelope was pleased to have gained information they hadn't previously had. After sharing a quick glance with Barnaby and Stokes, she fixed her gaze on Agatha's lined face. "Now, if someone who didn't know him asked, how would you describe Monty?"

Agatha frowned. "I expect in the same way all in society who knew him would. He was always pleasant, even-tempered to a fault, quite gregarious and jovial, and in general, an all-around good sort. I've never heard anyone say a bad word about him, and despite his and Pamela's marriage being arranged, he and she have made a good match of it." Her expression growing troubled, she shook her head. "It's most unsettling to think that a man as decent as he could meet with such a violent end."

"So you have no idea why anyone would want to kill him?" Penelope asked.

"None whatsoever, and I'm very puzzled by that." Leaning on her cane, Agatha met Penelope's eyes, then glanced at Barnaby. "As you no doubt know, within our circle, when deaths like this happen, there's almost always a story behind it. One already known. Some hint of bad blood between victim and killer, that sort of thing. But with Monty"—she shrugged—"there's nothing. Not a glimmer of enmity or hostility, not even the veriest whisper of scandal." Agatha leveled her shrewd, rather penetrating gaze on Penelope. "At least as far as I've heard."

Ignoring the invitation to share what she knew, Penelope smiled and rose. "I have to agree. Until Monty wound up dead, I had no idea that anyone at all wished him ill."

She helped Agatha to the door, then dispatched the footman, now on duty outside the room, to fetch Lord Morland.

For Morland, the first of Monty's victims to be questioned, Barnaby switched places with Penelope so that when Morland arrived and claimed the interviewee's chair, Barnaby was seated directly opposite.

Morland was in his late forties, a tall, broad-chested, physically imposing man with an unexpectedly nervous disposition that prompted him to do his best to fade into any background. He had a bumbling, blundering way about him, displayed in both manner and movement, and he was patently thrown off balance by the current circumstances, unsure of himself and plainly wondering what he should do and say.

He sat almost tentatively in the armchair and pressed his palms to his thighs.

Barnaby smiled reassuringly. "We're trying to get a sense of where people were at the time of Underhill's death, but to start with, can you confirm when you arrived at the Grange?"

Morland blinked. "On Sunday. Came down in my carriage. Must have got here about four."

"Other than socializing," Barnaby asked, "was there any purpose you hoped to achieve during your stay?"

Morland frowned. "Purpose? No." He grew slightly agitated and shot a glance at Penelope. "Well, I was invited, and I've been here before. Know the family quite well. And it's the sort of thing one does during summer, isn't it?"

There's something there. He did have some purpose in coming down here. Barnaby inclined his head. "Turning to Monday morning, when did you come downstairs?"

Morland looked relieved at being asked a simple question. "I came down about eight o'clock and breakfasted with the other gentlemen I found at the table."

"And after that?"

"I came in here to read the news sheets."

"When did you leave?" Barnaby asked.

"After we heard the scream." Clearly remembering, Morland paled. "There was a group of us here by then. Sitting about, reading, and making the occasional comment. We heard the scream, and an instant later, Percival thundered past the doorway toward the front door. We shook off our shock and followed him."

"I see. At any time that morning up to the moment you heard the scream, did you happen to notice anyone leaving the house?"

Morland hesitated, then said, "I assume Monty left, although I didn't actually see him step outside. He wandered in, did the rounds like the good host he was, seeing that we were all comfortable."

"When was that?" Stokes murmured.

Morland frowned. "Not sure. Sometime around nine?" He paused, then went on, "He chatted with us about the latest in the news sheets, then he said he was off for a ramble to check on something—he didn't say what." Morland sighed. "And off he went. He went out of the door and turned toward the front of the house...and that's the last I saw of him until the orchard..." Morland broke off and swallowed.

Barnaby let a second pass before asking, "How would you describe Underhill? How did he strike you?"

Morland instantly replied, "He was a good sort. You might say 'chummy.' We've known each other for decades, moved in similar circles all our lives..." He paused, then went on, "I would say he was a friend, but really, we weren't that close. Not personally. More like long-term social acquaintances. We were comfortable in each other's company, and he was an easy man to like and get along with."

When Morland returned Barnaby's gaze steadily and offered nothing more, Barnaby moved on. "Do you know of any reason someone would want to kill him?"

"No." Morland's perplexed expression testified to that being the truth. "Indeed, that he has been killed in such a vicious way is quite shocking. What is the world coming to?"

Barnaby glanced at Penelope. Accepting the cue, she gently said, "As it happens, we have reason to believe that Monty had something of a history as a blackmailer."

"What?" The incredulity reflected in Morland's face could not have been manufactured. He stared at Penelope. "No. No...you *must* be mistaken." The color slowly drained from his face as he grasped the personal implication. "Surely not." The last words were a whisper.

Penelope drew out the little black book. "We found this hidden in Monty's study." She opened the book, flicked through several pages, then read, "Under your name are listed several dates, starting just over three years ago. The most recent is May fifteenth this year. Against that date, Monty—this is all written in his hand—has noted the sum of fifty pounds."

Morland was white as a sheet. "Dear God."

From his expression, he was reviewing the past, starting to piece together some sequence of events. As he only grew more aghast, it seemed that nothing he saw in his mental landscape contradicted the notion of Monty as his blackmailer.

Her voice low, Penelope said, "We apologize, but we do need to inquire further. The notation Monty has placed beside your name is *I*, which we believe denotes 'infidelity.'"

As if in a daze, Morland choked out, "My wife, Cynthia, died five—

no, six years ago, but she was ill for years before." Morland swallowed and went on, his own voice lowering, "During that time, I…commenced a liaison with another lady. She's married, too, so we were very discreet." He grimaced. "Or so we thought. But somehow, the blackmailer—he found out." Morland's features started to firm, along with his voice. "He threatened to reveal the affair to my children as well as the lady's husband and family. But worse"—Morland refocused quite fiercely on Penelope— "he said he would make it sound as if the affair led me to do away with Cynthia. But I loved Cynthia—she was the love of my life—yet she was fading before my eyes and I…sought comfort in the arms of someone who understood, but he made it sound so tawdry. He swore that if I didn't pay, what he would reveal would make it certain that I was accused of murdering Cynthia!" He stared at Penelope. "And it was *Monty*?"

Abruptly clutching his head with both hands, he leaned forward. "I can't believe it!" He shook his head, but then stilled and, a moment later, more quietly said, "And yet…"

When he didn't continue, Penelope suggested, "Monty being the blackmailer fits?"

Head still between his hands, Morland nodded. "Looking back…yes, that fits."

Penelope glanced at the book, still open in her hands. "According to his record, you paid Monty ten times over the past three years."

Morland nodded. Releasing his head, he straightened. His expression suggested the revelation of his blackmailer's identity had rocked him to the core. "The alternative was simply too horrible to contemplate, and the amounts were never too much to manage." His lip curled. "Monty would have known how much I could withstand without being too hard-pressed."

Evenly, Stokes said, "Can you tell us how you made those payments? Perhaps the last few?"

The tale that fell from Morland's lips was a male variation of Regina's experience. Notes were delivered either to his house or to White's, and all the payment spots had clearly been chosen so as to be difficult if not impossible to monitor. When Barnaby commented on that point, Morland laughed cynically. "One of the earlier ones was at a race meet at Doncaster. I was told to leave the payment below a step in the stand just above the bookmakers' stalls. With all the men milling about the book-makers, it was impossible to see who picked up the packet." He paused, then added, "I did try, several times, to see who collected the payments, but then I realized he'd hired one of those boys you find on London streets, willing to do any job—like pick up a parcel from a certain place —for a few pennies. Quick as flashes, they are. No chance of catching them, and odds are, even if one did, the boys themselves could tell you very little. After that, I gave up and just paid." Glumly, he added, "It was easier that way."

Stokes looked meaningfully at Penelope, and she cleared her throat and asked, "There's a second letter beside your name. F. We were wondering whether that meant 'fraud.'"

"No—well, yes." Morland grimaced. "It means me playing my wife false. That's how he put it."

Gradually, Morland had regained his composure, and as the certainty of what they'd told him sank in, his ire was rising. His features setting in grim lines, he narrowed his eyes, then shook his head. "And it was Monty —bloody Monty Underhill—all along!" Then, his gaze fell on Penelope, and his color rose. "Your pardon, Mrs. Adair. But this news is…very hard to take in."

Penelope inclined her head. "We appreciate that. And you should know that Monty wasn't blackmailing only you." She held up the black book. "He had quite a talent for learning other people's secrets."

"Apropos of that," Stokes said, "we would ask that you keep the news that Underhill was a blackmailer to yourself."

Barnaby added, "With any luck, we can solve this murder in a way that ensures your 'secret' never becomes known."

Morland's relief was palpable. "I won't tell a soul."

"In that case"—Barnaby rose, bringing Morland to his feet—"thank you for your honesty. You've been very helpful, and it's unlikely we'll need to speak with you again."

Morland bowed to Penelope, nodded to Stokes, and allowed Barnaby to usher him from the room.

After closing the door behind his lordship, Barnaby returned to Penelope and Stokes. He halted by the empty chair and arched his brows at them. "He's still a bit dazed, and he's no actor."

Penelope nodded. "He's not the victim who turned on Monty."

"Agreed," Stokes said. "Not even Kemble could dissemble to that degree." He looked at Penelope. "So who's next?"

The answer was Miriam, Lady Kelly, Richard's other aunt and Agatha's younger sister.

Penelope didn't know Lady Kelly as well as she knew Agatha; she rose and watched with interest as Barnaby welcomed Lady Kelly and guided her to the interviewee's armchair.

Her ladyship was a smaller version of Agatha all around and rather sprightlier with it. She had the same blue eyes, but where Agatha's were shrewd, Miriam's were full of open curiosity and blatant interest. Iron-gray curls framed a sweet-featured round face, and her hands seemed rarely still, reminding Penelope of sparrows, forever flitting.

Combining what she knew of Agatha with what she could see in Miriam, Penelope suspected the younger sister was even more observant and wide-awake to everything happening around her, and Agatha was no slouch in that regard.

After Miriam settled, Penelope, Barnaby, and Stokes resumed their seats, and with Penelope once more in the central chair, she proceeded with their now-standard questions. As she'd hoped, while the gist of the answers was the same as those they'd received from Agatha, the details Miriam readily supplied were rather more fulsome.

"Oh, you see, we, our families—the Hurstbridges who hold the marquessate and our family—go back generations. We've always been close, at least in our memory. We're neighbors, you see, or were, so we grew up knowing each other well, and Agatha and I were contemporaries of Gordon, the late marquess. So we've known Pamela and Susan since birth. Theirs, I mean. Of course, all that was before our papa became Viscount Seddington and we moved to Lincolnshire."

"I see. And is that why you and Agatha chose this house party to attend?"

"Oh, my dear, we knew Pamela always holds such an event at this time of year, and with the Grange being in Surrey, it's so easy to reach, and given it was Richard we intended to drag down, we knew Pamela would be happy to include us and him on the guest list. And she already knew Mrs. Hemmings and her daughters—their family lives nearer here —so it was all very easy to arrange. Pamela understood our need perfectly and was happy to assist."

Miriam happily confirmed Agatha's timing of their descent from their room. "It was almost nine when we left our room, which is just by the stairs, and the clocks struck the hour as we started down, but of course, with her hip, Agatha has to take steps more slowly now, so it would have been a few minutes later when we saw Monty go out of the front door, and then Mr. Nevin-Smythe went across the hall and nodded politely our way. His choice of attire might be a trifle flashy, but at least his manners are sound."

She confirmed that she and Agatha had joined the other ladies and that Susan had left a little later. "I believe," Miriam said, "that must have been closer to nine-thirty. It wasn't as if Susan up and left the instant we settled to chat."

As for her opinion of Monty Underhill, while Miriam painted the picture that seemed to be the society-wide view of a genial, kind-hearted, always pleasant gentleman, at the end of her description, she tipped her head in a birdlike way and stated, "But that can't be all of him, can it?" Her bright gaze flitted from Barnaby to Penelope and on to Stokes. "In my experience, few totally innocent people have their skulls crushed in while strolling in their own orchard."

Penelope hid a smile and posed their final question. "Are you aware of any situation that might have prompted someone to kill Monty?"

Miriam met her gaze and blithely declared, "None at all, my dear Mrs. Adair, but I will confess I'm all agog to learn what the reason was. I'm sure it will prove to be quite eye-opening. With someone as universally well-regarded as Monty, it would need to be something quite startling, don't you think?"

Penelope refused to react and, instead, thanked her ladyship and, rising, helped her out of the deep armchair and accompanied her to the door.

After seeing Miriam out, Penelope exhaled, returned to the chairs, and laughed at the expressions on Barnaby's and Stokes's faces. Both looked distinctly drained.

Barnaby glanced at Stokes. "I have to admit this succession of interviews has been more demanding than I'd imagined."

Stokes grunted, sat up, and looked hopefully at Penelope. "I vote we break for lunch."

Still smiling, she turned toward the door. "I'll speak to the footman. I'm sure they can assemble something sufficiently sustaining to carry you two through to the next round."

Behind her, both men softly groaned.

CHAPTER 6

*R*ichard sat at the luncheon table beside Rosalind. He hadn't been surprised when Regina had claimed the place on his other side. Ever since speaking with the investigators, Regina had been quiet and subdued and had stuck close to Rosalind and Richard.

The company passed the platters of meats, breads, cheeses, and fruits and attempted to behave in a manner that echoed normality. Pamela, Cecilia, and Vincent had rejoined their guests, and Pamela had asked everyone to "carry on as well as we can while the investigators pursue dear Monty's killer."

Naturally, no one had quibbled, yet all three Underhills were somber and drawn and, at times, transparently distracted with thoughts of other things, but those around them tactfully averted their gazes and forged on with their conversations.

After the company had been consuming their selections for several minutes, Leith, seated opposite Richard, leaned forward and inquired, "How did you find your interview with our investigators?"

Richard briefly met Leith's eyes and read nothing more than simple curiosity behind the question, one that had attracted a good deal of attention up and down the board. Aware of that, Richard knew better than to try to avoid answering. He lightly shrugged. "It seemed quite straightforward. Just the usual things one might imagine they would want to know, such as when I arrived and what I did on Monday morning." That was true enough and not particularly concerning.

Leith nodded and sat back. "That was my take as well. They seemed to be checking our whereabouts over the critical period, perhaps"—he darted a glance up the table to where their hostess sat—"as a prelude to concluding they need to cast their net farther afield and search the area for itinerants or gypsies."

Richard doubted that but nodded equably. "Perhaps."

Leith regarded him for an instant, then ventured, "I must say that I found them—the investigators—a curious bunch. Two well-established members of the haut ton combining with a Scotland Yard inspector to investigate crimes. I can't imagine why the Adairs—as busy as they are— would give up their time to such an endeavor."

Can't you? Richard didn't react but merely nibbled on a piece of cheese and waited.

Leith shrugged. "I haven't heard of such an investigative team before."

I have. Richard could have warned Leith—and all those listening— not to underestimate the trio, but he left the words unsaid. He had a strong suspicion that all three investigators, and Penelope especially, preferred to be underrated.

When neither he nor Leith volunteered more, those listening, some- what reassured over what was in store for them, returned to their own low-voiced conversations.

Leith shifted his gaze to Rosalind. "Are you quite recovered from your ordeal, Miss Hemmings?"

Rosalind raised her gaze to his. "I am, thank you." She paused, then added, "Finding Mr. Underhill's body wasn't pleasant, but in a way, I'm glad I found him. He might otherwise have lain there for hours or even days, and that would have delayed the investigation considerably."

Graciously, Leith inclined his head. "Indeed. Have you had a chance to venture about the grounds as yet?"

"Only over the lawns and through the shrubbery. It's quite pleasant in the wood beyond." She glanced across Richard at Regina. "I believe there's a croquet green somewhere."

Her sister usually loved playing, and if anything could lift her spirits, a game of croquet would.

"There's a lovely green," Leith said. "It's in the opposite direction to the shrubbery. Quite a nice expanse and usually perfectly trimmed."

Regina's gaze rose from her plate—at last!—and she glanced hope- fully at Rosalind. "Perhaps…"

Alison Waterhouse, a pretty girl sitting beside Leith and quietly listening, leaned forward and replied, "Yes. Why not? Lady Pamela asked us to behave normally, so after lunch, we"—her sweeping gaze included several other younger members of the company sitting nearby—"should all go and play a round or two."

The suggestion was met with considerable eagerness by the younger crew and with some relief by their elders.

Consequently, as soon as the meal was deemed over, those intent on playing croquet swept out to the terrace, with Alison drawing Regina with her. Both Cecilia and Vincent Underhill joined the group, in a sense giving the event a measure of approval, and after rapidly gathering hats and parasols against the summer sun, the small crowd set off across the lawn.

Responding to the pointed look her mother sent her, Rosalind stepped out in the group's wake. She wasn't surprised to find Richard by her side but was mildly amazed when not only Leith but also Elliot joined them.

When the latter caught her faintly wondering gaze, he grinned. "I'm not used to sitting inside all day. I need to get some air."

"Hear, hear," Leith echoed as he walked on the other side of Regina, who had fallen back to walk beside Rosalind as she and the other more mature guests brought up the rear of the loosely ambling group.

"I hope you'll forgive my curiosity, Miss Hemmings." Leith leaned forward to speak to Rosalind across Regina. "But how did you come to find the body?"

Having expected that question from someone at some point, serenely, Rosalind replied, "I'd gone out to take a turn about the grounds and thought to venture into the orchard."

Leith's gaze fell to Regina. "Oh. I heard you were walking with your sister at the time. I apologize for bringing up the subject—I'd forgotten that."

"Ah..." Regina shot a wide-eyed pleading look at Rosalind and, beyond her, at Richard.

Rosalind smiled reassuringly at Regina and smoothly replied, "That was one aspect for which I'm grateful. Regina had been with me, but at that point, we'd parted ways, and she'd continued via a different route."

"Ah, I see." Leith's expression suggested that he, too, was grateful that his question hadn't caused Regina any undue distress. "Now," he said bracingly, looking ahead, "how is a company of this size going to manage a game of croquet?"

"It'll need to be a tournament, surely?" Richard did his part to redirect the conversation.

"But how will we select the teams?" Elliot, too, stepped in, and those walking ahead heard and turned, and the remainder of the distance to the green passed in a lighthearted discussion of increasingly nonsensical criteria for team selection that lifted the collective mood considerably and effectively swung all thoughts from the finding of a dead body in the orchard.

After the investigators finished their meal and Gearing cleared away the platters, they resettled in the armchairs. The men lounged while Penelope studied her list of guests.

Eventually, she ventured, "I believe we can place Richard and his aunts at the bottom of our suspects list."

Replete and comfortable, Stokes arched a brow at her. "We have a suspects list?"

The look Penelope sent him was severe. "Of course!"

Barnaby smiled. "She has a list for everything. Of course she has a list of suspects."

"If that's the case," Stokes returned, "then for my money, Lady Pamela doesn't rate highly, either."

"No, she doesn't," Penelope agreed.

"Based on what we know thus far," Barnaby said, "we can't discount Leith, but if we find corroborating evidence that he stayed within the house, he, too, will be out of contention."

Penelope waggled her pencil. "There was no hint of hostility toward Monty—not from Leith."

"So Leith's at least halfway down the list." Stokes glanced at his fellow investigators. "What about Morland?"

"While we might all agree that he had no idea Monty was his black-mailer," Penelope stated, "logically, he has to remain on the list for now. However, I suspect the gentlemen who were with him in the library at the time of the murder will provide him with a sound alibi."

"He's also not the type to crack open a man's skull in a fit of rage," Barnaby said.

Pencil raised, Penelope stilled, then said, "I hadn't actually thought of that—that the murderer was, almost certainly, seeing red at the time he attacked."

Stokes nodded. "Judging by the force behind the blow, he definitely was." After a moment, he added, "While I'm not sure what help that might be to us, it's worth bearing in mind." He met Barnaby's and Penelope's gazes. "Anyone needs a powerful motivation to cave in a man's skull, and blind fury fits the bill."

Penelope frowned. "By that reasoning, there has to be a more compelling motive than anything we've thus far heard. If any of the victims had learned Monty was their blackmailer, why not just threaten to expose him? In society's eyes, blackmailing is a far worse sin than minor peccadilloes such as kissing a footman or having an affair. He was at least as vulnerable as his victims to such pressure."

"You've just answered your own question," Barnaby said. "In the murderer's case, the secret of theirs that Monty discovered is too critical to the murderer for them to ever countenance another knowing it. The murderer simply can't live with the ongoing threat of their secret becoming widely known."

Stokes was nodding. "The murderer's secret is so damning they can't risk it ever coming out."

Comprehension lit Penelope's face. "The murderer's secret is something that will ruin them. Utterly ruin them, not just cause a minor scandal."

Barnaby tipped his head in acknowledgment. "And that's why Morland isn't a strong suspect. While from his point of view, keeping his secret buried—especially Monty's twisting of it—was worth paying the price Monty asked, that secret simply isn't sufficiently powerful. It's not the sort of secret that would push a man to murder."

"Remember what Percival said." Stokes duly repeated, "'There are more secrets within the ton than most will ever know, and many of those secrets are powerful ones.'"

"Indeed. And on the basis of the rage required," Barnaby said, "I think we need to leave Susan on the upper part of the list. Not at the top, perhaps, but she was outside, alone, and no matter how she tried to play it down, she deeply resented Monty refusing to support a match between Vincent and Samantha."

"I agree." Penelope jotted, then straightened and studied her list. "So, at the moment, we have only Susan on the 'likely, meaning actually might be' part of our list."

Barnaby exchanged a look with Stokes. "We knew this wouldn't be easy." He glanced at Penelope. "Who's next to be interviewed?"

"Lord Kilpatrick," she replied.

Barnaby rose and headed for the door.

Five minutes later, he greeted Kilpatrick and steered him to the central armchair facing the investigators' chairs.

Kilpatrick presented as an affable gentleman in his mid-thirties, eligible by all accounts, and apparently, he owned the property beyond the eastern boundary of the Grange estate.

As Barnaby reclaimed his chair, he reassured Kilpatrick, "We're posing the same questions to all the guests, purely to gain some sense of who was where and what was seen. In that vein, when did you arrive at the Grange?"

"I'm staying at home"—Kilpatrick nodded eastward—"at Kilpatrick Lodge next door. The easiest and fastest way here is across the fields, and generally, I walk over to join the company every morning, but on Sunday, I came across and arrived around four o'clock, in time for afternoon tea."

Penelope smiled at Kilpatrick. "Is there any particular reason you chose to attend?"

Kilpatrick almost squirmed. "Well, for a start, Lady Pamela invited me, and I wanted to remain on good terms with her." He colored faintly. "I suspect she needed me to make up her numbers, but"—lightly, he shrugged—"I'll have to look for a wife one day, and these events of Lady Pamela's aren't a bad place to start."

"Very true," Barnaby acknowledged. "So, shifting to Monday morning, did you join the company here for breakfast?"

"No. I breakfasted at home. I spoke briefly with my steward, then sometime after nine-thirty, I started across the fields."

Stokes looked up from his notebook. "You weren't in the house at the time of the murder?"

"Between nine and ten o'clock," Barnaby clarified.

Kilpatrick shook his head. "I must have been walking across the fields when it happened. When I arrived in the forecourt, the ladies were all clustered at the edge, looking toward the orchard. That's when I realized something...dramatic had occurred."

"While you were walking in, before you reached the forecourt, did you notice any other guests outside?" Stokes asked.

"No. No one." Kilpatrick faintly grimaced. "But I wasn't really looking, of course."

Penelope leaned forward, claiming his attention. "You must have known Monty Underhill reasonably well. How would you describe him?"

Kilpatrick hesitated. When he eventually spoke, his reluctance was plain. "I admit I wasn't his greatest supporter."

"Oh?" Penelope opened her eyes wide. "Why was that?"

Kilpatrick pulled a face. "We—the two estates—had an ongoing dispute involving water rights. Underhill insisted on taking the matter to court, and he—or rather the Grange estate—had the wherewithal to hire a QC, and I didn't, so that was that. They won the case." Kilpatrick's glum expression eloquently conveyed his feelings. "So now, if I want my orchards to survive the summer, I have to pay the Grange for water from the stream that runs between the properties." After several seconds of pondering that outcome, he shrugged fatalistically. "Nothing I can do about that now, but obviously, Underhill wasn't my favorite person."

Despite his apparent acceptance, anger rippled beneath his words and shimmered behind his eyes.

Barnaby let a moment slide by, then asked, "Are you aware of any dispute Underhill had with any other neighbors?"

Kilpatrick thought, then shook his head.

"Do you know of any reason anyone would want to kill Underhill?" Barnaby asked.

Kilpatrick's brows rose. "Clearly, someone felt they had sufficient reason, but it wasn't me." He paused, then went on, "Now Monty's gone, I can hope, in time, that Vincent will see sense and agree to reinstate the old arrangement of equal water rights that our estates used to have." Kilpatrick glanced at Barnaby. "Vincent and I have always got on. We share several pursuits, and we're both members of the local hunt."

Barnaby glanced at Stokes, then at Penelope, but both shook their heads. He looked at Kilpatrick. "Thank you." Barnaby rose, and Kilpatrick did, too, and Barnaby accompanied him to the door.

After shutting the door, Barnaby returned to the armchairs.

Penelope met his eyes. "Kilpatrick remains a definite suspect, given he was supposedly walking outside at the time of the murder, and despite what he said, his disagreement with Monty might have been much more heated."

"We've no idea how critical the water situation is to Kilpatrick's holdings," Stokes said. "However, while I agree he might have had means and opportunity as well as motive, is that motive sufficient to have moved him to murder—specifically murder in the grip of a sudden eruption of rage?"

"I think, at present, that's an open question," Barnaby said. "Let's leave Kilpatrick on our list for now and move on." He looked at Penelope. "Who's next?"

Penelope took point with Mrs. Hemmings, Rosalind and Regina's mother. A neat matron—neatly gowned and neat of figure—in her late forties, she was of average height and build, very much average in appearance with brown hair and eyes and with a practical air that stated she was very clear as to her role in life, namely, to guide her two daughters into sound marriages.

"That, of course, my dear Mrs. Adair, is why we are here." Mrs. Hemmings fixed Penelope with a direct look. "Mr. Percival's aunt, Lady Kelly, is a dear friend of mine, and she and Lady Campbell-Carstairs felt that Rosalind would make Richard a perfect wife, and as we all knew the Hurstbridges, Lady Pamela was entirely amenable to helping us make the necessary introduction in the supportive setting of her house party."

Penelope smiled understandingly and ran through their questions and got the same answers they'd received from Rosalind and Regina. The Hemmingses had arrived in their carriage on Sunday afternoon, and on Monday morning, they'd come downstairs with Lady Susan and her daughters and some of the other ladies at just after eight o'clock and taken breakfast with the group. Then, Mrs. Hemmings had gone to the morning room with the older ladies while Rosalind had gone upstairs to read, and Regina had joined the younger ladies making for the conservatory.

Mrs. Hemmings paled, and one hand rose to her lace fichu. "I was in the morning room when I heard Rosalind scream for help. I was so shocked that, for a moment, I didn't know what to do. All the other ladies were frozen as well. Then, we heard the men rush outside, and we followed."

"Before that occurred," Penelope said, "did you notice any of the company leave the house or see anyone outside?"

"No. But the younger ones had spoken of going for a ramble about the grounds at some unspecified time. I'm not sure if any of them had got that far when the…incident occurred."

"Did any of the ladies leave the morning room before you heard Rosalind scream?"

"Yes. Susan went out. I'm not sure to where or why, but she spoke to

Pamela before she did, and some of the others would have heard as well."
Mrs. Hemmings added, "Susan hadn't come back by the time we went
out, but I'm fairly sure she joined us in the forecourt, while we were
waiting to hear what had happened. She was definitely there when some
of the gentlemen brought us the news."

"Thank you." Penelope saw that Stokes had jotted that down. She
returned her attention to Mrs. Hemmings. "If you will, could you share
your view of Mr. Underhill?"

"Well!" Mrs. Hemmings appeared to expand with indignation, much
like a mother hen in defensive mode. Her eyes flashed as she declared,
"Obviously, my view of our late host has changed." She met Penelope's
eyes. "Regina told me all, of course. At my insistence, she made a full
confession regarding her nonsensical behavior and how that beast had
been blackmailing her! I was never so shocked in my life!" She went on,
"I can only wish that Regina had told me all earlier." She shook her head.
"Silly girl, but she was always the flighty one. Not nearly as grounded, as
mature, as Rosalind at the same age. I should have suspected that something was amiss, but..." She lightly shrugged. "With all the social orga-
nizing that having two daughters to establish entails..." She blew out a
sigh. "I just hope we've all learned our lessons."

Mrs. Hemmings refocused on Penelope. "But regarding Monty
Underhill"—every soft feature in her face sharpened—"I am utterly
shocked and appalled. And truth to tell, saddened, too. I'd always rather
liked him, but now, I feel that he preyed on my daughter and, through her,
our family. I have to admit I feel as if my confidence has been utterly
betrayed. I can't imagine how Pamela must feel, knowing he was blackmailing friends." She saw Stokes casting worried looks at Penelope and
rushed to assure him, "I gave the girls, and Richard, too, my word I
would breathe not a whisper of any of this to anyone until you give us
leave."

Stokes looked as relieved as Penelope felt. She arched a brow at him,
but he gestured at her to continue.

She turned back to Mrs. Hemmings. "Aside from the blackmailing, do
you know of any other reason why anyone might have wanted to kill
Monty?"

Mrs. Hemmings shook her head and straightforwardly stated, "Obviously, he blackmailed the wrong person." She shook her head again, this
time in disbelief. "Can you imagine? Blackmailing other members of the
ton. Well, it reeks of betrayal, doesn't it? To prey on your own kind—a

sort of cannibalism." She paused, then, in a faintly amazed tone, asked, "How on earth did he manage it?"

Penelope blinked, then slowly nodded. "Quite."

Deciding that they'd heard enough from the rather garrulous matron, Penelope smiled at Mrs. Hemmings. "Thank you. That's all our questions for the moment."

She rose, waited for Mrs. Hemmings to get to her feet and exchange nods with Barnaby and Stokes, then showed Mrs. Hemmings out.

Penelope returned swiftly to the armchairs and pinned Barnaby and Stokes with her gaze. "I know she meant the comment rhetorically, but it's a valid question. How on earth did Monty learn so many secrets? About people who are usually rather good at keeping those sorts of secrets? I can imagine that he might have stumbled across one or two such secrets in his time, but there were seventeen pages in his black book —eighteen if we include the one torn out."

Barnaby was nodding. "You're right. He must have had some sort of source."

Stokes finished jotting and looked at what he'd written. "Where and how did Underhill learn his secrets? At present, that's an unknown." He looked at Barnaby and Penelope. "Let's leave it for later cogitation and forge on. Who's next?"

Five minutes later, Barnaby ushered Lord Griffith to the central armchair.

Griffith was in his mid-thirties and, at least by birth and wealth, qualified as an eligible bachelor, yet within half a minute of him seating himself—with a flourish—in the interviewee's chair, it was apparent to all that he was a distinctly silly man.

Viewing Griffith critically as, plainly agog at the drama of being involved in a murder investigation, he gushed at Penelope, declaring himself only too willing to assist, Barnaby decided that the man wasn't acting even though his florid and colorful attire testified to a theatrical bent.

With his legs crossed and his hands clasped on his knees, Griffith leaned forward and earnestly confided, "It's all so very exciting! Please, tell me how I can help."

"The first piece of information we need," Barnaby said, "is confirmation of when you arrived."

"Oh! That's easy. I drove down on Sunday afternoon." Without further prompting, Griffith explained, "M'mother's a close friend of Lady

Pamela, and the two of them insisted—positively *insisted*—that I attend this gathering. And I'm so glad they did! A murder! Fancy!" His eyes gleamed, then with unexpectedly endearing self-deprecation, he glanced at Penelope and added, "I suspect my inclusion was more a matter of making up the numbers, but really, who knows what they might have planned?"

With a poorly suppressed grin, Penelope inclined her head. "We also need to learn what you did on Monday morning. When did you come downstairs?"

"Oh, I'm always rather early. I left my room at just after seven. I heard the clocks strike the hour before I made for the door, so I suppose it must have been about seven-fifteen when I reached the dining room." He paused, clearly recalling, then went on, "Percival, Carrington, Morehouse, Cordingley, and Elliot were all before me, and Leith left just after I arrived."

Barnaby owned to mild surprise at the detail and clarity of the answer. "And after you rose from the table?"

"Ah. I came in here and had a quick glance at the news sheets there—"

"What time did you leave the dining room?" Stokes rumbled.

Griffith paused, then said, "It was a few minutes after eight. I recall the clocks striking again before I decided it was time to move."

"So you came to the library…" Barnaby prompted.

"But I didn't remain here. Elliot, Morehouse, and Carrington had taken up residence and were deep in the news sheets, and I knew the older men who were still in the dining room would soon join them, and no one likes a chatterer, so I ambled around to the billiards room and started potting a few balls. After a time, Nevin-Smythe came in, and he and I played a game or two. We were chewing the fat when we heard Miss Hemmings scream. The sound was distant and faint, and at first, we weren't sure what it signified, but then, we heard the ruckus and came out to see what was up."

Barnaby asked, "At any time that morning before the scream, did you notice anyone else of the company outside?"

Griffith paused, then volunteered, "When I was in the billiards room, a little while after Nevin-Smythe joined me, I saw Lady Wincombe go walking rather determinedly across the rear lawn. Toward the east. From her expression, she seemed set on something, which I thought rather odd, but"—he grimaced—"she wasn't heading anywhere near the orchard, so I suspect that's of little use to you."

"On the contrary," Penelope assured him, "it helps us place Lady Wincombe during the critical period. With a company such as this, eliminating people is half the battle."

Griffith all but preened.

"Now," Barnaby said, "and we're asking everyone this question, what was your view of Mr. Underhill?"

Predictably, Griffith gushed, but nothing he said deviated from the general consensus of a genial, pleasant, entirely unthreatening gentleman.

As for knowing of any reason why someone might have wanted to kill Underhill, Griffith declared, "No! I own to being utterly mystified and am simply agog to find out why. Well, the whole company is, aren't they? Everyone knows there must have been some reason, and as no one has any inkling of what that might be, imaginations tend to run rampant, don't they?"

Barnaby didn't answer. He glanced at Penelope, who was still struggling to hide her amusement at Griffith's histrionics, then looked briefly at Stokes, who was wearing his most stoic expression. Returning his attention to Griffith, Barnaby rose. "Thank you." As Griffith rather uncertainly got to his feet, Barnaby waved him to the door.

As he reluctantly headed that way, Griffith looked over his shoulder and added, "If there's anything else I can do to assist…"

"We'll be sure to let you know," Barnaby stated.

Once he'd shown Griffith out and shut the door, he returned to the cluster of armchairs.

"He might have been a touch excitable," Stokes said, "but he was quite definite in what he remembered."

"His recollection of details was strangely impressive." Penelope rose. "I'll call in our next interviewee."

While they waited for Lady Carville to join them, Penelope shared what she knew of her ladyship. "She's not unintelligent and has been comfortably married to Lord Carville for decades. He's a Member of Parliament, and she's known as a minor political hostess and has steered their son and two daughters into very suitable marriages. She's widely regarded as an established matron of the ton, and there's long been a suspicion that she's Lord Morland's lover and has been for years."

"So," Stokes said, "she's the one Underhill was blackmailing Morland about?"

"Almost certainly." Penelope's lips thinned. "And Monty was also blackmailing her, presumably over the same liaison, but as with Morland, there must have been something else there for a more-or-less-known affair to be rendered blackmail-worthy. Something worth paying to keep hidden."

A tap on the door heralded Lady Carville, and Penelope rose and went to welcome her ladyship and usher her to the armchair at the focal point of the investigators' attention. Lady Carville was in her mid-forties, a well-preserved, well-turned-out matron with curly blond hair and an air of no nonsense about her.

Penelope resumed her seat and quickly led her ladyship through their opening questions.

Lady Carville confirmed that she'd arrived in her carriage at the Grange on Sunday afternoon. "As to why I'm here"—she shrugged— "I've known Pamela and Monty for an age, and she invited me, and it's the sort of thing people like us do in summer, isn't it?"

Penelope inclined her head. "And on Monday morning, when did you come downstairs?"

"I came down at just after eight o'clock with several other ladies. Many of the gentlemen had already breakfasted and left or were leaving the dining room. I remained there with the other ladies, chatting over the teacups, then when Pamela led most of the more-mature crew to the morning room, I diverted to the conservatory." Lady Carville met Penelope's eyes. "By then, I'd had a surfeit of chatter, and I have an interest in orchids, and Pamela has a few I have my eye on to add to my collection when next they're divided. I spent some time inspecting them and was still admiring them when I heard what sounded like a distant scream, followed by people rushing outside, and I went out and joined the other ladies who, by then, were on the front lawn."

"While you were in the conservatory," Penelope asked, "did you see any of the company outside?"

"The only person I saw was Susan. She came out onto the terrace and went down the steps and across the lawn toward the rose garden. That was no great surprise—she's fond of that rose garden, and like me, she can abide only so much chatter."

"How did you find Monty Underhill?" Penelope asked. "You said you'd known him as well as Pamela for years. How would you describe him?"

Lady Carville shrugged. "He was a decent sort, usually very genial and oozing bonhomie. A steady, reliable gentleman, predictably conservative in his ways. Widely well-regarded and liked. I've never heard a word against him."

Penelope glanced at Barnaby and Stokes. There'd been not the slightest hint in her ladyship's tone and manner to suggest she knew that Monty had been her blackmailer. Penelope returned her gaze to Lady Carville, who was waiting with outward patience. "Do you know of any reason why anyone would want to kill Monty?"

Lady Carville's face clouded. "No. None. And I must admit that fact troubles me on Pamela's and the children's accounts." She sighed. "I'm sure I'm preaching to the choir in saying that where there's smoke, there's usually some sort of fire. Ergo, when a man is murdered, and so viciously, there has to be a reason. A real and powerful reason. Just because we don't know what it is doesn't mean it isn't there."

"So you don't subscribe to the passing-vagrant theory?" Barnaby asked.

Her ladyship made a derisive sound. "Not that I can't see the attraction, but that's merely the sort of story one clings to in circumstances such as these, isn't it?"

Penelope had bent a questioning look on Stokes. When he nodded, she focused on Lady Carville and said, "We are aware you've been blackmailed for the past several years."

All color fled from Lady Carville's countenance.

Holding her gaze, Penelope continued, "Based on evidence we've found in Monty's study, we can only conclude that he was your blackmailer."

Her ladyship's eyes slowly widened. "What?" The word was whispered. Then, a species of horror washed over her ladyship's features. "No." Her gaze sharpened on Penelope's face, and her lips parted as if on a more definite rebuttal, then, she stopped and thought again.

Eventually, she met Penelope's eyes. "Really?"

From her expression, it was transparently obvious that Lady Carville was genuinely stunned.

"We found a small notebook in the desk in the study." Penelope drew the book from her pocket and held it up. "The entries are in Monty's hand, and he lists those who we believe have been his victims and gives details of payments and the dates they were made."

"Good Lord!" Lady Carville slumped back in the chair. She looked utterly floored, yet at the same time, she was clearly starting to reassess.

Penelope opened the book to the relevant page and quickly confirmed with her ladyship the date of the first demand just on two years ago and the continuing payments, in her case in cash, that spanned the period to the present day. When Penelope inquired as to how the payments were made, her ladyship told much the same tale as Morland and Regina.

Lady Carville grimaced. "I did try to learn who it was, but I was never able to spot them. Even when I hired a boy to watch over one packet, he reported that it was another boy—one of the street boys—who'd picked up the money." She paused, clearly thinking back, then shook her head. "I'm still having difficulty believing it was Monty, but I have to accept you know what you're saying." She tipped her head at the book in Penelope's hands. "And then there's that, which, by any stretch of any imagination, is still nigh-impossible to explain."

After a glance at Barnaby and Stokes, Penelope gently said, "He was blackmailing Morland as well."

"What?" Lady Carville looked incredulous, but then her features grew grim. "I suppose if he knew enough to blackmail me, then..." She shook her head in the manner of one greatly disappointed in another. "And Morland was his friend for even longer."

"We can tell from Monty's annotations that he was blackmailing you and Morland, separately, over your affair." Penelope met her ladyship's gaze. "Given the longstanding relationship and the...well, unstated acceptance among the ton, I admit I'm surprised you didn't brush the notion of blackmail aside."

"Oh, I would have—if it had been simply over the affair." Lady Carville paused, studying Penelope, then her gaze flicked to Barnaby and Stokes. After a second, she seemed to come to some decision. She returned her gaze to Penelope and said, "I would have weathered the affair coming out, but the compounding issue was that once—just once—I'd very stupidly borrowed a small amount from Morland. A small loan to cover some debts until the next quarter day. Carville was deep in some political business, and frankly, at that point, I didn't want him knowing I'd been playing cards. He wouldn't have approved, and I've never done it again. I'm useless with cards, anyway. So I learned my lesson over that, but to get out of it, I needed sixty pounds, and Morland readily gave me the cash." She paused, then said, "I paid him back next quarter day, and I've never got into debt again, but somehow, the blackmailer found out about that loan."

Penelope glanced at Stokes and Barnaby. Perhaps the *F* beside

Morland's name had meant "financing" and not "fraud" or "false" as Morland had thought.

Lady Carville's features hardened as she went on, "Of course, on the face of it, me borrowing such a sum from Morland wouldn't have raised much of a dust except for the twist the blackmailer threatened to put on the bare facts." She met Penelope's eyes, and her gaze was now fierce. "The blackmailer—*Monty*—threatened to say that I'd received money from Morland as payment for influencing my husband. Morland's in the Lords and from the other party, so…politically, the scandal would have ruined Sidney's career as well as mine and Morland's. All our reputations would have been shredded."

All four in the room took a moment to allow the full impact of Monty's threat to sink in.

Eventually, her ladyship refocused on Penelope. "So of course, I paid. And continued to pay." She paused, then added, "I did notice that, given the seriousness of the threat, the demands weren't as extortionate as I'd feared. They were all well within my ability to pay, and the demands often arrived just before quarter day, so I always had the funds."

Penelope checked the entries in the black book and nodded. She hadn't noticed that point before—another indication of how well Monty had known and understood his victims.

"One question, if I may," Barnaby said. "If we accept that your blackmailer was Monty, do you have any notion of how he came to learn of you borrowing money from Morland?"

Lady Carville thought, then her features hardened. "Wyndham Castle. It was there that I asked Morland, and he gave me the money then and there." Puzzled, she looked at Barnaby. "But that was in my room. I'm certain we didn't speak of it anywhere else, so how could Monty—how could anyone—have overheard?" Her puzzlement deepened. "Indeed, how could anyone have known I would ask him for cash at that particular moment in time?"

The investigators shared equally puzzled glances. At that point, they had no answer to that question.

Lady Carville's face darkened. "What I want to know is what Monty thought he was about. This will all come out, and the people who will have to face the music are Pamela, Vincent, and Cecilia. How dare he put his family through this?" She appealed to the investigators. "What on earth for?"

Somewhat grim herself, Penelope nodded. "That, indeed, is one point we will be seeking to understand. Meanwhile"—a glance confirmed that Stokes and Barnaby had no further questions, and Penelope returned her gaze to Lady Carville—"thank you for your frankness."

"And," Stokes said, "please keep all you've learned in this room to yourself."

Rising to join Penelope, Lady Carville said, "Of course. Not least to protect Pamela from the distress this will inevitably cause. No sense in precipitating that any earlier than need be."

"Exactly." Penelope ushered Lady Carville to the library door, then returned to Stokes and Barnaby and gave her verdict. "She's a sensible and well-grounded lady, and while I believe she would have the gumption and ability to murder Monty, I truly believe she had no idea he was her blackmailer."

Stokes nodded. "I agree. She's definitely low on our suspects list."

Barnaby rose and stretched, then bent an inquiring look on Penelope. "Who's next?"

The answer proved to be Lord Wincombe.

Barnaby had his lordship summoned and escorted him to the relevant chair.

Somewhere in his fifties, Lord Wincombe was a gentleman of average height and decent girth. A solid man tending portly, he was conservatively dressed, and his thinning brown-gray hair was combed over his balding pate. He settled somewhat fussily in the chair and was quick to tell them, "I'm here with m'wife, Georgina, and our niece, Harriet Cranton. Damned if I know why, but I've known Monty Underhill for decades and Pamela and Susan as well, so when the invitation arrived and Georgina saw it, she was all for pouncing on the opportunity to show off Harriet to the eligible young bucks, what?"

Barnaby knew his lordship as a hail-fellow-well-met sort who was devoted to foxhunting. On that subject, he was an acknowledged bore, but a harmless one. He was readily tolerated within ton circles but remained largely oblivious of much of what went on around him—not so much intentionally self-centered as blinkered.

In short order, Barnaby established that the Wincombes and Harriet arrived in their carriage in the late afternoon on Sunday.

When asked, Wincombe stated, "On Monday morning, I came down behind the gaggle of ladies at just after eight o'clock. Morland was heading down as well, and I joined him at the table. Griffith was just leaving, and Percival followed soon after. Can't remember which others were there. Morland and I had a comfortable meal, then headed here, to the library. The news sheets had been delivered, and Elliot, Morehouse, and Carrington were already settled and poring over them. Morland and I joined them—there were plenty of copies to go around."

"Did you leave the library between then and the time you heard Miss Hemmings cry for help?" Stokes asked.

"No. And the others—Elliot, Morehouse, Carrington, and Morland—didn't, either."

"Did you notice anyone leaving the house or walking outside?" Barnaby asked.

Wincombe started to shake his head but stopped. "Only person I think left the house was Monty himself. He came in—must have been around nine or so—and chatted a bit, as a host does, making sure we were all comfortable. Then, he headed off—I think he said something about strolling out to check on some estate matter—so I assume he left the house, although I didn't actually see him do so."

"Thank you," Stokes said. "That's very clear."

When Barnaby asked Wincombe for his view of Monty, they received a paean that, while at base the same as society's widely held view of Underhill, was delivered in significantly more glowing terms. "An excellent chap all around, don't you know? Sound fellow and a sad loss."

With no real hope, Barnaby asked, "Do you have any idea why anyone might have wanted to kill him?"

"No! Not a clue." Wincombe appeared entirely flummoxed, then he focused on Barnaby. "I say, it couldn't have been an accident, could it? A case of mistaken identity—that sort of thing? I mean, it's hard to wrap one's head around the notion of some beggar who knew it was Monty walking up and caving his skull in." Frowning, he shook his head. "That's so strange. So very strange."

Barnaby rose, thanked Wincombe, and showed him out.

Penelope watched until Barnaby turned back and looked at her inquiringly. "Lady Wincombe next."

While they waited, Penelope expounded, "Her ladyship is in her late forties and is a longtime friend of Susan and also Pamela."

"And"—Stokes consulted his notes—"she's the other one who was scheduled to make a payment on Monday."

Penelope nodded and rose as the door opened, and Lady Wincombe appeared.

Smiling, Penelope welcomed her ladyship and directed her to the interviewee's chair.

Another established matron, her ladyship wore her light-brown hair drawn back in a neat bun, and her blue eyes and pleasant if unremarkable features signaled both curiosity and uncertainty in equal measure. As Lady Wincombe settled in the armchair, she confided to Penelope, "I'm not sure what to expect, my dear Mrs. Adair, so do, please, bear with me."

Penelope considered her ladyship's attitude to be rather revealing. Normally, Lady Wincombe was surer of herself, a trifle arrogant and also ready to ruffle her feathers and take offense at the least little thing. Indeed, normally, she was a touch snooty, just like her good friend Susan.

A reassuring smile on her face, Penelope commenced with their now-standard opening questions.

"Oh, we—Lionel, myself, and Harriet, our niece—arrived in our carriage on Sunday afternoon. And our principal reason for being here is to spend time with our friends, meaning the Goodriches and the Underhills."

"On Monday morning, when did you come downstairs?" Penelope asked.

"Harriet and I came down with Susan and some others. I know what time Susan is liable to be heading for breakfast, and we time leaving our rooms accordingly." Helpfully, she added, "Susan usually leaves her room at just after eight."

"And after breakfast? Did you join the group in the morning room?" Penelope ingenuously inquired.

Lady Wincombe hesitated, then opted for the truth. "No. Truth to tell, I felt a trifle under the weather, so I went upstairs to my room, then I decided a quick stroll about the grounds would be more the thing to clear my head, so I went down again and out onto the terrace and so to the rear lawn."

Without looking up from his notebook, Stokes asked, "In which direction did you walk?"

Lady Wincombe eyed him, then replied, "I walked out to the croquet green. I wasn't looking for conversation and didn't think there would be anyone out that way, and there wasn't. I had the place to myself."

"So," Penelope prompted, "between nine and ten o'clock, you were...?"

"First in my room and then on the croquet green, or at least, going to it and returning. I felt much improved after walking around the green, and when I returned to the house, Harriet was waiting on the terrace. She and I then heard the scream and the ensuing brouhaha, and together, we walked into the house and spotted the other ladies making for the front door and joined them."

"I see." Penelope continued, "During your walk, did you notice anyone else—any other member of the company—also outside?"

"Well, from the croquet green, I spied Kilpatrick marching over the fields from next door. He was still some distance away when I turned back to the house. And of course, I met Harriet on the terrace. Apparently, she'd seen me go off, and the dear girl had waited on the terrace to make sure I returned safely."

Penelope made a mental note to check why Harriet had been so concerned for her aunt. "If you were asked to describe Monty Underhill, what would you say?"

Lady Wincombe's expression cleared. "He was always such a pleasant, jovial sort. A *nice* gentleman, one might say. He seemed an undemanding sort of person, very easygoing and likeable."

Bluntly, Penelope asked, "Do you know of any reason why anyone would want to kill him?"

The answer came immediately. "No. None at all." Her ladyship's gaze swept all three investigators. "I own to being quite bamboozled over why anyone would want to kill Monty, of all men, and indeed, in sympathy with Susan and Pamela, I'm really rather upset."

Penelope exchanged a quick glance with Barnaby and Stokes, then returned her gaze to Lady Wincombe and, while watching her closely, stated, "In searching Monty's study, we discovered a small book, hidden away, in which Monty had kept a record, one dating back several years, of what we've confirmed with others are payments made to him by people he was blackmailing." Lady Wincombe's eyes slowly widened as the meaning of those words sank in. Penelope continued, "All of his victims are members of the ton and include a large number of those who called him 'friend.' Including you."

Lady Wincombe's hands had drifted to the chair's padded arms, and now, she gripped them tightly, as if she was trying to stop herself from leaping up. She stared in patent horror and disbelief at Penelope, then she moistened her lips and, faintly, said, "What?"

Then, every last vestige of color fled from her face, her eyes rolled up, and she slumped in the chair.

"Good Lord!" Stokes struggled to his feet.

Penelope had already leapt to hers, simultaneously ferreting in her reticule. She hauled out a small vial, tossed the reticule on her chair, and after uncapping the vial, waved the open end beneath Lady Wincombe's nose.

Lady Wincombe frowned and snuffled, then weakly batted at Penelope's hand.

Penelope retreated a step and, smelling salts still at the ready, watched her ladyship gradually revive.

Finally, Lady Wincombe's blue eyes fluttered open, and she looked at Penelope and weakly smiled. "Oh, thank you, Mrs. Adair. Silly me!" She waved ineffectually as she struggled to sit upright again. "I thought you said *Monty* was…" Her words faded, then abruptly, she refocused on Penelope's face, and what little color she'd regained drained away. Eyes wide, her ladyship gasped, "Oh God! You did say that—that he was the blackmailer!"

Solemnly, Penelope nodded. "He was the person who was blackmailing you. Your name is in his book, along with the sums you paid him, as well as a notation that you were to pay him another thirty pounds on Monday."

But Lady Wincombe was shaking her head. "Oh no, dear. It just can't be. Surely not. Not *Monty!*"

Despite Penelope reiterating the evidence, Lady Wincombe continued to go around and around, apparently unable to accept that her friend's husband—her *nice* gentleman—had been the one steadily milking cash from her.

In the end, Penelope showed her the page in Monty's black book that related to her and her payments. Only then, as her gaze scanned the list of payments, did the ineradicable truth sink in and, finally, take hold.

"Dear God," her ladyship whispered and slumped in the armchair again.

Penelope studied her for a moment longer, then, deciding the threat of fainting was past, subsided into her chair. Catching Stokes's impatient look, she refocused on Lady Wincombe and stated, "You were due to make a payment on Monday."

Her ladyship was recovering her composure, and as sometimes happened, having had her acumen and judgment regarding Monty's character proved to be wildly wrong, she was growing angry. "Yes." Her tone was now rather clipped. "As usual, I received a note delivered to the kitchen door of our London house last Thursday. The note stated that I was to place thirty pounds in an envelope and leave it in the cupboard beside the croquet green—the one holding the mallets and balls and hoops. I was to leave the payment by half past nine on Monday morning."

Her features set, she looked at Penelope, then at Barnaby and Stokes. "It was always like that—a place that virtually anyone could get to—and from experience, I knew there was no point lying in wait and trying to see who picked it up. That never worked."

Gently, Penelope said, "I fear we must ask—the notation beside your name indicates that an indiscretion was the basis for the blackmail. But I confess, I can't quite see why, with your standing within the ton being so well-established, that the mere rumor of an affair would be so damaging that you felt compelled to pay to keep the matter concealed."

Lady Wincombe grimaced, then said, "It's because of Harriet." She sighed. "I had a silly little fling several years ago, and just after that, Harriet's parents—my dear sister and her husband—were killed in a dreadful carriage accident. I'd always promised my sister that if anything happened to them, I would look after Harriet and ensure she made a good match. So Harriet came to live with us, and I took it as my solemnly sworn duty to steer dear Harriet—and she really is a dear, dear girl—through the shoals of society and ensure she makes an excellent match."

Still puzzled, Penelope frowned. "And the threat of some illicit affair being made public would impact your ability to do that?"

Lady Wincombe sighed even more deeply. "The gentleman involved is much younger than I am, and at the time, he was recently wed himself, and on top of that, he's viewed as …well, rather risqué. At least according to his reputation. Suffice it to say that the news wouldn't have sat well with those into whose circles I needed to promote Harriet." She paused, then added, "And the sums demanded were never so great I would balk at paying them. All in all, to me, paying was the easier option by far."

Frowning, she went on, "My bigger concern was how the blackmailer learned of the incident. And it was just one incident. I could never under-stand it, and as you might imagine, that preyed on my mind."

"Allow me to guess," Penelope said. "Your fling occurred at Wyndham Castle."

Lady Wincombe stared at her. "Yes. How did you…? Oh!" Her face signaled she'd seen the connection. "Monty. He was there, too." A second later, her frown returned. "But I still don't see how he learned of it. It's not as if we weren't careful. Indeed, both of us were very discreet."

"It seems quite a few of his secrets were learned there," Barnaby said.

"Exactly how he managed it, we don't yet know, but there has to be some explanation."

Stokes stirred and, when Lady Wincombe glanced his way, asked, "You said you left your payment in the cupboard by the croquet green?"

"Yes." Lady Wincombe went on, "There's a box inside that holds the balls. I was to leave the envelope under the box."

Penelope caught Stokes's gaze. "Even if people have played a game since then, there's no reason they would have lifted the box." She glanced at Lady Wincombe. "Your payment should still be there."

Her ladyship all but bounced to her feet. "Let's go and see."

Penelope agreed, and Barnaby and Stokes were very ready to join them.

With Stokes bringing up the rear, as Barnaby walked with Penelope and Lady Wincombe to the door, he observed, "Your payment being where you say it is will also prove where you were when Monty Underhill was killed."

The comment only added to Lady Wincombe's eagerness, and she led the way out of the house, onto the terrace, down onto the lawn, and across to the croquet green, tucked behind a thick row of tall shrubs and effectively screened from the house.

Lady Wincombe led them directly to a green-painted wooden cupboard perched on short legs at one end of the green. She opened the door, looked inside, then stood back and pointed at the cupboard's base. "That's the box. The envelope should be beneath it."

The investigators crowded around, and after they'd taken note of the simple wooden box in which the wooden balls were piled, Barnaby reached inside and lifted the box a few inches, and Penelope slipped her fingers underneath and drew out a simple envelope.

"There!" Lady Wincombe beamed.

"It's still full." Penelope handed the packet to Lady Wincombe. "Just to be sure, if you would check that the money's all there?"

Her ladyship opened the envelope and peered inside, then flicked through the contents with her fingertips. "Yes. It's all here." She looked at Stokes and Barnaby. "Thirty pounds."

"Good." Stokes looked around, and Penelope and Barnaby did as well. Stokes said, "You mentioned seeing Kilpatrick. Where was he?"

Lady Wincombe walked along beside the green on the route she would have taken on her way back to the house. She stopped halfway along the green and pointed. "There. That section of the field visible through the gap in the trees. That's where he was, walking toward the Grange."

Along with Barnaby and Stokes, Penelope took note of the position. It was still a good distance from the Grange; it would have taken even Kilpatrick, with his long strides, several minutes to reach the front of the house. And judging by the timing of everything else, Monty had to have been dead by the time Lady Wincombe left her money in the designated spot.

"Thank you," Stokes said. "We have no further questions for you."

Penelope nodded at the envelope in Lady Wincombe's hand. "It's over now. You can forget your indiscretion. It will no longer be any threat to you in helping your niece make the match you and her mother would want for her."

Lady Wincombe met Penelope's gaze and smiled. "Thank you." She nodded to Stokes and Barnaby. "And thank you, as well." As they all turned toward the house, her ladyship sighed. "You have no idea how good it feels to finally be free of that weight."

CHAPTER 7

*I*n the warmth of the long summer afternoon, Richard sat with Rosalind, Mrs. Hemmings, Regina, Harriet Cranton, Leith, and Kilpatrick around one of the white-painted wrought-iron tables arranged on the rear terrace and partook of scones and raspberry jam and tiny cucumber sandwiches, washed down with cups of tea.

Sipping from his porcelain cup, Richard surveyed those at his table, then looked farther, scanning the rest of the company, all of whom, it seemed, had dutifully gathered for tea. No one was missing.

Safety in numbers, perhaps?

It was now more than twenty-four hours since their host had met his end, and given the company were prohibited from leaving until the investigation concluded, the general consensus appeared to be that maintaining some semblance of normalcy was the right thing to do.

While attempting to behave in a manner befitting such a summer house party created a superficial façade of calm in that everyone understood what options they had at any given hour, an unsettling undercurrent of uncertainty over what the next hour or day might bring underscored how fragile that assumed façade actually was.

Seated beside him and also surveying while she sipped, Rosalind murmured, low enough that only he would hear, "It's…interesting to see how our fellow guests are reacting to the situation."

Richard's gaze rested on his aunts, seated at a table farther down the terrace and chatting avidly with several matrons and a number of the older gentlemen. "Some seem more curious—even consumed by curiosity —while others are more watchful."

"They know they aren't the murderer and are wondering who is," Rosalind returned.

"Certainly those who've lived rather longer," Richard observed, "are avidly curious over what Monty did that led to his death."

"They're experienced enough to realize that there must have been something—some fire to give rise to the smoke—and they scent a sensation."

Wryly cynical, Richard added, "Or at least, are fervently hoping for one."

Rosalind threw him an amused glance, then returned her attention to the company. "Although everyone is trying to behave normally, I notice that no one has gone far from the house—for example, for a ramble about the grounds."

"No matter the comforting theory of a passing stranger being the killer, everyone suspects that the murderer is among us, and deep down, no one feels truly safe."

Sipping again, Rosalind nodded.

"I say." Kilpatrick leaned across the table. "Is it true you're acquainted with our investigators, the Adairs?"

Richard nodded. "I've known them for some time. Both are very well-connected."

"So," Leith put in, "do you have any notion of what point the investigation has reached?"

Richard smiled faintly. "Would that I did." After a second, he added, "However, with a group of this size and a murder of this nature, I daresay it will take several days for them to gain some understanding of what occurred about the time of the murder and where each of us was at the time."

Regina's cup rattled as she set it on her saucer. When everyone glanced her way, she blushed.

Leith, sitting beside her, glanced at her, then reached for a small platter. "Would you like one of these sandwiches? They're really quite delicious."

Regina smiled weakly, thanked Leith, and took one of the tiny sandwiches.

Kilpatrick engaged Richard in swapping tales of crop yields and improvements made to pastures, while Rosalind and Mrs. Hemmings spoke with Harriet about various walks in the extensive Grange grounds.

Leith, meanwhile, questioned Regina about her experiences thus far of the London theaters, using that point to segue into a description of some of the performances he'd witnessed. An experienced gentleman, he made his comments witty and entertaining and was ultimately rewarded with a spontaneous laugh, one that seemed to surprise Regina as much as her mother and sister.

Noting the somewhat relieved glance Rosalind and Mrs. Hemmings shared before returning to their exchange with Harriet, Richard deduced that, unsurprisingly perhaps, Regina's recently subdued demeanor wasn't her natural state. While Leith's conversation was entirely aboveboard and Regina's blush had long since faded, there was color in her cheeks and a tiny spark in her eyes that suggested that, with Leith's help, she was slowly emerging from the funk into which discovering the body had cast her.

All to the good, Richard thought as he returned his attention to Kilpatrick and his fields.

Later, as the company rose, leaving the empty cups and platters on the tables, and contemplated their next hours, Richard watched Mrs. Hemmings bustle about the table to where Leith was assisting Regina to her feet. Mrs. Hemmings thanked Leith for his kindness and suggested a turn about the rear lawn. Leith was happy to oblige, and the trio made for the steps, with Harriet and Kilpatrick falling in behind them.

Rosalind caught Richard's eye. "I suppose I should go, too."

He smiled and offered his arm. "We don't need to stick too close."

Smiling back, she looped her arm in his, and together, they walked to the steps and descended to the lawn.

As they strolled more slowly in the others' wake, Richard saw that Mrs. Hemmings was doing her damnedest to encourage Leith. *And really, who could blame her?*

To return from this house party with a firm understanding between Rosalind and Richard would be viewed as a very good outcome. To go home with the Earl of Leith with his eye fixed on Regina would, in ton terms, be nothing short of a notable coup.

∽

Penelope had presided over the tea tray Gearing had delivered to the library. Now, with nothing left of the scones and sandwiches but crumbs, she drained her teacup, set it aside, and gave her attention to their suspects list.

"It seems to me," she stated, "that Lady Wincombe and Lord Kilpatrick alibi each other. And Lady Carville saw Susan go out, which places Lady Carville in the conservatory, at least at that point, and it's difficult to see how she could have reached the orchard and committed the murder if that's so." She glanced at Barnaby and Stokes. "That leaves Susan highest on our list, and even she isn't that compelling in the role of murderer."

Stokes grunted and set down his cup and plate. "Let's move on. Time's ticking, and there's quite a number of the company we've yet to speak with."

Barnaby drained his cup, set it on the tray, then rose, hoisted the tray, and carried it to the door. He opened the door, handed the tray to the footman on duty, and asked for Mr. Elliot to be fetched.

On returning to the other two, in reply to Penelope's interrogatory look, Barnaby offered, "Elliot's in his late thirties and, being well-born and distinctly well-heeled, definitely qualifies as an eligible bachelor. He's widely known as a quiet, reserved sort and, I gather, is in fact on the lookout for a suitable wife, but unsurprisingly given his character, he's being wary and careful. He's an investor of some note, owns a decent estate, but doesn't make a show of his wealth."

Elliot arrived moments later, and Barnaby greeted him and showed him to the interviewee's chair.

Barnaby reclaimed the armchair opposite and embarked on their now-standard questions.

Quietly urbane, Elliot answered readily. "Having been encouraged by Pamela and Susan—both of whom I've known for some time—to attend, I drove down in my curricle and arrived in the middle of the afternoon on Sunday."

Barnaby inclined his head. "On Monday morning, at what time did you leave your room?"

"I came down to breakfast quite early. Percival was already there, as well as Morehouse, Carrington, and Cordingley, and Griffith arrived soon after. Monty came in a few minutes later, followed by his son and his friends, but I left soon after with Percival, Morehouse, Carrington, and

Cordingley. Morehouse, Carrington, and I came in here, while Percival and Cordingley headed upstairs."

Barnaby saw that Stokes was busily taking notes. "Thank you. That's very clear. What did you do next?"

Elliot replied, "I settled with a news sheet, and Morehouse and Carrington did the same. Leith was here when we arrived, glancing at a news sheet, but he left soon after, saying he had letters to write. Griffith looked in, cast his eye over a news sheet, and went out again—he didn't say to where—and after quite some time, Morland and Wincombe joined us. We five sat and read and occasionally traded comments." Elliot frowned. "About ten or so minutes after Morland and Wincombe came in, Monty arrived. He chatted and circulated, asked if we had all we needed —that sort of thing. Then, he said he had to check on some estate matter and was going for a stroll to attend to it and went out."

"That must have been, what?" Barnaby asked. "Ten or so minutes after nine?"

Elliot considered, then nodded. "Yes. About that."

"And neither you nor any of the others left the library after Underhill went out?" Stokes asked.

"No. We were all there until we heard Miss Hemmings scream for help."

"While you were in here, did you notice any of the company leave the house or see them outside?" Barnaby asked.

Elliot frowned. "Well, Monty headed toward the front door, so I imagine he went out that way. Other than him, the only person I saw leave was Percival, who must have been on the stairs when we all heard the scream. He went racing past the library doorway and out onto the porch. We—the five of us—followed him outside and across the lawn."

After glancing at Stokes, Barnaby returned his gaze to Elliot. "We gather you know the Underhills reasonably well. What was your view of Monty?"

Elliot took a moment to think, then offered, "He was always a genial, jovial soul, very amiable and good-natured. Never saw him lose his temper or even get close to that. I always thought that, socially speaking, he was the positive side of the marriage, while Pamela, with her abrupt manner and abrasive personality, was the negative. They balanced each other, and all in all, the alliance worked well." He paused, clearly debating, then he glanced at Barnaby and said, "Over the years, one thing I have wondered about is whether Monty resented the general assumption—correct in his case—that he married for money. While that might have been the truth, there are times when the truth can grate."

Barnaby saw that Penelope looked quite struck by that observation. He returned his gaze to Elliot. "Do you have any idea why someone might have wanted to kill Monty?"

"No. None whatsoever." Elliot's brow furrowed. "In truth, it seems quite inexplicable."

When Barnaby glanced at Stokes, he fractionally shook his head. Barnaby smiled at Elliot. "Thank you for your help."

Barnaby rose, as did Elliot, and after bowing to Penelope and nodding to Stokes, Elliot turned for the door, and Barnaby saw him out.

"Well!" Penelope said. "Would that all our interviewees were as refreshingly direct and straightforward."

Stokes nodded. "And factual. He didn't just tell us about himself but also where others were over that time. That's going to be a big help in placing those others at the time of the murder."

"He'll make an excellent witness if it comes to that." Barnaby arched a brow at Penelope.

She consulted her list. "Mrs. Waterhouse is next."

After Barnaby sent the footman to find Mrs. Waterhouse and returned to the armchairs, Penelope filled in, "The Waterhouses are a well-connected family within the Goodrich-Underhill orbit. That said, the Waterhouses tend to spend more time in the country than in town, but with a recently presented daughter, Alison, to establish, it's no surprise that Mrs. Waterhouse and Alison are attending this house party. Alison is a pretty girl with nice manners who, all things being equal, should make an acceptable match."

Two minutes later, Mrs. Waterhouse was shown into the room. She was of average height with wavy brown hair looped into plaits that formed a coronet about her head. With pretty but ageing features and a rather timid, self-effacing manner, she was the sort who tended to eschew attracting any attention.

Smiling, Penelope rose and welcomed Mrs. Waterhouse and guided her to the central armchair.

Mrs. Waterhouse tentatively sat and, finding herself the cynosure of three gazes, drew in a nervous breath.

Seeking to reassure her, Penelope quickly said, "We're asking everyone the same questions, purely to get some idea of who was where and when. Our first question is straightforward—when did you arrive at the Grange?"

"Oh." Mrs. Waterhouse's hands fluttered in her lap, then stilled. "We—Alison and I—came down in our carriage and were here by three o'clock on Sunday." She leaned toward Penelope a trifle and lowered her voice. "We're very grateful to have been included by dear Lady Pamela. I know you'll understand when I say that it's imperative that Alison meet with suitable gentlemen, and this event is simply perfect for that. We're very glad we're here…." Mrs. Waterhouse suddenly looked stricken and hurried to add, "Except for the murder, of course. That has been a horrible shock!"

She sat back, and Penelope gently asked, "On Monday morning, at what time did you and Alison leave your rooms and come downstairs?"

"We kept an ear out for the others—Lady Susan and her daughters and some of the other ladies—and we followed them down and joined them at the breakfast table."

"And after you rose from the table…?"

"I went with the other matrons and the two older ladies to the morning room. Alison—she and Cecilia are great friends. Did I mention that? She went off with Cecilia, Enid, Regina, and Samantha to the conservatory, no doubt to put their heads together and discuss the eligible gentlemen here."

"Did you notice if any of the company left the house? Did you see anyone walking outside?" Penelope asked.

Mrs. Waterhouse shook her head. "No—well, except for Susan. She went out to stroll in the rose garden. She didn't seem to want company, and I was comfortable with the other ladies, so I didn't offer to accompany her."

Penelope nodded. "What was your view of Monty Underhill?"

"Oh, he was everything that was amiable." Mrs. Waterhouse's fluttering hands came into play. "*Such* a pleasant gentleman. He was quite unexceptionable and so very easygoing. Nothing was ever amiss with him. In all honesty, I cannot fathom why anyone would want to kill him." She looked perturbed, then glanced at Penelope and leaned toward her again. "I admit I'm rather concerned, Mrs. Adair, as to whether this murder will reflect badly on the Underhills and, by association, cast a shadow over Alison and dim her hopes."

Smiling with faint cynicism, Penelope rose and reassured Mrs. Waterhouse, "By the time the ton returns to London, I suspect that any sensation generated by this murder will have faded from the collective memory."

"Oh. Yes." Mrs. Waterhouse rose. "We must, indeed, hope for that."

Penelope showed Mrs. Waterhouse to the door, then asked the footman to fetch Mr. Cordingley.

On returning to Stokes and Barnaby, Penelope sank into her armchair and observed, "Note that Mrs. Waterhouse's concern is driven by a suspicion that there is, indeed, some real and potentially sensational reason behind Monty's death."

Stokes nodded. "So what do we know about Cordingley?"

"He's somewhere around thirty, an eligible enough bachelor." Penelope looked inquiringly at Barnaby. "But other than that..."

Barnaby shook his head. "I've seen him at ton events, but I know very little about him."

When Cordingley entered, Barnaby rose, greeted him with a friendly smile, and ushered Cordingley to the central armchair. Cordingley was a trifle taller than average, although not as tall as Barnaby or Stokes, and possessed even if unremarkable features set in a pleasant face under a mop of shiny brown hair.

Once Cordingley sat, Barnaby resumed his seat and mildly inquired, "When did you arrive at the Grange?"

"I drove down on Sunday," Cordingley answered readily. Glancing at Penelope and Stokes, he seemed more curious about them and not nervous in any way. "I confess I started a trifle late and got here about five." As if sensing they'd seen his interest, he grinned. "I was hounded by my mother and aunts to come down here and cast my eye over the field, as it were. They're set on finding me a bride, but I'm only thirty-one. I'm really not interested in getting married just yet." He tipped his head, his smile engaging. "So, you see, I'm keen to learn all I can about the murder—all the sensational details—so I can report to them how coming down here brought me close to some violent killer and resulted in me being interviewed by Scotland Yard!" His grin was infectious as he looked at Penelope. "That should buy me a little time, don't you think?"

Penelope tried but failed to hide her smile. "That's...certainly an inventive use for news of a murder."

Stokes cleared his throat, and Barnaby duly asked, "Shifting to Monday morning, when did you come downstairs?"

"Oh, early, to beat the ladies. It was just after seven when I left my room, and I more or less followed Percival down."

"And after you rose from the table?"

"I left with several others—Percival, Carrington, and Morehouse. Oh, and Elliot. Percival and I went straight upstairs to our rooms. Percival said he had letters to write, and I wanted to continue reading a book I brought and had started the previous evening. The other three headed in here."

"What was the book?" Penelope asked.

"It's a fascinating tale of an adventurer's travels through Egypt and Mesopotamia." Cordingley sensed a kindred spirit, and his eyes lit. "It's by a fellow named Cannington. Have you heard of it?"

Penelope nodded and cast a swift glance at Stokes, confirming the book was real. "His journey makes quite a story."

"However"—Barnaby cut in before Penelope and Cordingley could head off on that tangent—"to continue with our questions, at any time after leaving the dining room, did you see anyone leave the house or notice anyone walking outside?"

Cordingley nodded. "The chair in my room is by the window, and I happened to look out and saw Lady Wincombe walking across the rear lawn, toward the east. She seemed quite intent on getting somewhere." He paused, then added, "Earlier, I heard voices—male voices, I think of Vincent and his friends—on the terrace, but I was deep in the book at that point and didn't look out, so I don't know if they went farther than that."

Stokes nodded as he jotted. "Thank you. That helps."

"On the subject of our late host," Barnaby said, "what did you make of him?"

Cordingley paused, then shrugged. "He seemed a good sort. Jovial. Easy to get along with. Truth to tell, I didn't know him that well—hadn't really met him other than to be introduced before—and I hadn't paid all that much attention to him over the time before he met his end."

"So you have no idea why he might have been killed?" Barnaby asked.

Cordingley shook his head. "None at all, I'm sorry to say." His insouciant grin returned. "I am, however, keen to learn what it was that got Monty murdered, not least so that I can wave it as a warning to make my mother and aunts desist from their matchmaking."

Barnaby glanced at Stokes, but he shook his head. He returned his gaze to Cordingley and smiled easily. "Thank you." Barnaby rose, bringing the younger man to his feet, and after Cordingley had bowed to

Penelope and nodded respectfully to Stokes, showed him firmly out of the room.

"Well!" Penelope grinned at Barnaby as he returned to his armchair. "He was a bit of light relief."

Barnaby replied, "You would have encouraged him to tell us all about Egypt. But regardless, who's next?"

Penelope consulted her list. "It was supposed to be Rosalind, but we've already spoken with her, so we may as well move on to Nevin-Smythe."

Stokes got up and went to the door to send the footman to fetch Nevin-Smythe.

On returning to the chairs, Stokes asked, "What do I need to know about this one?"

Penelope grimaced and looked at Barnaby. "Other than him being another of Monty's victims, albeit not one scheduled to make a payment while here, I know very little about him."

"He's another thirtyish eligible bachelor," Barnaby said. "He belongs to the right clubs, moves in the right circles, and styles himself as a bit of a dandy. Good family. Nothing adverse known about him."

"Except for the cheating Monty was blackmailing him over." Stokes sank into his chair. "Let me take the lead on this one—I'm feeling left out."

Barnaby and Penelope grinned, and when the door opened and Nevin-Smythe was shown in, Stokes rose, greeted him, and waved him to the armchair set before them.

Nevin-Smythe clearly fancied himself quite the dandy. His hair was coiffed and pomaded, his coat, in a solid shade of purple, bore large mother-of-pearl buttons, and his spotted-silk cravat ballooned about his chin before disappearing into the top of his silver-and-gray-striped waist-coat. He was quite an eye-catching sight as he glided forward, bowed with a flourish to Penelope, then with studied grace, inclined his head to Barnaby and Stokes before subsiding—elegantly—into the designated armchair.

Stokes began by stating, "We're asking the same questions of all the guests. To begin with, please tell us when you arrived at the Grange."

"I drove myself down on Sunday and arrived a bit latish—a little after five, I should think."

"And you're here because…?"

Nevin-Smythe hesitated, then admitted, "I believe I have to settle down soon, or so my sisters tell me. They're older than I am and arranged the invitation through parental connections with the Hurstbridges, so I'm here to cast my eye over the young ladies paraded before me and the other eligible bachelors present." He lightly shrugged. "That's what house parties like this are for, after all."

Stokes nodded in acceptance, then asked, "On Monday morning, at what time did you come downstairs?"

"Late. At events such as this, one must be either hideously early or inconsiderately late to have any chance of eating one's breakfast in peace, and I'm not an early riser. I came down just before nine o'clock. The others had all left by then, and I grabbed a cup of coffee and a piece of toast and left the staff to clear the board. When I left the dining room, I heard balls clinking from the billiards room—the sound called to me, and I headed that way. Griffith was there, and we amused ourselves by playing a few games."

"So," Stokes clarified, "between nine and ten o'clock, you were in the dining room briefly, then in the billiards room with Griffith."

"Yes."

"From the time you came downstairs to the time you heard Miss Hemmings scream, did you see anyone else leave the house or notice anyone walking outside?"

"As I left the dining room, I saw Underhill on his way out through the open front door." Nevin-Smythe paused, then evenly continued, "I suppose that might make me the last of the company to have seen him alive—except for his murderer, of course. Oh, and I saw the two old ladies—Lady Campbell-Carstairs and Lady Kelly—coming down the stairs as I crossed the front hall. I bowed to them, and I know they saw me."

"They did," Stokes confirmed. "And I gather neither you nor Griffith left the billiards room until after you heard the scream."

"That's correct. We heard someone rush down the last stairs and race outside—apparently, that was Percival—so we put up our cues and went to see what was happening."

Smoothly, Stokes continued, "How did you view Monty Underhill?"

Nevin-Smythe blinked, then rather carefully said, "I didn't know him all that well. As I said, the family connection is with the Hurstbridges—Pamela and Susan's family. I've only visited here once before, but I've often stayed at the marquess's principal seat at Wyndham Castle." He paused, then more airily added, "Truth be told, I hadn't really thought about Monty that much. He was of an older generation, and what little I saw of him painted him as a genial character, helpful and, overall, rather harmless."

Stokes arched a black brow. "So you have no idea who might have wanted to end his life?"

"Not a clue. I really have no notion of why anyone would want to bop him over the head."

Stokes paused, regarding Nevin-Smythe steadily. To his credit, the man didn't squirm, although a wary look entered his eyes. After a lengthy moment, Stokes said, "We now know that Monty Underhill was a blackmailer."

Nevin-Smythe's already pale faced blanched further. "What?" he whispered.

Inexorably, Stokes went on, "His victims were members of the ton, and according to the record he kept of those victims and the payments he demanded and that they paid, you were one of those victims."

Patently utterly dumbfounded, Nevin-Smythe just stared.

When Stokes simply stared back, waiting, Nevin-Smythe moistened his lips, then he blinked and shook his head. "No. It can't be…" His gaze went to Barnaby, then Penelope. When they looked steadily back and volunteered nothing, he returned his gaze to Stokes. "Monty? It was him?"

Stokes nodded. "It seems he believed you cheated in some fashion, and as you've been meeting his demands in order to buy his silence for rather more than a year, it seems you believe you cheated, too."

Still staring at Stokes, slowly, Nevin-Smythe nodded. "I did, God help me." His jaw set, then he blurted, "I only did it once! It was a card game, and I thought I had the winning hand and got in too deep, and I knew I couldn't afford to just up and walk away. I couldn't pay, so I had to recoup, and I cheated on one hand. Just one!"

From his expression, Nevin-Smythe had regretted that transgression for the past year and more.

Deflating, he shook his head. "Just once—and I paid for it. Again and again."

"Where was this card game?" Penelope inquired.

Nevin-Smythe looked at her blankly, then he refocused and uttered a harsh laugh. "At Wyndham Castle. At a major ball. And yes, Monty was there, in the card room, moving around the tables. He must have seen…"

Stokes arched a brow at Penelope and Barnaby, but both shook their heads.

Nevin-Smythe looked like he'd bitten into a sour lime. Stokes considered him for a moment, then said, "Please keep the news of Underhill's illicit activities under your hat. Not least because if you do, no one else will ever know of your own slip from grace."

"As matters stand," Barnaby said, "you won't be hearing from your blackmailer ever again."

Nevin-Smythe stared back for a moment, then nodded. "I won't breathe a word."

After the door closed behind him, Penelope sent the footman to summon Cecilia Underhill.

Penelope had wondered if the girl would be sufficiently recovered for them to question, but when Cecilia took her seat before them, Penelope was relieved to see that determination was etched in every line of Cecilia's rather plain face.

In her early twenties, Cecilia appeared less sulky than when they'd first spoken with her. Less arrogant, perhaps, now the reality of her father's murder had sunk in. Although she remained subdued, and her light-brown hair appeared lackluster and brittle and her features were drawn, there was enough awareness in her blue eyes to suggest that, normally, she was rather livelier.

Once Cecilia had settled, Penelope commenced by confirming that Cecilia had arrived at the Grange with her parents some weeks before, then gently inquired what hopes Cecilia had had of the house party.

From her expression, it was plain that Cecilia debated whether or not to answer truthfully, then she lightly shrugged and said, "I was hoping to forge an understanding with Lord Griffith or Mr. Elliot. Mama and Papa favored Mr. Elliot, but Lord Griffith is much more entertaining." She paused and tipped her head. "On the other hand, after a time, 'entertaining' might wear thin."

Penelope was quietly impressed by that unexpected sign of deeper thought and continued with her next question.

"I came downstairs with Mama," Cecilia said, "at a bit before eight o'clock. Mama makes a point of being early on the first morning of a house party so she can make sure all is running smoothly and all the guests—well, the female ones—have rested well. After breakfast, I went with Alison, Enid, and Samantha to the conservatory. We wanted to chat without our mamas being able to hear, but when we reached the conservatory, we saw Lady Carville was already there, so we went to the music room."

"Did you see anyone leave the house or notice anyone walking outside?" Penelope asked.

Cecilia shook her head. "I didn't see anyone venture outside."

Penelope paused, wondering at the wisdom of voicing their next question, but in the end, she asked, "How did you view your father?"

Cecilia straightened. "Papa was always a good sort—about everything. He balanced Mama, if you know what I mean. It wasn't that he wasn't strict, but he wasn't unreasonable about it."

"Do you know of any reason anyone would want to kill him?"

"No. None." Cecilia's features crumpled, and her lips quivered. "Truly, I can't believe he's gone."

Her last word was a faint wail. Before she could dissolve into tears, Penelope stood and rather bracingly said, "Thank you." She drew the now-wilting girl to her feet and helped her from the room.

Penelope was relieved to find Alison Waterhouse waiting in the hall and gratefully handed Cecilia into her friend's care.

Returning to Barnaby and Stokes, Penelope blew out a breath. "Phew! That was close."

"I thought she did well to remain so composed," Stokes said.

"She wants us to find who killed her father," Penelope said.

Barnaby sighed. "We all want to solve that mystery, but frankly, my head is spinning with all the details we've heard."

Penelope glanced at the clock on the library's mantelpiece. "It's getting rather late to call people in."

Stokes rumbled, "For my money, we need to call a halt and digest what we've learned. There are all sorts of pertinent snippets mixed in with otherwise irrelevant details."

"Such as," Barnaby said, "Nevin-Smythe giving Griffith an alibi and vice versa."

"And Cecilia and her friends placing Lady Carville in the conservatory," Penelope said. "That's almost enough to strike her ladyship off our suspects list." She paused, then went on, "It occurs to me that, in this case, with so many people in the house and moving about, given Monty was killed in the orchard, that means whoever killed him couldn't have been in the house at that time."

Barnaby nodded. "Theoretically, we should be able to identify the killer or at least get a strong sense of who he is by cross-checking where everyone was."

Stokes had been consulting his notes. "People saw others here and there. The orchard's far enough from the house that the killer had to have been outside and out of sight of any of the other guests for a substantial amount of the critical hour between nine and ten."

Penelope nodded decisively. "Our murderer will be unaccounted for during most of that time. And if he searched the study while everyone was distracted by the body in the orchard, he should also be unsighted by anyone during that interval as well." She tipped her head, considering that. "No one should remember him at the orchard with the other men or on the front lawn with the women."

"We have several guests with sound memories and acute observational skills," Stokes said. "But before we go too far with our thoughts and suppositions, I suggest we retreat to the inn and go over all we've heard thus far, then work out what we can be certain of in terms of where people were. Once we have that, we can come back tomorrow and interview the rest and see what confirmations we can get for those we've yet to definitively alibi."

"I agree." Penelope looked at Barnaby.

He nodded and pushed himself out of his chair. "But before we quit the premises, I suggest we report to Pamela."

They sent the footman to fetch his mistress and met Pamela in the front hall.

They kept their report brief, merely saying they believed they'd made some progress and would return the following day to interview those they'd yet to speak with and that after that, they hoped to have a clearer view of the events that had led to her husband's death.

Rather wan, Pamela thanked them and reiterated her support for their efforts.

With bows to her and thanks to Gearing, who had thought to summon their carriage, they quit the house, descended the steps, climbed into the carriage, and set off for the inn.

CHAPTER 8

*R*ichard walked into the drawing room at a few minutes after
six-thirty. The company was gathering there to spend the
traditional half hour chatting before going in to dine.

He spotted Rosalind and Regina standing along one side of the room,
attended by Leith, Cordingley, and Nevin-Smythe, and strolled to join the
group.

They turned to him as he neared. He half bowed to Rosalind and
Regina, then Nevin-Smythe leapt in to ask, "Have the investigators
gone?"

"A few minutes ago," Richard said. "I saw them in the hall, taking
their leave of Pamela. They said they'd return tomorrow to finish their
interviews."

Regina murmured, "I noticed they haven't yet interviewed the
younger guests."

"It seems they've been asking each of us where we were and who else
was there and who we saw wandering around," Cordingley said.

Regina studied the circle of faces, then, concerned, looked at Richard.
"Do they think Mr. Underhill was killed by one of the guests?"

A short silence fell, then, her tone even, Rosalind stated, "The family
is talking of a passing vagrant having taken it into their heads to wander
into the orchard and kill Monty and that, therefore, the killer will be long
gone by now."

Leith arched his brows, then glanced at Richard. "Is that likely?"

"It's a convenient tale," Richard replied, "but a highly unlikely one. I seriously doubt you'll find the inspector and the Adairs coming to such a conclusion."

"Well, I hope the investigators at least pursue the possibility," Nevin-Smythe declared. "Wouldn't do to chase their tails, hunting for clues among the guests while the real killer gets clean away."

Richard smiled thinly. "I suspect we'll discover the investigators have all possible avenues covered."

Rosalind raised her chin a trifle. "While at such a time, one has to feel for the family, I hope they'll push the investigators to solve the case regardless of who the killer proves to be."

"Indeed," Richard said, and the other men murmured agreement.

Gearing appeared in the doorway and announced, "Dinner is served, my lady."

Pamela rose from the chaise on which she'd been sitting, and as the ranking nobleman, Leith went forward to offer her his arm.

While the procession of couples to the dining room vaguely accorded with accepted precedence, allowances were made to foster the chance of the hoped-for understandings. Consequently, Richard was left to escort Rosalind to the table, and they were encouraged by all to claim chairs side by side, not quite halfway down the long board.

As Rosalind sat and Richard pushed in her chair, he saw her gaze track to where Regina, who had come in on Nevin-Smythe's arm, was being seated farther down the table amongst the other younger guests.

Richard claimed the chair on Rosalind's right and sat. The soup course promptly arrived and was consumed in relative silence, with only the occasional murmur breaking what was an almost-awkward moment. As plates were cleared and platters brought out and the courses progressed, frankly assessing glances were cast up and down the table. It seemed their interviews with the investigators had focused many of those present on the sequence of events that must have occurred, thereby awakening an understanding that the most logical conclusion was that one of their number was the killer.

The prevailing undercurrent of uncertainty and suspicion testified to that burgeoning presentiment.

The yet-to-be-interviewed younger crew was the only group untouched by the rising tide of foreboding. In chatting amongst themselves, they seemed distinctly more relaxed than their now-wary elders.

Under his breath, to Rosalind, Richard said, "The company seem to be growing increasingly tense."

"Hardly surprising," she returned, equally quietly. "I wonder how much longer it will be before your friends identify the killer."

"Difficult to say," Richard murmured back. "They won't make a move until they're sure. I know enough of them to be certain of that."

"Hmm." Rosalind darted a glance up the table. "I hope the murderer, whoever they are, has nerves of steel and will simply wait out this interlude without attempting to deflect or distract the police in some way."

Richard hadn't thought of that but admitted she had a point.

As he said so, he noticed that Leith, who was seated on the opposite side of the table, up a few places and flanked by Cecilia Underhill and Alison Waterhouse, had been watching him and Rosalind. Now, Leith caught his eye and, leaning forward a little, asked, "Did the investigators give you any hint as to the direction of their thoughts?"

Although he hadn't raised his voice, Leith's question instantly focused every eye on Richard.

He inwardly sighed, but with outward calm, replied, "No, but to them, this is early days yet. They'll be gathering every fact they can before deducing what actually happened." He paused, then, accepting that he was, in fact, speaking to the entire company, he added, "Mrs. Adair once gave me a description of how the investigators' collective mind works. She said their process is akin to assembling a jigsaw. One by one, you slot the pieces into place, and at some point, even if you haven't got every last piece, the picture is revealed, and you can clearly see who the murderer is."

That seemed to satisfy those listening. Many turned to their neighbors, and a livelier discussion developed regarding the facts the investigators had already assembled and what others they might yet be seeking.

Rosalind caught his eye and, sotto voce, murmured, "That was very well done. You've given them a novel perspective of the situation to dwell on."

He faintly smiled. "With any luck, the distraction will last through the rest of the evening."

She smiled back. "We can but hope."

In light of their host's absence, there was no suggestion the men would remain about the table, drinking his brandy, and as the covers were drawn and the company rose and repaired to the drawing room, Rosalind had to admit to having had a significant change of heart.

When she'd arrived at the Grange, she'd had no favorable view of what, through marriage, a gentleman—any gentleman—could offer her that she didn't already have. In return for her independence, what would she receive? Quite aside from the understanding that was being slowly borne in on her that the benefits accruing from marriage couldn't be measured solely in transactional terms, courtesy of the murder and the ensuing situation, she was coming to appreciate the comfort and reassurance that having an intelligent, sensible, and fundamentally powerful man at her side conferred.

As she accepted Richard's proffered arm and, together, they joined the exodus from the dining room, she was acutely aware of her mother's and his aunts' interested—indeed, hopeful—expressions.

Previously, she would have been irritated, but now...she inwardly shrugged.

Glancing from beneath her lashes at Richard's profile, she acknowledged that, throughout their time at the Grange, their interactions had invariably suggested he regarded her as an intellectual equal; unlike all other gentlemen she'd previously met, he treated her as a partner and not merely a pretty face with no real intelligence behind the façade.

Looking ahead, she smiled and inwardly admitted that she wholeheartedly approved.

Barnaby slumped onto the settle before the fire in their private parlor at the Red Lion Inn. As Penelope joined him and Stokes claimed the armchair to Barnaby's left, Barnaby observed, "This case is proving quite a slog. A different slog to having to rely on countless boots on the ground —as in the Sedbury case—but a slog nonetheless."

Stokes folded his hands over his stomach, plainly content after their excellent meal. "I have to admit that I'm finding so many interviews, one after another and all treading over the same ground, difficult to keep track of."

Sagely, Penelope nodded. "Too much information all at once."

"I can't recall any case like this," Barnaby went on, "where we know so little about the murderer. We know quite a bit about the murder itself and how it was carried out, and we now know enough about the victim, but when it comes to his killer, we have no sighting, nothing to point us his way, and only a presumed, not-yet-proven motive."

Stokes grunted. "All that confirms is that we need to keep on with our interviews. We have to trawl through all the dross to find nuggets of useful facts that, hopefully, will steer us in the right direction."

Penelope sighed. "And we can't risk skipping anyone, just in case they're the person who knows the vital clue."

"We can't go any slower, either," Stokes said. "We can't intersperse the interviews with other investigations because we're not going to be able to keep the entire company at the Grange for much longer. I give them until the day after tomorrow before they start agitating to leave."

"Us not having a clue as to who the killer is," Barnaby said, "will mean their imaginations run riot, and they'll grow increasingly fearful over with whom they're sharing a roof."

Sitting straighter, Penelope bracingly declared, "Well, we'll just have to forge on and find our murderer!"

Barnaby threw her a fondly amused glance. "I vote we start by reviewing what we've gleaned of how Monty managed his blackmailing scheme."

"Very cannily, by all accounts," Stokes returned. "He knew his marks well and knew how to twist his stories into more effective swords to hold over people's heads. Importantly, he was wise enough never to ask for too much—more than the mark could relatively easily part with."

"Yes," Penelope said. "That's been very clear. His knowledge of those he preyed on was central to his scheme's success, and I have to say that he demonstrated considerable inventiveness both in the way he trans-formed relatively innocuous secrets into potential scandals and in his selection of places to leave his payments. Not many would have thought of using a railway carriage!"

Barnaby was nodding. "He was bold but also careful and crafty."

Stokes grimaced. "And that resulted in his victims—all of them—not having a clue who their blackmailer was."

"Except"—Penelope tilted her head—"if we're correct in thinking it was Monty's blackmailing that got him killed, then plainly, whoever murdered him had learned *his* secret." Reflected firelight danced on the lenses of her spectacles as she looked at Barnaby, then Stokes. "How?"

Stokes raised his black brows. "Underhill slipped up somewhere, and one of his victims noticed enough to put two and two together."

"And," Barnaby added, "if our theory of rage fueling the deed is correct, then presumably, it was the realization of the blackmailer's iden-tity that ignited a blaze of murderous fury in our killer."

Stokes frowned, then ventured, "Acting on such an eruption of rage, which I agree is the most likely scenario with this murder, implies that the moment of ignition—of realization—had to have only just occurred." He looked at Penelope. "Within a matter of minutes before the deed."

Penelope, too, was frowning, no doubt reviewing the timeline of the murder in her mind. Her expression clearing, she focused on Barnaby's face, then glanced at Stokes. "That suggests that something happened at about nine o'clock on Monday morning that revealed to the killer that Monty was the blackmailer." She paused, then went on, "I did wonder if it could have been Monty looking for Regina's payment in the hollow tree, and the killer had somehow guessed and had been watching that place, saw him, and realized..." She grimaced. "But that won't wash, because Regina hadn't placed her payment into the hollow, so there was nothing to say that the hollow wasn't just a hollow or a bird's nest—nothing revealing at all."

Stokes had hauled out his notebook, flicked through the pages, and was studying his scrawl. "Multiple people have placed Underhill in the library at around nine o'clock. Prior to that, he was in the dining room at the breakfast table—nothing revealing about that, I would have thought. And after he chatted with the gentlemen in the library, he went outside, and shortly after that, his killer found him in the orchard at the hollow tree and struck."

"I agree," Barnaby said, "that something that exposed Monty as the blackmailer to one of his until-then-ignorant victims had to have happened around that time, most likely in the library. But what?"

Stokes flipped through several pages, stopped, read, then said, "There were five gentlemen in the library at the time—Elliot, Morehouse, Carrington, Morland, and Wincombe. All were there before Underhill walked in, and all remained until after the Hemmings girl screamed. All five have told us that Underhill came in, chatted and inquired if all was well, then he said he was going outside to check on some estate matter and left. Subsequently, the two old ladies—Lady Campbell-Carstairs and Lady Kelly—saw Underhill go out of the front door, and Nevin-Smythe did as well."

Penelope stated, "We need to ask the five gentlemen exactly what Monty said..." She grimaced. "But all five remained in the library, so the critical revelation didn't lie in Monty's words."

"Nevertheless"—Stokes jotted a note—"we should confirm that all five remained in the library throughout, and one didn't go out for a few minutes, then return, and the others haven't thought to mention it."

A rap on the door had the three of them twisting to look that way, and Barnaby called, "Come."

The door opened, and Morgan stuck his head around the panel. He saw them, grinned, stepped inside, and shut the door, then he crossed to halt beside Stokes's chair and snap off a salute. "Just came to report, guv." He nodded to Penelope and Barnaby. "Sir. Ma'am."

Morgan returned his gaze to Stokes. "I'd spelled Walsh in the study, and he relieved me just now. But earlier, I spoke with the gardeners about that stake, and they all agree it's one of theirs and that the number means something, but none of those around today knew what. However, they said the head gardener will know, but he was off at some market today. He'll be back tomorrow, and apparently, he'll be able to tell us what that thirty-five painted on the stake means. The other gardeners all felt sure it'll tell us where in the grounds the stake came from."

"That's something at least." Stokes added another note in his book, then looked up at Morgan. "Follow up with the head gardener tomorrow. Report as soon as you learn anything useful." Morgan nodded, and Stokes went on, "So Walsh is back in the study?"

"Aye, guv. I'll go over in the small hours and relieve him, like I did this morning."

"Good. In that case, you'd best be off to have some dinner and get some sleep."

Morgan saluted, nodded to Penelope and Barnaby, and left.

As the door closed behind him, Penelope remarked, "I must admit that learning that Monty was an established blackmailer is a fact I'm still struggling to fully assimilate. I'm sure there'll be consequences I've yet to see."

Barnaby felt much the same. "One point—all his victims are members of the ton. No staff or people of lesser social standing. That might be an outcome of him using people's visits to Wyndham Castle to glean their secrets—"

"And *that* suggests," Penelope concluded, "that the killer will most likely be someone who has stayed at the castle at some point."

Stokes scrawled a note. "That might be a way of winnowing our suspects list." He glanced at Penelope. "Once we finish the interviews and have it complete, we should ask Lady Pamela and Lady Susan which of those on the list have visited the castle. It seems likely they will know."

Frowning lightly, Penelope nodded. After a moment, she said, "Regarding who was where at the time of the murder, the guests seem to have had certain gathering places, which is helpful for us. After leaving the breakfast table—and everyone had by the time of the murder, even Nevin-Smythe—most guests went to the library, the billiards room, the morning room, the conservatory, or the music room. Only a handful went off on their own—three upstairs to their rooms, where they say they remained throughout the hour, Lady Susan, who went to the rose garden, and Lady Wincombe, who went upstairs and then to the croquet green, and her niece Harriet, who trailed after her." Her frown deepened. "We have several guests yet to interview, but thus far, there are not many who might have been Monty's killer."

Barnaby offered, "The five in the library saw Monty go out into the hall and turn toward the front door, and Nevin-Smythe and Richard's aunts saw him go outside. We know that much, but not what happened next."

A knock on the door was followed by O'Donnell looking inside. Stokes waved at his sergeant to join them, and O'Donnell came in, shut the door, and, looking distinctly weary, plodded over and nodded respectfully to the three of them.

Then O'Donnell looked at Stokes. "I spoke with all the gamekeepers round about. They seemed the most likely to know if any stranger was lurking in their woods, and they all swear there isn't a one." He visibly drooped. "I circled the whole estate, went into all the nearby villages, found the gamekeepers of all the surrounding properties, and chatted with the locals as well—the farmers and farmhands. No one has spotted anyone they can't put a name to, and no one was anywhere they weren't supposed to be." His lips twisted, and he met Stokes's eyes. "Seems a right law-abiding neighborhood hereabouts."

Barnaby, Penelope, and Stokes understood O'Donnell's skepticism, but their only interest was in some unknown stranger.

"Thank you for being so thorough." Stokes dismissed O'Donnell with an appreciative nod. "You'd better join Morgan in the tap and get yourself a good dinner."

"Aye, guv. I'll do that." O'Donnell nodded to them all and dragged himself to the door.

As the door shut, Penelope observed, "So much for our fictional passing homicidal maniac."

Stokes snorted. "Indeed. But that makes it as good as certain that our murderer is still at the Grange and, given Underhill's choice of victim, almost certainly one of the guests."

Penelope nodded. "Even if we imagine that another of Monty's victims, one not at the house party, somehow realized their blackmailer was him and came down here intending to kill him..." She grimaced. "It's hard to see that happening, isn't it? The property is large, so how could someone from beyond its boundaries know that Monty would be in the orchard at that time?"

"Even if they'd been watching the house from the cover of the woods, why be there watching in the first place? Surely not on the off chance that Monty would obligingly wander out alone and walk into the orchard?" Barnaby shook his head. "No. Someone intent on murdering Monty coming from outside the estate doesn't make much practical sense."

"Also," Penelope went on, "if the motive for the murder is Monty's blackmailing activities—and as yet, we've found no other possibility—then a murderer coming from outside the estate implies that person had learned but *only just* learned that Monty was their blackmailer."

"We're a bit more than an hour from London," Stokes observed. "That scenario might be possible."

Barnaby inclined his head. "But while it's possible, is it plausible? Given how long Monty had been blackmailing while successfully concealing his identity?" He paused, then added, "I really can't see it. And we still have the difficulty of someone from outside the estate just happening to be in the right place at the right time to find Monty outside and alone." He looked at Stokes. "No one's mentioned Monty taking a regular morning walk around the grounds. Quite the opposite. He told people he was going out to check on some estate matter. As it turned out, that was his code for picking up payments from two different victims."

"At least two victims." Penelope arched her brows at Barnaby. "We don't know what was written on the torn-out page."

Barnaby tipped his head her way. "True."

Silence fell as they considered where that left them.

Eventually, Stokes said, "I can't see any viable alternative to our thesis that the motive for the murder is Underhill's blackmailing activities. We shouldn't forget the necessary incitement of violent fury inherent in this murder, and as yet, we've found no hint of any other reason powerful enough to have provoked the required degree of rage."

Penelope pointed out, "Mrs. Hemmings used the word 'betrayal.' That's a powerful emotion and would almost certainly have been in play had our killer just learned that Monty was his blackmailer."

Stokes was studying his notes. "If we accept that Rosalind Hemmings is effectively alibied by her sister, Regina, who found Monty dead before Rosalind reached the orchard, and as we know Regina couldn't have struck the lethal blow, then over the relevant time, the members of the company as yet unvouched for by others are Lady Susan, Leith, Percival, Lady Carville, and Cordingley. All three gentlemen were, apparently, in their rooms upstairs. Lady Carville was in the conservatory and was seen there by the young ladies, but no one saw her later, so she remains on our list for now. Lady Susan was the only one outside, supposedly in the rose garden, alone. And the rose garden is on the same side of the house as the orchard, so she's still a definite possibility."

Penelope pulled a face. "I truly can't see Susan being sufficiently enraged to do the deed. She's too…calculating, and she knows and loves—I would even say is devoted to—Pamela as much as to her own family. The sisters have always been very close. And probably better than anyone else, Susan knows how much Pamela's status relied on Monty's. Susan has a similar marriage—one of that sort of convenience —so her understanding of Pamela's need of Monty is bolstered by her own experience and commensurately deep." She met Stokes's gaze, and her lips twisted. "Even if she was profoundly angry with Monty for vetoing the proposed alliance between Vincent and Samantha, knowing and understanding all that Susan does, would she kill Monty and deprive Pamela of her social crutch?" Penelope shook her head. "I doubt it."

Stokes faintly grimaced. "Be that as it may, we should check where she, Lady Carville, and the three gentlemen were at the time they heard the scream. We didn't specifically ask that during our interviews, and the replies might allow us to find others who can corroborate their story and definitively place them at that moment and, thus, rule them out of contention."

Barnaby nodded. "For instance, Richard says he was on the stairs when he heard Rosalind scream. That's confirmed by the others who saw him run past the library doorway, and subsequently, they followed him to the orchard. For him to have gone outside, killed Monty, and made it back inside in time to come downstairs at that moment…" Barnaby grimaced. "I suppose it's possible, but the timing would be very tight."

"I know we don't believe Richard is the killer," Penelope said, "but to be thorough and rule him out, we should check that he did, indeed, leave letters on the hall table, as he says he did. He said he was upstairs writing those letters, and if they do exist, then…if he hadn't been writing them but, instead, had gone outside and killed Monty, returned to his room, and brought down prewritten letters to serve as proof of what he'd been doing during the critical hour, that suggests a high degree of planning, and we all agree that this murder was a spur-of-the-moment, fueled-by-sudden-fury attack."

Stokes was nodding. "An excellent point. We should follow up with Gearing about those letters."

"We still have a good handful of guests to interview," Barnaby said, "and I agree that our fastest and surest route to identifying the killer lies through proving where everyone was during the crucial hour." He glanced at Penelope. "We might need to interview the staff."

The look she returned wasn't encouraging. "At a large house party, at that time of the morning, the entire indoor staff would have been run off their feet. They would have been scurrying here, there, and everywhere and fully focused on their duties. We'll be very lucky to find anyone who noticed anything useful."

"That leaves us with our as-yet-to-be-interviewed guests." Stokes studied his list. "I make it nine we've yet to speak with, but they're all the younger crew."

Penelope said, "Perhaps we can go faster with them by focusing on the critical times and who they saw where."

Stokes nodded. "That's the information we need. Our murderer has to be unvouched for by anyone else from nine until close to ten o'clock." He looked at Penelope. "And possibly later than that. If your conjecture that he searched the study while everyone else was focused on the orchard is correct, he won't have been among those gathered at the front of the house, either."

Barnaby had been thinking. "If our thesis is that the murderer only discovered that Monty was the blackmailer minutes before the murder—thus accounting for the murderer's eruption of overwhelming rage—then the murderer had no reason to search Monty's study earlier." He tipped his head toward Penelope. "We know the study was searched, we believe by the murderer—the page torn out of Monty's book of victims with the book left for us to find and no money or valuables taken supports that—ergo, the search had to be carried out after the murder. While everyone else was outside."

"And," Penelope stated, "that, despite the risk, the killer seized that very moment to search the study also suggests that he believes Monty has some physical evidence of his secret. Also, the killer's secret, whatever it is, isn't anything so mild as a liaison or cheating at cards, and he's quite desperate to keep it hidden."

Stokes arched a brow at her. "You don't think that in searching the study, the killer was after Monty's black book, intending to erase any mention of him in it, thus covering his tracks for the murder?"

Penelope thought for a moment, then shook her head. "No. The book was hidden. How would the killer know of its existence in order to search for it? He couldn't have known he wasn't Monty's sole victim and that there were others Monty had to keep track of as well, hence the black book." She paused, then shook her head again. "No. I believe the killer was searching for the evidence of his secret that he believes Monty has."

Barnaby had been following her logic. He nodded. "I agree. That's the only explanation that's a good, solid fit. In theory, other explanations for the search might be possible, but none are anywhere near as probable."

"But physical evidence is a difference between the killer and Monty's other victims," Penelope pointed out. "With all the victims we've spoken with, his 'evidence' was purely knowledge of their secret, not anything tangible."

"Those are all excellent points," Stokes said, "and I don't disagree with any of them. But we need to move expeditiously tomorrow and get our final interviews over with as soon as we can. With that as our aim, I believe we need some sort of map showing where everyone was or says they were over the critical hour."

Penelope rose. "Let me fetch pencil and paper, and we can put together all we've thus far learned."

Ten minutes later, as she sat at the parlor table and commenced her latest list, she murmured, "As sure as eggs are eggs, someone is lying, and in this case, there are simply too many people moving around that house for the murderer, albeit by his absence, not to stand out."

CHAPTER 9

*T*he following morning, Penelope led the way up the steps to the Grange's front door with a clear plan for the day fixed in her mind: Interview the remaining nine guests, combine their information with the facts she, Barnaby, and Stokes had already learned, and see who was still unaccounted for. Reinterview as required, then study the final picture that emerged.

She was entirely happy with that plan and confident that, by the end of the day, they would have a very firm idea of who the killer was.

With a determined and enthusiastic smile on her face, flanked by Barnaby and Stokes, she swept into the front hall.

And immediately came to a halt as Gearing, transparently agitated, came hurrying toward them.

"Thank God you're here, Inspector!" Gearing all but gasped. "Grimshaw, Mr. Underhill's valet, has been attacked!"

Stokes stepped forward. "When did this happen?"

"Last evening!" Gearing visibly drew in a deep breath, gathered himself, then more calmly explained, "Grimshaw was set upon yesterday evening, upstairs. He was hit quite viciously and fell unconscious, and he only regained his senses this morning and raised the alarm."

Stokes exchanged a glance with Barnaby and Penelope, then asked Gearing, "Where is Grimshaw?"

"We have him in the kitchen under Cook's eye. He'd gone upstairs yesterday evening because the mistress had asked him to select clothes for laying out the master's body once it's returned to us. Grimshaw went into the master's dressing room, not expecting anyone to be there, and was coshed over the head."

"We'll speak with Grimshaw immediately," Stokes said, "and then we'll need to examine the dressing room."

"Yes, of course." Gearing stepped back, gestured toward the green-baize-covered door at the rear of the hall, and led them in that direction. "I mentioned the assault to your constable when he arrived this morning, and he sent up the constable who'd kept watch in the study overnight to keep an eye on things upstairs."

"Good." Stokes followed at Gearing's heels. "Let's see what Grimshaw can tell us."

As they strode along the narrow corridor beyond the baize-covered door, from his position at the rear of the small procession, Barnaby asked, "Who else have you told of the attack?"

Gearing glanced over his shoulder. "I reported the incident to her ladyship at once, and she suggested it would be best to keep silent about the matter until the inspector was informed."

Stokes grunted in clear approval, and facing forward, Gearing added, "Constable Morgan assured me you would be along shortly, or else I would have sent word."

The corridor ended in a very large kitchen that, to Penelope's eyes, was neat, clean, and efficiently run. At that hour, maids and footmen were ferrying breakfast dishes into the scullery from which emanated sudsy sounds punctuated by the clinking of cutlery and crockery mixed with the clang of pans being scoured.

An older footman was sorting silverware on a bench along one wall, and a pair of kitchen maids were making what Penelope thought was dough for scones, while a younger maid was sieving berries for a sauce. The delicious aroma of baking bread filled the already warm room.

Gearing led them down the long, freshly scrubbed deal table to where, at the far end, a solidly built, middle-aged man sat slumped on a stool, his elbows propped on the table with his bandaged head held between his hands. Behind him was the massive hearth, and the cook stood nearby, polishing a copper bowl while keeping a careful eye on the injured man.

"Grimshaw," Gearing said as they neared. "The inspector and the investigators are here."

Moving carefully, Grimshaw shifted his head enough to look up at them, then he tensed to stand.

"No, no." Penelope waved him back to his stool. "Please remain seated. You're in no condition to stand."

The intervention earned her a grateful look from the cook.

With a pained grimace, Grimshaw complied. "I won't argue with that. My head's still splitting."

Judging from what she could see of the bandage, Penelope concluded he'd taken a powerful blow to the rear of his head.

Stokes sat on the end of the nearest bench so he could see Grimshaw's face without forcing the man to lift his head completely. "Tell us what happened."

Grimshaw moistened his lips, then stated, "Last evening after we'd had our tea, I went to the master's dressing room. Her ladyship had asked me to pick out suitable clothes for... Well, I'd been steeling myself to do it since the morning, when she asked me, so I thought I'd better get it done before I went to bed."

"Is there a door to the dressing room from the corridor?" Penelope asked.

Grimshaw started to nod, then caught his breath and said, "Aye, ma'am. That's the door I used. There's another from the master's bedchamber and, opposite that, a door leading to his bathing chamber, but when he's not in the house, I always use the corridor door."

"To be clear," Barnaby said, "all three doors leading into the dressing room are at the corridor end of the room?"

"Aye. That's right."

Stokes asked, "As near as you can remember, what happened? Walk us through it."

"I went up the main stairs and along the corridor. I opened the door... I paused then, steeling myself. It was the first time I'd been in there since..."

"All right," Stokes said. "And then?"

"I pushed the door fully open, stepped inside, and turned to shut the door. That's when he rushed in and hit me. He came from the bedroom— I'd put my back to that door as I shut the one from the corridor, and the door to the bedroom was open, now I think of it. Shouldn't have been. I usually leave it shut so I can go in and out of the dressing room without disturbing the master." Grimshaw paused, then added, "Can't say as I remember much more."

Barnaby had circled behind Grimshaw enough to visually examine his bandaged head. He winced. "That's a very nasty lump."

"Aye. It was a tremendous blow, I can tell you that."

Stokes looked at Barnaby. "Just the one?"

Barnaby nodded. "Looks like it."

"I only remember one, of course." Grimshaw met Stokes's eyes. "I've been in my share of dust-ups, and I don't normally go out that easily. You learn how thick your skull is from experience, you know?"

When Stokes nodded, Grimshaw went on, "So this time, I tried to cling to my wits, at least long enough to get some sense of who the attacker might be, but the pain was so bad, I couldn't focus, and my wits just slipped away."

"You said 'he,'" Penelope stated. "Are you sure it was a man?"

Grimshaw tipped his head enough to faintly smile at her. "Aye, ma'am. I'm sure. Not many women strong enough to deliver such a hammer blow, and I got the sense—just before he struck me—of a body bigger than mine."

Penelope studied him, then gently asked, "If you can, do you think you could manage to stand? Just for a moment so we can get some idea of how tall you are and how large is bigger than you?"

Grimshaw winced, but gamely placed his palms on the table, and Gearing and the cook rushed in to help him to his feet.

Once he was upright, Stokes, Barnaby, and Penelope studied him. Unlike most valets, many of whom were short, and in keeping with his solid frame, Grimshaw was a touch above average height.

After checking to confirm that Barnaby and Stokes had seen enough, Penelope waved Grimshaw back to the stool. "Thank you, Grimshaw. That will help us identify your attacker."

Stokes glanced at her, then looked at Gearing. "I'm officially advising Grimshaw to rest up and take things easy for the next several days."

"Until his headache eases off, preferably to nothing," Penelope said and received a grateful nod from the cook.

"Not only is that a very nasty knock," Barnaby said, also catching Gearing's eyes, "but we would all feel better if Grimshaw remained with others, including having a footman sleeping on a pallet in his room, until we have your master's murderer—who was almost certainly Grimshaw's attacker—by the heels."

The cook sucked in a breath. "You think the dastard might come after Grimshaw again?"

"It's possible," Stokes said. "He won't know if Grimshaw saw and will remember something that gives us a clue to his identity, and he might well want to be sure." He looked at Grimshaw, who was even paler than he had been before. "So no going about the house by yourself. Stay down here and use the servants' stairs, but even then, keep someone with you all the time. We don't want another murder on our hands."

Penelope looked at Gearing. "I'm sure Lady Pamela will agree."

Gearing and the cook looked at Grimshaw with stern and sober determination. "We'll do as you say, Inspector," Gearing assured them.

Stokes rose from the bench, then paused. "One last question." He caught Grimshaw's gaze. "Do you know what time it was when you went into the dressing room?"

Grimshaw, Gearing, and the cook exchanged glances, then the cook murmured, "Had to be about nine. It was a bit after the tea trolley went out. That, I do know." She looked at Stokes. "That was at eight-thirty."

Gearing nodded. "I delivered the trolley to the ladies in the drawing room and waited to see if Lady Pamela had any further orders for us, then at about a quarter to nine, Grimshaw and I did the rounds of the gentlemen, who were in the billiards room, offering brandy. After that"—he glanced at Grimshaw—"we came out into the hall, and we parted at the foot of the stairs. I came back to the kitchen, and Grimshaw went upstairs."

Grimshaw frowned. "I can't remember if the clocks had struck the hour, but when you live with that happening all the time, you don't really pay attention anymore."

"About nine o'clock is good enough." Stokes finished jotting in his book, looked up, and nodded to Grimshaw. "Thank you. Your information will help."

Penelope nodded kindly to Grimshaw. "Best you get some rest."

Stokes looked at Gearing. "We'll take a look at the dressing room now."

With Penelope, Barnaby followed Stokes and Gearing up the main stairs and along the corridor of the sprawling house's central wing. Gearing led them to where Constable Walsh was standing before a plain door toward the end of the corridor.

"Thank you, Walsh." Stokes nodded to his constable. "You can get back to the inn and your bed."

Walsh had been on guard in the study over much of the night. Plainly relieved, he saluted. "Yes, guv."

With a nod for Barnaby and Penelope, Walsh stepped past them and strode for the stairs.

Gearing had paused before the door. "This is the master's dressing room, and as you'll see, his bedchamber lies to the right and his bathing chamber to the left." Gearing opened the door and stepped back, and Stokes led the way inside.

Barnaby followed Penelope into a typical gentleman's dressing room. Halting behind Penelope and Stokes just inside the room, Barnaby surveyed the scene.

One long wall of the narrow room played host to chests of drawers, while the opposite wall held two wide wardrobes. At the far end of the room, before the single central window, a well-padded gentleman's chair sat to one side with a tall cheval glass angled in the other corner.

Gearing, who had remained in the corridor, shifted. When Barnaby glanced his way, Gearing weakly smiled and confessed, "The staff need to set up for morning tea."

Over her shoulder, Penelope flung him a smiling glance. "No need to stay. We won't be long."

Stokes leaned to look past the door. "We'll return to the library shortly. If you need us again, you'll find us there."

"But please station a footman at the library door, as you did yesterday," Penelope instructed. "That was a great help."

"Of course, ma'am. And thank you. All of you." Gearing bowed and left them and hurried back to the stairs.

Stokes pushed the door to the corridor shut. "Do my eyes deceive me, or has this place been searched?"

Penelope went forward and pulled open a drawer. She looked inside, then shut it. "Thoroughly searched." She pulled out another drawer at random and examined the contents. "There's not that much disturbance, but there's no chance Grimshaw would have left cravats rumpled."

Barnaby went to the open doorway to his right. "The attacker came from here."

Penelope bustled up and past. The curtains in the bedroom were drawn, rendering the chamber gloomy and dark. She went to the window and drew back the heavy damask, revealing a four-poster bed flanked by two small bedside tables. A pair of armchairs stood angled before the hearth at the far end of the room.

She crossed to the nearest bedside table. "I expect he will have searched here as well." She pulled out the single drawer, then huffed and closed it. "He did."

Barnaby walked to a tallboy set against the wall opposite the windows. He glanced inside the top drawers, then checked the lowest. "It appears he's been through every drawer."

Stokes, who had remained in the dressing room, called, "He's even moved the coats and jackets and turned out the pockets."

Penelope returned to the dressing room, and Barnaby followed.

Stokes stood before one open wardrobe. Penelope pointed over his head. "He's even moved the hat and boot boxes and put them back. They're out of alignment."

Stokes looked, then shut the wardrobe doors and turned to Barnaby and Penelope. "What does this tell us?"

Promptly, Penelope replied, "That he—the murderer—is still in the house."

Nodding, Barnaby added, "And that at least to the time he searched in here, he hadn't found what he's after."

"Presumably," Stokes said, "the evidence he believes Underhill held of his misdeeds, whatever they are."

"I think," Penelope said, "that this also reinforces the notion that the murderer hadn't previously known that Monty was his black-mailer. If he'd known that prior to coming to this house party, he could easily have arranged to search the house—all of it—while the family was absent, for instance, when they were recently at Wyndham Castle."

Barnaby nodded. "There would have been only a skeleton staff here—much easier to avoid."

Stokes's features firmed. "You're right. Everything we're seeing fits with our theory that the murderer only learned Underhill was his black-mailer while here, at this house party."

"So," Barnaby said, "sometime since Sunday afternoon, once everyone was here."

Penelope glanced around, then walked to the dressing room door. "Also," she said, opening the door, "the attack on Grimshaw is proof positive that we're not dealing with the actions of a passing vagrant, demented or not."

Barnaby and Stokes shared a cynically amused glance, then followed Penelope into the corridor.

~

With Barnaby and Stokes, Penelope descended the stairs to the front hall to find Richard and Rosalind waiting.

As Penelope stepped off the stairs, Rosalind glanced up the flight. "What's going on?"

Penelope looked at Stokes. He met her gaze, then Barnaby's, before turning to Richard and Rosalind and waving the pair toward the library. "Come and join us, and let's see what we can make of our latest developments."

Richard and Rosalind looked eager, and soon, the five of them were settled in the armchairs at the far end of the library, well away from the door and any sharp ears.

Stokes regarded Richard and Rosalind. "You're both sensible enough not to panic, so it's better you know that the murderer—whoever he is—is still among the company here."

Penelope clarified, "He's almost certainly one of the guests."

"And also almost certainly," Barnaby added, "one of Monty's victims."

Rosalind darted a glance at Richard, then, pressing her palms together in her lap, stated, "I want to help. If that's possible." She met each of the investigators' eyes. "I believe it's uncontestable that until the murderer is identified and exposed, Regina—and her future—will remain under a cloud."

Penelope saw no grounds on which to argue. "Perhaps..." She glanced at Barnaby and Stokes. When both nodded, she returned her gaze to Rosalind and Richard. "The pair of you are perfectly placed to watch and listen to the other guests. In particular, if you could keep your ears open for any mentions of where people were when the murder was committed—say between a quarter of an hour after nine o'clock and ten or so minutes before ten. We're asking them that, of course, but what they tell us and then reveal to others might not always be exactly the same."

Richard was nodding. To Rosalind, he remarked, "Everyone remembers where they were at the moment when some shocking event occurred."

"Also take note of any unexpected behavior," Barnaby said.

"And most importantly," Stokes stressed, "tell us the instant you hear or see anything odd."

Her expression stern, Penelope instructed, "Find us, wherever we are. Don't dally."

Rosalind and Richard regarded her with faint surprise, but then both saw that Barnaby and Stokes were equally serious, and their demeanors grew more solemn.

Tight-lipped, Richard nodded. "If we learn anything, we'll bring it to you immediately."

"Good," Stokes said. "Whoever this murderer is, they and the threat they pose are not to be taken lightly."

With nods confirming their understanding, Richard and Rosalind rose.

"The rest of the guests are presently taking their ease on the rear lawn." Rosalind glanced at Richard. "That's as good a place to start as any."

Richard agreed, and the pair left the investigators to their day and quit the library.

As the door shut, Penelope drew out her list of guests. She scanned it, then looked at Barnaby and Stokes. "Best we get to it. We only have the younger crew to get through, and as none were Monty's victims, with any luck, interviewing the lot won't take too long."

Barnaby rose and headed for the door. "Who's first?"

"Mr. Angus Carrington," Penelope replied.

After dispatching the waiting footman to fetch Carrington, Barnaby returned to the cluster of armchairs.

Looking at Stokes, Penelope said, "Carrington is about thirty. He's a perfectly eligible bachelor who hasn't yet shown any signs of wanting to alter his marital state."

One black brow arching, Stokes said, "I presume that's why he was invited. To nudge him into taking action."

Penelope nodded. "That would have been the intention."

When Carrington presented himself, Barnaby could find nothing about the amiable, urbane, well-dressed man to contradict Penelope's insight. Carrington settled in the central armchair and exuded an air of being completely relaxed regarding his present situation and a trifle curious as to how the investigation was proceeding.

In response to Barnaby's initial question, Carrington replied, "I drove down with Morehouse. His leader had gone lame the day before, and I was happy to have the company. We arrived at about five o'clock on Sunday." With a disarming smile, Carrington glanced at Penelope and added, "I'm supposed to be casting my eye over the available young ladies with a view to seeing if any strikes me as a potential bride, but in truth, I'm in no hurry to marry."

Mildly, Stokes asked Carrington to describe his movements on Monday morning.

"I came down to breakfast with Morehouse at just after seven o'clock. We joined Percival at the table, and soon after, Cordingley, then Elliot, joined us. After a companionable time spent downing our coffee, bacon, and eggs, the five of us quit the table."

"When was that?" Stokes asked.

Carrington screwed up his face in thought. "Not long after seven-thirty? Something like that." Without prompting, he added, "Percival and Cordingley went upstairs, and Morehouse, Elliot, and I headed for the library. Leith was already there, flicking through the news sheets, but he left soon after we arrived—said he had some letters to write."

"And for the hour before ten o'clock?" Barnaby asked.

"We three—Morehouse, Elliot, and I—remained in the library, reading and chatting about stories in the news sheets. Griffith looked in, but then went out again, and Morland and Wincombe turned up at some point and remained, like us, scanning the news sheets."

"While you were in the library," Stokes asked, "did you notice anyone outside or see anyone leave the house?"

Carrington paused, then said, "Well, there was Monty, of course. He came in after we'd been there for a time and chatted and asked if we had everything we needed—just being a good host—then he mentioned going for an amble outside to check on something to do with the estate. And off he went."

"Did any of the four gentlemen who were in the library with you leave and return at any point?" Penelope asked.

Carrington shook his head. "No. We were all quite settled until we heard the scream."

"What happened then?" Barnaby asked.

"We heard someone—it proved to be Percival—leap down the last stairs and race out, past the library doorway and out through the open front door. We five looked at each other—we were rather startled. We'd all been deep in the news sheets at the time. But then, we set them aside, leapt up, and rushed after Percival. When we got outside, we saw him running across the lawn toward the orchard—toward where Miss Hemmings was calling for help—so we followed him."

Barnaby glanced at Stokes, who nodded, and Barnaby returned his gaze to Carrington. "What was your view of Monty Underhill?"

Carrington shrugged. "Genial chap. Good host. Older generation, of course, but not stuffy or disapproving. Very easygoing fellow. Truth to tell, I've never heard anyone say a bad word about him."

"Do you have any idea why anyone might have wanted to kill him?" Barnaby asked.

Carrington pursed his lips and shook his head. "Damned strange, that. I have no idea what he might have done to provoke such an attack. Quite shocking in its unexpectedness, you know?"

Barnaby inclined his head, then thanked Carrington for his assistance. After showing the younger man out, Barnaby returned to the armchairs.

Penelope looked up. "We've heard exactly the same story from all the gentlemen in the library."

Barnaby nodded. "Next?"

Penelope looked at her list and sighed. "As much as our remaining interviewees are unlikely to reveal anything of note, I suppose we have to put them through their paces."

Stokes nodded resignedly. "We do, for appearances if nothing else, and especially as, as yet, we have no threads to tug on to unravel the mystery surrounding this killer."

"And who knows?" With a slight smile, Barnaby said, "By now, we ought to have learned that critical clues often come from the most unlikely sources."

Penelope arched her brows. "I doubt we'll get much from Alison Waterhouse, but she's next."

While the footman fetched Miss Waterhouse, Penelope informed Barnaby and Stokes, "Alison is generally viewed as a pleasant young lady who happens to be a very close friend of Cecilia Underhill. Alison is considered to have an…ameliorating effect on Cecilia's less socially acceptable tendencies. By which I mean Cecilia's propensity to sulk or to be overweeningly arrogant. Alison is in her early twenties and expected to make a good match quite soon. To date, she's been biding her time, considering her options, and has been careful to give no indication of partiality for any particular gentleman. However, she is well-regarded and well-connected, so her parents will have high hopes."

When the door opened and Miss Waterhouse walked tentatively into the room, Penelope rose, greeted the younger lady with a smile, and directed her to the interviewee's armchair.

Of average height, Alison had blue eyes and glossy brown ringlets, and her features were quietly attractive, and her figure was sufficiently curvaceous to draw male eyes. However, at present, she appeared somber and subdued, a circumstance she immediately explained.

As she sank onto the cushions, her gaze on Penelope, she murmured, "I doubt I can help your investigation, but I'm happy to do whatever I can to assist in finding whoever did this to poor Mr. Underhill. Cecilia and her mother are so upset—I suppose we all are, albeit to a lesser extent."

The level-headed tone of that observation reassured Penelope; Alison seemed the sort of young lady who could be relied on to behave in a steady, sensible manner. Penelope duly embarked on their standard questions, and Alison responded not only with transparent candor but also with a conciseness and clarity that sped matters along.

"We drove from London in our carriage and arrived on Sunday afternoon. I was looking forward to spending a pleasant week with Cecilia—it's so much quieter and less hectic here than in town." Alison colored faintly and met Penelope's eyes. "As I'm sure you realize, Cecilia and I were also hoping to spend a little time getting to know some of the bachelors attending."

Penelope smiled understandingly. "Naturally. Now, on Monday morning, when did you come downstairs?"

Alison's reply confirmed her mother's account—they'd come downstairs just after hearing other ladies go down at soon after eight o'clock and had joined Lady Pamela, Lady Susan, Cecilia, and the Goodrich girls at the table. Alison added, "Many of the gentlemen had already left or were on the point of leaving."

"And after breakfast?" Penelope asked.

"The four of us—Cecilia, Enid, Samantha, and I—went to the conservatory, but Lady Carville was already there, looking at the orchids. So we went on to the music room—it's a little farther along that wing." Alison blushed slightly and admitted, "We wanted our discussion to remain private, you see."

"Of course." Penelope could imagine. "Now, while in the music room, did you see anyone outside or notice anyone leaving the house?"

A faint frown furrowed Alison's fine brown brows. "A little after we settled in the music room, I saw Lady Wincombe set off across the rear lawn."

Realizing from Alison's curious gaze that she was now wondering whether that had any connection to the murder, Penelope smiled reassuringly. "Thank you. That confirms Lady Wincombe's account. Now, I gather you've known Mr. Underhill for some years."

Alison nodded. "For as long as I've known Cecilia, really."

"How would you describe him?" Penelope asked.

Alison's face clouded. "He was a very nice man. Always jovial and comforting, but never in a way that made one uncomfortable."

Penelope nodded. "And do you know of any reason why anyone might have wanted to kill him?"

"No." Alison's features firmed. "None. And it's been thoroughly upsetting and shocking to know that someone—with no reason—just up and killed him in such a terrible way."

Penelope resisted the impulse to correct the assumption that there had been no reason—no motive—behind the killing.

As if knowing she was biting her tongue, Barnaby smiled and smoothly thanked Alison, and Stokes added a rumbling expression of gratitude, then Penelope rose and, in kindly fashion, showed Alison from the room.

After instructing the footman to find and deliver Mr. Morehouse, Penelope returned to the armchairs and nodded at Barnaby. "Your turn."

As the younger gentlemen were more than seven years his junior, Barnaby had little prior knowledge of them to share. He greeted Morehouse and directed him to the central chair. As Barnaby resumed his seat and Morehouse settled in the large armchair, Barnaby saw a gentleman very much of the same ilk as Morehouse's friend, Carrington. Around thirty years old, with straight dark-brown hair, brown eyes, even features, and a pale complexion, Morehouse, like Carrington, was sufficiently handsome to pass muster yet not striking enough to stand out from the crowd. Yet from the quality of his clothes and the ease with which he wore them, he was plainly one of the rather large number of well-heeled eligible bachelors currently gracing the ton.

Morehouse fixed an inquiring gaze on Barnaby, polite yet faintly curious. He projected a genial, likeable persona, appearing relaxed and confident without being arrogant. It wasn't difficult to understand why Lady Pamela had invited Morehouse and Carrington. Both were personable, unexceptionable bachelors who just might be tempted into marriage.

Barnaby commenced with the first of their standard questions, and Morehouse confirmed what Carrington had told them regarding their arrival and the reason for their inclusion on the guest list. "Although I do assure you," Morehouse added with a swift glance at Penelope, "that I'm in no hurry to tie any knot."

His account of his Monday-morning activities tallied with Carrington's, including seeing Richard and Cordingley go upstairs after they'd quit the dining room. When asked if, while in the library, he'd noticed anyone leave the house, Morehouse replied, "Well, Underhill said he was going out, but of course, I didn't actually see him go through the front door, although he did turn in that direction." Morehouse paused, then added, "I was sitting facing the open doorway, and for what it's worth, I didn't see anyone else but Monty head toward the front door. Not until Miss Hemmings screamed and Percival raced past."

"What was your view of Underhill?" Barnaby asked and found he was actually interested in hearing the answer. Morehouse seemed to have a sound head on his shoulders.

"Lovely old chap," Morehouse declared. "Easygoing, which, I can tell you, not all of his age are. He seemed...genuinely interested in life. In the people and society around him."

"Are you aware of any reason why someone might have wanted to kill him?"

Morehouse frowned. "No. None." He met Barnaby's eyes. "And in all honesty, that's rather disturbing."

Barnaby nodded in understanding, then rose, thanked Morehouse, and showed him out.

"Miss Cranton, please," Penelope called, and Barnaby relayed the request to the footman.

Before that young lady arrived, Penelope shared her observations of Harriet Cranton. "I've seen her at events in London, and she appears a quiet, rather reserved, slightly nervous young lady. The latter is likely an outcome of her having lost her parents a few years ago and being Lady Wincombe's niece and ward and, consequently, not wanting to do anything that might reflect poorly on her aunt and uncle. She seems wary of putting a foot wrong, so to speak. All that, however, suggests that she might well be more observant and aware than the other young ladies here."

Shortly after that, Miss Cranton arrived. A slim young lady with neat brown hair and blue eyes, with wary politeness, she nodded in response to Penelope's greeting and almost gingerly sat in the interviewee's chair. As Penelope embarked on their questions, her reading of Harriet seemed borne out. When asked what she hoped to achieve during the house party, Harriet softly but straightforwardly explained, "I expected to spend time with Cecilia, Alison, and the Goodrich girls. We're all part of the same group—Cecilia, Alison, and I made our come-outs together."

"I see." Recalling that neither Cecilia nor Alison had mentioned Harriet as being one of the group who'd taken refuge in the music room, Penelope skipped asking when Harriet had come downstairs and leapt ahead to the question, "So when the ladies left the dining room…"

"I went with the other young ladies to the conservatory, but we saw Lady Carville already there, so the others made for the music room. But I'd come down with a nagging headache, and I decided to rest quietly for a while. Everyone was planning to go for a ramble later—well, all the younger people—and I didn't want to miss that. So I went upstairs to my room."

Her gaze on Harriet's face, Penelope tipped her head. "So were you in your room over the whole hour from nine to ten o'clock?"

Harriet's lips thinned fractionally, and she shook her head. "I was at first, lying on the bed, but after a time, I heard Aunt Georgie next door. I decided I felt better, so when I heard her go back downstairs, I decided to go down, too. I was going to join the group in the music room, but I saw Aunt Georgie ahead of me, going down the stairs. I expected her to go to the morning room, which was where the other matrons were, but instead, she took the hall to the door to the rear terrace. I…wasn't sure what she was doing, and I just followed, and I saw her go down the steps to the lawn and stride off toward the croquet green." Harriet colored and shot a glance at Penelope. "I don't know why, but I went out onto the terrace and waited for her to come back."

Did she suspect something? Or was this the reaction of a young girl who'd had parents go away and not come back?

Penelope studied Harriet, then inclined her head. "I see. While you were out on the terrace, or even earlier when you were upstairs or moving through the house, did you see anyone outside?"

"Well," Harriet said, "I went out, as I said, and Aunt Georgie was ahead of me. Other than that, I didn't see anyone else outside, and Aunt Georgie was only away for ten or perhaps fifteen minutes at most. I was there, on the terrace, when she came walking back. She was nearing the terrace steps when we heard Rosalind scream for help."

"Thank you. That's most helpful." Penelope noted that Harriet's account tallied with her aunt's and also those of the other girls. "Now, how did you find Mr. Underhill?"

Harriet's expression suggested she found the question easy to answer. "All the young ladies found him pleasant and comforting. He was always reassuring and…well, kind."

She looked at Penelope in patent confusion. "Why would anyone want to kill him?"

Penelope lightly grimaced. "That was my next question to you. I take it you have no idea?"

Vehemently, Harriet shook her head. "None at all. It seems quite incomprehensible. He was such a kind man."

Penelope thanked Harriet, rose, and showed her to the door. Before returning, she sent the footman to summon Mr. James Patterson.

Resuming her seat, Penelope said, "I gather Patterson is a good friend of Vincent's, which I expect is why he's here. Along with Andrew Fentiman. Compared to the other bachelors present, Patterson, Fentiman, and indeed, Vincent are not in the same league of eligibility, primarily because of their age. The trio are about twenty-six years old and, in the grandes dames' eyes, not yet up to scratch."

Barnaby nodded, then rose to greet Patterson and steer him to the central armchair.

Patterson was of average height and build, well-dressed, albeit a trifle flashily, as was the current fashion among gentlemen his age. He had brown hair, brown eyes, and features regular enough and pleasant enough to render him attractive.

Once Patterson had settled, Barnaby started with their regular first question.

Patterson replied readily, with an open, honest air. "I drove down with Fentiman, and we arrived at the Grange late on Sunday afternoon." With the faintest of smiles, he added, "We've visited before, quite often, actually, and knew not to be late and risk the wrath of Lady Pamela."

In response to the question of why he was at the Grange, Patterson said, "Fentiman and I are here purely to spend time with Vincent. None of the three of us are hunting for a bride—not yet—so we were looking forward to simply relaxing and having a jolly time." Without prompting, Patterson continued, "The three of us are sharing Vincent's room—it's huge—so we came down to breakfast together at about half past seven. We wanted to be done before the ladies arrived with all their chatter—it's a bit much, first thing, you know?" Apparently only then remembering

Penelope was there, sitting on Barnaby's right, Patterson threw her an apologetic glance as if hoping he hadn't offended her and rattled on, "When the ladies arrived en masse, we left and took refuge on the terrace. We smoked cheroots and chatted about this and that, then Vincent suggested we take a look at his new gelding and the latest litter of pups in the kennels, so we headed over there. To the stable and the kennels. They're across the rear lawn and through that band of trees bordering it."

Barnaby sensed both Penelope and Stokes, seated on either side of him, come alert. He clarified, "So between nine and ten o'clock, you—and Vincent and Fentiman—were outside at the stable and kennels?"

Compared with what the investigators had seen thus far of Vincent, Patterson's direct answers and straightforward manner cast him as more grounded and sensible than the son of the house. "Yes. We were on our way back for the proposed ramble when we heard the scream for help."

Stokes stirred. "Did you notice anyone else—any of the company—who were outside the house during that time? Between nine and ten?"

Patterson paused, then, faintly frowning, said, "I think one of the gentlemen—I assume it was one of the guests—was walking into the woods to the east, beyond the side door. I just caught a glimpse through the trees. I couldn't tell you who he was…" Patterson's eyes widened on Stokes. "Could that have been the vagrant who killed Vincent's pater?"

Flatly, Stokes returned, "We seriously doubt that."

Penelope leaned forward, drawing Patterson's attention. "But you are sure there was someone there? Some man?"

Patterson took a moment to consult his memory, then he refocused on Penelope and, his jaw firming, nodded. "Yes. There was definitely someone there. I would swear to that."

Glancing up from his notebook, Stokes asked, "When was this?"

"When we were on our way to the stable and kennels."

"Which was about what time?" Stokes asked.

Patterson thought, then grimaced. "I really can't say with any exactitude, but somewhere between eight-thirty and nine."

Barnaby exchanged a meaning-laden glance with Stokes and Penelope, then returned his attention to Patterson. "What was your view of Mr. Underhill?"

Patterson's expression sobered, then he shrugged lightly. "He was Vincent's father and a surprisingly good sort. Always encouraging and jolly."

When Patterson offered nothing more, Stokes asked, "Do you know of any reason why anyone would want to kill Mr. Underhill?"

"No. None." Plainly puzzled, Patterson added, "It seems deuced odd. He was such an easygoing chap that it's hard to see why anyone would want to murder him."

After glancing briefly at Penelope and Stokes, Barnaby thanked Patterson, rose, and showed him out. On returning to the armchairs, he rested his hands on the back of the central chair and looked at Penelope and Stokes. "Do we press on or…?"

Penelope glanced at the clock on the mantelpiece, which showed it was nearly eleven o'clock. "Tea," she declared. "I need tea and sustenance if I'm not to develop a headache."

When Stokes grunted in agreement, Barnaby smiled and returned to the door to request the footman to fetch some tea.

Within minutes, Gearing arrived, bearing a well-stocked tray. Given the speed, it was clear he'd anticipated their need. After seeing the plates set out and confirming that they required nothing more, he left them to imbibe and consume in peace.

For several minutes, they did just that, then Penelope settled back, sipped, and observed, "That was the first mention of someone whose identity we don't yet know being outside the house."

"And whoever he was," Barnaby pointed out, "he was leaving, presumably having exited via the side door at, say, eight forty-five. Time enough to circle around to the orchard and meet Monty there."

Stokes reached for another slice of cake. "Other than those three, no other guests were in that area at that particular time. Lady Susan, Rosalind, Regina, and Lady Wincombe all went out later and via the terrace, not the side door."

Barnaby nodded. "So Patterson, Fentiman, and Vincent are the only ones likely to have seen the mystery man leave the house. There was no one else on that side of the house until later."

Penelope set down her empty cup. "We need to learn what Fentiman and Vincent saw. Luckily, we're almost at the end of our interview list, and they're two of the four remaining." She met Barnaby and Stokes's gazes with renewed determination. "So let's get to it."

Stokes sighed and leaned forward to place his cup on the tray. "At least there are only four left. My pencil is worn to a nub."

Barnaby grinned. He stood, picked up the tray, and arched a brow at Penelope. "Who's next?"

She consulted her list, and armed with the name, Barnaby crossed to the door, handed the tray to Gearing, who had been about to enter, and asked for Miss Enid Goodrich to be summoned.

Before Enid arrived, Penelope filled in Barnaby and Stokes with what little she knew of the elder Goodrich girl. "She's plain and suffers from the same unattractive disposition as her mother and her aunt. Given her age, she's definitely actively seeking an offer, which is why she's here, hoping to capture and fix the attention of one of the eligible gentlemen present."

The door opened, and summoning a reassuring smile, Penelope rose and went to greet Enid, who, plainly hesitant, entered exceedingly tentatively.

With a slightly dumpy figure and rather horsey features, Enid was blessed with glossy dark-auburn hair—her redeeming attribute. Her complexion was pale, which showed her hazel eyes to good effect. Penelope felt Enid would do rather better for herself if she would only add a little vibrancy and vitality to her expression. Instead, she seemed intent on clinging to sullen impassivity.

Once she had the girl installed in the central chair, Penelope resumed her seat, noting as she did that Enid fixed her gaze tightly on Penelope, ignoring Barnaby and Stokes.

Enid was definitely not as composed as Cecilia or Alison or even Harriet. She fidgeted, but then Penelope caught a gleam of surprisingly avid curiosity in Enid's slightly protuberant eyes, suggesting a deep vein of morbid inquisitiveness.

Deciding that taking charge was the only way to deal with an interviewee as flighty and sensation-seeking as Enid, in a direct and no-nonsense manner, Penelope asked, "When did you arrive at the Grange?"

"I came with Mama and my sister in our carriage. That was on Saturday. We came early to spend some private time with Aunt Pamela and Cecilia."

"And you're at the house party because...?"

Enid blinked. "Well, because we were invited, of course."

"Let me rephrase," Penelope said. "Is there a purpose behind your visit? Do you hope to achieve anything while here?"

Enid stared, then moistened her lips and cast an uncertain glance at Barnaby and Stokes, both of whom attempted to look uninterested in the proceedings. "Ah." She returned her slightly goggle-eyed gaze to Penelope. "Well, I'm supposed to be getting to know Mr. Cordingley. Or Mr.

Carrington or Mr. Morehouse. Mama told me one of those three would suit, and I should concentrate my efforts there."

Penelope inclined her head. "Your mother is a sensible lady. Now, on Monday morning, when did you come downstairs?"

"I came down with Mama, Samantha, and several other ladies, and we went in to breakfast. That would have been at just after eight o'clock—we always come down about then."

"And after breakfast?"

"I went with Cecilia and the other younger ladies to the conservatory, but we didn't stay there and, instead, moved on to the music room."

"So between nine and ten o'clock?"

"We were in the music room, chatting and telling tales and laughing."

"While in the music room, did you notice if anyone left the house?'

"No." Enid looked surprised to have been asked. "But I wasn't looking outside, and I had my back to the windows."

Penelope nodded and changed tacks. "You've known Mr. Underhill—your uncle Monty—all your life. How did you see him?"

Enid's eyes clouded with genuine emotion, and her features wavered. "He was a nice uncle—I liked him, and I'm quite upset that someone has killed him."

Penelope was struck by the strong resemblance between Enid, her mother, and her aunt in the stubborn jut of a squarish chin in an attempt to hold back her feelings.

Penelope hesitated, but on the off chance Enid knew something relevant, asked, "Do you know of any reason why someone would have wanted to kill your uncle?"

Enid blinked again. "No, but then, I suppose a passing itinerant or a gypsy doesn't need a reason, do they?"

The sudden avid interest in Enid's gaze as it locked on Penelope's face had her crisply replying, "Thank you, Enid. That will be all."

Enid looked surprised, indeed, taken aback. Then, she darted a glance at Barnaby and Stokes as if expecting them to question her. When neither said anything—Stokes busy with his notebook and Barnaby looking supremely bored—Enid's lips tightened. "Oh, all right."

She rose almost grumpily as Penelope got to her feet, and briskly, Penelope showed her to the door.

Closing the door behind Enid, Penelope glanced back at Stokes and Barnaby, her expression signifying they'd just had a lucky escape, then she opened the door and sent the footman to fetch Mr. Fentiman.

Three minutes later, Barnaby sensed rising eagerness in his coinvesti-gators when the door opened, and he rose to welcome Fentiman. While they'd waited for the young gentleman to appear, Penelope had informed him and Stokes that she knew little more of the young man than she'd already imparted, other than that he hailed from a good family whose holdings lay in Norfolk.

Fentiman had dark-brown hair, bright brown eyes, and an engaging demeanor. Of similar build to Patterson, he was, perhaps, a fraction taller. Nevertheless, he and Patterson—as well as Vincent—were plainly cut from the same cloth. Aside from all else, the three obviously shared the same tailor.

After steering Fentiman to the central armchair, Barnaby sank into the chair directly opposite and briefly considered the younger man. Fentiman appeared willing to be helpful—even eager—yet there was a hint of wari-ness and caution, as if he was worried about saying the wrong thing or, perhaps, revealing too much.

Instead of embarking on their customary questions, thinking to reas-sure Fentiman, Barnaby opened by asking, "How did you come to know Vincent and the Underhills?"

Fentiman visibly relaxed. "Vincent and I—and Patterson—met at Eton. We were in the same form and, well, it's safe to say none of us were teachers' pets, not being all that skilled at the books. That said, we're not dunces, either, as we all ended up at Oxford. At Balliol."

"I see. And you drove down with Patterson?"

Fentiman nodded. "We lodge together in London—with Vincent, too, when he's not here—and we arrived latish on Sunday afternoon." Fentiman grinned. "We're always happy to support each other through these sorts of events." Then he sobered. "Just as well, as things have turned out."

"So you're here purely in support of Vincent?" Penelope gently inquired.

Fentiman looked at her in faint horror. "Lord, yes! None of us are ready to even think about a wife."

Barnaby could see the smile Penelope struggled to hide and, drawing Fentiman's gaze, asked, "What are your recollections of Monday morn-ing? From the time you came downstairs."

Fentiman's account matched Patterson's in every respect. He concluded, "We'd just started on our way back when we heard the scream."

Keeping a tight rein on his hope, Barnaby mildly asked, "Did you see any of the company outside the house while you were going back and forth to the stable and kennels?"

"Yes." Fentiman's answer was quite definite. "There was a man walking through the wood. Judging by his coat, he—whoever he was— was likely a gentleman. He was definitely not any itinerant or passing vagrant. He was striding along quite purposefully, not skulking about." Fentiman grimaced. "That said, I only caught a glimpse. I couldn't tell you who he was."

Leaning forward, Penelope clarified, "This was while you were on your way to the stable."

Fentiman shook his head. "No. I know Patterson thinks he saw a man walking away from the house, out past the side door, while we were crossing the lawn on our way to the stable, but I didn't see anyone then. That said, I wasn't looking that way." He drew breath and went on, "The man I saw was, at first, striding through the wood toward the house, toward the side door, quite intently, as I said. But then he paused and… sort of loitered in the trees. He shifted, and I couldn't see him after that, but this was after we'd heard the scream and were pelting back toward the house. We hadn't reached the lawn and couldn't see the rear terrace yet, but we could see across the lawn to that section of the wood, and I swear I saw someone—this man—there. And he was heading toward the house, not away."

Caught in his memory of the moment, Fentiman added, "Initially, I thought it might be one of the gardeners, but his coat was far too well-cut. And I would think most gardeners or any estate workers would have come running after hearing that scream."

Barnaby exchanged glances with Penelope and Stokes, then asked, "What was your view of Vincent's father? You must have interacted with him a fair bit over the years."

Fentiman nodded. "He was a good sort. I always thought Vincent was lucky to have such an easygoing—even indulgent—pater, but it's always different when it's not one's own parent, isn't it?"

"Do you know of any reason why anyone would want to kill Mr. Underhill?" Stokes asked.

Fentiman frowned. "None at all. It seems rather strange. As far as I've ever heard, Mr. Underhill was universally well thought of."

Barnaby arched his brows at Penelope, but she shook her head, as did Stokes; they had no further questions.

Returning his gaze to Fentiman, Barnaby smiled. "Thank you for your assistance." He rose, as did Fentiman, and Barnaby showed the young man out.

When he returned to the armchairs, Penelope was leaning toward Stokes, plainly eager to discuss what they'd heard.

Barnaby halted behind the interviewee's chair and widened his eyes at his coinvestigators. "Well, that's a new and potentially revealing part of the puzzle."

"If," Penelope said, "we credit both Patterson and Fentiman's accounts—and there's no logical reason we should discount either—then someone, most likely a gentleman and therefore most likely a guest, left the house via the side door at somewhere between eight-thirty and nine o'clock, *before* Monty was killed, and someone, and surely that has to be the same gentleman, returned through the woods to the side door *after* Rosalind found Monty dead in the orchard."

Stokes was madly flicking through his notebook. "We need to work out who was where and which of the guests our mystery gentleman could have been."

Penelope straightened. "We have two more to interview. While I'm inclined to say let's leave them aside and forge on with what we've recently learned, given we didn't expect to get anything useful from the younger crew—"

"We'd be wise not to dismiss any potential gift horses before we even examine them," Stokes stated unequivocally.

Barnaby nodded. "A tortured analogy, but I agree. Let's get the last two in and done, then see what we have." He looked at Penelope. "I've lost count. Who's second last on our list?"

She told him, and Barnaby returned to the door and dispatched the footman to fetch Miss Samantha Goodrich.

As Barnaby returned to the armchairs, Penelope said, "Samantha is Susan's younger daughter. I don't think she's twenty yet. Her reputation paints her as very young, flighty, and somewhat silly. However, from the few occasions on which I've encountered her, while the young, silly, and flighty might, indeed, be true, I would say she's also highly observant and wide awake to everything that goes on around her."

"So"—Stokes looked hopeful—"we might be pleasantly surprised?"

Rather primly, Penelope replied, "We can hope."

She rose as the door opened, and Samantha walked confidently in. The wide-eyed blue gaze that scanned the three investigators as the men politely got to their feet testified to the accuracy of Penelope's observations.

To Penelope's eyes, Samantha was like a curious bird, eager to find a worm.

She was very young, with a figure that had yet to fully blossom, and her brown hair was put up in a simple knot. Her features were less aggressive than her sister's and mother's, and her attitude as she readily took the chair to which Penelope waved her was distinctly sunnier.

Firmly, Penelope took Samantha through their opening questions, eliciting answers that mirrored her mother's and sister's. Asked to divulge her reason for attending the party, Samantha smiled and, in a light, melodic voice, assured Penelope, "I'm too young to be bothered with anything other than enjoying myself and watching everyone else having to go through the awkwardness of learning about each other."

Having herself been the youngest of four sisters, Penelope comprehensively understood and, indeed, sympathized. Aware that Stokes preferred to keep the questions rolling in their agreed order, she led Samantha through her movements on Monday morning, to the point of leaving the dining room with the other young ladies.

"We went to the conservatory—it's brighter there, and we wanted to sit in the sunshine and chat—but Lady Carville was already there, admiring Aunt Pamela's orchids, so instead, we went to the music room and settled there."

"And you and the others remained there until you heard Rosalind scream?"

"Yes. We'd been chatting and laughing. Well," Samantha confided, "I was mostly just listening while the others compared notes on the eligibles here."

"While you were in the music room, did you notice anyone outside?"

"As a matter of fact, I did." A puzzled frown tangling her brows, Samantha went on, "As we were leaving the music room, after we heard the scream and decided we'd better find out what had happened, I forgot my handkerchief. I'd left it on the chair, but when I got to the door, I remembered and ran back to pick it up. As I bent to get it, through the side window, I saw a gentleman striding toward the house. He was in the wood, and I thought he must have heard the scream, too, and was coming back to find out what had happened."

Holding her breath, hope welling, Penelope asked, "Could you see which gentleman it was?"

But Samantha shook her head. "It was all shadowy under the trees. I couldn't see his face clearly."

"But you're sure he was a gentleman?" Barnaby pressed.

"Oh yes." Samantha's tone rang with confidence. "He wasn't a vagrant or a gypsy or anyone like that. His coat was far too well-tailored. And there's a certain way a gentleman strides along, if you know what I mean?"

Penelope nodded. "Indeed." She exchanged a swift glance with Barnaby and Stokes. It now seemed incontestable that one of the gentlemen was returning to the house when Rosalind screamed.

"Just a few more questions." Penelope returned her gaze to Samantha. "You've known your uncle Monty all your life. What did you think of him? How did you see him and find him?"

Samantha's lower lip trembled, and suddenly, she looked much younger. She blinked her large blue eyes, now shining with unshed tears, then drew in a tight breath, tipped up her chin, and gamely replied, "He was a lovely uncle, and I'm very sad he's gone." Her eyes sparked, and her lips and chin firmed. "And I'm not at all in charity with whoever killed him."

Penelope seized the opening to ask, "Do you know of any reason why anyone would want to kill him?"

Samantha's frown was patently genuine. "No. None. He was a good, kind man, and it seems so strange that anyone would think to even hurt him."

Penelope glanced at Barnaby and Stokes, then rose. "Thank you, Samantha." As the younger woman got to her feet, Penelope assured her, "You've been a very real help."

The words pleased Samantha. With a polite nod to Stokes and Barnaby, she followed Penelope to the door.

After Penelope dispatched the footman to find and deliver Vincent to them and she returned to sink into the chair beside Barnaby, he observed, "Well, it seems that, finally, matters are growing a little clearer."

His tone hard, Stokes repeated, "We can hope." He glanced toward the door. "Let's speak with our last interviewee and see where we end up."

The instant Vincent Underhill walked into the room, Barnaby, rising to greet him, saw that the young man was much more somber than he'd previously been. His dark gaze held a bleakness it hadn't before. Clearly, the reality of his father's death had started to sink in.

As Vincent took the chair Barnaby indicated and nodded soberly to each of them, it seemed that Vincent was evolving—maturing—before their very eyes, as if the weight of his inheritance falling squarely on his shoulders was forcing him to change and grow.

Added to that, sorrow had scored new lines in his face. His feelings over losing his father, and in such a way, could not be doubted.

"We'll try to make this as quick as we can," Barnaby said, "but we're asking everyone the same questions. First, when did you arrive at the Grange, and what did you hope to take away from the house party?"

Vincent faintly grimaced. "I live here some of the time. When I'm not in town. I came down with the rest of the family—that was just over two weeks ago, after we'd been visiting at Wyndham. As for what I hoped to gain from the week, it was simply to spend time with my friends—Patterson and Fentiman." His next grimace was stronger. "It doesn't do to try to skive off—Mama won't stand for it—so I have to be here." He shrugged. "Best I could make of it was to invite Patterson and Fentiman to join me. At least I have good company."

Barnaby nodded understandingly. "On Monday morning, when did you come downstairs?"

"We three left my room at just on seven-thirty. We were rushing to beat Mama and all the females and their noise. Then…" Delivered in a low monotone, his account matched Fentiman's and Patterson's exactly.

"What time did you head off for the stable and kennels?" Stokes asked.

Vincent frowned. "I really can't say. It would have been after eight-thirty, I think—say five or ten minutes after that."

"And between nine and ten o'clock?" Barnaby gently probed.

"We went to the stable first, then after we'd looked over my new gelding, we went on to the kennels. We left there—it must have been going on for ten by then—thinking to get back in time for the ramble that someone had suggested. We'd left the kennels and were on the path that cuts through the trees and leads to the rear lawn when we heard the scream. We paused for a second, then we started running for the house. We couldn't tell where the scream had come from, but it was in that direction."

"Did you see anyone else outside the house during that time?" Barnaby asked.

Vincent frowned. "When we were walking to the stable, I thought I glimpsed someone in the wood to the east, beyond the side door. But when I looked more closely, I didn't see anyone, so…" He shrugged. "It might have been a trick of the light, a shifting of shadows under the trees."

Stokes caught Barnaby's gaze, then to Vincent, said, "Patterson saw the man, too."

Vincent's expression turned puzzled. "He did? When we were heading out? Not later, like Fentiman?"

Barnaby exchanged a glance with Penelope, then looked at Vincent. "It seems some man was going out at the same time as you three were heading for the stable, and he was returning when you heard the scream and came running toward the house."

Vincent's expression stated he hadn't made the connection with his father's murder. Again, he lightly shrugged. "I suppose that makes sense."

After a moment of wordless communication with Stokes and Penelope, Barnaby continued, "If you had to describe your father to others, what would you say?"

Vincent hesitated, then offered, "He was all right. I can't complain. All things considered, he was a pretty decent father. He didn't get angry easily, and he usually listened to what one thought, what one had to say." After a moment, he added, "He steered rather than pushed."

When Vincent glanced at him, Barnaby nodded understandingly. "Last question—do you know of any reason why anyone might have wanted to kill your father?"

"No." Confusion darkened Vincent's eyes and was reflected in his expression. "It seems so strange, so unbelievable that someone would want to kill him. He was never the sort to stir up trouble, and I can't recall him ever being aggressive or mean or nasty. He simply wasn't like that…" Vincent paused, then tipped his head. "Well, except for the disagreements about money, but that was entirely within the family. Really just between Mama and Papa. Cecy and I tried our damnedest never to get involved."

"Disagreements over money? What were they?" Penelope inquired.

Vincent faintly grimaced and shifted in the chair. "I expect it's common knowledge that in our family, the funds flow from Mama, not Papa. Just like Cecy and me, he managed on a quarterly allowance. The reins for the funds are wholly and firmly in Mama's hands, and there was always—as far back as I can remember—a sort of tension between them over that, if you know what I mean. Understandable, I think. I can imagine how Papa must have felt, always having to ask Mama for any extra he might need."

"But your father managed the estate?" Barnaby asked, seeking confirmation.

Vincent nodded. "He did. He managed everything to do with the Grange estate, but the title deeds are in Mama's name. All the profits, every quarter, get paid to her, and she always made sure Papa handed the lot over. Her father saw to it that she understood accounts well enough to oversee them, but otherwise, she's not particularly good at—or interested in—managing money. Every quarter, she takes whatever Papa hands over, pays our allowances from it, takes what she wants, then puts what's left into the bank. That's how they worked their finances, and as I understand it, that's how it was from the first—from the day they married."

He paused, then added, "It might seem strange to anyone outside the family, but Cecy and I can vouch for the fact that just as much as Papa was financially dependent on Mama, she needed his social standing to properly claim her place in the ton." Vincent met their eyes. "They balanced each other, you see?"

Penelope assured him they did.

Vincent nodded in acceptance, then his puzzlement returned. "So, you see, there's no earthly reason anywhere that explains why someone killed Papa."

For several moments, silence held sway, then Barnaby rose. "Thank you, Vincent, for being so frank. Your insights will help us understand the situation as we work to unravel that mystery."

Vincent looked at Barnaby, then nodded and rose. With a bow to Penelope and a polite nod to Stokes, Vincent allowed himself to be ushered to the door.

On opening it, Barnaby was pleased to see Patterson and Fentiman lurking in the hall, plainly waiting to take Vincent in hand and support him as they could.

With an approving nod to the pair, Barnaby handed Vincent into their care, then closed the door and returned to the armchairs.

He dropped into his and looked at Penelope, then at Stokes. Both met his gaze, then collectively, they exhaled and sat back.

After a moment, Stokes said, "We did well, getting through that lot, and now, we've got a lot more pieces to fit into our puzzle."

Penelope nodded. "Never has the analogy of solving a mystery being like putting together a jigsaw been more apt." She looked at the mantel-piece, at the clock ticking there. "Best of all, we managed that marathon in time for lunch. I suggest we reward ourselves with a short break to eat and recoup."

Barnaby and Stokes immediately agreed, and Barnaby rose and crossed to the bellpull to summon Gearing.

CHAPTER 10

*R*ichard sat beside Rosalind on a large rug in a pretty clearing in the wood to the west of the Grange. It was the perfect spot for a picnic, and about them, the company were relaxing on similar rugs and attempting to strike the right balance between somber memory and getting on with life. In the center of each rug, an array of delicacies provided by the Grange's cook had been arranged by attendant footmen to tempt the appetites of the assembled guests.

The remaining members of the Underhill family had elected to join the gathering, bolstered by Lady Susan and her daughters. The unvoiced opinion of the guests seemed to be that, while mourning had its place, the peculiar circumstances and the as-yet-unresolved murder that hung over the house made Lady Pamela's, Vincent's, and Cecilia's attendance understandable and acceptable. Despite the unexpected death, as hosts of the event, their responsibilities to their guests persisted, especially as, courtesy of the investigation, the guests were forbidden from decently departing.

The Underhills and Goodriches shared the large rug to Richard's left, along with Elliot, Nevin-Smythe, Patterson, and Fentiman.

In addition to Rosalind, the circle around Richard included Regina, Mrs. Hemmings, Cordingley, Kilpatrick, and Leith. Mrs. Hemmings sat on Richard's other side with Kilpatrick lounging beside her. The pair were quietly discussing various features of the locality, with Mrs. Hemmings drawing Kilpatrick out regarding his neighboring estate.

On the opposite side of the rug, Regina and Cordingley were discussing London pursuits, with Leith indulgently looking on.

On Richard's right, Rosalind leaned a fraction closer and murmured, "Two days on from the murder. Is it my imagination, or are its gripping effects starting to ease?"

Keeping his voice low, Richard replied, "The tension has definitely lessened, although it hasn't gone away. And we shouldn't forget the investigators' warning. The murderer is still here, among us." He glanced around at the idyllic setting. "Even here."

Briefly, Rosalind met his gaze. "That's a very sobering thought."

Richard gave a small nod. "Indeed."

As the warmth of the afternoon wafted beneath the canopies and wrapped them in its embrace, with the victuals largely consumed and glasses of champagne emptied, a semisomnolent postprandial drowsiness was taking hold. Conversations stuttered and slowed, and silences grew longer.

After glancing at the others on their rug, Rosalind again met Richard's eyes. A faint interrogatory lift of her fine brows effectively conveyed the same question circling in his brain. *Surely this is an opportune moment to do a little probing?*

Before he or she could decide where to start, Kilpatrick looked across the rug at Leith. "I was just telling Mrs. Hemmings about that last party at Wyndham Castle. You were there, weren't you?"

"Indeed, I was." Leith smiled affably. "Have you mentioned the contretemps over the brandy?"

Kilpatrick grinned. "I was attempting to explain why the difference between brandy and whiskey is so…acute."

Still smiling, Leith glanced at Regina, then shifted his gaze to Rosalind and Richard. "Someone mixed up the decanters. It caused quite a comedy, with some swearing the brandy in the whiskey decanter was, in fact, whiskey, just from a different region, and others maintaining that the whiskey in the brandy decanter was, indeed, brandy but produced by a different fermentation process. That left those who could correctly identify both liquors—like myself and Kilpatrick here—not quite knowing what to say."

"In the end," Kilpatrick said, "the marquess had both decanters emptied and refilled from the correct tuns under the eye of all the gentlemen about the table."

"That was the only way to settle the arguments," Leith said. "The sheepish faces when those who'd been so adamant about which liquor was which realized what had actually happened made for a very memorable moment."

Richard seized the opening to observe, "I daresay this house party will also be remembered by all attending, albeit for quite a different sort of moment." Mildly, he glanced around the circle of faces. "Speaking for myself, I doubt I will ever forget the instant when I was coming down the stairs, feeling quite carefree, and heard Miss Hemmings scream for help."

Cordingley readily nodded. "I was in my room, reading, but I had the window open and heard the scream, too. Quite set the blood racing and had me rushing to the stairs. The gentlemen who'd been in the library had come into the hall and were looking out"—Cordingley tipped his head at Richard—"and we all followed you, Percival, across the lawn."

Kilpatrick sighed. "I missed it all. I was walking to the Grange from the manor at the time." To the ladies, he explained, "Coming over the fields is the quickest and easiest way, so I was on the other side of the house, and the scream didn't reach that far. I didn't realize anything was wrong until I got to the forecourt and found everyone gathered outside."

Mrs. Hemmings artfully shuddered. "I was with the other matrons in the morning room, and I can tell you that hearing that scream gave us quite a shock. Then, we gathered ourselves up and followed the gentlemen outside, but at that point, we had no idea what had happened, and we stopped on the lawn just beyond the forecourt to wait for news."

When everyone's gazes shifted to Leith, he also sighed. "I, too, missed the excitement, such as it was, entirely. I was in my room, putting the finishing touches to several letters, and unlike Cordingley, my room is in the east wing, and the window was shut, so I didn't hear any scream. I did, however, hear the commotion downstairs, and ultimately—and, I admit, reluctantly—I put aside my pen and came down to see what was going on. By then, most of the company were clustered on the front lawn."

Smoothly, Leith turned to Regina and, with a kindly smile, asked, "And where were you, my dear?"

Along with everyone else, Richard looked at Regina, then bit back a curse. Her expression was that of a rabbit bailed up by a fox.

It was Rosalind who, equally smoothly, replied. "Regina and I had left the house via the rear terrace. We'd walked around the grounds, circling the house. Regina had had enough, but I wanted a longer walk, so we parted in the shrubbery, and Regina headed back to the house while I went on to the orchard."

Rosalind directed a smiling—encouraging—glance at her sister, and Regina managed a wooden nod. "Yes," she rather breathlessly said. "I… was still in the shrubbery when I heard Rosalind scream, and I… I just didn't know what to do."

Her tone, her expression, and her tightly gripped fingers testified to that being the truth and that the recollection upset her.

Mrs. Hemmings reached across and bracingly patted Regina's hands. "Indeed, dear. That's hardly surprising. We all had a dreadful shock that morning."

Rosalind said, "I do hope the investigators find the murderer soon so that everyone here, and the Underhills, too, can start to put this experience behind them."

Taking the hint, obligingly, Cordingley offered, "The book I was reading is about Egypt. Quite a fascinating place, it seems."

"My uncle traveled there recently," Kilpatrick said. "He's something of an amateur adventurer."

"Oh? How did he find it?" Cordingley asked.

"Hot." Kilpatrick grinned. "But he did say he found lots to see."

Cordingley shifted to face Kilpatrick. "Such as?"

As the conversation moved on, Richard glanced at Rosalind and saw that she was looking at Regina.

Leith, too, had his gaze fixed on the younger sister's face. Under cover of Kilpatrick's account of his uncle's recollections, Leith caught Regina's gaze and, his expression comforting, asked, "Do you have any ambition to walk in Lady Stanhope's shoes, Miss Hemmings?"

Regina sucked in a breath, then considered and replied, "I really don't think I'd enjoy traveling over sand dunes on a camel." Rallying, she added, "I prefer cool woodland"—she gestured about them—"like this."

Rosalind volunteered, "I, too, prefer cooler climes, but I'm sure Lady Stanhope craves the adventure and new sights rather than the heat."

"Very likely," Richard said. Regina had calmed, and the awkward moment had passed. Somewhat relieved, he lent Rosalind his support in guiding the conversation into clearer waters.

~

In the library, Barnaby collected the last flaky crumbs from the slice of delectable game pie he'd consumed. "Everyone here, even Monty's victims, viewed him in the same way as all of society—as a genial, innocuous, well-meaning, and entirely harmless older gentleman."

Seated behind the desk in the library at which they'd eaten, Penelope added, "Not someone likely to inspire anyone to viciously murder him."

"Except"—Stokes set his empty plate on the desk—"for the blackmail."

Sitting back, Barnaby looked at his coinvestigators. "Is there any other motive that might apply? Or are we correct in assuming one of his victims realized he was their blackmailer and killed him in a fit of rage?"

"The latter, I think." Penelope scrunched up her face, then stated, "While theoretically, the killer might have been hired by someone else— Vincent or even Pamela—for some reason we've yet to learn, the search of the study and the attack on Monty's valet argues that the correct motive is Monty's blackmailing. It was that that led to his death."

Stokes was soberly nodding. "I believe we're on solid ground in assuming the blackmailing is the foundation of our murderer's motive. There's the dispute with Lady Pamela over Underhill's lack of independent income, but that appears to be a longstanding issue, so if that was the cause, why now? Also, that dispute is surely more a motive for Underhill to murder Lady Pamela rather than the other way around. From all we've learned, including from Lady Pamela herself, she valued what Underhill brought to the marriage, and she doesn't seem the sort to cut off her nose to spite her face."

"You're definitely right there," Penelope said. "I really can't see Pamela, Vincent, or even Susan committing this crime. It wouldn't suit any of them, in the sense of creating more problems than it solves."

"However"—Barnaby tipped his head—"the lack of personal funds might well be what drew Monty to blackmail. Even if he wasn't in any sort of debt, and there's no hint that he was, the temptation of having a nest egg of his own could well have proved too great to resist."

Penelope said, "That would fit with the care he took to hide his identity and also explains why he never asked for too much—for more than his mark could easily pay. He made it as easy for them as he could. He wasn't blackmailing them to hurt them or even exercise power over them. His sole purpose was to accumulate some funds he could call his own."

Stokes nodded. "I agree. So the blackmail, it is—that's the root cause of this murder."

"Most if not all of his victims were friends of the family," Penelope pointed out, "and it seems likely he used their stays at Wyndham Castle to gather his intelligence—to learn their secrets."

Stokes frowned. "I have to wonder if there's any particular reason that makes Wyndham Castle a good location to learn of people's secrets." He looked at Penelope and Barnaby. "Is there anything special about the place?"

Penelope arched her brows. "It's a drafty old castle. The modern house—and it's not that modern—is built within and around the ancient shell, which I understand dates to early medieval times."

Barnaby was staring into space. "I wonder..." After a moment, he looked at Penelope and Stokes. "Let's get Vincent back in. He might be able to shed some light."

Barnaby rose and walked to the door.

While one footman went to fetch Vincent, another came in and cleared away their luncheon plates and platters.

Several minutes later, Vincent arrived. He shut the door behind him and walked to join them where they were again occupying the conversational grouping of four armchairs. He looked from one to the other. "You wanted to speak with me?"

"Yes. Just a quick question we're hoping you might be able to help us with." Barnaby waved him to the central chair, and once Vincent had sat, Barnaby asked, "If you wanted to learn people's secrets, is there any reason you might choose Wyndham Castle as the place to do so?"

Vincent frowned. "Learn people's secrets?" Then his face cleared, and he looked at Barnaby, Penelope, and Stokes. "The secret passageways. From them, you can listen to people and, in some rooms, spy on them as well."

"Secret passageways?" Penelope inquired.

"The old staff corridors from when it was a medieval castle," Vincent explained. "They've been closed up for years. Probably full of cobwebs. When we were little, Cecy and I used to play in them with Enid and Samantha. I doubt anyone's been in them since then." He studied their faces. "Why do you ask?"

Penelope smiled innocently. "It was just an idle point that came up regarding the castle. Now you've explained, we can see where the information fits. Thank you—that's a help."

Barnaby rose, and more slowly, Vincent came to his feet. He regarded them suspiciously but then inclined his head. "I'll leave you to your investigation. If you need me again, I'll be in the billiards room."

Barnaby showed Vincent out, then returned to the armchairs. "Well," he said, dropping into his chair, "that explains that."

Stokes was studying his notes. "If we accept that Underhill learned his victims' secrets via the secret passageways of Wyndham Castle, then what are the odds that most of those here have, at some point, visited the castle?"

Penelope grimaced. "Excellent, I would say. Pamela and Susan, together and also independently, host several events and even a house party or two there every year. Their cousin, the current marquess, is a widower, and his sons and their wives live in the north, so he's happy to have the daughters of the previous marquess continue to use the castle socially and keep the place alive. That's how he described it to me the last time we spoke."

Still studying his notes, Stokes rumbled, "Is there any point interviewing the Grange staff?"

Penelope tipped her head one way, then the other, then said, "I doubt we'll gain any value from that—at least not at this stage. From breakfast to the time of the murder, they would all have been very busy, more than usual with so many guests in the house. There would be rooms to tidy, beds to make, curtains to be neatened, water jugs refilled, basins emptied, and a host of other chores. And that's just upstairs."

"It'll be more use," Barnaby said, "to speak with Gearing and pertinent staff once we have some specific question to pursue. Such as if they saw Mr. X leaving the house before nine o'clock."

A tap fell on the door, and when Barnaby called, "Come," Morgan entered, closely followed by an older, heavyset man wearing old-fashioned gaiters on his sturdy legs and with a battered cloth cap perched on a head of bountiful gray curls.

Morgan carried the iron stake believed to be the murder weapon, and judging by his expression, he bore good news. He confirmed that with a jaunty salute and a "You'll want to hear this, guv."

The constable halted before the chairs, and whipping off his cap, the older man stopped by his shoulder. Morgan gestured at the man. "This is the head gardener, Winston."

Winston had a weather-beaten face and shrewd brown eyes. He nodded respectfully to the investigators, then tipped his head at the stake in Morgan's hand. "That's definitely one of ours. There's a collection of 'em. They were used by the old lord—the one who had the arboretum out front planted. The stakes were used to steady the young saplings, and the number painted on each stake identifies which tree it was. There's a plan somewhere that matches the numbers to the trees, saying what type of tree they are. Even though, now, the trees are well-grown, we've left the stakes in the ground." Winston shrugged. "Might be useful to someone sometime to know which tree is which."

Stokes asked the vital question. "Do you know which tree that stake was supporting?"

"Oh, aye." Winston half turned to the door. "If you need to know, come outside and I'll show you."

They found themselves in the thick band of trees bordering the front lawn. Winston led them through the shade beneath the massed canopies, weaving between thick trunks on a path that ran roughly parallel to the right-hand façade of the huge old house.

"Here's thirty-three." Winston tapped the head of a stake as he passed. A step farther on, he pointed at a tree on the outer rim of the arboretum, closer to the lawn. "And that's thirty-four over there." He looked ahead, then halted and pointed at a large dark-green spiky-leaved tree a few paces on. "Thought so. That yew is number thirty-five, and you can see the hole that stake should've been in."

Stokes, Barnaby, and Penelope went cautiously forward, careful of where they were placing their feet.

A yard from the yew's trunk, they saw the small mound of disturbed dark earth marking the hole from which the stake had been hauled.

Carefully, Stokes and Barnaby studied the ground. Although it had been dry for the past few days, where it wasn't covered in leaf mold, the ground under the trees was dark and soft.

"When last did it rain here?" Stokes asked Winston.

"We had a good bit of rain Sunday night," the gardener promptly replied. "Heavy enough to soak in."

Continuing to scan the ground, Stokes nodded. "We might find something, then."

Barnaby had drifted out from the yew, past the hole. He stopped, staring down. "Here." He crouched to study the ground more closely.

Stokes and Penelope came up, and with a pointed finger, Barnaby outlined the print he'd found in a patch of softer earth. "A man's shoe with a leather sole. Not a work boot."

"And shallow, suggesting it was left recently, since the last rain," Stokes said.

Barnaby grimaced and rose. "It's an average-sized gentleman's shoe. That won't help us identify who left the print."

Stokes looked at where the shoe's toe pointed, then nodded in that direction. "He made this when he was striding for the orchard, stake in hand."

Stokes turned to Winston. "Thank you for your help. It'll make a real difference to the investigation."

Winston tugged his cap. "Pleased to be able to help." He paused, then added, "The staff all liked Mr. Underhill. If this helps you catch who did for him, I'll be right happy."

With that, Winston bowed to them all and walked off through the trees, making for the side of the house.

"So," Stokes said, looking between the hole and the shoe print, "our killer was here immediately before the murder. Why was he out here?"

Penelope walked closer to the lawn, to where she could see the house clearly. She almost stood on another set of shoe prints, but caught herself just in time. "He was standing over here, it seems." She looked at the house. "Perhaps staring at the house." She looked upward at the thick overhanging branches shading the spot. "He would likely have been shaded sufficiently so that anyone in the house, looking out this way, wouldn't have spotted him."

With Morgan trailing them, Barnaby and Stokes came up and crouched to study the fresh set of prints.

After a moment, Barnaby nodded and rose. "He stood here for some time, facing the house."

Stokes grunted and straightened. "That's why these prints are more deeply indented."

After glancing at the house, Barnaby stepped carefully forward, placing his shoes over the prints so that he was standing in the exact same spot, facing in the same direction as the murderer had been. He studied the house. "From here, I can see through one of the library windows."

"Into the library?" Penelope asked.

"If I had a spyglass, yes. I can see movement without a glass, but to make out anything inside the library clearly, one would need a spyglass."

"I wonder if any guest has a spyglass in his possession," Penelope said.

"Or," Stokes said, "if there's one in the house that's been moved or gone missing."

"That's a question we can ask the staff." Barnaby stepped free of the prints and looked at Stokes and Penelope. "No time like the present."

They left Morgan to watch over the site and strode quickly back to the house.

By luck, they found Gearing in the front hall, replacing the large vase of flowers on the central table.

Penelope smiled at the butler. "Gearing, is there a spyglass in the house? One that's small enough to carry about on one's person?"

They all saw the surprise that flared in Gearing's eyes. "A spyglass, ma'am?" There was an odd note in his voice as well.

Studying him, Penelope tilted her head. "Yes, but what's strange about that query?"

Gearing colored faintly. "It's just odd you ask that, ma'am." He nodded toward the library. "There's one in there. Let me show you."

They followed Gearing into the long library, and he led them to the mantelshelf. Halting before it, he pointed at the small, collapsible brass-and-walnut spyglass standing at one end.

"That glass is usually always there, in that spot. But when Milly, the parlormaid, came in to dust yesterday morning, it was gone. She told me straightaway and showed me, and we looked all over this room, thinking one of the guests had picked it up and put it down somewhere else, but we didn't find it." Gearing drew in a breath and continued, "And then, late yesterday afternoon, after you had left, Milly came in to straighten and dust, and there it was. In that spot. She called me to see, and it was just sitting there"—Gearing gestured at the glass—"as you see it now. So we reasoned that one of the guests had borrowed it and taken it away and used it for whatever they needed it for, then brought it back."

Gearing looked at Barnaby and Stokes, who was busy jotting notes.

When Gearing's gaze moved on to Penelope, she nodded. "I think that's exactly what happened, Gearing." She smiled at the butler. "Thank you."

Stokes shut his notebook, tucked it away, then reached out and picked up the spyglass. To Gearing, he said, "We're officially borrowing this for now. We'll return it—into your hands—once we've finished with it."

Gearing was puzzled, but half bowed. "Of course, sir."

Barnaby shared a glance with Stokes, then said, "We'll be heading off to the inn shortly, Gearing. If we're needed, send for us there."

Gearing bowed again. "Indeed, sir."

He followed them out of the library and headed down the hall, returning to his duties.

Meanwhile, with poorly concealed eagerness, Penelope, Barnaby, and Stokes walked briskly across the front lawn to where, they were now quite sure, the murderer had stood and watched something happen in the library.

They reached the trees, ducked under their cover, and made their way to the critical spot.

Barnaby placed his shoes in the prints again, then raised the spyglass to his eye.

After barely a second, Penelope impatiently demanded, "What can you see?"

"Strange," Barnaby replied. "I can see a vase. Very clearly. It's perfectly framed by the window."

After a moment, he lowered the glass and looked at Penelope. "It's that Chinese vase on one of the display shelves among the bookcases on the other side of the library, opposite the windows."

Penelope's face cleared. "I remember it." She started back toward the house. "Let's go back and examine it."

There was no one about to see them reenter the house. They went into the library, and Penelope went straight to the large white-pink-and-green vase. As Barnaby had said, it sat on a shelf directly opposite the window through which he'd been looking.

Stokes had paused to look about the front hall. He joined them with, "Obviously, it's easy enough to move about this house without being seen."

Penelope reached for the vase, carefully lifted it, brought it to her, and peered inside. "Hmm." She frowned into the vase. "There's always dust in these things." Tilting her head, she studied the vase's interior. "And in this case, the coating of dust within has been disturbed relatively recently. Not as if someone cleaned, mind you. More like something—a packet of some sort, perhaps—had been placed inside, then taken out."

She straightened and offered the vase to Stokes. "If you look carefully, you'll be able to see the marks."

Stokes accepted the vase and looked, tilting the porcelain this way, then that. Eventually, he nodded. "I see what you mean. There are straight lines streaked in the dust on either side."

As he handed the vase to Barnaby, Barnaby observed, "Given what the other victims told us of the places Monty stipulated for leaving their payments, this vase certainly fits his bill."

After studying the vase, Barnaby returned it to the shelf.

"Except"—Stokes was looking out of the window toward the distant trees—"this time, Monty made a mistake. He didn't realize he could be seen from outside."

Penelope added, "And several witnesses say he came in and moved around the room, chatting to them, before he went outside." She looked at the vase. "I wonder if he approached the vase?"

Barnaby had been studying the various groupings of chairs. "Recalling where all the chairs were when we arrived—before we moved those four—then if he did approach the vase, he would have been between the vase and those sitting in the armchairs, so he would have been able to remove a packet from inside the vase without any of those others seeing."

Stokes checked the angle from the window to the vase. "But with that spyglass trained on him, the murderer would have seen Underhill's arm move, at the very least, and most likely seen him take the packet from inside the vase and slip it into his pocket."

Barnaby was assessing the various possibilities. He grimaced. "All the guests were here from the evening before. The murderer had plenty of time—literally the entire night—to place his payment in the vase with no one the wiser."

Penelope was staring at where the spyglass had sat only feet away from the vase. Slowly, she nodded. "And when he left his payment, he realized what Monty hadn't—that the window would allow him to keep watch and see who picked up the packet. See who his blackmailer was." She pointed at where the spyglass had been. "And the spyglass he needed to do that was right there, waiting for him to take and use."

Stokes looked deadly serious. "We need to stop and think"—he met Barnaby's and Penelope's gazes—"and put together everything we've heard and learned before we race ahead."

Barnaby nodded, and more reluctantly, Penelope did, too.

"So," she said, "let's head to the inn. We can start sorting through all the information from our interviews before we break for dinner."

❧

At the Red Lion, Penelope led the way into their private parlor, and Barnaby and Stokes followed.

As Stokes shut the door, Penelope said, "What I want to know is what possessed Monty to use his own house to collect payments?" She dropped onto the settle facing the fireplace and looked at Barnaby and Stokes as they joined her. "Up to this point, he'd been so careful. Surely, arranging for payments at Patchcote Grange was a risk?"

Barnaby sank onto the cushion beside her. "I think you just answered your own question. He'd operated for years without a hitch, and he'd grown complacent." He glanced at Stokes as he claimed the nearby armchair. "There's also the possibility that Monty didn't see the Grange as *his* home but rather as Pamela's house and, therefore, just another ton venue."

Stokes added, "He favored crowds for confusion, and there were so many people in the house, he might have felt it was safe enough. Comfortable enough for him. Thirty guests and family, plus just as many staff, and probably more visiting staff, and for all the victims knew, any one of the entire cohort could have been the blackmailer."

Penelope wrinkled her nose. "I suppose, at least with the payments being left outside, in the orchard and on the croquet lawn, they might have been picked up by literally anyone."

"Don't forget," Stokes said, "that occasionally, he used third parties, and several victims were aware of that. There was no reason for his victims to imagine the blackmailer was one of the company, much less their host."

"If you think about the fateful payment he arranged to be left in the library vase," Barnaby said, "if it hadn't been for that window, he would almost certainly have retrieved that payment with no one the wiser. He made one mistake—just one—but it was with the wrong victim, one quick-thinking enough to see the opportunity and capitalize on it."

Reluctantly accepting that, Penelope inclined her head. After a moment, she looked at Stokes. "So how are we to approach the mountain of information before us and tease out the pertinent points?'

Stokes arched a brow at her. "Logically, as always, I expect. And apropos of that, I think our first question should be: Are we correct in believing that the murderer is the person named on the page removed from Underhill's black book?"

Penelope was already pulling out her lists. "All Monty's female victims are either alibied by others or, like Regina, incapable of the deed. So assuming the killer is one of Monty's *male* victims, did he find the book and tear out the page? Or did Monty tear out that page at some earlier time for some other reason, and the killer is one of those still named in the book?"

Barnaby nodded. "I've been wondering about that, but the only male victims presently at the Grange whose names remain in the book are Morland and Nevin-Smythe, and neither were due to make payments while here."

He looked at Penelope as she flicked through her lists, comparing and cross-checking.

After a moment, she replied, "On top of that, Morland was with the other gentlemen in the library the whole time, and Nevin-Smythe, who was seen in the front hall on the way to the billiards room as Monty left the house, remained in the billiards room with Griffith until everyone heard Rosalind scream."

Stokes nodded in satisfaction. "Good. That's one point settled. The killer tore out the page that referred to him in the black book and left it for us to find, intending to cast suspicion on the other victims among the company." He met Barnaby's and Penelope's gazes. "That option best fits what we know thus far. It also suggests we're dealing with a cold-blooded and calculating character."

Barnaby steepled his fingers before his face. "Let's accept that as our foundation—that the murderer was one of Monty's male victims, and after murdering Monty, he found the black book and tore out the page referring to him."

Penelope's eyes narrowed. "Given none of the victims we've spoken with were aware that Monty was their blackmailer, can we assume that, when the murderer arrived at the Grange, he likewise did not know his blackmailer's identity?"

Stokes stirred, then offered, "I think we can and should assume that. At the most, he might have suspected, but he didn't know, or else he would have come much better prepared."

"Nor would he have been so enraged on learning his blackmailer was Monty," Barnaby observed.

Stokes nodded. "My instincts say he had no clue, any more than the others did. But of course, he was desperate to know, which is why he seized on the chance afforded by the positioning of the vase and why, as you say, he was so enraged on learning the blackmailer's identity. This was a hot-blooded, opportunistic slaying, not a planned execution, and we know that, in his cooler moments, even under pressure, as he would have been while searching the study, our killer is careful and clever. Normally, he thinks before he acts."

"So," Barnaby concluded, "learning the blackmailer's identity was a massive shock, one the blackmailer hadn't anticipated or foreseen in any way, which was why he reacted so forcefully and ferociously. He's not otherwise given to impulsive acts."

"Actually"—Penelope tipped her head—"that's a point to note. Whoever our murderer is, he felt…a lot, but mostly, I suspect, he felt immensely betrayed. Given Monty's image, the one everyone has of him, that he was a sound and solid friend to all, that makes some sense."

"Regardless," Stokes said, "we need to verify that when Underhill entered the library and chatted with the men there, he actually approached the vase in a way that would have allowed him to extract the payment."

Barnaby said, "So we have our murderer standing in the trees, watching with the spyglass through the library window, and he sees Monty go to the vase and remove the payment our murderer had earlier deposited in the vase. The murderer is poleaxed to discover that *Monty* is his blackmailer, and rage overcomes him—and before he has a chance to cool down and think, Monty walks out of the house and strolls off toward the orchard."

"And our murderer sees his chance to vent his fury." Penelope took up the tale. "He seizes the iron stake conveniently near him and stalks after Monty."

Stokes nodded. "Our murderer didn't come to the Grange expecting to kill anyone, but events collided, and he reacted."

Frowning, Barnaby said, "I can't see that we'll have any luck trying to track who placed the payment in the vase. There are too many opportunities prior to any of the other men entering the library on Monday morning, including during all of the previous night."

"All we can say," Penelope stated, "and really, all we need to know is that our victim-turned-murderer placed his payment in the vase, saw the window and recognized the chance it offered, then saw the spyglass, picked it up, and later, used it to watch Monty pick up the payment."

"And," Barnaby said, "he returned the spyglass to the library the following day, and again, there are too many hours during which he might have done that unobserved to get us any further."

After a moment of ruminating, Stokes said, "As I see it, the critical point is that at the time Monty picked up the payment and left the library and then the house, the murderer was in the trees. He was out of the house and out of sight of all others during that time."

Penelope added, "And it seems he didn't return to the house until after Rosalind screamed, and everyone else rushed outside."

"As to that," Barnaby said, "the mystery gentleman Vincent and Patterson saw leaving the house via the wood to the east—and later, after Rosalind had screamed, Fentiman and Samantha saw returning via the same route—is almost certainly our killer. He had to have left the house before nine o'clock to circle around and be in position in the trees to see his blackmailer pick up the payment, and later, after killing Monty, he returned the same way. If you think about it, it's possible to move under the cover of trees the whole way. He never had to step into the open except for the few paces to and from the orchard entrance arch, and at the time, there was no one else around to see him."

"True." Penelope went on, "But once he'd returned to the house, he didn't go outside and join the others on the lawn. Instead, by then, he'd started thinking more clearly, and he seized the moment of universal distraction to slip into the study and search…" Brows rising, she looked at Stokes and Barnaby. "For what, exactly? It couldn't have been Monty's black book, because the killer couldn't have known such a record existed."

"No," Barnaby agreed. "It wasn't the black book—that was an incidental and lucky find for him. Presumably, he was searching for some evidence he believes Monty had of his malfeasance—the basis for the blackmail. And because the killer hadn't known Monty was his blackmailer, the search couldn't have occurred before that moment." He glanced at Penelope. "So yes, the search definitely occurred at that time, and while everyone else was outside at the front of the house, the killer was in the study."

Penelope nodded. "So he won't have been seen by anyone else between ten o'clock and sometime after ten-thirty or even later—whenever the company returned indoors."

"Even more importantly," Stokes said, scribbling a note, "is that the evidence of malfeasance Underhill held must still exist, although where he might have hidden it for safekeeping is anyone's guess. It might not even be in this house."

Frowning, Penelope ventured, "Tangible evidence—documentary

evidence—doesn't fit with the killer's crime being an indiscretion or something of that nature."

"No," Barnaby agreed. "Tangible evidence that the killer believes Monty held makes the killer's secret significantly more serious." He met Stokes's gaze. "Serious to the point of pushing a man to murder to keep it concealed."

Penelope's frown deepened. "I'm trying to think of whom among the guests might have such a secret and coming up with no idea." After a moment, she suggested, "Let's compile what we know of our murderer." She raised one hand and started counting on her fingers. "He's a cold-blooded and calculating character."

"Except when in the grip of unexpected rage," Barnaby added.

"And sadly," Stokes said, "that doesn't exactly single him out."

Undeterred, Penelope continued, "He's been a guest at Wyndham Castle."

"Again," Stokes remarked, "that doesn't appreciably narrow our list of suspects."

Penelope moved on to her third finger. "He has a secret of the order that would drive him to kill to keep it hidden."

Stokes inclined his head, conceding the point.

"Next"—Penelope tapped her fourth finger—"the killer was outside from before eight forty-five to close to ten o'clock, the times he was seen leaving and returning to the house. He was therefore not among those gathered on the front lawn or near the orchard." She touched her first finger again. "And he was in the study, searching from about ten o'clock for perhaps as long as an hour." She looked at Barnaby. "He might have risked continuing to search even when the others returned to the house, on the grounds that, in the circumstances, no one would think of going to the study."

Barnaby nodded. "Very possibly."

Penelope rolled on, "Then, on Tuesday evening at nine o'clock, the killer was upstairs in Monty's bedchamber, still searching. He was surprised by Grimshaw coming into the dressing room and knocked the poor man out." She looked at Stokes. "That's six points we know about our murderer. And what's more, his searching in Monty's bedchamber suggests he might not yet have found the evidence he's convinced Monty held."

Stokes nodded. "As he's killed to keep that evidence hidden, it's unlikely he'll stop searching for it."

"Although," Barnaby said, "if he hasn't found it yet, given we're often in the house and we've set a guard on the study, he might well lie low until we depart." He met Penelope's eyes. "He is, after all, a careful person when not in the grip of overwhelming rage."

She nodded, and Stokes fixed his gaze on her and Barnaby and asked, "So who fits our bill?"

Penelope smoothed out her lists of where people were and when. "Adding the information we gleaned today…"

She busily scanned the sheets, her spectacle-focused gaze tracking from one sheet to the other and back again.

Stokes and Barnaby exchanged a glance and waited, not exactly impatiently, but they knew when to hold their tongues.

Eventually, Penelope straightened. Her gaze on her lists, she stated, "Strictly speaking, those for whom we have only their word for where they were between nine and ten o'clock are Regina, who was in the grounds and out of sight of anyone over the critical time, Rosalind, who was in the gardens, looking for Regina, Leith, who was writing letters in his room, Susan, who was walking in the rose garden that's on the same side of the house as the orchard, Richard, who was also writing letters in his room, but was on the stairs when Rosalind screamed for help, and Cordingley, who was reading in his room but says he saw Lady Wincombe on the rear lawn when she crossed to the croquet green, which suggests he was in his room at that time… Yet if he was the murderer and returning toward the house, heading toward the side door but still in the wood, he could have spotted Lady Wincombe *returning* and so would have known that she'd been outside and would almost certainly have crossed the rear lawn earlier, on her way out." She frowned at her lists. "I think Cordingley needs to remain as a suspect for the moment. And then there's Lady Carville, who the young ladies saw in the conservatory before nine o'clock, and she says she saw Susan leave for the rose garden via the terrace, but she might have heard that Susan had gone out and added that to her story, and we have no other confirmation Lady Carville remained in the conservatory between nine and ten."

Penelope scanned her lists one more time, then nodded decisively and looked at Stokes and Barnaby. "Everyone else was either with others or seen by others in the places they say they were."

Barnaby pointed out, "It wasn't a woman who stood in the trees and watched Monty take the payment from the vase. The footprints make that indisputable."

Penelope regarded him. "True." She turned back to her list. "Eliminating the women leaves us with…Leith, Richard, and Cordingley."

Barnaby glanced at Stokes. "Richard mentioned dropping the letters he'd written on the hall table as he raced out of the house in response to Rosalind's scream."

"I know none of us imagines Richard is the murderer," Penelope said, "but for completeness's sake, we should check with Gearing. He'll know if the letters were, in fact, there."

Stokes nodded. "The same applies to Leith. He said he was writing letters the entire time, so either he's given Gearing letters to post, or they're on the desk in his room."

Barnaby nodded. "We can check with Gearing—either way, the staff will know."

Penelope was frowning. "If the gentleman Vincent and Patterson and then, later, Fentiman and Samantha saw in the wood is our murderer, which of our three suspects could that have been?"

"Obviously," Barnaby said, "any one of the three could have slipped down the rear stairs and out and back via the side door…" He paused, then voice firming, went on, "Except that Richard couldn't have completed the return journey."

"No." Penelope's face cleared. "Patterson and Samantha both said they saw the mystery gentleman heading toward the side door *after* they'd heard Rosalind's scream. At that time, Richard was on the stairs, then racing through the front hall, and many members of the company saw him and followed him outside."

Barnaby looked at Stokes. "So Richard's off the list as well. That leaves only Leith and Cordingley."

Stokes grimaced. "As much as I hate to say it, we have to allow for the possibility that the man sighted in the wood was, in fact, two different men. None of the witnesses saw the man well enough to say much about him on either occasion. So Richard not being able to have been the second man doesn't rule him out as the murderer—he could have slipped out, killed Underhill, then returned earlier, in time to be on the stairs and respond to the scream."

"But Richard couldn't have searched the study," Penelope pointed out. "He was outside in full view of most of the company while that search was underway."

Stokes held up a hand. "I agree Percival is not a good candidate for the role of murderer—on a host of counts—but there's an outside chance that the search was committed by someone other than the murderer."

Penelope narrowed her eyes on Stokes. "You're determined to play devil's advocate, aren't you?"

Fleetingly, Stokes grinned. "I'm just more used to the lawyers' arguments and judges' questions than you. But if for no other reason than to make our investigation appear utterly thorough and even-handed, can we leave Percival on the list for the moment? At least until we have confirmation that he did, indeed, drop a handful of letters on the hall table for Gearing to post?"

Penelope sighed. "All right." She studied her list. "So we're down to three suspects—Leith, Richard, and Cordingley." She looked at Barnaby and Stokes. "Will the confirmation of the existence of letters by Gearing be enough to alibi Leith and Richard?"

Stokes and Barnaby frowned, then Stokes offered, "It depends on when he wrote the letters and how many there were…" After a moment, Stokes sighed. "I really can't see Percival as our killer." He looked at Penelope. "He was seen going upstairs, I believe?"

Penelope consulted her notes. "Yes. By Morehouse and Carrington at about seven-forty."

"So to be in the trees, watching the library, by nine o'clock," Stokes said, "he would have had to leave his room and the house at some point, then return very quickly from the orchard to his room—without being seen by anyone—to seize the letters, go to the stairs, and be on the way down when Rosalind screamed."

"But," Barnaby said, "Richard couldn't have known that Rosalind would find the body and scream for help, and it's simply too convenient to imagine that he had letters written and ready to leave on the hall table to establish what he'd been doing. That smacks of a degree of planning that we've agreed didn't apply in this case."

Penelope nodded. "This murder was a spontaneous act of rage, not a planned killing."

"Perhaps," Stokes said, "we simply leave Percival on the list until we confirm the existence of those letters. We still have the list down to just three, which, in the circumstances, is astonishing."

"But what about Leith?" Penelope persisted. "If we learn that he wrote several letters on Monday morning, does that eliminate him?"

Barnaby and Stokes both thought, then Stokes asked, "He wasn't sighted or mentioned by anyone, was he?"

"Carrington said Leith was in the library when he—Carrington—went in there with Morehouse and Elliot at a little after seven-thirty," Penelope replied, "but that Leith left soon after, saying he had letters to write. After that"—she scanned her lists—"we have no further mention of Leith."

"That doesn't necessarily mean he's guilty," Barnaby said. "Cordingley hasn't been mentioned by others, either, not after he went upstairs."

Stokes nodded. "So we're down to those three, and in reality, that's as far as we can go at this point."

Barnaby observed, "In light of the plethora of guests, the multiplicity of Monty's victims, and the mountain of minutiae we've had to trawl through, getting our suspects list down to just three—and really only two —is a notable accomplishment."

"Yet considering who those suspects are, we still have to find incontrovertible proof that one of them is our killer." Stokes studied his notes, then said, "We should follow the obvious trails. Ask Gearing about letters from Percival and Leith."

Barnaby added, "Ask the gardeners and also the indoor staff if any of them saw our three possibles anywhere outside their rooms during the nine-to-ten-o'clock window."

"We should also ask," Penelope put in, "whether any of the staff saw anyone going into or out of the study after the scream and the ensuing commotion."

Nodding, Stokes was jotting. "Further to that point, we should also see if, after everyone reacted to the scream, any of the guests or staff remember Leith or Cordingley joining the groups on the front lawn. We know where Percival was at that time, and both Cordingley and Leith said they came downstairs—Cordingley soon after the scream and Leith later, sometime after he heard the commotion. Someone ought to have seen them."

After a moment, Stokes went on, "We should also check who was where at nine o'clock on Tuesday evening." He looked at Penelope. "What would the company have been doing at that time?"

Penelope grimaced. "In light of the murder, they might well have retired early. The ladies, at least." She looked inquiringly at Barnaby.

"Difficult to predict," Barnaby said, "but I doubt the gentlemen would have retreated to their rooms at such an early hour. More likely, they congregated in the library or billiards room." He tipped his head at Stokes. "But you're right—that's a point we should check."

Stokes studied his notes, then shut the book. "Right, then." He looked at Barnaby and Penelope. "We're very close. Let's focus solely on Percival, Leith, and Cordingley. We have several supposed facts for which we need corroboration." He held up his hand and, as Penelope had earlier, marked the points off on his fingers. "First, when he spoke with the gentlemen in the library at around nine o'clock, did Underhill approach the vase close enough to reach inside? Second, on Monday morning, did Percival leave letters on the hall table when he rushed from the house, and is there evidence Leith wrote letters in his room? Did he leave any to be posted? And third, did Cordingley or Leith join the others gathered on the front lawn, or were they searching the study at that point? We acknowledge that's something Percival couldn't have done, but we're leaving him on the list for the moment."

Penelope observed, "We know the murderer isn't Richard, but he could be a useful stalking horse of sorts and including him at this point shows we're not playing favorites."

Stokes nodded. "Keeping him on the list will make sure we're ticking all the boxes in provably logical fashion. But we have one more test for our putative murderer. We need to determine where Percival, Leith, and Cordingley were at nine o'clock on Tuesday evening." He met Barnaby's gaze. "If we can get answers to all four questions—"

"We'll have our killer." Barnaby nodded confidently. "I can't imagine we won't."

"What I honestly can't imagine," Penelope said, "is what secret would be major enough to push either Cordingley or Leith to kill to keep it hidden."

Barnaby admitted, "I can't, either. Nevertheless, one of those two has just such a secret, and he's our killer."

CHAPTER 11

$\mathcal{T}$he following morning, immediately after breakfast, Richard accompanied Rosalind and Regina in taking a turn about the Grange's well-stocked conservatory.

Rosalind had been tasked by Mrs. Hemmings to keep her sister close. At the very least, under her eye. Mrs. Hemmings was still in two minds about the murderer possibly being a lurking vagabond—a notion that still held currency among the older matrons—and had taken to fussing over Regina's safety, something Regina didn't appreciate but bore with a long-suffering air.

Consequently, Richard was ambling beside Rosalind, keeping pace as she, in turn, followed her idly strolling sister along the wending paths between the potted plants that transformed the glassed-in room into a jungle of verdant green.

In truth, Richard was keen to engineer a moment alone—preferably two or more—with Rosalind. He wanted to…explore the sense of like-mindedness, the camaraderie of sorts that had steadily grown between them over the past few days. He wanted to see if she was, by any chance, thinking along the same lines he was.

There was nothing quite like being involved—too closely involved—in a murder investigation to strip away all superficialities, revealing people for who they really were behind their glossy social façades. Courtesy of the events of the past days, he'd come to understand and appreciate Rosalind—her personality and her strengths—in ways he never otherwise would have. And somewhat to his surprise, he'd found himself in complete agreement with his aunts' assessment. Rosalind Hemmings would make him an excellent wife.

The only fly in that ointment was that he wasn't sure if she was so inclined. Despite his extensive experience of ladies—earned via the string of well-born lovers of whom he'd long ago lost count—nothing in that history had prepared him for how to take the next step.

Hardly surprising. I never imagined marrying any of them.

So now, he paced beside Rosalind—close but not too close, just close enough that her skirts occasionally brushed his trouser legs and the scent from her hair wafted and teased his senses—and wondered what his next move should be.

They were admiring the orchids, several of which were in bloom, when Alison Waterhouse walked in. On seeing them, Alison paused, but when Rosalind smiled encouragingly, Alison smiled back and joined them.

"Hello," Rosalind said. "Are you looking for ways to pass the time?"

Alison's grin was quietly confident. "I think most of the company are. Everyone's waiting to see what the investigators do next."

Regina smiled warmly at Alison and indicated a pretty pink-and-white orchid. "Isn't this just perfect?"

Alison agreed and fell in beside Regina, and the pair continued down the line of pots, examining blooms and commenting on the variety of colors.

Richard caught the sidelong glance Rosalind threw his way. Their gazes met and held and, as had happened frequently over the past days, it seemed they were both thinking along the same lines…

Then, Regina and Alison walked on, and with what sounded like a half-stifled sigh, Rosalind looked ahead and followed.

Richard was wracking his brains to find some way of creating the moment it seemed both he and Rosalind desired when, after a whispered conversation, Regina and Alison turned, walked back, and halted before Rosalind and Richard.

"Alison and I need to stretch our legs rather more," Regina said, "so we're going for a stroll in the gardens."

"Just for half an hour or so," Alison put in. "It will be a relief to get out of the house."

"You don't need to worry—we'll stay together," Regina said. "And we'll keep within sight of the house so we won't get lost."

It was plain that Alison and Regina did not want to be supervised. Over recent days, the pair had become friends, and Alison appeared to have a sound head on her shoulders.

Richard glanced at Rosalind and saw that she was debating whether or not to agree, torn between strictly following her mother's injunction and allowing her sister reasonable freedom while also seizing some time for herself and him…

He murmured, "That should be safe enough."

Rosalind slid a glance his way and met his eyes. After a moment, she returned her gaze to Regina and Alison. "Yes. All right. But make sure you're back before morning tea, or Mama will fret."

Regina beamed. "Yes, of course."

Alison looped her arm with Regina's. "We promise to be back by then."

Rosalind inclined her head, and the pair rustled off toward the conservatory doors, heads already dipping close.

As they passed out of the room, the sound of their tinkling laughter drifted back to Richard and Rosalind.

She glanced at him. "In the circumstances, that's a nice sound to hear, and truth be told, their burgeoning friendship is something of a relief. Alison's a sensible girl, and I'll be happy if Regina follows her lead."

As Rosalind swung to face him, he arched a brow at her. "You're sensible, too. And reliable and well-grounded."

She blinked in surprise and met his eyes.

He smiled understandingly, but knew he had to seize the chance Fate had offered. "As it happens—as I think you know—I've been wanting to speak with you about"—on impulse, he opted for the shockingly direct—"whether you might be inclined to sensibly follow the direction suggested by your parents and my aunts and consider marrying me."

She blinked again, then her lavender-blue gaze grew more intent, and she studied him unabashedly. After several heartbeats, she asked, "Is that a proposal?"

He tipped his head this way, then that, then confessed, "Actually, it's more a straightforward question." He held her gaze. "It's simple, really—do you think that marrying me would be a good idea?"

She eased back a trifle, closely scanning his expression, his eyes, then her lips twitched. "I suppose that depends."

"On what?"

More confidently, she tipped up her chin. "On what the boundaries of the role are, at least in your mind." When she met his gaze, hers had turned challenging. "Perhaps, given we are—for once—blessedly alone, we might discuss your requirements?"

His grin was entirely genuine. "Yes," he agreed. "Let's."

Once again, Penelope led Barnaby and Stokes into the front hall of Patchcote Grange. The tattoo of her heels striking the tiles reflected their determination to ask what they hoped would be their final questions, the answers to which would shine an unforgiving light on the murderer in the company's midst.

The previous evening, they'd debated whether to return immediately and pose those questions, but as most would be directed to the staff, who would be frantically busy during the evening, they'd reluctantly decided against what might prove an unproductive foray. As Stokes had pointed out, they needed considered, accurate answers, not replies flung at a run.

Now, as the hall's cool shadows embraced them, Penelope acknowledged that their forbearance had been wise. As Barnaby had remarked, there was an outside chance that they'd missed some vital clue and the killer was someone other than their three—really two—prime suspects. If so, then actively investigating literally under the avid attention of the entire company could well give the guilty party a chance to cover his tracks or even escape. Consequently, albeit reluctantly, they'd elected to play their cards close to their collective chest and arrive to pursue their investigations at a more normal hour.

They paused in the otherwise empty hall, and when a footman duly appeared in response to the sounds of their arrival, Penelope instructed, "Please fetch Gearing. We'll be in the library."

The footman bowed. "Yes, ma'am. At once."

She turned toward the library. Stokes opened the door and held it, and she swept inside.

By the time Gearing arrived, they'd arranged themselves in their now-customary armchairs. He half bowed to them, then looked at Penelope. "Yes, ma'am?"

"We realize," Penelope said, "that on Monday morning, the staff would have been in something of a tizzy, but do you recall picking up any letters that had been left on the hall table?"

Gearing looked relieved. "Why, yes, ma'am. On that morning, there were three letters left on the salver for me to post. All were from Mr. Percival. One was addressed to Viscount Seddington, who I believe is Mr. Percival's ward."

Penelope smiled. "That's correct. Now, has the Earl of Leith left any letters for you to post?"

"No, ma'am." Then Gearing amended, "Not as yet."

Penelope widened her eyes. "Perhaps he hasn't brought them down yet. Do you know if he's been writing letters in his room?"

Gearing hesitated, then no doubt remembering his mistress's instructions to render all assistance possible to them, he offered, "I could ask the maid who tidies his room if there are any letters there, perhaps unfinished or yet to be addressed?"

"Thank you, Gearing." Penelope inclined her head. "That would be helpful."

Stokes clarified, "Whether just started, half finished, or even discarded. We'd like to know if there's any evidence of letter writing in Leith's room."

Gearing bowed. "I'll find Gemma—the maid who tends those rooms —and ask and return with her answer."

Barnaby nodded. "Please do."

Gearing bowed again and departed.

After the door closed, Stokes stated, "That's our second question in hand, and Percival is looking less and less suspicious."

"Which of our questions should we tackle next?" Barnaby asked.

Stokes considered the list in his notebook. "It'll be faster if we split up, and"—he glanced up and met Barnaby's and Penelope's gazes—"I'm getting that itching between my shoulder blades that insists time is of the essence."

Barnaby grimaced. "You, too?"

Grimly, Stokes nodded. "Let's get this last round of questioning done as quickly and efficiently as possible. Questions three and four need to be directed to the staff, both indoor and outdoor. I'll take O'Donnell and speak with the indoor staff about whether anyone noticed Leith, Cordingley, or Percival outside the house or near the study immediately after the alarm was raised, and also whether they spotted any of those three upstairs on Tuesday evening before or after nine o'clock. Meanwhile, I'll have Morgan ask the gardeners if any of them saw Leith, Cordingley, or Percival outside the house before the murder or around the time Miss Hemmings screamed. With luck, someone will have spotted our mystery gentleman and have some clue who he is."

Penelope looked at Barnaby. "That leaves you and me to put our questions to the gentlemen of the company. First, did those in the library on Monday morning when Monty came in see him approach the vase?"

Barnaby rose. "And our second question for the gentlemen is who was where on Tuesday evening at nine o'clock."

Penelope and Stokes got to their feet.

With determination etched in every line of his face, Stokes stated, "If we can get clear and unequivocal answers to those questions, we'll know the identity of Underhill's killer."

Despite being driven by the same determination infecting Stokes, Barnaby and Penelope made first for the morning room.

They walked in, and Barnaby swiftly scanned the occupants. Ensconced in armchairs in the middle of the room were Pamela, Susan, Percival's aunts, Lady Wincombe, Mrs. Hemmings, and Lady Carville. Of the older ladies and matrons, only Mrs. Waterhouse was absent, although an empty chair suggested she was expected.

To say that Barnaby and Penelope's arrival was greeted with interest would have been a gross understatement. Conversations cut off midsentence, and every eye instantly fixed on them, while the expressions trained on them ranged from the faintly concerned to the avidly expectant.

Penelope smiled winningly. "We have a few last questions we would like to pose in the hope that, as a group, you might be able to shed some light."

Lady Campbell-Carstairs gestured expansively. "Ask away, my dear. We're agog to see you in action."

Penelope's smile only brightened. "Our primary question concerns what the company did on Tuesday evening."

The ladies looked puzzled; plainly, news of the attack on Grimshaw hadn't percolated to their ears. Mystified as to why they were being questioned about Tuesday evening, they glanced at one another, then Lady Kelly clarified, "Tuesday evening—the second evening after the sad event?"

"Exactly," Penelope confirmed.

"Oh, well..." Lady Kelly glanced around the circle. On receiving encouraging nods from all, she returned her gaze to Penelope. "We retired early, all of us."

Sensing more was needed, Susan added, "More or less immediately after we'd dealt with the tea trolley."

Penelope ventured, "So around eight o'clock?"

"About that," Pamela said. "As far as we know, all the men remained downstairs, presumably in the library or the billiards room. I'm not aware of who went where."

"We weren't feeling very convivial," Mrs. Hemmings said, "as I'm sure you can understand."

"Indeed." Penelope inclined her head to the company. "Thank you." Then, she shifted her gaze to Pamela and Susan. "One last question. Can you tell us who among those presently here have also been a guest at Wyndham Castle?"

That hadn't been on their list of questions, but Barnaby could see why his clever wife had posed it.

Pamela shared a look with Susan, then said, "The Wincombes, certainly, and Lady Campbell-Carstairs and Lady Kelly, of course. The Hemmingses, Leith, Kilpatrick..."

"Nevin-Smythe," Susan put in, "and Lord and Lady Carville and Morland."

"Oh, and Griffith," Pamela stated, "and Mr. Elliot, and Vincent's friends, Mr. Patterson and Mr. Fentiman." She looked at Penelope. "And, of course, all the members of Susan's and my families."

By her expression, Penelope was mentally striking through names on the guest list. Eventually, she said, "So not Morehouse, Carrington, Cordingley, or Percival."

"No." Pamela was quite definite. "We haven't had the pleasure of those gentlemen's company at the castle as yet."

Lady Campbell-Carstairs snorted. "Not for want of trying in Richard's case. We've done our best to inveigle him into attending several house parties there, but he's as slippery as an eel when he wants to be and never obliged."

Penelope smiled and inclined her head to the company. "Thank you. That's really all we needed from you." She paused, then asked, "Mrs. Waterhouse?"

"You just missed her, dear," Lady Kelly said. "She slipped upstairs to fetch a shawl. If you want to speak with her, I'm sure she'll be back at any minute."

No doubt noticing the gleam in several pairs of eyes, Penelope shook her head. "No, no. I was just curious."

Barnaby half bowed, and he and Penelope quit the room before they could be detained and interrogated. As they reentered the hall, he felt the heightening of the impending urgency they and Stokes had earlier acknowledged. To Penelope, he murmured, "It seems we're closing in."

"It does," she returned. "But attendance at Wyndham Castle, while indicative, can't be considered conclusive."

"No, but it does focus the mind."

The clack of billiard balls drew them down the corridor to the room from which the sound was emanating. There, somewhat to their surprise, they found what, at first glance, appeared to be the entire company of gentlemen.

The older men were sitting in armchairs crammed around the room's perimeter, while the younger crew stood about in groups, idly chatting and watching Cordingley and Patterson, who were engaged in a game.

Of course, when Barnaby and Penelope walked in, all conversation ceased, and all eyes swung their way. Then, in deference to Penelope, the gentlemen seated started to rise, but she quickly waved at them to remain seated, and they gratefully subsided. Cordingley, who had been leaning over the table, lining up a shot, straightened, cue in hand, and, like everyone else, looked expectantly their way.

A quick scan of the company showed that most were present with two notable exceptions.

Penelope turned her head and whispered, "Leith and Richard aren't here."

Sotto voce, Barnaby murmured back, "That might make this easier."

He raised his voice. "We have a few last questions. First, for those who were in the library on Monday morning, prior to the murder." He focused on the cluster of older men.

Helpfully, Penelope added, "That's Lord Morland, Mr. Elliot, Mr. Morehouse, Mr. Carrington, and Lord Wincombe."

All five gave them their undivided attention, plainly eager to assist.

Barnaby asked, "Thinking back to when Underhill came in and chatted with you all, can you describe where in the room he stood?"

Faintly mystified, the gentlemen involved glanced at one another, then Carrington offered, "Well, he came in and stopped by the three armchairs closer to the door. Elliot, Morehouse, and I were sitting there, reading, and Underhill chatted a bit, then"—Carrington tipped his head toward Morland and Wincombe—"moved on down the room to where Wincombe and Morland were sitting."

The other four men were all nodding, and Elliot added, "He was just circling about like any good host, exchanging a few words with each of us, then moving on."

"So," Barnaby prompted, "he merely moved around the armchairs?"

Lord Wincombe frowned. "Well, he did cross to that vase. Ruddy great thing on a shelf farther down the room." He glanced at Morland. "Remember?"

Morland and the other three all nodded.

Morehouse volunteered, "He said it was one of Pamela's prize posses- sions, and it wasn't sitting quite right, and she was very particular about that, so he went and straightened it."

Barnaby didn't dare look at Penelope, knowing he'd see triumph in her eyes if not her face. "Thank you." Wanting to move the men's minds away from the vase, smoothly, he continued, "Now, if you would, cast your mind back to Tuesday evening. After dinner and tea in the drawing room, we understand that you, as a group, congregated…where?"

"We were all in here." Morland looked around the room. "More or less as we are now." He glanced at Barnaby. "With you two and the inspector chappie commandeering the library, we weren't sure if we should go in there, and with the study out of bounds as well, we all came here."

The other men nodded.

Penelope managed not to sigh. "This might be a bit tedious, but please, bear with us. We need you to tell us who you remember being here."

"We need to know," Barnaby clarified, "who came in when you made your way here and remained here until at least nine-thirty."

Penelope nodded at Cordingley, who happened to be standing at the end of the billiard table and was closest to Barnaby and Penelope. "If you would, Mr. Cordingley, did you come in with all the others, and who do you remember came in with you and remained until nine-thirty?"

Cordingley glanced around, then said, "I walked in with Carrington and Griffith, and Fentiman, Vincent, and Patterson were ahead of us. We were playing rounds and chatting for most of the time, and I'm fairly certain all of us remained until we went up at some time after ten." He glanced at Barnaby and Penelope. "Others were here as well, but I didn't interact with them, so I'm not sure when they left."

Penelope smiled at him. "Thank you. That's exactly the information we want to hear." She shifted her gaze to the next gentleman. "Mr. Patterson?"

Barnaby listened intently as they worked their way around the twelve men in the room. Helpfully, there were no arguments over who was present or who wasn't, with most confirming each other's presence and many mentioning Richard as being there.

"Quite a dab hand with the cue, you know?" Griffith observed of Richard. "Not one you'd want to challenge for any meaningful wager."

Judging by the earnest nods from the younger men, Richard had left a lasting impression.

When the last man, Wincombe, had given his account, which tallied with everyone else's recollections, Penelope arched a brow at Barnaby.

Returning a slight nod, he swept his gaze over the faces, then spoke to the room at large. "None of you have mentioned Leith. Do any of you recall him being here?"

Morland frowned. "He arrived with us from the drawing room. I'm sure of that. But later…" He shrugged. "I can't remember seeing him."

Others were nodding thoughtfully, clearly reviewing their memories and not finding Leith in the billiards room.

Kilpatrick, who was standing at the far end of the room, shifted. "I don't remember seeing him in here, but I think he must have been for a time, as I was." Kilpatrick had stated, and others had verified, that fifteen minutes or so after they'd settled in the room, he'd left the company and the house to walk across the fields to his home. Kilpatrick went on, "When I left to go home, I spotted him on the stairs, heading up. He saw me and said he had letters to finish. I waved good night and went on to the side door. I assume he continued up the stairs to his room."

Barnaby resisted the urge to look at Penelope. "Just remind us, at what time was that?"

Kilpatrick blew out a breath. "Well, if we got here at a little after eight"—he glanced around, and the others nodded—"then I must have left at the latest by eight-twenty." He paused, plainly calculating, then stated, "It must have been about then, because I reached home at eight-forty-five, and it's a good twenty-minute walk."

"Thank you." Penelope beamed at Kilpatrick, then swept the company with a smile. "That's all very clear."

"Indeed." Barnaby nodded. "You have our thanks."

With that, he quickly ushered Penelope from the room while pretending not to hear Lord Wincombe ask whether they'd found the murderer yet.

Penelope fought to contain her exclamations until they were safely behind the library's doors.

But before she could expostulate, Barnaby held up a staying hand. "We should wait to learn what Stokes discovers."

She frowned at her spouse. "But on several counts, it's increasingly clear that the murderer is *Leith*." She swung away and started pacing. "What I can't for the life of me imagine is why. What on earth can he have to hide?"

"Let's see what the maid who tends Leith's room says about his letter writing." Barnaby frowned. "Although he does seem to have been writing quite a sheaf of letters, or else they're proving difficult to pen. But if he was truly writing letters, then perhaps we've missed something."

"We haven't," Penelope all but growled. She started pacing along the bookshelves. "But I still can't make sense of it, and given Leith's rank, unless we find some real proof as to why he would do such a thing…" She huffed. "Well, it's not going to be easy to prod the Commissioner into charging Leith with Monty's murder."

Barnaby sighed. "I know, but patience. We'll get there in the end. We always do."

Penelope reached the far end of the bookshelves. She swung around and started pacing back, then abruptly halted. She stared—almost ferociously—at a tome on the bottom shelf.

Puzzled, Barnaby asked, "What is it?"

"You know when something is just not right, and no matter how much you try to ignore it, your eyes keep returning to it, and you simply can't not see it?"

"Yes."

She pointed at the hefty tome. "While we were interviewing everyone and I was sitting in the armchair, watching our interviewees, this book was just inside my line of vision. I'd noted it more or less as soon as we arrived, and I knew it was…well, *wrong*."

Barnaby walked to where he could see the offending volume. It was a tall, inches-wide tome covered in faded red leather. "Wrong in what way?" It looked perfectly normal to him.

"It's stupidly misshelved! Who puts *The Collected Works of Shakespeare* with maps and geography?" Shaking her head, Penelope swung and pointed at a shelf behind her. "It belongs there, with the other works of poetry and literature. There's even space for it there." She scowled at the irritating book. "I'm going to reshelve it where it belongs."

She marched to the tome, bent, and wriggled it free, then hefted it. "Oh!"

"What?" Barnaby closed the distance between them.

Slowly, Penelope replied, "It's not a book. Or at least, it might once have been a book, but now, it's one of those book-safes. A box to hold valuables that masquerades as a book." She tipped her head, fingertips exploring the longer side. "The catch should be somewhere here... Ah, there it is!"

The lid of the book-box released. Balancing the tome on one hand, she flipped back the lid. "What have we here?"

"Sit down and let's see." Barnaby steered her to the cluster of chairs they'd used to interview the company.

Her gaze fixed on the contents of the box, Penelope fell into the first chair and set the box on her lap.

Barnaby sat in the chair alongside and leaned across, watching as she lifted a thick folded parchment from the box.

With bated breath, Penelope unfolded the parchment, then her eyes widened, and her breath left her in a rush.

"What is it?" Barnaby angled to see.

She tilted the document so he could read what she had. "It's the last will and testament of Augustus Frederick Armstrong, the late Earl of Leith. And if memory serves, this was written mere days before he died."

In stunned amazement, they stared at the document.

After a lengthy pause, Penelope admitted, "I never imagined—never would have imagined—that Leith's secret might be something like this."

Barnaby nodded. "Of this magnitude." After two more seconds, he tipped his head at the document. "We're going to have to read it and learn what it is that the man currently holding the title is so desperate to conceal."

"Indeed." Penelope drew in a deep breath and, holding the document so Barnaby could read it as she did, turned over the front page.

It didn't take them long to realize what they held.

Penelope met Barnaby's eyes. "Good Lord!" She looked across the room, staring unseeing at the fateful window through which Leith had watched Monty Underhill retrieve his last payment. "I can only vaguely recall Jonathon. Do you remember him?"

"Only distantly. He was several years behind me at Eton." Barnaby thought, then added, "He vanished from the ton when he was about twenty, soon after he came on the town."

Barnaby looked at the parchment, and his features hardened. "You wanted to know what secret Leith could possibly have that would be worth killing for. This document definitely qualifies."

Holding the will, Penelope lifted the box and sprang to her feet. "We need to show Stokes." She dropped the book-box onto the chair.

Barnaby joined her, and they strode to the door. He opened it, and Penelope rushed out, and he followed at her heels.

He strode after her as she hurried toward the baize-covered door at the end of the hall.

She was almost there when the door was flung wide, and Stokes, his features grimly set, strode through.

"It's Leith!"

It took a second for them to realize they'd spoken in unison.

Stokes blinked, then demanded, "What have you found?"

Penelope all but jigged with impatience, yet still insisted, "You first."

Barnaby added, "Trust us, it'll make more sense that way."

Stokes stated, "While Leith's been here, he hasn't written any letters of any sort. Not one. Not even a note. And a tweeny saw him leaving his room on Tuesday evening at a little after eight-thirty."

"That fits with what we learned," Barnaby said. "On Tuesday evening, Kilpatrick saw Leith head upstairs at about eight-twenty, ostensibly to write letters. Both Cordingley and Percival were in the billiards room throughout the relevant period."

"And neither Cordingley nor Richard have ever stayed at Wyndham Castle, but Leith has," Penelope said.

She paused, then whirled to look at Barnaby. "We forgot to ask whether anyone remembered seeing Leith on the lawn after the murder."

Barnaby nodded at the will. "I don't think that matters now."

"What is that?" Stokes reached for the will.

Penelope let him take it. "It's what Leith killed to hide."

She opened her mouth to explain but stopped as Alison Waterhouse rushed into the hall from the direction of the rear terrace.

Plainly distraught, Alison skidded to a halt before Penelope. "Do you know where she is?"

"Who?"

"My mother! I was told she'd taken a fall."

Penelope glanced at Barnaby. "The other ladies said she'd gone upstairs to get a shawl—"

On a gasp, Alison whisked around and set off up the stairs.

Frowning, Penelope called, "But she should have come back down by now."

Alison didn't hear and didn't stop in her headlong rush up the stairs.

Penelope, Barnaby, and Stokes watched her disappear, then a moment later, they heard a wail. "Mama!"

The investigators looked at one another, then hurried after Alison.

Stokes was in the lead as they rushed through the gallery and into a long corridor.

Halfway along, Penelope saw Mrs. Waterhouse stretched out on the runner as if she'd fallen forward, face-first.

Alison was struggling to help her mother up.

"Wait!" Stokes called. "We should check for injuries first."

Penelope swooped on Alison and raised her and drew her to the corridor's side to allow Barnaby and Stokes to crouch on either side of the fallen lady.

Barnaby gently inspected the back of Mrs. Waterhouse's head, then looked at Stokes. "She's been hit, but I think not too hard. Just enough to knock her out."

"I'm awake now," Mrs. Waterhouse weakly protested.

His features set, Stokes nodded to Barnaby, and together, they gently helped Mrs. Waterhouse to her feet.

She swayed, but gradually steadied. Penelope released Alison, who rushed to her mother's side.

Alison peered into her mother's face. "What happened?"

"I…I suppose I must have stumbled on a fold in the runner, lost my balance, and fallen." Mrs. Waterhouse frowned. "My feet seemed to go out from under me, and I fell forward…and my head hurts *so*!"

Penelope had been studying the runner. "You didn't stumble. That's what you and we were supposed to think." She pointed farther down the corridor to the end of the runner, which lay rumpled. "It's been jerked quite powerfully. That's what caused you to fall."

With her hand gingerly held to the back of her head, Mrs. Waterhouse squinted at Penelope. "Someone did this to me?"

Penelope's lips set. "I fear so. They made you fall, then hit you on the back of your head to make sure you were incapacitated, at least for a little while." She looked at Stokes and Barnaby. "I believe we know who, but why…?"

Footsteps climbed the stairs, then turned in their direction, and Richard and Rosalind came into view.

Walking toward them, Richard explained, "We were coming to find you to tell you our news, and we heard your voices and came to see…"

He halted and stared at Alison, who was wholly engaged in comforting her mother, then Richard looked at Rosalind.

Rosalind's gaze had also fixed on Alison. "Alison, where's Regina?"

Alison glanced up. "Leith came to tell me that Mama had taken a fall…" Alison frowned and looked at her mother. "I expected to find half the household here."

Her tone rising, Rosalind prompted, "And Regina?"

"It's all right," Alison assured her. "I left her with Leith. We were out near the shrubbery. He said he'd walk back with her."

Horror washed over Penelope. She met Barnaby's and Stokes's gazes, then looked at Richard and Rosalind. "Leith is the murderer."

"What?" Rosalind stared at Penelope.

"Oh God!" Richard spun and raced for the stairs. "And Regina is with him."

Stokes and Barnaby were on Richard's heels as he rushed down the stairs. Penelope and Rosalind followed as fast as they could.

On reaching the hall, Stokes peeled away, pushed open the baize-covered door, and bellowed for his men and Gearing.

Barnaby paused only to confirm that Penelope and Rosalind were behind him, then yelled after Stokes, "We'll start searching from the shrubbery!"

Poised in the doorway, Stokes waved them on. "Go! I'll turn out everyone else and follow."

CHAPTER 12

*D*esperately searching for some sign of Regina, Richard halted just inside the shrubbery.

He listened intently, but heard no sound, no rustle, no crackle of a leaf.

Chest heaving, dread pounding in his veins, he waited for Barnaby, Penelope, and Rosalind to catch up with him.

When they arrived, his hands on his hips, he swung to face them. "I don't think they're here anymore. Given the time it would have taken Alison to get to the house, Leith and Regina could be anywhere. He might even be at the stable."

Rosalind hauled in a huge breath.

"No!" Penelope slapped a hand over Rosalind's lips. "Don't call out to her!"

Above Penelope's fingers, Rosalind's eyes widened. When Penelope drew her hand away, Rosalind whispered, "Why not?"

Beyond grim, Barnaby replied, "Because she's walking with a murderer who almost certainly has designs on her life. Even if she's close enough to hear, he won't let her respond."

"And showing him how close we are might force his hand with whatever he's planning." Penelope, too, was scanning the hedges and bushes all around. "That's the last thing we want to do."

"If possible, we need to find and join them without giving Leith a chance to put whatever plan he's concocted into action." Barnaby walked deeper into the more formal section of the shrubbery.

Frowning, Richard asked, "How do you know he has a plan?"

"Because," Penelope replied, "while Monty's murder was spur of the moment and very much *un*planned, this time, Leith isn't overcome by rage. He's cold-bloodedly calculating. He tumbled Mrs. Waterhouse and knocked her out to distract and divert Alison and get Regina alone. Believe me, he didn't do that for no reason."

Rosalind looked at Richard helplessly, and he reached out and took her hand.

He squeezed her fingers. "Trust them—they are the experts in this."

Penelope was frowning increasingly direfully. "What *is* he planning?" Frustration edged her words.

Barnaby had been casting about, peering through the trees and checking along the hedged avenues. Returning to them, he stated, "The estate's too extensive, the grounds far too large to mount any swift and effective search." He raised his head and looked toward the house. "Stokes has his troops fanning out across the rear to the north, east, and west. Some will come tramping in this direction soon."

Like a weathervane in an uncertain breeze, Penelope had been aimlessly turning this way, then that.

Richard focused on her face. "So what is he planning?"

Rosalind pleaded, "Where would he take her?"

Behind her spectacles, Penelope's eyes flew wide. *"That's it!"* Her face cleared, and she swung to face Barnaby. "The orchard. That's where this started. That's where he'll take her. He's clever enough to have guessed that Regina was supposed to leave a payment in the apple-tree hollow. He's trying to throw us off the scent by making it seem *she* was Monty's killer!"

Barnaby blinked and made the deductive leap. "Dear God!" He bolted for the orchard.

Richard released Rosalind's hand and raced after Barnaby.

Penelope hiked up her skirts and, with Rosalind beside her, raced after the men as they streamed along the outer hedge of the shrubbery and pushed on across the lawn to the archway into the orchard.

≈

Barnaby ran flat-out through the archway. Ahead, by the fateful apple tree, he saw Leith, his face contorted into a murderous mask and his hands locked about Regina's throat as he squeezed the life from her.

"Let her go!" Barnaby yelled and barreled on.

At his heels, Richard swore. "You bastard! Unhand her!"

Leith's head came up. He saw them, and his grip slackened.

Then he snarled and, as Barnaby and Richard neared, flung Regina's limp form at them.

Barnaby caught her.

Richard sidestepped and launched himself at Leith as he turned and attempted to flee.

The flying tackle brought Leith crashing down.

But he wasn't about to surrender. He rolled, taking Richard with him, and fought to get free.

Leaving Leith to Richard, Barnaby gently laid Regina down. Relief coursed through him when she coughed, then hauled in a painful breath, and her brows drew into a frown. He sensed her awareness returning and life reinfusing her limbs.

In a flurry of skirts, Penelope and Rosalind arrived.

Rosalind fell to her knees. "Darling!" She reached for Regina and gathered her in, cradling her sister's head and shoulders.

Penelope met Barnaby's eyes and tipped her head to where Richard was grappling with a furious, desperate, and heavier Leith. "Go!"

Barnaby surged to his feet and started toward the brawling men. Leith had bulled his way farther down the row of trees, but Richard had managed to maneuver around so that he blocked Leith's path deeper into the orchard.

As Barnaby approached, Richard landed a solid blow to Leith's chin.

Leith reeled back and fell.

Barnaby saw Leith's face as he struggled to his feet. Lips drawn back in a snarl of unrestrained rage, Leith saw Barnaby coming for him, and with a rush of strength, Leith surged upright, drew a knife—a dagger—from his coat, and rounded on Richard.

"Knife!" Barnaby warned.

Richard saw the blade flashing in the morning light as Leith lunged toward him, the knife at chest height.

At the last instant possible, Richard twisted away from the strike.

Leith saw and attempted to correct his aim, yet his blade scored only Richard's upper arm.

The shift in positions gave Richard the advantage, and he hammered a right hook into Leith's chin and followed that with a powerful punch to the side of Leith's head.

The would-be earl went down, collapsing face-first into the grass.

Chest heaving, Richard stood over him, then, finally convinced the miscreant was, indeed, down and out for the moment, as Barnaby joined him, Richard met Barnaby's eyes and faintly smiled. "I haven't brawled like that since I was at school."

Barnaby nodded at the fallen man. "Obviously, you haven't forgotten how."

Richard glanced to where the ladies sat in a froth of skirts in the orchard's grass. "Yet another thing I've learned about myself while here."

Barnaby followed Richard's gaze and smiled to himself.

Regina was sitting up on her own and delicately massaging her throat. Her gaze was alert, and her color appeared to be returning.

Looking over the orchard wall, Barnaby and Richard saw Stokes and his men, followed by virtually everyone else, streaming across the lawn toward them.

Leith groaned and stirred, drawing Barnaby's and Richard's attention.

Having heard the groan, Rosalind rose, and her expression that of an avenging angel, she stalked past Richard to Leith's side and administered a well-aimed kick to his ribs. "You monster! How dare you!"

"Shh." Richard caught her and drew her into his arms and pressed a kiss to her temple. "We caught him in time. That's all that matters."

Leith groaned again and rolled. He raised his head enough to slant a bleary-eyed glance up at them as if, even now, weighing his chances of winning free.

His features reflecting open disgust, Richard looked at Leith and shook his head. "You're a despicable excuse for a gentleman. How on earth are you an earl?"

"He's not." Barnaby watched as Stokes and his men cleared the archway and strode toward them, then Barnaby glanced at Richard and Rosalind. "That's what this has been about."

No stranger to the contortions of inheritance, Richard widened his eyes. He looked at Leith. "Really?"

But Leith was studying Barnaby. Hoarsely, Leith asked, "You know?"

Barnaby met Leith's gaze as Stokes came up, and O'Donnell and Morgan reached down to haul Leith to his feet. "We've worked it all out," Barnaby coldly informed him. "And we have the proof."

Leith read the conviction in Barnaby's eyes, and the desperate hope that had sustained him drained, and he slumped in the policemen's hold.

Leaving O'Donnell and Morgan to take Leith in charge, Stokes nodded to Richard. "Good work."

Richard smiled. "I wasn't about to let the bastard escape."

Rosalind hugged him.

With Richard's arm around her, the pair walked back toward the apple tree beneath the spreading branches of which Regina still sat, and Barnaby and Stokes followed.

Penelope was crouching beside Regina, supporting and encouraging the younger woman, but rose as they neared. Her gaze swept Richard—and fixed on the bloody gash in his coat sleeve. "You've been cut!"

"What?" Rosalind pushed out from under Richard's arm and swung to see. "Where?"

Penelope saw the intensity of Rosalind's reaction and smiled knowingly as all Rosalind's pent-up concern focused on a new target.

Richard met Penelope's eyes and half glared at her, then gave his attention to assuring Rosalind that he wasn't about to bleed to death from a relatively shallow cut.

Mrs. Hemmings arrived, supported by Lady Carville, and Penelope handed Regina into their care.

As she did so, something beside the apple tree's trunk caught Penelope's eye, and forever curious, she went to see what it was. She peered into the grass at the base of the trunk, then turned, waved to catch Stokes's attention, and beckoned. "You need to see this."

Stokes and Barnaby ducked beneath the branches and, followed by Richard and a slowly calming Rosalind, walked to where Penelope stood.

She pointed at the coil of strong rope half hidden by the grass. "This proves what his plan for Regina was."

When, after taking stock of the rope, the others looked at her, patently waiting for her to expound, she obliged. "I believe he intended to partially strangle Regina, enough to render her unconscious, then he was going to hang her from this tree." With her gaze, she measured the distance between the thicker branches overhead and the ground. "There's just enough clearance to imagine that she might have done it herself, and the bruising from the rope would have obscured the marks of strangulation." After pausing to allow that to sink in, she added, "I suspect he would have then 'found' her, no doubt claiming that he'd seen her safely back to the house, but that when he'd left her inside, she'd appeared 'troubled.' Something along those lines."

His voice low so only they would hear, Barnaby filled in, "He'd read Monty's black book and knew Regina was one of Monty's victims. He meant us to see the evidence of Monty's own record of Regina making a payment that morning—and somehow, Leith had guessed that she was the one who was supposed to have left a payment in the tree's hollow, and that was what Monty was looking for when Leith struck him."

"Leith saw how unsettled Regina was when the conversation turned to everyone's whereabouts at the time Monty was killed." Richard looked at Rosalind and lightly hugged her. "Remember?"

Rosalind nodded. "During the picnic yesterday, especially." She looked at the others. "Regina was obviously uncomfortable when the discussion touched on that subject."

"Right." Stokes kept his voice down. "So he was going to string her up as if she'd taken her own life because she was guilty of murdering Underhill." He looked at Penelope. "That's diabolical."

She nodded. "He intended to use her as his scapegoat. The one thing he failed to realize was that Regina's too short to have landed the blow he had." She glanced at Leith, drooping between O'Donnell and Morgan. "That simply wouldn't have occurred to him."

Stokes huffed. "It wouldn't have occurred to many at all." He, too, directed a steely look at Leith. "Few would have doubted his word."

"At least at first," Penelope said. "And really, that's probably all he would have needed to walk free, unsuspected of any crime. Monty's evidence of his misdeeds, which we've discovered but have yet to share, would likely have remained hidden, possibly for decades."

Leaning heavily on her mother's arm, Regina took careful steps toward them. "Inspector?"

Stokes turned and, instantly solicitous, walked to her side. "Yes?"

Regina drew in a deeper breath and managed to rasp, "He said something. When he started to…" She weakly waved at her throat, where the white skin was mottled by deepening bruises. "He said, 'You, my dear, are the perfect scapegoat.'"

Eyes still reflecting the shock of her ordeal, Regina looked at Stokes. "I thought you should know."

"Thank you." Gravely, Stokes inclined his head. He hesitated, then, no doubt judging that it might help Regina to hear it stated, he added, "We believe he intended to use your death as his ticket to freedom."

Regina's lips quivered, but then her chin firmed, and she nodded. "I thought it must have been that."

Vincent approached. His expression severe, he stared hard at Leith, then turned to Stokes. "Inspector. Do you and your men need any assistance?"

Grateful for the offer, Stokes arranged to have Leith temporarily held in a cellar storeroom.

At Stokes's nod, grim-faced, O'Donnell and Morgan marched Leith out of the orchard. The entire company and many of the staff had gathered in one large crowd on the lawn. They parted, creating an avenue to the forecourt, and the policemen steered Leith, with his hands now bound, his head hanging, and his gaze on the ground, to the house as comprehension, disbelief, and scandalized horror appeared on every face as the reality sank in that the Earl of Leith was Monty Underhill's murderer.

"Hold still!" Rosalind glared at Richard as, shirtless, he leaned back against one of the raised benches in the conservatory.

Pots of greenery had been moved aside to provide space for the bowls and balms and bandages Rosalind and Lady Pamela had deemed necessary to tend Richard's wound.

Using a damp cloth to firmly dab at the inches-long cut, Rosalind flicked a glance at Richard's face. "You're distracting enough without moving."

Richard grinned. "I'm relieved you've noticed."

Rosalind colored faintly but, her eyes on the wound, murmured, "I'm not blind."

Richard decided to let that comment pass unchallenged.

Several minutes later, after she'd dabbed ointment on the wound and bandaged it neatly, Rosalind stepped back and raised one hand to her temple to push aside a dangling glossy brown curl.

She met Richard's eyes, studied his subtly amused, dark-blue gaze, then rather waspishly insisted, "This is not funny! I don't find seeing you hurt amusing in the slightest!" Unbidden, the shock of realizing he'd been injured and was bleeding rolled through her again, and she swatted at his shoulder. "You didn't need to let him cut you."

His amusement deepening, although he did his best to hide it, Richard replied, "It was that or have him stab me in the chest. I chose the less damaging option."

"You could have let him run. He would have been caught."

Richard sobered. "I couldn't let him get away, not after what he did to Regina." He paused, then added, "What he was planning was beyond despicable."

Rosalind met his gaze, then sighed. "I don't even know why I'm arguing with you." She looked at the bandage. "You're as healthy as a horse, and I expect that will heal with no lasting damage."

Smiling gently, Richard reached for her. "I expect so, too." He drew her into his arms and looked into her lavender-blue eyes. "But truth be told, it's rather nice to have you fussing."

She primmed her lips, then, still holding his gaze, ventured, "I've heard that reacting as I did to you being wounded...says something. About how I feel."

Richard readily nodded. "I've heard the same." As she leaned against him, and something inside him purred with pleasure, he said, "I suspect that means we really should get married."

Smiling up at him, she arched a brow. "And not just dance around the subject?"

"Exactly. I feel we've discussed the possibilities sufficiently. We've already agreed we suit." Looking into her eyes, he arched his brows back. "So, when do you think we should tie the knot?"

"After today?" Rosalind's lips firmed. "As soon as possible."

Richard laughed. "I agree." Smoothly, he tightened his arms about her and bent his head, and she stretched upward, and he found her lips with his.

The kiss commenced innocently enough but quickly evolved into a deeper, hungrier pleasure.

Both knew what they wanted and could now have, and together, they set out to explore their new landscape.

Much later, when they emerged from the conservatory and joined the rest of the company for luncheon, Rosalind's lips were rosy red, and her eyes were sparkling, and Richard's cat-who-had-found-the-cream-jug smile spoke volumes.

~

The necessary denouement occurred later that day.

Immediately on returning to the house, the investigators repaired to the cellar storeroom, hoping to inveigle Leith into filling in the gaps in his story. Initially, Leith—more correctly, plain Frederick Armstrong—resisted all Stokes's and Barnaby's invitations to provide further details of what had occurred. Even when confronted with his late uncle's will, he simply set his lips and refused to say a word.

Then, Penelope lit on the strategy of filling in those details herself in increasingly outlandish fashion, and ultimately recognizing the unvoiced threat—that her inventions would henceforth shape the world's view of him—and accepting the utter futility of maintaining his silence, Frederick gritted his teeth and started to correct her.

Fact by fact, Penelope teased and extracted the complete story from him.

Eventually, armed with what they believed was a solid understanding of all that had occurred and knowing that attempting to leave the Grange without sharing the relevant parts of that understanding with all those present would cause an uproar, they decided on what they would reveal and what they wouldn't, then requested that everyone gather in the drawing room. Penelope asked Gearing to serve the company afternoon tea, if for no other reason than to give people something to do with their hands during what was likely to prove a lengthy dissertation.

Barnaby suggested that Gearing and Grimshaw attend as well so that later, they would be able to report to the staff.

Finally, the three investigators stood in the hall outside the closed drawing room doors. From inside the room, they could hear the hum of polite conversation spiced with excitement mixed with relief. The oppressive uncertainty that had afflicted the company since Monday had lifted, and all tension had dissipated, leaving everyone, for the moment, relaxed and rather eager to hear what had actually gone on.

Barnaby looked at Penelope. "Ready?"

She met his gaze. "As ready as I'll ever be."

"Right, then." Stokes opened the door and waved her in.

With a firm and deliberate tread, Penelope walked into the room and proceeded at the same steady pace all the way down the long chamber, and Barnaby and Stokes followed.

Gearing closed the door behind them, and Penelope went straight to the large fireplace, halted, and turned to face the assembled company.

Barnaby took up a position on her right, and Stokes flanked her on her left. They were there to assist with the later details, but Penelope was the arch-storyteller, and she would lead them in telling the tale.

Agog, the company had set their cups on their saucers and shifted to get an unobstructed view.

Her expression mild, Penelope swept the company with her gaze. The matrons filled the sofas and nearer armchairs, while the older gentlemen and the young ladies were seated on straight-backed chairs arranged in a large, elongated oval with, by design, the fireplace at one end being the focal point for the company. The younger gentlemen stood in clusters around the chairs, their gazes as fixed as any on the investigators.

Penelope noted the avid interest in every eye. In a clear voice, she commenced, "I'm here to tell you a story, one that could be described as a perfect illustration of the curse of ill-gotten gains."

With those words, she seized and held the entire company's intent and unwavering attention.

"For it was," she told them, "Monty Underhill's discovery of an ill-gotten gain and his subsequent pursuit of his own ill-gotten gain that led to his murder." She paused, then went on, "But the story didn't begin on Monday. Its genesis lies more than two years ago. That was when Augustus Armstrong, the late Earl of Leith, died, leaving, or so everyone believed, the title to his nephew, Frederick Armstrong.

"But Frederick stepped into the earl's shoes only because Augustus and his son, Jonathon, had had a falling-out years before, and Jonathon had vanished from the ton. After years passed with no sign of Jonathon, Augustus moved to have Jonathon officially declared dead. Subsequent to that, Frederick became Augustus's heir.

"However, as Augustus grew older, he pined for his son, and having never believed in his heart that Jonathon was truly dead, Augustus hired agents to search until they located Jonathon. Ultimately, after many years of fruitless endeavor, the agents succeeded in tracking Jonathon to New York. He had carved out a new and successful life for himself and was living in comfort, even luxury, there. As per Augustus's instructions, the agents did not inform Jonathon of his father's interest but instead dispatched the information to Augustus.

"Augustus received the news that his son was alive and well after Augustus had fallen ill and mere weeks before he died. During that time, Augustus wrote a new will. He knew his time was running out and, rather than chance waiting for his solicitor to attend him at Leith Hall, he used his previous will as a template and hand-wrote a new last testament leaving the title and entailed fortune to Jonathon and including directions of where Jonathon could now be found."

"Augustus had the new will witnessed by his estate manager and a tenant farmer who happened to be in the house, with neither man knowing what the document was, then Augustus left the new will along with the agents' letters in the drawer of a desk in his upstairs sitting room, a room he rarely used. Although he knew he was failing, he believed he would have ample time to hand the new will to his solicitor when the man responded to the summons Augustus had already sent. Presumably, he hoped the solicitor would take on the burden of informing Frederick that he was no longer Augustus's heir. But then, Augustus's heart gave out, and he died."

Penelope paused and glanced swiftly over her audience; they were captivated and hanging on her every word. "So Augustus's final testament and the knowledge of Jonathon's whereabouts, along with the correspondence relating to Jonathon being found alive, remained hidden in the drawer of the desk in the rarely used sitting room at Leith Hall. And per Augustus's previous will, his nephew, Frederick, became the Earl of Leith."

"Frederick—whom we know as Leith—lived in London. Augustus hadn't summoned him, and Frederick knew nothing of the new will or of Jonathon being alive. Other than a quick trip to Leith Hall for Augustus's funeral, over the months immediately following Augustus's death, the business of taking control of the earldom's estates kept Leith fully occupied in town. Eventually, however, he went to Leith Hall and set about working his way through all of Augustus's papers. That process took several visits over several months. It was only toward the end of that process that Leith thought to look in the drawer of the desk in the sitting room his uncle had rarely used. That's when Leith discovered his uncle's final will and realized that he wasn't, in truth, the earl at all."

To say that the company was riveted would have been a gross understatement. Satisfied, Penelope continued, "Leith made that discovery on a day when, that afternoon, he was due to join a large party for the annual Hunt Ball at Wyndham Castle. Thrown into complete turmoil by his discovery, Leith had to leave within an hour or so. Rather than leave the will—the document that effectively disinherited him—where someone else might find and read it, when he left for Wyndham Castle, he took the will with him.

"Unsurprisingly, the will captured and held his attention to the exclusion of all else. At the castle, in the room he'd been given, which happened to be in the old part of the building, Leith paced and read and paced some more—then it was time to go downstairs, or he'd be late, so he thrust the will into his bag, then left the room and locked the door behind him.

"Early the next morning, after the ball ended and Leith finally returned to his room, he was too exhausted to do anything other than fall into bed. And the next morning, when he looked for the will in his bag, it had vanished. He had no idea who could have taken the document or how anyone could have got past the locked door. But there was a huge contingent of staff brought in for the ball, as well as a host of guests who had attended. Assuming they'd somehow gained entry to the room, anyone could have found the document, realized what it was, and taken it.

"Leith now faced a dilemma. He hadn't told anyone of the final will, and he no longer had it. He couldn't prove it existed, and he didn't want to face the prospect of being disinherited. Perhaps unsurprisingly, he did nothing. He continued for several months, steadily growing ever more comfortable in his role as earl. Then, he received the first blackmail demand."

Penelope paused, then added, "Although he didn't say so, I suspect that in some corner of his mind, he must have been expecting it. He paid, of course, for the sum demanded wasn't that large, not relative to the earldom's coffers. He did, of course, try to identify his blackmailer—and by what the blackmailer had written, that person definitely held the late earl's final will—but the blackmailer was too clever and slippery, and Leith never caught any hint of who he was. None at all. And as the months went on and the demands continued, Leith continued to pay. However, parting with the money wasn't the worst of it. The knowledge that, at any moment of any day, Leith might be exposed as the imposter he was—indeed, as he has been today—weighed on him and undermined his enjoyment of his life as the Earl of Leith. More and more, the prospect of the will surfacing weighed on his mind, and there was nothing he could do to ease the pressure. And as the months passed, the pressure only grew.

"Then, Leith was invited to Patchcote Grange for this house party. And on the heels of that invitation came another demand from his blackmailer, and this time, the payment was to be made while Leith was here."

A ripple of expectation passed over the company, and several members looked at one another in speculation while others looked anxious. As if unaware of the latter, Penelope rolled on, "As directed, Leith made the payment early on Monday morning, but in designating the spot where he should leave it, his blackmailer made a fatal error."

Penelope glanced at Barnaby. They'd arranged that after she set the stage, he would step in and lead the company through the subsequent events.

He stepped forward, drawing the company's attention. "As you will by now have guessed, Monty Underhill was Leith's blackmailer." They'd agreed to, as far as possible, omit all mention of the others Monty had victimized.

Barnaby inclined his head to Lady Pamela; they'd warned the family of the substance of what they would reveal, and after recovering from the shock, stony-faced, Pamela had consented to the disclosure, which, regardless, would inevitably be made public at Leith's trial. In an even tone, Barnaby continued, "It appears that Monty had grown tired of never having any money to call his own. Blackmailing Leith was his choice of how to rectify that. We must stress that, no matter the circumstances of his death, in turning to blackmail, Monty committed a criminal act. However, to explain what happened on Monday morning, the spot Monty had nominated in which Leith was to leave his payment was the large Chinese vase that stands on a display shelf in the library."

The revelation caused muted exclamations from the gentlemen who had seen Monty go to the vase in the library that morning.

Smoothly, Barnaby continued, "In selecting that place, Monty didn't realize that someone with a spyglass, standing across the lawn in the cover of the trees, could keep the vase under observation." He paused, then added, "And that's what Frederick Armstrong did."

Barnaby glanced at Stokes, who stepped forward and stated, "Through all your interviews, you gave us the vital clues to piece together Armstrong's movements and conclusively prove that only he could have killed Underhill in the orchard. In essence, the locations of all the rest of you were either vouched for by someone else or could be proven by other facts. What occurred was this. After placing the money in the vase, Armstrong saw that the vase was in line with one of the windows. He also saw a collapsible spyglass sitting on the mantelpiece. He borrowed the spyglass, and knowing he'd been told to leave his payment in the vase before eight-thirty and also realizing that, in this instance, his blackmailer wouldn't want to leave as much money as he'd just placed inside the vase for a maid to accidentally come upon, after telling several people that he was going upstairs to his room to write letters, instead, Armstrong left the house via the side door and circled around into the band of trees that faces the house. In doing that, he was noticed by Mr. Patterson and Vincent Underhill as they made their way to the stable. Leith's footprints confirm that, from the trees, he watched the vase through the library window and waited. Eventually, as the five gentlemen who were in the library at the time can attest, Underhill came in, chatted genially to his guests, then crossed to the vase, ostensibly to straighten it. In doing so, he removed the packet of money Armstrong had placed inside.

"From the trees, Armstrong saw Underhill go to the vase and remove the money. Immediately thereafter, Underhill went out for a stroll and left the house via the front door. When Underhill stepped outside, alone, and walked across the lawn under Armstrong's eyes, Underhill's fate was sealed. To understand Armstrong's overwhelming rage, you need to appreciate that, until that moment, he'd considered Underhill not just a good friend but a mentor of sorts. Someone who, for decades, Armstrong had thought of kindly, and who he believed thought of him kindly."

"To realize that Monty was his blackmailer was a terrible shock," Penelope stated. "And while that doesn't in any way excuse what Frederick did, it does explain his violent reaction."

"In short," Stokes said, "in the grip of a towering rage, Armstrong seized the nearest weapon to hand, an iron garden stake, and stalked after Underhill as he strolled toward the orchard. We believe that, with the orchard's grass so thick, Underhill didn't hear Armstrong approaching. Underhill was examining a hollow in a tree when Armstrong came up behind him and hit him over the head with the iron stake, killing him."

"Subsequently," Barnaby stated, "Armstrong did his best to cover his tracks while also searching for his late uncle's will, a document he couldn't afford to allow to fall into anyone else's hands. He was convinced Monty had it and had hidden it somewhere. On returning to the house, once again via the side door"—Barnaby tipped his head toward the younger crew—"with his return witnessed by Patterson and Miss Samantha Goodrich, Armstrong didn't join the rest of the company on the lawns but instead slipped into Monty's study and comprehensively searched for the will. He even found the key to the safe and looked in there, but he didn't find the will.

"He was frustrated, but not about to give up. On Tuesday evening, when Armstrong told Kilpatrick, who was leaving the house to walk to his home, that he was going upstairs to write letters, Armstrong went to

Monty's bedchamber. He was searching there when Monty's valet"—Barnaby nodded down the room to where Grimshaw stood with Gearing before the closed doors—"came into the adjoining dressing room. Armstrong struck the valet unconscious before he'd had a chance to see who the intruder was. And Armstrong continued to search.

"However," Barnaby went on, "after that, with a constable on guard in the study and us interviewing in the library, Armstrong decided to lie low for the moment. But he grew increasingly concerned at what we might learn, and so he concocted a plan to offer us someone he hoped would be a believable scapegoat. He'd learned that after walking with her sister, Rosalind, and then parting from her, Regina Hemmings had been alone in the shrubbery at the time Armstrong had killed Monty. Regina didn't have an alibi for the murder, and so Armstrong decided to lure her to the orchard. To do that—to separate her from Alison Waterhouse, with whom Regina was walking—Armstrong caused Mrs. Waterhouse to fall in the corridor upstairs and followed that by striking her sufficiently hard to render her unconscious, then he used news of her mother's accident to send Alison flying to the house, leaving Regina to walk alone, with Armstrong, supposedly back to the house.

"But instead, Armstrong, who as we all know can be charming when he wishes, led Regina to the orchard, to where he'd set his scene. Luckily, mere moments before, in the library, we'd discovered the vital will and realized the murderer was Armstrong. Consequently, we set about hunting him down—and caught up with him just in time to prevent him staging Regina's death so that it would appear to everyone that she'd committed suicide, presumably driven by guilt over having killed Monty."

"Only," Penelope said, "we'd already established that Regina couldn't have delivered the blow that killed Monty. She's too short. But that's what was behind the incident you all saw with your own eyes in the orchard this morning."

They had, Penelope thought, covered every base and accounted for the facts the company knew in a way that spared Monty's other victims.

"There really is little more to the tale," Penelope stated. If she saw relief visibly flow through several of her listeners, she gave no sign. "As I said in my opening," she continued, "this was a case illuminating the curse of ill-gotten gains. If on finding his uncle's final will, Leith had immediately taken steps to share it with the family solicitor—as he should have done—there would have been nothing for him to be blackmailed about. And if Monty hadn't taken steps to collect his own ill-gotten gains

—if he hadn't stolen the will from Frederick's bag, read it, and decided to use it for blackmail rather than deliver it to the proper authorities—he would be alive today."

"Both these men either have paid or will pay the price for making those decisions." Stokes looked around the room. "Frederick Armstrong is, even now, being taken from this house and removed to Bow Street. He will stand trial for the murder of Mr. Underhill, and he will be convicted. Of that, there is no question, no doubt."

"Despite"—Penelope tipped her head—"or perhaps because of the curse of ill-gotten gains, justice will be served."

With that, she graciously inclined her head to the company, and Barnaby and Stokes did the same.

Then, they walked straight up the room and out of the door Gearing rushed to hold for them and left the company at Patchcote Grange avidly discussing the events and speculating on the principle and prospects of the curse of ill-gotten gains.

EPILOGUE

SEPTEMBER 18, 1841. SEDDINGTON GRANGE, LINCOLNSHIRE.

he celebration of the union of Richard Percival and Rosalind Hemmings was an unusual event. To begin with, for a ton wedding, the guest list was surprisingly short. For another, many of the guests hailed from strata of society not normally seen at ton gatherings.

And then there were the children.

Not only were Richard's much-loved nephew and niece there, but they were joined by a coterie of others drawn from both the Percival and Hemmings families and the Percival-connected Glendowers. The small army ranged in age from twelve down to infants-in-arms, and Barnaby and Penelope's sons, Stokes and Griselda's two, and Montague and Violet's children readily joined with Rose and Thomas's brood in flinging themselves into the festivities with unrestrained abandon.

The ceremony, held midmorning in the small church on the grounds of the Grange, had been attended by many locals and staff as well as the invited guests who had traveled from London and elsewhere for the event. With so many children among the congregation, the proceedings were necessarily short and to the point and had culminated in Richard and Rosalind leaving the church under a hail of rice with huge smiles on their faces.

After half an hour or so of chatting and exclaiming—and with much made of the laudable good sense displayed by the bride and groom in acknowledging the wisdom of their elders who had suggested they would suit—the guests joined the wedding party in streaming over fields carpeted in late-summer wildflowers to the clipped lawns that surrounded the grand old house of Seddington Grange, Richard and William's ancestral home.

The wedding breakfast, held in the first-floor ballroom with its long windows framing a spectacular view over the nearby sea, was an unabashedly joyous affair, brimming with laughter and good cheer. It was patently clear that, as was the case in the bright-blue sky outside, there were no clouds hovering on Richard and Rosalind's now-shared horizon.

After the sumptuous feast was dispensed with and the toasts were duly made, while those inclined to dance circled on the parquet floor, Penelope, Griselda, Violet, and Rose, dutifully followed by Barnaby, Stokes, Montague, and Thomas, took their children out to run and play on the balcony outside the ballroom's long windows. The sunshine was simply glorious, and a light sea breeze flirted with the ladies' ribbons and curls. The eight adults stood and idly chatted while they supervised their children gamboling and frolicking on the flagstones.

Gradually, Penelope, Barnaby, and Stokes gravitated together. Barnaby and Stokes leaned against the balustrade, while Penelope stood in their wind-shadow and, with a maternal smile lighting her face, watched Oliver and Pip as they helped the other boys and girls build a fort from the chairs and tables that had stood at one end of the balcony.

Despite her preoccupation, she spared a glance for Stokes. "Have you heard when Leith will go to trial?"

"They've just set the date for late October," Stokes replied. "His case threw the Law Lords into a bit of a quandary. Should he be tried as a lord or not? But now, they've heard from Jonathon Armstrong, the legitimate Earl of Leith. Apparently, he'd had no idea his father had died nor that he'd been declared dead, let alone formally resurrected and reinstated as the earl's heir. After learning of Frederick's usurpation of the title, Jonathon decided to return to England and step into his father's shoes, so Frederick is back to being Mr. Armstrong, and his trial will therefore proceed at the Old Bailey."

Pensively, Barnaby murmured, "If only he'd done the right thing as soon as he found that will."

"But he didn't," Penelope said. "And with him and Monty both doing the wrong thing, one might say they've ended up doing for each other."

Stokes nodded. "Leith will definitely hang, so they've effectively killed each other."

A gruff voice said, "It's too beautiful a day for you lot to be discussing murder."

Penelope turned, and Barnaby and Stokes straightened and looked at the newcomer.

All three smiled at the stocky, neatly and conservatively dressed man, and Penelope held out her hands. "Curtis! We saw you slip into the chapel at the last minute. You've been playing least in sight."

Curtis squeezed her hands and released them and nodded to Barnaby and Stokes. "Gents." Returning his gaze to Penelope, he admitted, "Ton weddings are a little out of my league, but after what Percival and I went through that time we crossed paths with you three, when he told me you'd all be here—friendly faces and all—I decided I should come and support him." He glanced through the windows into the ballroom, still crowded with happy, laughing guests. "But if those two old-lady aunts of his— Lady Campbell-Carstairs and Lady Kelly—are to be believed, it seems he's made a wise choice. And I have to say, Rosalind seems a good sort all around—friendly and not superior."

"She is, indeed," Penelope assured him. "She's exactly the sort of wife Richard needs. She and I are encouraging him to stand for Parliament."

Curtis thought, then nodded his large head. "Aye. I could see him there. He'd be good at it, too."

"So we think." Penelope beamed.

Curtis studied her for a moment, then looked at Barnaby. "Those lads of yours are working out a treat. Quick-witted, all of them, and they certainly know London's streets. Off their own bats, several of my agents have taken one of the lads under their wings to see how they do and train them up, as it were, but most are too young to be sure of as yet. We'll see how things pan out."

Barnaby was pleased, and Stokes looked approving as well. Curtis owned and ran the Curtis Inquiry Agency, which specialized in making discreet inquiries for London's wealthier citizens. His experience was considerable, his expertise unparalleled, and circumspection was the watchword for him and his men. If a lord wanted information on his son's acquaintances, or a banker wanted intelligence on a large debtor, or a company director had questions regarding another director, it was to Curtis they turned.

"And I wanted to mention," Curtis went on, "that older lad—Julian Alder—is one I'm definitely keeping on. He's beyond sharp-eyed, and his brain is, far as I can tell, always engaged. He sees and puts things together far beyond his years. I'm taking him on myself."

Barnaby smiled. "Excellent." To Stokes, he said, "Julian was the lad who brought us the information on Sir Ulysses Moubray in the Thomas Cardwell case."

Stokes's expression cleared. "The very prompt alibi that helped us get along rather faster." He looked at Curtis. "You're right. He's a promising lad for your business."

"So I think." To Penelope, Curtis added, "Julian's a good lad in other ways, too. Devoted to his widowed mother, it seems, so there's a solid family foundation there, which I always find bodes well."

Penelope nodded. "I quite agree." She glanced at her sons, still busy with engineering works, then smiled a touch impishly at Curtis. "But, Curtis, where's your hat? I almost didn't recognize you without it."

Barnaby and Stokes chuckled. Curtis invariably wore a low-crowned hat, a particular style that had become something of a personal hallmark.

Curtis mock-glowered and growled, "Aye, I feel half dressed without it, and my head is cold in this sea breeze, but that damned butler insisted on taking it. All I can say is he better give it back!"

Penelope, Barnaby, and Stokes laughed, then Thomas and Montague, having noticed Curtis, came up to shake his hand, and the conversation spread to wider fields as the ladies came to join them, and the children cavorted and played knights and castles at the other end of the balcony.

Surveying the scene, Penelope leaned against Barnaby.

When he glanced down at her and arched an inquiring brow, she smiled and murmured, "Friends, family, a wonderful wedding. This is the life. May it never end."

"Amen," he whispered.

The smile they shared was private and full of mutual satisfaction, then they turned back to the discussion and this group who were now such a large part of their lives.

∼

∼

Dear Reader,

The Honorable Richard Percival first appeared in one of the early volumes in *The Casebook of Barnaby Adair* series, *Loving Rose,* and was always destined to have his day in the sun, romance-wise. Given Richard's degree of involvement in that long ago case and his consequent connection with Barnaby, Penelope, and Stokes, then it was always likely that Richard's wider life would, once again, cross the investigators' paths.

And where more likely than at a summer house party for Richard, the erstwhile rakehell, to stumble upon the fated love of his life, along with a dead body, a situation that immediately triggers Richard's protective instincts? And naturally, those instincts would prompt him to send for Barnaby, Penelope, and Stokes with all speed. I hope you've enjoyed returning to one of the classic venues of ton life in this latest installment in the continuing adventures of Barnaby, Penelope, Stokes, and friends.

As for what's coming next, in *Who Killed the Earl of Moran?* (March 19, 2026), we return to Mayfair, to the heart of the London social scene, with our investigators called in by Curtis, of the Curtis Inquiry Agency, to help solve the case of a powerful man disliked by many found murdered in his study.

Information about earlier volumes in THE CASEBOOK OF BARNABY ADAIR series—*Where the Heart Leads*, *The Peculiar Case of Lord Finsbury's Diamonds*, *The Masterful Mr. Montague*, *The Curious Case of Lady Latimer's Shoes*, *Loving Rose: The Redemption of Malcolm Sinclair*, *The Confounding Case of the Carisbrook Emeralds*, *The Murder at Mandeville Hall*, *The Meriwell Legacy*, *Dead Beside the Thames*, *Marriage and Murder*, *and The Murder of Thomas Cardwell*—can be found following.

Barnaby, Penelope, Stokes, Griselda, and their friends and supporters continue to tackle the solving of crimes with undimmed enthusiasm. I hope they and their adventures solving mysteries and exposing villains will continue to entertain you in the future just as much as they do me.

Enjoy!

Stephanie.

For alerts as new books are released, plus information on upcoming books, exclusive sweepstakes and sneak peeks into upcoming novels, sign up for Stephanie's Private Email Newsletter http://www.stephanielaurens. com/newsletter-signup/

Or if you don't have time to chat and want a quick email alert, sign up and follow me at BookBub https://www.bookbub.com/authors/stephanie-laurens

The ultimate source for detailed information on all Stephanie's published books, including covers, descriptions, and excerpts, is Stephanie's Website www.stephanielaurens.com

You can also follow Stephanie via her Amazon Author Page at http://tinyurl.com/zc3e9mp

Goodreads members can follow Stephanie via her author page https://www.goodreads.com/author/show/9241.Stephanie_Laurens

You can email Stephanie at stephanie@stephanielaurens.com

Or find her on Facebook
https://www.facebook.com/AuthorStephanieLaurens/

COMING NEXT:
WHO KILLED THE EARL OF MORAN?
The Casebook of Barnaby Adair #13
To be released in March, 2026.

Mrs. Mary Alder, in discharging her last duty to her mistress, the Dowager Countess of Moran, goes to deliver a list of the ageing countess's engagements for the following day to her son, the earl, in his study, only to discover that the earl has been bludgeoned to death. When Mary is accused of the crime, her son, Julian, rushes to his employer, Curtis, of the Curtis Inquiry Agency, for help, and Curtis promptly enlists the aid of Barnaby and Penelope Adair and Scotland Yard's Inspector Stokes. Not that the trio needed much summoning as they've already been instructed by the Police Commissioner to solve the case with all speed. With the victim being a powerful nobleman and a major political player, from the first, the pressure is on to find who had dared kill the earl. While the investigators quickly rule out Mrs. Alder as a suspect, they soon discover that the other major suspects—the rest of the earl's family —were all in the Moran House drawing room at the time of the murder, under each other's eyes. And while it quickly becomes clear that quite a few people wished the earl dead, which one actually did the deed remains a tantalizing mystery.

Available for pre-order by January, 2026.

RECENTLY RELEASED:
The eleventh volume in
The Casebook of Barnaby Adair mystery-romances
THE MURDER OF THOMAS CARDWELL

#1 NYT-*bestselling author Stephanie Laurens returns with a perplexing case in which her favorite sleuths must untangle a web of interconnected motives to identify the man who killed Thomas Cardwell.*

When Thomas Cardwell, an upstanding man-of-business, is murdered, Roscoe enlists the aid of the best investigators in London – namely Barnaby and Penelope Adair and Inspector Stokes of Scotland Yard – to solve the puzzle of why anyone would want to kill a man as honest as Cardwell.

Dispatched by Roscoe, London's gambling king, to learn what "nefarious activity" an upstanding man-of-business has stumbled upon, Jordan Draper—Roscoe's own man-of-business—arrives at Thomas Cardwell's office to discover Cardwell very recently murdered.

Soon, Jordan finds himself working alongside the Adairs and Inspector Stokes as they search for clues as to why anyone would kill a man as unthreatening as Cardwell. Unexpectedly, Jordan finds himself drawn to Cardwell's family, especially Thomas's sister, Ruth, and as the investigation progresses, the greater Jordan's compulsion to find the murderer and bring the family resolution and respite grows.

Clue by clue, motive by surprising motive, the investigators seek to identify Cardwell's murderer and, along the way, uncover the "nefarious activity" he'd sought to bring to the authorities' attention. But in a case cluttered with intertwined motives and a web of potential suspects related to each other as well as the victim, finding the kernel of truth amid the chaff is no easy matter. Only through enlisting the help of the investigators' wider circle of supporters do they make any headway, and on the heels of uncovering a cascade of crimes, they finally—*finally*—close in on the man who murdered Thomas Cardwell.

A historical novel of 77,000 words interweaving mystery, crime, and a touch of romance.

**The tenth volume in
The Casebook of Barnaby Adair mystery-romances
MARRIAGE AND MURDER**

#1 NYT-*bestselling author Stephanie Laurens returns with a puzzling case in which her favorite sleuths must untangle a slew of secrets to expose a coldblooded murderer.*

When a middle-aged spinster is found strangled in her country cottage and scurrilous gossip implicates Henry, Lord Glossup, he appeals to Barnaby and Penelope Adair along with Inspector Stokes to unravel the mystery of who killed Viola Huntingdon.

Henry, Lord Glossup, arrives on Barnaby and Penelope Adairs' doorstep and begs their aid—and that of Stokes—in identifying the murderer of Viola Huntingdon, a middle-aged spinster who lived a largely blameless life in a country cottage in a tiny village close to Henry's home. As Stokes has already been tapped to take the case, the investigators travel to Salisbury and thence to Ashmore village and throw themselves into the case.

While initially Henry was touted as a suspect, he is quickly eliminated, and with the help of the victim's sister, Madeline, the investigators set out to discover all they can about the victim and who might have wished her ill. In such a small village, with a commensurately small population, the list of possible suspects is short, but the existence of Viola's 'secret admirer, H' has everyone stumped. First, how could Viola, living in such a small community, have had a secret visitor, a man no one saw except at a distance? And who on earth is he, this H?

As the investigators piece together the clues of missing jewelry and sightings of H and follow the leads generated by opportunistic thieves, dodgy jewelers, and local moneylenders, a picture emerges that points to only one conclusion. But in small villages, things are rarely as they seem. Have the investigators got the right man in their sights, or have they been led astray?

A historical novel of 82,000 words weaving mystery and murder with a touch of romance.

The ninth volume in
The Casebook of Barnaby Adair mystery-romances
DEAD BESIDE THE THAMES

#1 NYT-bestselling author Stephanie Laurens returns with a confounding case that sees her favorite sleuths acting to save a friend wrongly accused of murder.
When a detested viscount is found murdered by the banks of the Thames and Charlie Hastings becomes the prime suspect, Barnaby and Penelope Adair join forces with Stokes to discover the real story behind the unexpected killing.

Charlie Hastings is astonished to find himself accused of murdering Viscount Sedbury. Admittedly, Charlie had two heated altercations with Sedbury in the hours preceding the man's death, but as Charlie is quick to point out to Stokes – and to Barnaby and Penelope – there are a multitude of others in the ton who will be delighted to learn of Sedbury's demise.

As Penelope, Barnaby, and Stokes start assembling a suspect list, Charlie's prediction proves only too accurate. Yet the most puzzling aspect is who on earth managed to kill Sedbury. The man was a hulking brute, large, very strong, and known as a vicious brawler. Who managed to subdue him enough to strangle him?

As the number of suspects steadily increases, the investigators are forced to ask if, perhaps, one of their suspects hired a killer capable of taking Sedbury down. With that possibility thrown into the calculations, narrowing their suspect list becomes a futile exercise.

Their pursuit of the truth leads them to investigate the many shady avenues of Sedbury's life, much to the consternation of Sedbury's father, the Marquess of Rattenby. Rattenby does not want Sedbury's distasteful proclivities exposed for all the world to see, further harming the other family members who Sedbury has taken great delight in tormenting for most of his life.

In the end, the resolution of the crime lies in old-fashioned policing coupled with the fresh twists Barnaby and Penelope bring to Scotland Yard's efforts.

And when the truth is finally revealed, it raises questions that strike to the very heart of justice and what, with such a victim and such a murderer, true justice actually means.

A historical novel of 62,500 words interweaving mystery and murder with a touch of romance.

The eighth volume in
The Casebook of Barnaby Adair mystery-romances
THE MERIWELL LEGACY

#1 NYT-bestselling author Stephanie Laurens returns with her favorite sleuths to unravel a tangled web of family secrets and expose a murderer.

When Lord Meriwell collapses and dies at his dining table, Barnaby and Penelope Adair are summoned, along with Inspector Basil Stokes, to discover who, how, and most importantly why someone very close to his lordship saw fit to poison him.

When Lord Meriwell dies at his dining table, Nurse Veronica Haskell suspects foul play and notifies his lordship's doctor, eminent Harley Street specialist Dr. David Sanderson. In turn, compelled by a need to protect Veronica who is at Meriwell Hall as David's behest, David calls on his friends Barnaby and Penelope Adair for assistance.

However, as the fateful dinner was the first of a house party being attended by the local MP and his family, the Metropolitan Police commissioners also consider the Adairs' presence desirable, and consequently, Barnaby and Penelope accompany Stokes to Meriwell Hall.

There, they discover a gathering of the Meriwell family intended to impress the visiting Busseltons so that George Busselton, local MP, will agree to a marriage between his daughter and Lord Meriwell's eldest nephew, Stephen. But instead of any pleasant sojourn, the company find themselves confined to the hall and grounds while Stokes, Barnaby, and Penelope set about interviewing everyone and establishing facts, alibis, and the movements of those in the house.

To our investigators' frustration, while determining the means proves straightforward, and opportunity reduces their suspect list, motive remains elusive, and their list of suspects stays stubbornly long.

Then the killer strikes again, but even then, the investigators are left with the same suspects and too many potential reasons for the second death.

What did the killer hope to gain?

More importantly, will he kill again?

At last, the investigators stumble on a promising clue, yet following it requires sending to London for information, and their frustration builds. As the clock ticks and they doggedly forge on, they uncover more and more facts, yet none allows them to identify which of their prime suspects is the murderer.

Will they get the breakthrough they need, one sufficient to exonerate the innocent?

When the answer arrives, they discover that the Meriwell family legacies are more far-reaching than anyone realized, and that the crimes involved and the motivation for the murders is far more heinous than anyone imagined.

A historical novel of 78,000 words interweaving mystery and murder with a touch of romance.

PREVIOUSLY RELEASED IN THE CASEBOOK OF BARNABY ADAIR NOVELS:

Read about Penelope's and Barnaby's romance, plus that of Stokes and Griselda, in
The first volume in
The Casebook of Barnaby Adair mystery-romances
WHERE THE HEART LEADS

Penelope Ashford, Portia Cynster's younger sister, has grown up with every advantage - wealth, position, and beauty. Yet Penelope is anything but a typical ton miss - forceful, willful and blunt to a fault, she has for years devoted her considerable energy and intelligence to directing an institution caring for the forgotten orphans of London's streets.

But now her charges are mysteriously disappearing. Desperate, Penelope turns to the one man she knows who might help her - Barnaby Adair.

Handsome scion of a noble house, Adair has made a name for himself in political and judicial circles. His powers of deduction and observation combined with his pedigree has seen him solve several serious crimes within the ton. Although he makes her irritatingly uncomfortable, Penelope throws caution to the wind and appears on his bachelor doorstep late one night, determined to recruit him to her cause.

Barnaby is intrigued—by her story, and her. Her bold beauty and undeniable brains make a striking contrast to the usual insipid ton misses. And as he's in dire need of an excuse to avoid said insipid misses, he accepts her challenge, never dreaming she and it will consume his every waking hour.

Enlisting the aid of Inspector Basil Stokes of the fledgling Scotland Yard, they infiltrate the streets of London's notorious East End. But as they unravel the mystery of the missing boys, they cross the trail of a criminal embedded in the very organization recently created to protect all Londoners. And that criminal knows of them and their efforts, and is only too ready to threaten all they hold dear, including their new-found knowledge of the intrigues of the human heart.

FURTHER CASES AND THE EVOLUTION OF RELATIONSHIPS CONTINUE IN:

The second volume in
The Casebook of Barnaby Adair mystery-romances
THE PECULIAR CASE OF LORD FINSBURY'S DIAMONDS

#1 New York Times *bestselling author Stephanie Laurens brings you a tale of murder, mystery, passion, and intrigue – and diamonds!*

Penelope Adair, wife and partner of amateur sleuth Barnaby Adair, is so hugely pregnant she cannot even waddle. When Barnaby is summoned to assist Inspector Stokes of Scotland Yard in investigating the violent murder of a gentleman at a house party, Penelope, frustrated that she cannot participate, insists that she and Griselda, Stokes's wife, be duly informed of their husbands' discoveries.

Yet what Barnaby and Stokes uncover only leads to more questions. The murdered gentleman had been thrown out of the house party days before, so why had he come back? And how and why did he come to have the fabulous Finsbury diamond necklace in his pocket, much to Lord Finsbury's consternation. Most peculiar of all, why had the murderer left the necklace, worth a stupendous fortune, on the body?

The conundrums compound as our intrepid investigators attempt to make sense of this baffling case. Meanwhile, the threat of scandal grows ever more tangible for all those attending the house party – and the stakes are highest for Lord Finsbury's daughter and the gentleman who has spent the last decade resurrecting his family fortune so he can aspire to her hand. Working parallel to Barnaby and Stokes, the would-be lovers hunt for a path through the maze of contradictory facts to expose the murderer, disperse the pall of scandal, and claim the love and the shared life they crave.

A pre-Victorian mystery with strong elements of romance. A short novel of 39,000 words.

The third volume in
The Casebook of Barnaby Adair mystery-romances
THE MASTERFUL MR. MONTAGUE

Montague has devoted his life to managing the wealth of London's elite, but at a huge cost: a family of his own. Then the enticing Miss Violet Matcham seeks his help, and in the puzzle she presents him, he finds an intriguing new challenge professionally…and personally.

Violet, devoted lady-companion to the aging Lady Halstead, turns to Montague to reassure her ladyship that her affairs are in order. But the famous Montague is not at all what she'd expected—this man is compelling, decisive, supportive, and strong—everything Violet needs in a champion, a position to which Montague rapidly lays claim.

But then Lady Halstead is murdered and Violet and Montague, aided by Barnaby Adair, Inspector Stokes, Penelope, and Griselda, race to expose a cunning and cold-blooded killer…who stalks closer and closer. Will Montague and Violet learn the shocking truth too late to seize their chance at enduring love?

A pre-Victorian tale of romance and mystery in the classic historical romance style. A novel of 120,000 words.

The fourth volume in
The Casebook of Barnaby Adair mystery-romances
THE CURIOUS CASE OF LADY LATIMER'S SHOES

#1 New York Times *bestselling author Stephanie Laurens brings you a*

tale of mysterious death, feuding families, star-crossed lovers—and shoes to die for.

With her husband, amateur-sleuth the Honorable Barnaby Adair, decidedly eccentric fashionable matron Penelope Adair is attending the premier event opening the haut ton's Season when a body is discovered in the gardens. A lady has been struck down with a finial from the terrace balustrade. Her family is present, as are the cream of the haut ton—the shocked hosts turn to Barnaby and Penelope for help.

Barnaby calls in Inspector Basil Stokes and they begin their investigation. Penelope assists by learning all she can about the victim's family, and uncovers a feud between them and the Latimers over the fabulous shoes known as Lady Latimer's shoes, currently exclusive to the Latimers.

The deeper Penelope delves, the more convinced she becomes that the murder is somehow connected to the shoes. She conscripts Griselda, Stokes's wife, and Violet Montague, now Penelope's secretary, and the trio set out to learn all they can about the people involved and most importantly the shoes, a direction vindicated when unexpected witnesses report seeing a lady fleeing the scene—wearing Lady Latimer's shoes.

But nothing is as it seems, and the more Penelope and her friends learn about the shoes, conundrums abound, compounded by a Romeo-and-Juliet romance and escalating social pressure...until at last, the pieces fall into place, and finally understanding what has occurred, the six intrepid investigators race to prevent an even worse tragedy.

A pre-Victorian mystery with strong elements of romance. A novel of 76,000 words.

The fifth volume in
The Casebook of Barnaby Adair mystery-romances
LOVING ROSE: THE REDEMPTION OF MALCOLM SINCLAIR

#1 New York Times bestselling author Stephanie Laurens returns with another thrilling story from the Casebook of Barnaby Adair...

Miraculously spared from death, Malcolm Sinclair erases the notorious man he once was. Reinventing himself as Thomas Glendower, he strives to make amends for his past, yet he never imagines penance might come via a secretive lady he discovers living in his secluded manor.

Rose has a plausible explanation for why she and her children are residing in Thomas's house, but she quickly realizes he's far too intelligent to fool. Revealing the truth is impossibly dangerous, yet day by day, he wins her trust, and then her heart.

But then her enemy closes in, and Rose turns to Thomas as the only man who can protect her and the children. And when she asks for his help, Thomas finally understands his true purpose, and with unwavering commitment, he seeks his redemption in the only way he can—through living the reality of loving Rose.

A pre-Victorian tale of romance and mystery in the classic historical romance style. A novel of 105,000 words.

The sixth volume in
The Casebook of Barnaby Adair mystery-romances
THE CONFOUNDING CASE OF THE CARISBROOK
EMERALDS

#1 New York Times *bestselling author Stephanie Laurens brings you a tale of emerging and also established loves and the many facets of family, interwoven with mystery and murder.*
A young lady accused of theft and the gentleman who elects himself her champion enlist the aid of Stokes, Barnaby, Penelope, and friends in pursuing justice, only to find themselves tangled in a web of inter-family tensions and secrets.

When Miss Cara Di Abaccio is accused of stealing the Carisbrook emeralds by the infamously arrogant Lady Carisbrook and marched out of her guardian's house by Scotland Yard's finest, Hugo Adair, Barnaby Adair's cousin, takes umbrage and descends on Scotland Yard, breathing fire in Cara's defense.

Hugo discovers Inspector Stokes has been assigned to the case, and after surveying the evidence thus far, Stokes calls in his big guns when it comes to dealing with investigations in the ton—namely, the Honorable Barnaby Adair and his wife, Penelope.

Soon convinced of Cara's innocence and—given Hugo's apparent tendre for Cara—the need to clear her name, Penelope and Barnaby join

Stokes and his team in pursuing the emeralds and, most importantly, who stole them.

But the deeper our intrepid investigators delve into the Carisbrook household, the more certain they become that all is not as it seems. Lady Carisbrook is a harpy, Franklin Carisbrook is secretive, Julia Carisbrook is overly timid, and Lord Carisbrook, otherwise a genial and honorable gentleman, holds himself distant from his family. More, his lordship attempts to shut down the investigation. And Stokes, Barnaby, and Penelope are convinced the Carisbrooks' staff are not sharing all they know.

Meanwhile, having been appointed Cara's watchdog until the mystery is resolved, Hugo, fascinated by Cara as he's been with no other young lady, seeks to entertain and amuse her...and, increasingly intently, to discover the way to her heart. Consequently, Penelope finds herself juggling the attractions of the investigation against the demands of the Adair family for her to actively encourage the budding romance.

What would her mentors advise? On that, Penelope is crystal clear.

Regardless, aided by Griselda, Violet, and Montague and calling on contacts in business, the underworld, and ton society, Penelope, Barnaby, and Stokes battle to peel back each layer of subterfuge and, step by step, eliminate the innocent and follow the emeralds' trail...

Yet instead of becoming clearer, the veils and shadows shrouding the Carisbrooks only grow murkier...until, abruptly, our investigators find themselves facing an inexplicable death, with a potential murderer whose conviction would shake society to its back teeth.

A historical novel of 78,000 words interweaving mystery, romance, and social intrigue.

The seventh volume in
The Casebook of Barnaby Adair mystery-romances
THE MURDER AT MANDEVILLE HALL

#1 NYT-bestselling author Stephanie Laurens brings you a tale of unexpected romance that blossoms against the backdrop of dastardly murder.
On discovering the lifeless body of an innocent ingénue, a peer attending a country house party joins forces with the lady-amazon sent to fetch the victim safely home in a race to expose the murderer before Stokes,

assisted by Barnaby and Penelope, is forced to allow the guests, murderer included, to decamp.

Well-born rakehell and head of an ancient family, Alaric, Lord Carradale, has finally acknowledged reality and is preparing to find a bride. But loyalty to his childhood friend, Percy Mandeville, necessitates attending Percy's annual house party, held at neighboring Mandeville Hall. Yet despite deploying his legendary languid charm, by the second evening of the week-long event, Alaric is bored and restless.

Escaping from the soirée and the Hall, Alaric decides that as soon as he's free, he'll hie to London and find the mild-mannered, biddable lady he believes will ensure a peaceful life. But the following morning, on walking through the Mandeville Hall shrubbery on his way to join the other guests, he comes upon the corpse of a young lady-guest.

Constance Whittaker accepts that no gentleman will ever offer for her —she's too old, too tall, too buxom, too headstrong…too much in myriad ways. Now acting as her grandfather's agent, she arrives at Mandeville Hall to extricate her young cousin, Glynis, who unwisely accepted an invitation to the reputedly licentious house party.

But Glynis cannot be found.

A search is instituted. Venturing into the shrubbery, Constance discovers an outrageously handsome aristocrat crouched beside Glynis's lifeless form. Unsurprisingly, Constance leaps to the obvious conclusion.

Luckily, once the gentleman explains that he'd only just arrived, commonsense reasserts itself. More, as matters unfold and she and Carradale have to battle to get Glynis's death properly investigated, Constance discovers Alaric to be a worthy ally.

Yet even after Inspector Stokes of Scotland Yard arrives and takes charge of the case, along with his consultants, the Honorable Barnaby Adair and his wife, Penelope, the murderer's identity remains shrouded in mystery, and learning why Glynis was killed—all in the few days before the house party's guests will insist on leaving—tests the resolve of all concerned. Flung into each other's company, fiercely independent though Constance is, unsusceptible though Alaric is, neither can deny the connection that grows between them.

Then Constance vanishes.

Can Alaric unearth the one fact that will point to the murderer before the villain rips from the world the lady Alaric now craves for his own?

A historical novel of 75,000 words interweaving romance, mystery, and murder.

ABOUT THE AUTHOR

#1 *New York Times* bestselling author Stephanie Laurens began writing romances as an escape from the dry world of professional science. Her hobby quickly became a career when her first novel was accepted for publication, and with entirely becoming alacrity, she gave up writing about facts in favor of writing fiction.

All Laurens's works to date are historical romances, ranging from medieval times to the mid-1800s, and her settings range from Scotland to India. The majority of her works are set in the period of the British Regency. Laurens has published over 80 works of historical romance, including 40 *New York Times* bestsellers. Laurens has sold more than 20 million print, audio, and e-books globally. All her works are continuously available in print and e-book formats in English worldwide, and have been translated into many other languages. An international bestseller, among other accolades, Laurens has received the Romance Writers of America® prestigious RITA® Award for Best Romance Novella 2008 for *The Fall of Rogue Gerrard.*

Laurens's continuing novels featuring the Cynster family are widely regarded as classics of the historical romance genre. Other series include the *Bastion Club Novels*, the *Black Cobra Quartet*, the *Adventurers Quartet,* and the *Casebook of Barnaby Adair Novels.*

For information on all published novels and on upcoming releases and updates on novels yet to come, visit Stephanie's website: www.stephanielaurens.com

To sign up for Stephanie's Email Newsletter (a private list) for heads-up alerts as new books are released, exclusive sneak peeks into upcoming books, and exclusive sweepstakes contests, follow the prompts at http://www.stephanielaurens.com/newsletter-signup/

To follow Stephanie on BookBub, head to her BookBub Author Page: https://www.bookbub.com/authors/stephanie-laurens

Stephanie lives with her husband and a goofy black labradoodle in the hills outside Melbourne, Australia. When she isn't writing, she's reading, and if she isn't reading, she'll be tending her garden.

www.stephanielaurens.com
stephanie@stephanielaurens.com

www.ingramcontent.com/pod-product-compliance
Ingram Content Group UK Ltd.
Pitfield, Milton Keynes, MK11 3LW, UK
UKHW022142071025
8260UKWH00013B/534